THE NIGHT FOLLOWING

THE NIGHT

FOLLOWING

Morag Joss

DELACORTE PRESS

THE NIGHT FOLLOWING
A Delacorte Press Book / March 2008

Published by Bantam Dell
A Division of Random House, Inc.
New York, New York

Permission to reproduce *"I live in a world I have not created"* by Elizabeth Jennings, from her collection RELATIONSHIPS, published by Macmillan, is granted by David Higham Associates Limited.

Book design by Carol Malcolm Russo

Library of Congress Cataloging-in-Publication Data
Joss, Morag.
The night following / Morag Joss.
p. cm.
IBSN-13: 978-0-385-34118-9
1. Married people—Fiction. 2. Murder—Fiction. 3. Murder victims' families—Fiction. 4. Loss (Psychology)—Fiction. 5. Murderers—Fiction. 6. Deception—Fiction. 7. Psychological fiction. I. Title.
PR6060.O77N54 2008
823'.914—dc22   2007034711

Printed in the United States of America
Published simultaneously in Canada

www.bantamdell.com

10   9   8   7   6   5   4   3   2   1
BVG

FOR
PATRICK

ACKNOWLEDGMENTS

I am immensely grateful to Kate Burke Miciak at Random House for her clear, generous, and insightful editorship, which has enabled me to produce a better novel than the version she first read. She is that rare gift to any writer, an editor who is exacting and inspiring in equal measure. I thank her for her unending care of and belief in *The Night Following,* which have done more than she may realize to sustain me through some dark periods when writing was a struggle.

I am indebted also to my two wonderful agents, Maggie Phillips at Ed Victor Limited in London and Jean Naggar of the Jean V. Naggar Literary Agency in New York. They are so much more than agents; I appreciate deeply their warmth, kindliness, optimism, and faith.

Permission to use the *Mimosa* poem, written by Maria G. Bracchi-Cambini and dedicated to her daughter Joan, was very kindly given by the late Joan's brother Bert and her daughters Sue, Anne, and Carol. Thank you.

Finally, I wish to thank my friends and my daughter Hannah, who in their various adorable ways kept me going during the writing of this novel.

I live in a world I have not created
inward or outward. There is a sweetness
in willing surrender: I trail my ideas
behind great truths. My ideas are like shadows
and sometimes I consider how it would have been
to create a credo, objects, ideas
and then to live with them. I can understand
when tides most tug and the moon is remote
and the trapped wild beast is one with its shadow,
how even great faith leaves room for abysses
and the taut mind turns to its own wanderings.

Elizabeth Jennings
(from *Relationships*, published by Macmillan)

THE NIGHT FOLLOWING

Something tells me it's important not to look dangerous. You would think I'd be beyond it by this time, the old dread of making scenes, but I do want to get it done quietly, with the niceties observed. With some respect for finer feelings, though whose exactly it's hard to say at this point. If I could be sure of that, if I could be sure they'd take me with an attitude of courteous regret, of sorrow even, that reflects my own, I'd do it today. I would.

My hair and shoes are a little unfortunate but I could make myself tidy. I could practice the proper face in a mirror first. There's not much

I can do about the bones around my eyes that have a bluish, knuckly look about them now, but I think I could upturn my face so it resembled the mask expected of reasonable women entering this supposedly balanced and amiable chapter of middle age. I could clear my throat and imitate the rounded, sprightly cadences of such women's voices and say—what?

Suppose for instance I said, in that singing-out manner, Oh, excuse me! Could you help? I'm afraid something has happened.

As if I'd dropped a jar at the checkout. Would that be the correct thing?

There must be a right way and a wrong way, as there is for everything. I believe turning up at a police station might be customary, insofar as my particular circumstances are customary. But police stations aren't in obvious places anymore and I could waste all day looking for one. Or I could dial 999, although call boxes aren't in obvious places anymore, either. And they would ask me what's happened because how else are they to know who to send—police, ambulance, or fire engine—and I couldn't begin to go into it all on the telephone. But what is the emergency, they'll insist. All I could tell them is that I think I am. I may be the emergency. It's true that I would be emerging. I would be appearing unexpectedly after a spell of concealment. Surely I must be the emergency. What else could I say? That there's been an accident?

Once they saw I wasn't dangerous, I suppose for a time at least they'd prefer to think of me as sick. Indeed, I could just walk into a hospital. That worked before, after a fashion. I could just walk into a hospital, and nobody would ask if I actually believed I could ever find help there for what afflicts me.

The truth is I'm neither sick nor dangerous. I'm merely displaced. Not that that makes me unique. You've seen me, or someone like me, anywhere out of the way and out of season, run-down, closing down and in decline, though I may have escaped notice unless you happened to catch me in a small space between thoughts of your own. You will have seen me in odd, deserted places: a woman alone on a bridge, or standing by the roadside at a strange and hazardous point where weeds are sprouting, perhaps just loitering near an inexplicably derelict bus stop. I'll remind you of loneliness or old age, or that winter's setting in.

But most often I'll be in restless places, the passing points of departure and arrival between various somewheres. I'm the one apart and hesitant in the waiting rooms of stations, under the arc lights of ticket halls and in the corner booths, hovering at turnstiles and gates, never quite joining queues nor scanning information boards, yet never unaware of the human traffic. I stay in by the wall, sidestepping the tide of those in genuine and deliberate transit, dazed yet somehow impervious, lost but not utterly bewildered. I drift just outside the echoes and thrums of journeys that are not mine, the endings and beginnings of missions, diversions, pilgrimages, expeditions. I observe lives unlike mine, full of imperative planned destinations, and I envy people this apparent conviction that their myriad tiny events, their moving toward events yet to be, are of some importance. Neither a proper impetus to travel nor a true purpose in remaining where I am falls my way. I lack reasons either to go or to wait, and this looks like failure in me.

Not that I am at all disgraceful. I am never drunk. I don't mutter. I don't carry my belongings in a bundle. It may be stained and tatty but I do have luggage, and I tend also to have an address, albeit it's always temporary. I manage to keep out of hostels, mostly. Once a day I endeavor to eat at a table, wherever there's a bargain (jumbo platter, hot drink, £3.99) and whether or not it's a proper mealtime. Also once a day I'll spend up to an hour nibbling on most of a sandwich and then wrap and pocket the crusts for later. I'm a hoarder, not a scavenger; I admit I never spend money on a paper (and actually it suits me not to read the news before it's old and discarded) but I would not dream of polishing off abandoned cups of coffee. It's true that I'm not above helping myself to forgotten gloves and scarves. Once in winter I took a man's coat, left on a bench.

So my vagrancy is unspectacular. I wear a taint of rationing, that's all. I have the thready, ashamed look of a reduced person who assumes there is worse reduction to come, who lingers until the last minute where it's warmest before boarding the final bus or train, or who walks away from the dark station as the grilles rattle down because nobody waits for her in the evenings.

But tomorrow, though it's hard for me to speak loud enough for you to hear, I'll try again. I'll take a sly, off-center interest in your moments of parting and greeting, look too closely at your clothes, the magazine you carry. Your polite glance when you ask if the seat next to me is free I'll take as an invitation.

Yes! Though it's none too clean.

No. Oh well, it'll do.

I'm overglad to be spoken to, so that far too soon and whether you replied this way or not, I'll turn to you with a remark too intricate, an anecdote too unlikely and revelatory. Yes, the pigeons here are awful, aren't they? I met a woman once who got worms off a bench, from the droppings, she said. Filthy, it was. Much worse than this! After that she wouldn't sit anywhere in public without spreading the seat with news-paper first. Once she stood an entire night because she hadn't got any. But you can't win, can you, because that played merry hell with her veins, which was worse than the worms. Or so she claimed.

And you'll look away. You'll dread that anyone might overhear and think something in you encouraged the likes of me to babble to you in this manner, in a hurrying voice and staring straight at your eyes, using the sincere and zealous hand gestures of a person who expects to be disbelieved or motioned to shut up before her story is finished.

I don't blame you. I'll watch you walk away just as I might have been about to ask if you knew where the nearest police station is, or if there is a telephone nearby, or a hospital. I know I'm unsettling. Maybe it's because I know something you don't, though it secures me no ad-vantage. It's only the knowledge that some other knowledge eludes me. It's nothing more than an awareness of questions that the happen-stance of some lives and not others—mine, say, and not yours—poses for some people and not for others.

Such as, where do I pick up the story of a life that should be over, but isn't? If events have halted a life's narrative as utterly as death it-self, how do I go on as if I believed in mere continuation, never mind solace and amends? You won't know. So I won't detain you by saying, Oh, excuse me! Could you help? I'm afraid something has happened.

I won't call after you to tell you how weary I am, I'll settle back and wait out another day. To pass the time, from somewhere in my baggage I'll bring out bundles of thumbed papers secured under rubber bands and I'll fret over ordering and reordering them, rereading this or that grubby old letter as if it might contain something new. And I'll sink into wondering again, asking myself the same questions and finding them still unanswerable.

Dear Ruth

Were the flowers satisfactory? I just got white ones, you know I'm no good with colors. Were they the right thing?
Writing this isn't my idea it's Carole's. You don't know Carole.
Well can't think of anything else for now.

Arthur

D id it begin that morning? If it did, could I have known? Suppose that morning the butter had been purple and the sparrows blue and flying backward, was I too preoccupied with writing my shopping list (*eggs, raspberries*) to notice? If clouds had arranged themselves over the garden spelling out a warning in big vapory letters and loomed through the window, might I have been turning away at that precise moment and failed to see? I go on wishing that if what happened was fated to happen I could have been given a second's notice, just long enough to take a step out of its path. But that would amount to its not having been fated after all, and I would probably have missed such a warning, anyway. I had been unattuned to signs for so long.

Because of course it began long before the condom wrapper in the glove compartment. I must have missed those signs, the slight, prosaic symptoms of near-comic, midlife adultery: an unexplained and distant air of satisfaction, some extra fastidiousness about hair and fingernails, a renewed determination to lose some weight. Did he take longer to answer when I spoke to him? How many times did he look at me and wish he were with her, or slip away to ring her in a small, timed absence? I missed the little signs, but maybe I missed huge and laughably obvious ones, too. Maybe he had been living in a state of priapic delirium right under my nose but I had stopped seeing anything at all when I looked at him.

So the day began small. It was a Thursday in late April and set to be the same day again, the one I lived over and over, small and ordinary as I liked all days to be, though this one was to have one of those small and ordinary variations. We were switching cars. Jeremy was taking mine to be serviced and leaving me his so that I should not be inconvenienced. He would leave my Renault at the garage in Salisbury, walk to the hospital, and pick the car up at the end of the day. Small and ordinary arrangements had been made. Small, ordinary, and half-joking warnings not to scratch his precious Saab convertible were given and taken, after which we exchanged a small and ordinary good-bye.

No, that's not it, either. Too innocuous a beginning—my car being due its service—to be truly a beginning. Nor is a Thursday in April very much to the point, although it was, as would be said later, a proper spring day: sharp and blustery, one of those boisterous, unpredictable mornings randomly bright and dark when cold sweeps of cloud pass and clear across the sun, a day when your eyes water in the wind and you wish the weather neither warmer nor cooler, just less sudden.

I drove to the supermarket. I knew Jeremy's gym bag and rackets would be in the trunk so I didn't bother to open it; it was too small to be much use even empty. I unloaded as fast as I could and filled the floor on the passenger side with bags. I wanted to get on; often I ran into someone I knew and I didn't especially want to, out of slight embarrassment, perhaps. The Saab was bright yellow. Without telling me, Jeremy had sold the Volvo and cashed some bonds and bought it on his fifty-fifth birthday. I hadn't said anything at the time. I considered my not taking much notice of what Jeremy did to be one of my virtues and anyway, smug people often are naturally indulgent. He said he'd always been bored by station wagons and I would still have my little Renault if that was the issue. A sign.

I placed the last bag with the fragile things in it on the passenger seat, walked around to the other side, and got in. I had started the engine and put the car in gear before I noticed a dark liquid pooling in a corner of the bag and a shocking red ooze escaping from it onto the seat. I snatched the bag up and at once the split in the bottom of it yawned open. The raspberries and a box of eggs already disintegrating in raspberry juice dropped out and broke into the puddle that was forming in the hollow of the dove gray suede upholstery. The raspberry carton, minus the lid, tumbled out along with more juice. The bag was still swinging from my hand. Then the second carton of raspberries and the lid of the first flipped through the shreds of plastic and landed on top. That's why I was looking for a tissue.

Dear Ruth

A few came to the house afterward. What's-her-name Marsden from across the road and your group got it organized. Sandwiches, etc. It passed off all right. I stuck leftovers in freezer. Do egg sandwiches freeze?

Arthur

PS Funny to think you don't know Carole, you know everyone.

I fished in the glove compartment for something to mop up the eggs and raspberries. No tissue. My fingers landed on the empty little foil wrapper torn halfway across the letters DU and REX.

I don't like surprises, but my natural propensity is always to avoid making a scene. So I didn't burst into tears or sink my head onto the steering wheel or even swear. I wasn't angry. What happened was not the result of anger. Nor was I quite shocked. I was overwhelmed, if anything, by detachment. As if caught in a freak rush of air, I felt all at once swept off my feet and placed somewhere cooler, elevated, and separate. Of course I hadn't really moved and I sat there for maybe only two or three minutes, but I felt my breathing ease and my heart lighten with every beat. As time ticked by, I watched my life, or my idea of it at least, shift and re-form; I saw the old encumbered sense of who I was and all the ponderous certainties of the piled-up, married years lift and blow away from me. Maybe they never had been so certain after all, or of much use. I gave them one last audit as they flew past, disintegrating as they went: engaged at twenty to Jeremy (ten years older, anesthetist, dependable). No children, history of miscarriages, cause unclear. No career worth mentioning, some dabbling once as agent for a catalog selling artists' supplies, a little voluntary work in galleries. Inclined to be fanciful, if not highly strung. These days she paints, in watercolors of course and with enthusiastic mediocrity, the same butterflies and flowers and landscapes painted by all unconvincing, wishy-washy women; she sets great store on capturing the curve of wings and petals, the gleam of weak skies and pools of shallow water.

All the traditional wisdoms about fidelity, security, even happiness, came loose, too, and went flapping after them. They grew shimmery and fell away to nothing, and when they had gone I marveled that I had ever thought them real.

This new lightness both exhilarated and relaxed me. I switched off the ignition. I sat with the condom wrapper in my hand and saw what must have gone on like a sequence of illustrations from a story I'd been carrying around in my head, untold, for more than half my life. Look, here are Jeremy and his wife, married all these years. Jeremy is an anesthetist; his wife is artistic. He rescues human beings from pain, she notices the reflections of clouds in puddles. Here is their tasteful house in Beaulieu Gardens, a leafy cul-de-sac. They do not look unhappy, and why should they? They acquired long ago a lightness on the subject of childlessness and they have no troublesome friends or worries about money. They have everything from a double garage to a self-cleaning espresso machine. But if they are happy they are not ecstatically so. Ecstasy is not in the picture. What's on the next page?

Ah! Here is Jeremy again, tipped back in the gray suede driving seat of his prized yellow Saab convertible. He is not alone. A woman who is not his wife is stroking a condom over Jeremy's erect penis, in accordance with the instructions on the packaging, which almost certainly call it that, although this woman is using other words for it. Indeed, she is dallying, taking Jeremy's aforementioned between her lips, whispering playful threats and promises of what's going to happen. See here? Jeremy again. His eyes, shiny with joy, are fixed unseeing on the roof of the car. Yes, here it is, here's the ecstasy now. She's across him like a crab, claws waving, impaled. And here is Jeremy's wife, is it days, weeks, months, or even years further along in her married, leafy, cream-carpeted, cul-de-sac life, sitting in the yellow car alone, holding the condom wrapper that Jeremy left in the glove compartment. What does she make of this?

The parade of images faded. I pulled down the sunshield and looked at myself in the mirror, wondering if the calm I felt inside couldn't be what I was feeling at all and my face might reveal actual distress. Perhaps I wanted to watch myself deciding what to feel. But my face bore no more than a shadow of preoccupation. Should I not feel at least mild consternation? I was surprised. I hadn't expected it of Jeremy, or rather, of *a* Jeremy; from a Jerry, from a man of my mother's type, with many rings and a leather coat, gray hair over the collar, maybe. But this seemed an implausible story for any Jeremy to have got himself into, let alone an anesthetist Jeremy of fifty-eight suffering from problematic nasal hair and occasional tinnitus, a Jeremy with meaty, antiseptic hands and a quasi-surgical attitude to sex. (Not clinical, exactly, but with a fastidious emphasis on equipment, technique, and procedure: always in bed, straight to the relevant sites, and nothing said—he working reliably, I respectful of his concentration—until afterward, when he would express satisfaction not so much at passion spent or even appetite sated but at a job done. It's surprising, really, he didn't talk about outcomes.) At least that was how he was with me, and with diminishing frequency. Was it possible that he had discovered, squashed up with this woman in the yellow Saab, that sex—that he, Jeremy—could be grand and wild and dirty and magnificent?

How much younger than me was she? I ruled out her being a pros-titute—Jeremy would never have compromised the dove gray suede on the backside of a common tart—so what made it necessary for them to do it in the car? Simple unstoppable urgency?

I turned the wrapper over and over in my hand and felt traces of the lubricant from the silvered inside soften the pads of my fingers. Did they wrest the condom from it with hands intertwined and fum-bling? I checked its torn foil edges for teeth marks. Did he hiss at the sight of her long nails, groan as she eased it on, instruct her, take over? Did they cry out at the ludicrous little pulsating moment of crisis as they came, and afterward, capsized and contorted across the uphol-stery by the frantic passing squall in their groins; did they smile? Joke about where her knickers had got to? Or did he talk—really talk—to her?

I rubbed my fingertip and thumb together to feel that strange, clingy slip, neither oil nor powder, between them. I dipped my hand in the pool of bright cold slime on the passenger seat and rubbed that be-tween my fingers, too, squashing a handful of raspberries and egg to-gether, letting clear slippery albumen and creamy orange and grainy rags of fruit run down and stain my arm. With the engine switched off the car was already warm, and now the air filled with a new smell that quite overwhelmed the silicone tang of Jeremy's dashboard cleaner. It was raw, and tight with sweetness, fat with yolk and seed and juice. I thought of heat, of skin licked bare of perfumes and smelling only of it-self, salty and animal, and I thought of teeth and saliva and damp hair. I thought of the shoving and sighing, the sucking and shuddering, of sweat and come. And I thought, thanks to her husband, here is the anesthetist's artistic wife pausing in the car park after the supermarket shop, thinking so intensely about fucking of a kind she's never experi-enced that it is making her wet.

And I felt grateful, if a little envious and excluded. I did not even take any avenging pleasure in the Technicolor ruin of the passenger seat. Normally the raspberry and egg disaster would have upset me to the point of nausea but it aroused no feelings I could put a name to. All

I could do was study the colors. I sat and watched them seep into one another for a while. Here is Jeremy's wife contemplating a major spillage. Jeremy's wife considers that these marks will never come out.

But then came a realization, and with it a flood of pleasure as pure as anything sexual. The realization was that my calm did not require justification. Quietly and naturally I accepted that I did not mind about Jeremy's infidelity and so need not pretend to. Quietly and naturally I understood that my discovery severed a redundant bond, not because I cared where Jeremy's penis had been but, very particularly, because I didn't. I need not pretend that anybody's safety or happiness was at stake; nothing at all, finally, depended upon the continuation of our marriage to each other, and this was not a calamity. Rather it should be celebrated; here is proof of a union's unlooked-for but unmistakable meaninglessness, its sudden, clear freedom from having to go on appearing to have a point. This seemed so simple and unambiguous I did not feel it was something I had concluded for myself. It felt like a truth nesting within our marriage all this time like a late and overprotected egg. Now at last it was hatched, and emerging from it was something perhaps ungainly, but unmistakably itself.

I could not wait to tell Jeremy. I was sure it would be such a relief to him, too, to be let off any more of this. My desire to share it with him was, I think, wholly generous. I was sure that when I saw him and explained it all I would, albeit a little bitterly, thank him. I would go straight to the hospital. I could wait and perhaps catch him between the day's -ectomies: splen- or hyster- or append-, whatever bits of offal came out on Thursdays, I had no idea. We didn't talk about his lists anymore.

27 Cardigan Avenue
bed
still 9th May
day after

Dear Ruth

Today is taking much longer than usual. After all the recent coming and going it's very quiet. They've all told me I "must be exhausted." They've all told me I have a right to be angry. They are, they say.
I can just hear what you'd have to say to all this.

Arthur

PS Actually I can't. Not a word. It is very quiet.

M aybe I was a little upset and distracted by the mess on the seat beside me. As the car moved, the colors wobbled and pulsed like blood flooding the corner of my eye. I began to feel almost afraid of it, this wet heap beside me. I didn't dare stop noticing it, as if I could keep it from getting bigger by concentration alone, as if, should my awareness falter, it would bulge and swell and fill all available space, leaving nowhere that was not lurid with color.

I had taken one of the winding back routes to Salisbury, not specifically to avoid the main road, but for something like privacy. I wanted a little time to get used to myself as a wronged wife—as the phrase applicable to me, rather than the fact—because I was bemused at the cliché of it. I wasn't driving faster than usual. Between villages, the road rose and fell between fields and hedges, and here and there narrowed to a single lane. As always, it was almost deserted.

Up a hill on the left side was an orchard bordered by a low wall. I drove toward an overhanging line of trees in blossom whose ornamental acid pink was pressing hard into the blue of the sky. Set back from the road before the trees stood a pair of modern pebbledash cottages, each with a carport and a satellite dish. In the garden of the first one stood a caravan; in the other the sun was glancing off the glassy, dead surface of an artificial pond. Unremarkable as the houses were, I noticed them particularly, as if I knew I should later be unable to forget any detail of the moments just before. I passed by them and up toward the trees whose moving shadows cut like slate across the tarmac. The road was rising toward a bend beyond the trees and an even higher stretch of ground between garish spring fields. The green of these fields in the distance stung my eyes with almost chemical sharpness, the fresh bitterness of sap in new leaf, new grass. Green can be too green.

Perhaps I did wince as the pink branches bobbed above, almost in my face, or I may have blinked as a splinter of sunlight sliced at my eyes. And I'm not sure if I truly remember this or have constructed it after the event—after learning what the event must have been—but I can describe a jolt and a bang and the car bucking like an animal, and a black bulk thrown up and looming at me and blotting out the sky, and two or three ghastly, weighted thumps and then noises of scraping and rasping all around me. The windshield crackled and crumped inward. The bulk disappeared and the sun burned back through the crazed glass in fragmented darts of light that pricked my eyes like a fistful of thrown needles. I have no idea how I stopped the car.

This I do remember. In silence I walked—I did not run—toward the shape on the road. It was sprawled a shockingly long way back. It wasn't black. She was dressed in a russet checked jacket and navy trousers. She lay on her front, irretrievably broken. I went close enough to see that her head was the wrong shape, and I saw the crimson purée growing under it. It no longer fitted correctly on her neck. One side was flattened so it seemed to be lying in a hollowed-out bowl in the tarmac. I went close enough to see the off-center rictus of a dislodged dental plate forcing a mad smile out of one side of her torn mouth. I saw on her face a look of slight surprise, a single backward glance arrested indelibly in an eye that was drowsy and glistening with the filmy, departing gaze of a drunkard, or a very tired baby. I did not hear if the spinning rear wheel of the bicycle on the side of the road was making the usual cheerful ticking noise. All seemed quiet until I became aware of a soft, lamenting whine coming from my own lips. Beyond us, the wind flicked some sheets of paper across several spilled books on the road. A ring binder lay splayed, its cover showing a cartoon of a quill pen and the words *Woman Wise——Monkwell Women Writers Group*. A shopping bag caught and torn in the fractured spars of the bicycle bore a facsimile of Shakespeare's signature and the words **As You Like It**. Daffodils and clumps of grass at the base of the orchard wall shivered in little flurries of wind and I saw an empty blue hat on the side of the road begin to stir and roll among the waves of frayed yellow and green. Just then the silenced birds in the pink trees started up again.

The wind got up, too. A sudden gust blew the loose papers on the road upward into the light and shadow and for a few moments I stood transfixed by their swirling, indecent exuberance, the loveliness of bright white paper as the sun caught each flapping page. Then, perhaps to stop myself from screaming, I chased after them through the scattering wind, grabbing them in midair or where they dropped momentarily to the ground. I don't know what I thought I was saving, or for whom. All I saw was that every sheet bore the heading THE COLD AND THE BEAUTY AND THE DARK, and all I knew was that I could not bear that a single paper should be swept into the dirt and blood. I would not let a single word be smirched. By the time I'd picked the pages all up and bundled them in my arms, I was weeping.

I think my whimpering stopped in the second or two before my mouth dried. I didn't faint or fall but all at once I wanted to be down on the ground. I was clutching the papers against my body and they were suddenly unbearably heavy. I was going to have to sink down next to her and stay there forever, or I was going to have to move. I ran back to the car, opened the door, and threw the papers into the back. With my hand reaching for my purse—I was about to get my telephone, surely I was?—I turned and looked up, hearing a raucous hacking sound above me. A crow swooped out of the trees, skimmed over the wall, and alighted in a tatter of wings on the small of the woman's back. Two more landed on the road nearby. The first one, watched by the others, lifted its wings and tidied them over itself like a pair of oily folded hands. It hopped up the length of her body until it stood on her hair. Prayerfully, it dipped its head and began to peck. In the sunlight its feathers gleamed rainbow black. I drove away.

Dear Ruth

For obvious reasons it's no good me asking where the pressure cooker is. I wish I knew. I've never understood the new microwave. I could cope with the last one, this one really gets my goat. Far and away too fancy.

kitchen later

Window cleaner's just been here. Cheeky bugger. Acted like he hadn't heard the news. Actually whistling. Well, I wasn't about to enlighten him. I'm sure he knows and he's taking advantage. How much is he supposed to get? He told me £15. I paid up, just this time I told him, I won't be ripped off like that again.

I'll have something to say if he tries that again. The situations some people are capable of taking advantage of. Unbelievable.

A.

PS The police haven't been back. Unless you count Victim Support Officer. So nothing to report there

As I drove, I knew the sun would still be shining through the windy trees, painting the road in moving daubs of shadow. Daffodils and a lost hat would still waft together on the grass. Horror that should have quite overwhelmed me was somehow at bay, though I sensed that it was massing, growing in a place in my mind where it would wait and visit later when its full force had gathered. For the moment I was calm enough to know my calm for what it was: merciful, sedating shock, the kindly muffling of the brain that slows the world down following the rush of a disaster. And so what first horrified me was not what had happened, of itself, but that it was already receding, as a dream evaporates within seconds after waking. The event, though catastrophic, was already turning vague while new events, banal but new—a hat rolling in daffodils, clouds buffing and dulling the ground—claimed my attention irresistibly.

I thought about the wind flipping the strewn pages on the road and teasing the woman's hair. I thought about her wrecked body and my incidental, obliterating swipe that had punched the life out of it, and I realized that our being caught up in this together would never, ever be explained. How could two strangers be bound to each other forever as we now were by an event so haphazard, yet so crucial and so intimate? A husband was unfaithful. A shopping bag was punctured by the edge of a carton. A wife made too stark a discovery, on a day already angular and confusing with blades of shadow slicing through trees. But these were not reasons, merely circumstances: routine car maintenance, routine adultery, broken eggs, spilled fruit, a day of wind and sun. No divine or other congruence, no preordained astral spinning, could possibly be in motion either to prevent or determine that this conjunction of trivia would cause anyone to drive under a flickering arch of pink blossom toward a single, injurious, cataclysmic encounter with a stranger on a bicycle. Why should it?

People vanish as if they never had been more than apparitions and all the life in them little more than a movement that caught the eye. A woman invisible among the watery shadows on a lane in spring, my uncle walking away from me into a snowy night long ago. My grandmother in the early morning, pegging out washing and playing hide-and-seek behind the sheets: all vanished. Not a word comes back and not a breath remains, though the rippling of laundry on a clothesline can still make me wonder if she lingers there, teasing me with that old game, not knowing it was years ago and I've outgrown it, for the dead have no idea how long they've been gone.

But the sheets hang still after all, and so it was, of course, just a fancy to imagine she was there. And if we don't believe in ghosts, how can we trust their opposites, real people with their loud voices and certainties, their intentions for the day, ideas about their future and their happiness, to possess the same reluctance to relinquish this life, to be any more fleetingly present than they? And so the world proves itself as shadowy, as unreliable as anything glimpsed and dismissed as a trick of the light, and people pass over the surface of it the way they tiptoe out across the edges of a memory, or a dream.

And in the instant the dreamer wakes, already the separation is beginning from even the worst and strangest of nightmares, and the infinitesimal moment has passed when the dream's fragments might have all come together into something complete, albeit terrible. Revelation eludes us; even as our eyes are opening, the knife falls from the hand and voices expire on the shore of sleep. We are awake after all and alive in the solid world, and it seems so understandable and constant, and the time remaining to us so unwearyingly long. There are trees and fields all the way to the horizon and a pebble-sized heart beats in every flying bird. Yet we take only a moment to perish. We vanish under the surface the way a drop of water flicks from the tail of a fish, sparkles, and falls back into a river. Once you know that, you know that the will of a body to remain unbroken is itself piteously breakable.

Perhaps the woman on the road measured the last minute of her life in a calculation of how long it would take her to pedal to the top of the rise. Perhaps there was no more than a minute between the thought that soon she would stop to rest and the moment she became carrion. Perhaps this is what an accident is.

Dear Ruth

Sorry for silence, been busy.

Re: pressure cooker, I don't think it's here at all. Obviously it's not in stuff laid out for the Belle Aurore Atlantis, *I wouldn't expect you to take a pressure cooker on a cruise.*

I checked through all the stuff already packed in the spare room anyway, though. Not there.

But it's not in any of the boxes packed for next six months in Australia either—mistake, surely, as we could do with it there I'd have thought.

Been right through the attic and garage and everywhere else I can think of, no joy. Uncovered other stuff that might be handy however, it's amazing what you collect.

Also came across pages of this—your writing group stuff I suppose, some novel is it?

If I could ask your permission to read it I would. I don't see it makes a difference now. Also I'm not getting out to the library so it'll pass the time.

Arthur

THE COLD AND THE BEAUTY AND THE DARK
1932

Chapter 1: Beats Working In't Mill, or So They Say

At six a.m. on the 18th of January 1932, the blast of a dozen factory sirens over the roofs of Aldbury in Lancashire signaled the end of the night shift. A few moments later a crowd of chattering women and girls poured out from the Brightaglow Electric Apparatus factory into the raw winter morning. Among them was Evelyn Leigh. Slightly built, her girlish dimples and rosy complexion were offset by abundant dark curls that belied her twenty-nine years. She moved as if she were afraid of being jostled and her shoulders stooped with tiredness. But these days her dimples came and went more often, in private half-smiles. As the two hundred night workers clattered through the gates, their scarved and shawled heads bowed under the icy rain, Evelyn drew herself away from the tide and paused, looking up at the sky and letting her eyes adjust to the daylight.

It's like a dirty leaky ceiling up there, she thought to herself, trying to focus. It did seem to be raining gray, as if an upstairs pipe had burst and the clouds were wads of wet newspaper stuffed into the dripping cracks. She screwed up her eyes but still she couldn't make out anything clearly. The dirty rain just went on dripping down all around her, mucking everything it landed on. The walls of the factory were a wet dark blur, and beyond the gates nothing could be seen except for the mass of people moving through the street. Evelyn turned up the collar of her coat and walked slowly on toward the tram stop, blinking through the rain. She was tired and already her headscarf was soaked through.

Her eyes were stinging as they always did following the nine-hour shift in the Testing Division as a bulb checker, making sure that all sets of fancy lightbulbs were in working order before they were packed. It wasn't onerous work but in the eighteen months she had been there Evelyn had found it increasingly exhausting. Still, there was no choice, you worked where there was work, and at least it was quieter than the weaving sheds in the mills, and you didn't choke on the cotton dust.

The work wasn't heavy. First she had to assemble a box from the pile of flat cardboard sheets at her feet, folding and fitting the tabs in a matter of seconds. Then she would take a set of lights from the never-ending supply, regularly topped up by the lads from Assembly, in a carton on the floor at her side. She would hold the bare end of the brown snake of flex and touch it against the socket on the bench, and as long as the whole string of bulbs flared in a blaze of colored light, she would wind it around her crooked arm as she had been taught and pack it neatly in the box. The duds went into another carton for adjustments and retesting.

Every half hour, another lad from Dispatch would come along wheeling a deep basket on castors, and take the stack of packed boxes from the other side of her bench. A note would be made on her work sheet of the number of packed boxes she achieved and the supervisor's beady eye would peruse those sheets at the end of each shift, so it was just as well she had mastered the folding and packing quickly so that she could do it without really looking. Dazzled by each flash, she could see nothing for several moments afterward, except a starry afterimage.

Not until the end of her shift would Evelyn look up from her work and notice the shimmering, glassy air of the Testing shed and the strange, hard, salty smell of electricity. The space above her head seemed laden with tiny shocks that sparked against the white glazed bricks lining the walls and glanced back like arrows. Like a headache waiting to happen, Evelyn thought. Then she would rub her eyes and long for the fresh air. Every one of the hundreds of bulb flashes would smolder on in her vision for hours afterward, erasing detail as if they had made ragged red and gray holes like cigarette burns across the surface of her eyes.

Today, out in the freezing rain, she marched on briskly. She had more important things to think about than sore eyes. She would not let even the most dismal January she could remember interfere with her good spirits. After all, it would soon be spring, and she would be getting married. Then there would be the baby and so what if a few people talked? It wasn't unheard of, a honeymoon baby coming early, most folk wouldn't probe. The fuss wouldn't last. It would be a shock for Mam, and Evelyn hated the thought of upsetting her, but she would make her understand and she'd come round in time. Stan would settle down fine and there would be nothing more to worry about.

As she walked, a voice from behind interrupted her

thoughts. "Oy, Evelyn Leigh, hang on, can't yer!" She turned and waited for her friend, Daphne Baker, to catch up. "Heck, you're in a hurry!" she puffed. "Where's the fire?"

A grinning Daphne came lumbering toward her in her shapeless coat and tight stockings, careless as always of her lack of elegance. She had inherited, as she said herself, "me Dad's build and me Mam's legs, worse luck." It was true that she had his strong, square shoulders and short arms, and her legs were, like her mother's, almost elephantine below the knee. There was a medical name for it that Daphne had told Evelyn once and she'd forgotten, but a medical name didn't mean there was a remedy. Daphne laughed it off, as the only girl in a family with three teasing brothers, Paul, Colin, and Jem, had learned to do. "I'm as strong as an ox," she said. "And who looks at your legs if you've got a nice friendly face?"

The two friends linked arms and made their way to the tram queue where they stood patiently. There was no letup in the weather. The tram came, a dark shape appearing out of grayness, and it struck Evelyn that it too had lost its color, as if the rain had washed off its dark green paint and it had soaked away down the street drains. On board they had to stand as usual for the first few stops, but once past Coronation Mills they found spaces to sit. The motion and noise of the tram made talking difficult. Daphne brought out her cigarettes.

"Fancy one of mine?" she said, offering the pack to Evelyn.

"Oh, no, not for me, ta all the same," she said.

"Please yourself. Still off the cigs, are you?" Daphne lit one for herself and blew out the match with her first exhalation of smoke.

Evelyn turned away, trying to take her mind off feeling sick. She knew every bend and halt of the tram route by now and she didn't need to see through the grimy windows to know where they were. Soon they would be at Canal Street, the stop where occasionally the odd woman got on. Not that she was all that odd, not at first glance, she was just what Evelyn thought of as "different" and what Daphne called "not all there." She blended in all right as far as clothes and general appearance went but you could tell she wasn't from Unsworth's, where the other people getting on at Canal Street worked. For one thing, she wasn't regular enough, only boarding the tram on maybe two days in every six. Evelyn supposed the woman worked casual hours, maybe as a char. Daphne said she'd heard from somebody that she'd lost a son and had funny turns. She was generally considered to be harmless but definitely not all there. Nobody seemed to know her name.

Not that she drew attention to herself, rather the opposite. On the tram, whether she was standing or sitting, she would close her eyes and a smile would settle on her lips. She'd stay like that for the entire journey. The tram would creak along, jolting at every stop and juddering on again.

Now and then somebody might address a remark to her. "Mind if I get past you?" or " 'Scuse me, is anybody sitting there?" and the woman would usually reply quite sensibly. But not once would her eyes open or her smile falter.

Today she got on and took the seat opposite Evelyn.

Her eyes weren't closed in sleep or obvious tiredness, or squeezed tight against something unpleasant. As usual they were just shut and smooth, though her face was blotchy with cold. Her smile, even on her wintry, pinched face, made Evelyn think not for the first time that she knew well enough where she was, in a smoky tram surrounded by drab, glum passengers, and had just decided to spare herself the sight of it.

But today as Evelyn watched, all at once the smile vanished and the woman's eyes flew open in agitation. She blinked round the tram for a moment, her mouth working furiously. Evelyn was ashamed in case the woman had seen her staring. She tried to look away, but it was too late.

"Bloody look at it! I tell yer! Bloody look at me!" the woman suddenly shouted. She waved a grayish frozen hand toward the rain-streaked window. "Look! It's enough to make you, make you . . . it's enough to make you . . ." Her voice tailed off and the hand dropped in her lap. Her lips were trembling. People exchanged glances. Composing herself, she sighed and spoke again, quite calmly this time, and to nobody in particular.

"I'll tell you. Look at it. It's enough to make you go to bed New Year's Eve and not get up afore Easter." Apparently satisfied, she surveyed the carriage, smiled, folded her hands together, and closed her eyes.

A few people looked around nervously and one or two, including Evelyn, nodded. A gruff voice further down the tram muttered, "Aye, don't blame you, missus."

Daphne nudged Evelyn. "Only sensible thing she's ever said. She most definitely is not all there," she whispered. "Look. Get her now. Butter wouldn't melt!"

"Maybe she feels better for getting it off her chest."

"Maybe. Wouldn't mind it myself, sleeping New Year till Easter. Wouldn't be missing anything, would I?"

Evelyn smiled. "Rum kind of Sleeping Beauty you'd make, Daphne Baker."

Daphne laughed wryly. "Aye, but I'd catch up on my sleep, wouldn't I? You'd die of old age waiting for Prince Charming round here. I'm past all that, anyway. Getting too old, me."

"Do you mind? I'll thank you to remember I'm two years older than you, young lady."

"Aye, but you don't look it. And you've got your Stan. You're not stuck on't ruddy shelf like me, not that I'm bothered. They're all the same, men."

"Oh, Daphne Baker, you are not over the hill. You'll see. Somebody'll be along and sweep you off your feet. Mr. Right."

Daphne grunted. "I'm not worried. I'm better off. At least you won't catch me at a man's beck and call. I'm nobody's unpaid skivvy. You're a fool, Evelyn Leigh, getting married. Come on, this is us."

After they'd clambered off the tram at Station Road, Daphne had said "Ta-ta" and set off on the short walk to her home in Chadderton Street. Evelyn let out a deep sigh. Daphne could be so tactless. And she only pretended not to care. To hear her talk you'd think she'd seen a hundred Januarys, not twenty-seven. She was too young to come out with half the things she said, but that was what Daphne was like nowadays, bitter. She was becoming a bitter old spinster, a type all too recognizable since the terrible Great War, which had taken so many of the young men of their generation. Now there were simply too few to be the sweethearts and husbands of all the women who remained, many of whom were now resigned to spinsterhood, all their hopes of youthful romance and wife and motherhood dashed. Evelyn knew she was one of the lucky ones.

She turned to gaze in the direction Daphne had taken but she couldn't see her. After only a few yards the walls and pavements of Station Road melted into a thick blur. She rubbed her eyes and set off toward Roper Street, protesting inwardly at Daphne's words that were still echoing in her head.

It wasn't true that getting married meant ending up somebody's unpaid skivvy. She wouldn't. It wasn't true that men were all the same. Stan was different. Stan didn't want a skivvy. He was principled. He believed in equality and the rights of the working man. And this January was different from other Januarys, not freezing and colorless at all if you only looked a little deeper, beneath the cold, ashy surface of the world.

Dear Ruth

I'm not sure these letters are right. Carole says there isn't a right or wrong, the idea is I just write what I want, whatever I'm thinking. I can express anything I feel. Including anger, she added.

Write what I want? What does that mean? I said to her, You don't appreciate the situation, Ruth's the one for the words, not me. I'm no good with words. Not the letter writing kind, anyway. Oh, give me rainfall bar charts for Derbyshire since the second world war or an ornithological distribution map of the British Isles and I'll bore for Britain on those, I said. I'm on safe ground there. But as I told Carole, you were the English teacher, I was only Geography. I looked out some Overdale photos and showed her. Even found some Overdale poems your kids did.

Carole won't let it go though, she says of course I don't have to if I don't find it helpful, but she'd like me to persevere with the letters. Just write whatever I'm thinking, express anything I'm feeling. It's well known, she said, to be a useful tool in grief management.

Huh, I can't even think straight so how can I feel straight? Let alone write it down? I told her, Ruth's the one with the words, or aren't you listening, I said.

Maybe you are angry, she says. You don't need qualifications or special language to say you're angry. Or to write to your wife. Just use ordinary words.

Use ordinary words to say what? I don't see how telling you about window cleaner, pressure cooker etc can be a useful tool for anything. I never was the writer. Nor the talker. You were. What would the listener have to say after all this time?

Carole says whatever I write it's for you, not her, but I asked her to read this just the same. She thinks it's a start. I asked her to leave. Told her I was tired.

Well, no more for now.

Arthur.

Ps later——STILL *no sign of pressure cooker yet.*

I would rather omit this. I observe it now only reluctantly and without hope of forgiveness, because nothing should be omitted. Though I have braced myself time and again to go back over it, as I might make myself watch a film with shocking scenes that I thought I ought to try to understand, I don't remember, to begin with, that I did actively decide to close the garage doors behind the wrecked car. Until that day I had always left the garage doors open for Jeremy's return in the evening, but this day was unlike any other, and certainly I was now quite unlike myself. So I can't know if my reason for closing them was to conceal my shame, or the evidence of the collision, or because some part of my mind had already planned what was to happen next. Was I at that point angry or frightened, rational or deranged? I must in some way have chosen to do what I did next but I have no idea if I was in control of my actions or not. I can't locate a memory of anything as deliberate as motivation, so any finer distinction such as the shading between compulsion, intention, calculation, and desire simply has no meaning for me in this instance.

I was aware nevertheless of a single swift moment of puzzlement, and intense regret, that I should be reaching up to pull a hammer, a crowbar, and a heavy chisel from their hooks on the garage wall at roughly the same time as I would ordinarily have been lifting this or that delicate paintbrush—a tiny, fairylike bunched tail of sable, itself so exquisite—and stroking another smoky, barely pigmented sweep of color across one of my diluted studies of petals and stamens, or butterflies. But that was all. I did not pause. I did not consider, let alone reconsider. I wasn't thinking at all.

I didn't stop until the hood was hammered in, the doors were smashed, and my feet were crunching through the orange and red chips of glass littering the floor from the busted lights. The front bumper was split and hanging off, the grilles were shattered, the tires ripped. The windows and windshield had gone except for a frill of broken glass. I was gasping and sweating, and when I paused to rest I caught my reflection in the window in the back wall. I could see I had changed. My eyes were larger and brighter but I wasn't sure if that made me look younger and prettier, or just insane. Then I noticed a smell of fruit and gasoline, and a chinking sound, quieter than silence, as a few bits of glass dripped from the windshield like little cubes of melting ice and landed on the hood and dashboard and shopping bags. I took a deep breath and thought, Oh, thank God. It's over, thank God. Whatever it is, it's all done now. It's all stopping.

I was wrong. I raised the crowbar in my hand and lowered it gently, gently. Then I heard myself scream. I lifted the bar again and smashed it down hard again on the hood, a number of times, and I followed that with several blows of the hammer. Then I doubled over and yelled, but

I couldn't hear myself above the din I'd made. It was like standing inside a splitting bell. I straightened and tossed the bar and the hammer onto the roof of the car. They banged across it, slithered off, and clanged on the floor. Then I reached in through the ragged passenger window, opened the glove compartment, found the condom wrapper, and placed it carefully in the center of the pitted roof. I could hardly see. After a few moments the noise changed into a kind of fuzzy echo that set my skull vibrating and shivering under my hair. A distant ringing started up from even deeper and lower inside me. I stood watching the loose bits of glass hanging in the windshield until they stopped swaying and glinting.

When all was still and quiet again, I wheeled from the corner of the garage an old barbecue we hadn't used for years (too basic for Jeremy now, just a metal basin on legs) and brought it to the middle of the floor. I returned to the shelves and rummaged until I found what I needed and then, using some sticks of kindling and a slosh of liquid lighter fuel, I set a small fire going in the barbecue.

Then I reached into the back of the car and gathered up the pages I'd picked off the road. I began automatically to put them in order, as if my destroyed, methodical self was struggling obstinately to discover some system at work in all this mayhem. I concerned myself only with the numbers. Whatever the words were about, I didn't have a complete set. The beginning was missing; the first page I had was number 94 and was headed **Chapter 15: 1962 Christmas Eve**.

One by one I fed them into the flames and watched them flare and blacken and turn fragile and silvery. The garage filled with hot smoke and a choking smell, but the rhythmic lift and turn of each page as it met the flames soothed me. By the time the last one was collapsing into the pile of rectangular gray veils, I was quite calm again.

Dear Ruth

On entering spare bedroom couple of days ago, saw someone had been in. Whole place ransacked. Got a bit of a shock, I got straight on the phone.

Don't worry, I wasn't in a panic. Didn't even ring 999. The policeman that's been before left his card by phone and he told me I could ring him anytime I needed updating. So I did. When did the police start getting business cards?

For that matter, when did they start talking about "needing updating"? Made me sound like a 5-year old car.

He wasn't in, of course. I got some girl. She wanted to know all kinds of stuff. When had I last left the house unattended, did I find the property secure on my return, any signs of forced entry, etc.

In the course of trying to accommodate her, I cast my mind back. I hadn't been out since I don't remember when. Had to get rid of her, so I said someone was at the door and put phone down.

Realized it was me, you see! A while back, searching for pressure cooker—not sure when—I must've upset all the packing. In haste to find it, I suppose I hadn't noticed stuff falling all over the place. Or maybe I was just too frustrated by wild goose chase after pressure cooker to care, because I STILL haven't found it. Everything from the cases is now scattered everywhere, sorry to say, including a great deal of your paper. Was surprised you'd decided to take so much of that gobbledygook (your word for it!) of yours with you, given how heavy paper weighs.

It's all very colorful isn't it, cruise wear. I can't see either one of us in those colors now. I wonder I ever could.

Got to go.

After midnight or thereabouts
Got a bit upset there. To continue: on day after said phone call (see

above), my policeman came again. No headway on your case—if you ask me they've given up. But can't fault them on promptness this time. Just follow-up, he said. That girl I spoke to had left a few loose ends, obviously. I let him check the spare room window but he didn't say much, only gave me more advice on locks.

Later on comes yet another, the woman from Victim Support. I've a feeling she's been before. I don't register faces much these days. She was the last straw—I let rip. Left her in no doubt what I thought of the hit-and-run bastard. She was quite shaken, I believe, didn't stay. Good riddance.

They're all coordinators of something, these visitors. Units, networks, support groups, you name it, they coordinate it. Must mean I'm getting the top people. Anyway I'm inundated. Keeping curtains closed doesn't do a lot to deter.

Especially not Mrs. Marsden across the road. She pops over with alarming frequency. Is she a Mary or a Rosemary, I've forgotten. No, I never did know, never had cause. No good asking you now.

I can't think what else to say so I will close now.

Bye, Arthur

After the smoke died away, my first thought was incongruously, and in the circumstances I felt unforgivably, exactly what Jeremy's would have been. Although perhaps it wasn't altogether strange; perhaps it was at least explicable, after more than twenty years' assimilation of his honed, palliative urges, that suddenly I very badly wanted a cup of tea. I walked slowly from the garage, rubbing my eyes.

I entered the kitchen and was at once surrounded by the smell of clean house, mildly leafy with an undertow of carpet and new bread and paint. It was as pervasive as a sound; it was the layered, burnished

scent of a house not merely recently cleaned but kept, on principle, pi-
ously and improvingly stainless, as if every day I sprayed some attar of
the domestic virtues—Order, Constancy, Thoroughness—into all the
corners and then went around with a cloth. The worktops were wiped
and shining, oranges and lemons (more than I needed, acquired for the
look of them) glared from a bowl sitting next to a stack of green tins. I
could see my obedient herbs flourishing in their terra-cotta containers
on the decking outside the kitchen window; I could see sparrows and
finches swinging at the birdfeeder. Above the slow *tack-tack* of the
kitchen clock and the rising purr of the kettle I could hear a mower
growling a few lawns away.

It was no good. I knew how smug and how fugitive it all was: the
arranging of fruit in a display of bogus generosity, the offhand cherish-
ing of little wild birds, the taming of gardens. It amounted to no more
than the application of an unimaginative respect for hygiene, habit,
sentiment, and surface. And I knew now the dangers of the fatal absence of spirit that that concealed, and how flimsy it was as armor
against it; I felt afraid and nauseated, and I began to shake again. Glass
will splinter as easily as it will send back a polished shine. Bodies tear,
blood spills. I had just wielded a metal bar as lightly as I would flick a
duster. I rushed to the back door and got myself outside just in time to
be copiously sick into a pot of marjoram.

When I was calm once more, I wandered through the house. I
think I was memorizing it as it was, because as soon as Jeremy came
home everything would change again, though it had changed already,
and I couldn't detect what it was in the silence now that prevented it
from being peaceful. What was it I couldn't touch or see or smell or
taste or hear that charged the air in every room with aggression? There
had always been something about our house that made it difficult even
to raise a voice. I had always kept loud noises at bay, along with dust,
upsetting odors, and objects challenging to the eye. The very walls and
carpets and furniture seemed to be in on it, contributing their so coor-
dinated, so understated, solidity and hush to the solidity and hush of
our marriage and its traditional patterns, its established and exquisitely

intimidating courtesies. It was as if the house itself knew that Jeremy disapproved of shouting. Did I? I approved of his disapproval, certainly. Shouting meant being not just too loud, but in the wrong. Solid, hushed people such as we were did not resort to shouting. Until today, shouting was the worst thing I had ever had to apologize to Jeremy for.

It was nearly seven o'clock when I heard the Renault turn into the drive. I sat waiting in the sitting room. He came in from the garage and stood in the doorway, staring. He was holding the condom wrapper. We were both horribly embarrassed. I tried to say something, but whatever it might have been came out in a voice that I hadn't used all day and was no more than a whisper. Jeremy's mouth opened and closed. Then he burst into tears and turned away from me. I heard his sobs juddering as he rushed upstairs. A few minutes later came the unmistakable bumping and scraping of drawers and cupboards being emptied, and then all was quiet. About half an hour after that another vehicle, one of those scaled-down, tarted-up versions of a jeep, drew up and parked outside. The driver didn't get out.

Jeremy struggled downstairs with our two biggest suitcases and left them in the hall. Then he marched into the sitting room and placed my car keys on the mantelpiece. Though his eyes were red, his face was again smooth, fixed with a look of aloof regret that I imagined he used for the relatives of dead patients. A heart might have stopped forever while Jeremy was in charge of keeping it beating, but that rueful, authoritative half-smile avowed that his part in any such death would always be blameless. He looked as if he knew he wasn't in danger of shouting at me, and was proud of it.

He made a short speech about the rest of his belongings, every word of which I forgot at once. Then he paused to compose himself with some learned breathing technique, before speaking again. It didn't take him long to deliver himself of the reasons why he was leaving me. He had tolerated years of "emotional neglect" and now (and apparently coincidental to my discovery of the condom wrapper) he had had enough. I didn't take in the details of what he told me about his new living arrangements, which were, of course, intricately bound up with the circumstances of the driver of the waiting jeep-ette. I was too taken aback by the realization that he thought that all of this was happening because of his affair. My hammering his yellow Saab convertible pride and joy to bits, his insistence that *he* was leaving *me:* these were what he thought important. Because his affair hadn't crossed my mind for hours, I said I simply didn't understand why he was getting so worked up. I suppose that was what made him slam the door on his way out.

I climbed upstairs to the landing window to see him go. The front path was empty. He must have paused under the porch, maybe to wipe his eyes in the silence after the slam, more likely to check he had everything he needed. Suddenly I couldn't bear to watch, and I closed my eyes. Then came the sound of his feet on the path and the trundle of the cases. Of course he was in a hurry to be gone. Of course they both must have been; I heard the car start before the opening and closing of the trunk and the passenger door were quite done with. I opened my eyes only at the burr of the engine at the end of the cul-de-sac, when they would be out of sight. I imagined the disappearing wisp of exhaust as they turned onto the main road and I knew that to Jeremy, as he was driven away, I was invisible now, not just physically but in the sense of ceasing to be anywhere at all, even in his mind. To Jeremy, I was not present, nor sentient; I was barely living. I was nowhere. I did not stand at this window, I did not listen, or grieve, or wonder.

But I stayed there for a long time, collecting and ordering in my mind the scrape of feet and squeak of wheeled luggage, the cough of an engine, a slammed car door, the distant mingling of traffic and birdsong above the roofs of the cul-de-sac. Sounds overheard have a deliberate music, a pacific and sequential logic that's absent from the noise of unwitnessed behavior. Jeremy's departure played sounds that I might want to remember one day and run over in my head, like a tune.

Dear Ruth

Did you see the car before it hit you?

This may sound harsh but Carole misses the point. I didn't ask her inside the last couple of times she visited and again yesterday she's on the doorstep.

This time saying she's a bit concerned. SHE'S *a bit concerned???* I try to tell her I STILL *have somehow to establish whereabouts of the pressure cooker so I'm* MUCH *too busy to sit about talking to her. She says if I don't want to talk, would I like her just to sit with me a while. Well, what'd be the good of* THAT, *forgive me for asking. That'd be an even bigger waste of time (see what I mean about missing the point?). She forgets there's a great deal to be sorted out. Especially given the suddenness. This whole situation is all up in the air and somebody has to get a hold on matters. I have to raise my voice to get her to see that.*

Next and don't ask me how, she's over the threshold, saying the pressure cooker seems to "represent a more important loss" and does it have special associations, and I shout yes, associations with Irish Stew start to finish in thirty minutes, veg. in under two. Or has she never heard of TIME AND ENERGY SAVING?

When did you use it last? I seem to remember it was a wedding present.

Well hoping it turns up

Arthur

On the day after the accident I awoke to a morning full of dangers. In the shower, water broke around me like beads of wet glass on stones and my throat stiffened with steam and soap fumes. I emerged with something undesirable still clinging. I got dressed and went downstairs masquerading as a person who belonged here, a person who might have a legitimate connection with a tranquil house in Beaulieu Gardens on another sunny spring day. When I put on the kettle and poured cereal for myself, my hands shook.

I wondered if I could reinstate a former manageable smallness as the order of the day. I knew very well the advantages of going through the motions; if I didn't do it anymore, what would I go through instead? If I didn't, how was I going to become again what I had been for so long: absorbed, unseen, relieved?

But the air in every room I entered was suspended like breath held in anticipation of something splintering. I tried to think about housework, but I struggled to remember how I had ever been able to touch ordinary objects, for what might they become, in my hands? I could render anything and everything in the house lethal. Daylight burned on the edges of furniture, revealing them as unbearably raw. Ordinary colors punctured my eyes. I wandered the floors in fear of scalpels hidden under surfaces, of straight lines turning into blades. The emptiness of rooms glimpsed through doorways terrified me; I was afraid to walk under the lintels for fear of what I might bring in with me.

Yet I did not blunder from room to room, clumsy with distress. Despite what I felt, despite what I had done, I moved smoothly and did not disturb the quiet. It seemed I was still to appear, at least, to be part of the unchanged surface of the world. But I could never resume my old harmless life, not if I were also to be part of the new day upon whose ration of catastrophe the sun had already risen, just as it had yesterday. Because of me, a woman was dead. Somewhere, a family was in ruins. *I* was the one who deserved to be dead, they would think, and I didn't know why I wasn't; it seemed implausible, incredible even, that I should be able to go on breathing while disgust and hatred, justifiably without limit, mounted against me. They would want me caught and punished, of course; they would want me to suffer. The search would be already under way. Should I not simply give myself up? But whatever happened then, I wouldn't pay enough for the woman's life. I could never suffer as they did. Something was inadequate about the notion that any consequence less than my own death could counterweigh for hers. Something was askew, simply, in my remaining alive. It was a mistake, an oversight that should be corrected.

Anything could happen. I went back to bed and stayed there,

frightened of the purposeless way angles fill houses, frightened of all the minutes and hours of light that fill a single day, flaunting themselves, so brightly colored and jagged with risk, so available for the infliction of damage. I closed my eyes until it was dark.

When night came I got up. The moon reached in through the windows and painted luminous squares across the floors, lit the landing and stairs, laid a white path along the kitchen tiles to the back door. I went outside and kneeled on the ground. I was thinking of nothing, except to wonder if such emptiness of mind is felt by those about to be executed. Damp needles of cold pricked my legs and I pressed my palms down and stretched forward and rested my forehead on the grass, pushing it into the earth till my head was numb. May I not please also be dead? The mushroomy sop of the ground, an ancient, resurrected smell from deep below, seeped into me. I pressed my skull harder and harder into the gritty slide of soil and moss and worm cast, I tore up lumps of turf and rubbed them into my head, as if I could grate myself clean. I had to resist a desire to stuff my mouth with handfuls of mulch. I wanted the earth to soak in through my hair and skin and replace me, cell by cell, and if I couldn't be replaced I wanted to disintegrate.

Of course, none of these things happened. The garden all around me trembled in the wind. If it had been daylight I might have panicked and run away, but the moon shone and so I stayed, and soon, from the shadows, differing shades of dark emerged and receded, revealing themselves as wavering shapes: soft pillowy mounds and clusters of improbable, irregular domes. After a while my eyes were able to judge more than the simple presence of the trees and shrubs. Under the moon they had become vessels for hoarded light. Around their floating penumbrae I perceived something of their daytime solidity and distance, yet they imposed themselves so gently on my sight, wearing their white haloes like ghosts hinting palely at previous selves. They were so benevolent and colorless. I couldn't close my eyes against their beautiful absence of color.

The dark and the moonlight shimmered together; leaves hung as chill as the scent of the grass. I released my breath slowly. Again and again I ran my hands through the earth. Whatever might once have been buried here, and however long ago, and whether one night to be exhumed or not, to be seen again or never again uncovered, it all came to the same. All the uncountable particles once so fantastically joined up as to be living people were drawn to this end, reduced to one sodden compound with its familiar, equalizing, watery smell. Every glance and touch and hope, every driving beat that stabbed the heart when love failed, was atomized, finally. I thought of the woman's body softening and darkening, all its fleshly dreams and shocks melting into some patch of cool degenerative earth solemnly breached and laid open to take her.

I covered my face with my hands and remained there, kneeling on the grass. Time tucked its head under its white wings; all the time in the world lay floating on the lake of the night. I could stay here undisturbed until daylight came bobbing at the edges, bright with malice.

Dear Ruth

Carole's been again.

I let her in just for the sake of peace. Was going to show her the latest on letter writing front but realized in nick of time I couldn't let her read the last one. I'm not especially enamored of the woman but there's no need to hurt her feelings.

She seemed interested in my big cleanup of attic, drawers, cupboards etc. She did have to wade through a bit of stuff to get to a chair but even so I don't think it's quite her business to start picking papers up off the floor. MY papers off MY floor. Papers mainly yours in fact, a load of bumf looking like bits of poems, but you know what I mean. It's the principle of it. Snatched them away from her before she could get a look-see.

She means well but how can anyone else have a clue what all this is like?

However, getting off the point. Which is—as I'm not up to a regular laundry day, finding myself short on socks and whatnot, I raided spare room and put on some of the new stuff. Can't say it appeals, but it's a criminal waste all that new cruise wear hanging about in there getting trodden and crumpled. You'll remember I was forced to undo all your packing looking for pressure cooker. Of which still no sign, by the way.

Spare room still a mess but my new look is up and running!

I had on a green shirt and that light blue sweater with the anchor when Carole came. She seemed a bit shaken by the change of style.

I tried to make a joke about it. I was telling her about the cruise and then I remembered she's from CRUSE! You know, those coping with loss people, they had a fund-raiser not that long ago. Carole takes it all very seriously anyway. Delivered a stern lecture on the word "cruse"—did I know it's an Old Testament word for a widow's jar of oil that never ran dry, blah blah, the point being that support was there as long as it was needed? That's just the kind of thing Ruth would know, I told her. Then she wanted to know if I cry much. Nosey parker!

Still, changing subject again, can report headway of sorts. Often as not I see Mrs. Marsden from across the road coming out to catch Carole just as Carole's going, holding her up chatting, not very considerate of her.

Anyway, the Mary or Rosemary dilemma solved! Not that she minded me not calling her anything, or not talking at all, but it preyed on my mind. So, brainwave!—now I call her Mrs. M, in a light-hearted manner of course.

She noticed the new look too! She agreed apricot was unusual on a man except for golf but she said these slacks were really a kind of burnt apricot. She said you had a good eye for a bit of style, in a quiet sort of way. Then her eyes filled with tears.

Mrs. M's bossy. Says she keeps her front room gas fire on low till May so I should do the same. Oh, and getting huffy with it—she found something or other of hers in our fridge when she was throwing out the milk (gone smelly, she found it at the back) and got all offended. Didn't I care for either her leek and potato soup or her sausage casserole? I said, Not really and you can get rid of them along with the milk while you're at it, thank you very much. Then she peered at me and asked did I have an allergy, my forehead seemed to be breaking out. Psoriasis? Or maybe eczema? I pointed out it wasn't yet against the law for a man to scratch if he had an itch and if my appearance offended that was her problem, not mine. If looks could kill.

Bye for now
Arthur

Ps Suppose I can't let Carole see this letter either. So it's just you and me then. Nicer, I suppose.

PPS Am not letting her see any of that story you wrote, either, don't worry. Private, between you and me.

———

THE COLD AND THE BEAUTY AND THE DARK
1932

Chapter 2: At Mam's

A little before seven o'clock Evelyn let herself into the quiet house on Roper Street. As usual Mam had left her two slices of bread and margarine and put a hot water bottle in her bed. It was kind of her, though also as usual, the bread was curling and the hot water bottle was tepid. Evelyn ate quickly, then in the chilly room she changed into her long flannelette nightdress and bed socks. As she rubbed her toes on the cooling stone bottle and closed her eyes, she thought how funny it was that even a cold hot water bottle was better than nowt. Just the kindness had a bit of warmth to it. It wouldn't occur to Stan that you came off the night shift with freezing feet. But once she explained, he'd be sure to oblige.

She got up again at two o'clock in the afternoon. She was grateful, these days, for the house being empty when she woke. For the past few weeks she'd been sick first thing, but today she felt fine. She must be getting past the sickness stage and she was grateful for that, but it meant that before long she'd be showing. She *had* to get a date out of Stan, and soon.

By the time Mam came in it was getting dark but at last the rain had gone off. Evelyn sat Mam down while she made the tea. Mam called out to her above the wireless with snippets of news and gossip. She always had what she called "the latest" from her work at the Co-op. Everybody went to the Co-op so she didn't miss a thing.

"They're laying off another fifty at Worleyford's," she said. "That'll be it for Meg Throckmorton's Harry. He's for it this time."

"That'll not please Meg. He managed to hold on last time."

"No, it'll be hard."

"Happen they'll be teking on again at Marsden's soon. He might get took on there, her Harry."

Mam didn't seem to notice that Evelyn ate very little. Stan was meant to be coming down after tea, so after she'd washed up, Evelyn went to her room to change. Although she didn't much feel like going out, she made the effort, re-arranging her hair and putting on a fresh blouse and some lipstick. She had just dabbed some "Nuits de Mimosa" on her wrists and was wondering if real mimosa smelled anything like the cloudy, flowery scent from the bottle, when the knocker clacked against the door. She dashed downstairs, pulling on her coat as she went.

She might have guessed the minute she opened the door and saw him, she thought later. Stan stayed astride his bike instead of fiddling to get his padlock and chain around the downpipe against the house wall, which he would do if he'd had any intention of getting the bus with her down to the Roxy Palace. Added to that, his head was hanging forward the way it did when he had a drink or two in him. Still, he was wearing the bright red scarf she had knitted him for Christmas (with the fancy cable pattern in it, though all he cared about was the color). But maybe she was seeing what she'd wanted to see. Maybe he really meant it when he said the wearing of red was a political act and who knitted it wasn't important. Maybe his hair wasn't done nice and careful for her. More like it was only plastered down with the rain and the back of his hand.

On top of that he was late. Then she realized he wasn't on his own. A sudden tiny flare drew her gaze past Stan and she made out the shape of his crony Alan O'Reilly lurking over at the curb on his bike, lighting up under the street lamp. She crossed her arms and gave Stan a look.

"Oh, so you've got Alan O'Reilly in tow. Coming up the Roxy, too, is he?" she said, trying not to sound too sarcastic. Stan didn't go in for sarcasm. "Who's he stepping out with tonight, then?"

Stan didn't reply. Evelyn turned back into the tiny hall and set about getting her hat on, a nice little maroon toque.

"It's gone quarter past already. Remember main picture starts at twenty to, Stan," she reminded him, turning to smile so he couldn't say she was nagging. Brightening her smile even more, she called past him, "Evening, Alan! Who's the lucky one tonight, then?"

She was hoping Alan had just met up with Stan on the street and biked along with him. It was possible, just about. Hat fixed, handbag on her arm, Evelyn stepped onto the pavement. Stan wheeled back a little.

"Can't stop, sorry. Roxy's off. Change of plan," he said. Alan O'Reilly was glowering over his cigarette. He had a way of screwing up his eyes when he inhaled. Mean-looking, Evelyn thought.

"Where'd you say we've to be tonight, Comrade?" Stan said.

"Told you." Alan pulled a sheaf of papers from inside his jacket, and read aloud, "Extraordinary meeting called under Clause 7, right of Ordinary Members to call special or emergency meeting for any purpose including but not limited to those listed under Article 14 of Constitution."

He dragged again on his cigarette and stared at Evelyn, smoke leaking down his nose. Stan was smirking now, in the way that told her he definitely had already had a few.

"Another of your ruddy meetings? No, don't tell me," she said, "planning the revolution again, is it? You and the ruddy comrades? We had arrangements for this evening, Stanley Ashworth."

Alan O'Reilly threw his cigarette end into the gutter. "Come on, Stan, it's gone five."

"Nobody asked you, Alan O'Reilly," Evelyn said. She crossed her arms. "So, this meeting of yours'll be at the pub, I suppose? Stan?"

"I've got to go," Stan muttered. "I'm seconding him for Secretary, we're ousting Percy Johnson. And for your information it's in the Co-op Rooms."

Evelyn fought back tears. That Alan O'Reilly was a bad-tempered so-and-so and he was getting Stan the same way.

"Very well, then. Go to your ruddy meeting. You're welcome. But if you think you can make a fool out of your fiancée, you'd better think again!"

"If a meeting's called, a meeting's called. There's no point maithering on," Stan said, rolling his eyes in Alan O'Reilly's direction. "Come on, Evie."

"Don't you 'Evie' me! We've got certain matters to discuss, Stanley Ashworth, may I remind you?"

"There's time enough for that," Stan groaned. "I won't be nagged, woman!"

Alan O'Reilly chimed in, "Got a temper on her, ain't she? You want to watch yourself, Comrade. Come on."

"Good riddance," Evelyn muttered through her tears. She went upstairs to her room. Stan knew tonight was her last evening off before next week when she changed shifts. He knew they needed to set the date.

But she wasn't one to mope. Once she'd washed her face she came back downstairs. Mam had dozed off in her chair, her knitting on her lap. Evelyn took it up and finished the row, then worked one or two more. She was in no mood tonight to get on with her own knitting, which was a pullover for Stan in the same red as the scarf. Mam was making socks in dark green and the light was poor but the needles flew swiftly and smoothly in Evelyn's hands. She didn't need to see what she was doing, only to count the stitches. They were all good knitters on Mam's side, and they all had the same dimples, too. Knitting came as easy as smiling to the Leigh girls, people said.

Later, she washed through some stockings in the scullery and then she got Mam up to bed with a cup of tea. Afterward she sat on in front of the fire. Some evening out, she thought. I should go to bed myself.

But then, she reflected, Stan might just call in late on his way back from the meeting if he saw a light on. So Evelyn waited, yawning from time to time and half-listening to the voice on the wireless introducing a dance band from some-where or other. The rain came on again, harder than ever. She went to the window and pulled the curtain aside. Even the lamp right in front of number 58 on the other side of the street was hard to make out. Surely it was unusual for it to rain so hard you couldn't even see a street lamp? Raining ink, she thought. Evelyn watched it pour down the window till the glass looked as if it were melting. Then she drew the curtain back, put out the light, and returned to her chair, thinking of Stan pushing his bike past, glancing at the window, and thinking she'd gone to bed. In the dark, she began to cry again.

He'd be out there, caught in the rain. He could catch his death, and serve him right. But then her baby would never know its father. So in that respect the little mite would be like her, although not quite; Evelyn had been twelve years old when the telegram had come about her Da, "Missing in action, presumed killed," so she always felt that she should have kept hold of something more of her father to remember than the slow-moving, silent figure she hardly dared speak to. Over the years she tried to forget how the rasp of his boots in the yard and the click of the back door latch struck terror into her. She tried to forget his cruelties, a savage clip round the head or a snarled remark, and also his drunken rages when it was positively dangerous to be around him. She preferred to imagine that he might have come back from the War changed somehow, kind and smiling. She was careful to remember him only from the telegram, a few photos, and four postcards sent from the Belgian front.

She leaned back in her chair with her eyes closed. Suppose Stan did die and their baby grew up without him.

There wouldn't be much difference, in the end. It didn't matter whether your Da got a chill on the lungs after a soaking, or laid down his life in the Great War, he was dead and gone just the same. You wouldn't know his voice. You wouldn't be able to tell the back of his head in a crowd. You'd never know if he might have been the best father in the world. Whether his name was among The Fallen on the War Memorial or not, you'd just go without.

I should go to bed, Evelyn thought, blinking. Sometimes it felt as if her eyelids didn't keep the light out anymore. When she closed them, fireworks started going off across the insides, dots bursting in the blackness. It sounded pretty put like that, colored stars on the insides of your eyes, but it wasn't. It could be hard to get to sleep with lights pricking away all the time, popping off like at work, fancy lights flashing all night long. Some of the other girls at Brightaglow said it happened, some people got the flashing lights and some didn't, but it went after a bit. It hadn't bothered Daphne past her first three weeks, after all. She would just have to stop going on about it.

When she woke in her chair, the broadcast had finished and the wireless was crackling. The sound, like a match put to paper and kindling, had sent her into a half-dream that she was lighting a fire. Her eyes were watering now at the fading firelight, and she closed them again. When the stinging subsided, she read the clock. It was gone eleven and the fire had burned down to a few coals. The only other light in the room was coming off the wireless dial, dull and cool and greenish, as if from shining from under water.

She should have given herself an early night instead of waiting up on the off-chance Stan would drop in. He'd feel bad about tonight when he stopped to think about it. After all, they were getting married. He'd agreed.

Evelyn went to the kitchen to put the kettle on in the dark for her hot water bottle, and stood thinking her sad thoughts in the soft blue light from the gas. She had turned the gas off and was filling the bottle before it occurred to her it was foolish not to have put a light on. But she managed it fine, as easily as if she could see. She smiled. It was like Mam often said about this little chore or that, turning the heel on a sock or crimping the edge of the pastry on one of her famous meat and potato pies, Oh, I could do it blindfold.

Evelyn got the stopper on and stood for a while, pressing the bottle against her stomach.

The earthy aroma of warmed stone and the smells of damp brushes under the sink, burnt matches and potato peelings and gas were as familiar to Evelyn as the back of her own hand. She could breathe those smells anywhere and she'd be straight back in Mam's kitchen, but nevertheless tonight she felt a bit lost. It definitely did make you a bit nervy and weepy, being in the family way, she thought. She tiptoed upstairs, avoiding the creaky spots. As soon as she was in her bed with her feet on her bottle, she would feel as right as rain.

Dear Ruth

Is it going to be sad all the way through, this story?

I remembered something. You had some poem about mimosa. Where would that be lurking?

Tried to unearth it but no sign of it in any of the boxes of books or papers. Though would I know it for what it was, if I found it? Occurred to me I might not be clear about what I was looking for.

Instead, found heaps of stuff from Overdale! Ruth, was it at Overdale you told me about mimosa?

Later
Been looking further, still no sign.

Maybe you took it with you somehow. That's how it seems. Plus you took away a lot of words on other subjects as well.

Excuse scrawl, light poor, bulb dead.

Legs giving trouble.

Arthur

I'd done it before, watched from an upstairs window as someone left, and then waited on long enough afterward to feel a reverberating absence imprison me like a circle of spears. But that April evening I was a grown-up married woman, who had struck and killed another human being, so the parallel was a surface similarity only. In fact it wasn't the same kind of situation at all.

I was six the night the man I knew as my great-uncle left. He stalked out in a riot of hurled missiles, insults, and breaking glass, leaving a trail of strewn belongings and wrapped presents that shed their bright ribbons and paper across the snow. It was Christmas Eve of

1962. Whenever my mother talked about it, she made a great deal of that. Christmas bloody Eve, can you believe it, *Christmas bloody Eve*, she would say, as if he had chosen the moment so that particular and perpetual outrage at his sense of timing would stain the day forever, obliging her to rename it. She forgot that he didn't choose it at all, and he wasn't around after that to correct her, but left because she threw him out. Not literally, for he was a foot taller than she was and strong, even at his age; what she actually threw (as well as the Christmas presents he had shown up with), straight through the windows of the confectioner's and tobacconist's corner shop that he owned and my mother ran, were several glass jars of sweets from the shelves behind the counter, some clothes and shoes, two ashtrays and a lighter, a radio, a suitcase, a set of hairbrushes, and a collection of cigarette cards in a biscuit tin. If she could have lifted the cash register, that would have gone, too.

The part I don't remember is before. He must have turned up very late; the shop was long since shut and my grandmother and I had gone to bed. I remember my intention to stay awake to see Santa Claus. I remember staring at my bedroom door but I don't remember seeing it open. Would I, sleepily, in the dark, have mistaken one for the other? Would I have not known the wondrous, real Santa Claus from my great-uncle with his nicotine breath and damp lips, guiding my hand and whispering that maybe he had a sweetie for a good little girl in his pocket?

I don't remember anything until I heard weeping and shouting and the stumbling of feet on the stairs. My room on the top floor had only a skylight facing the back so I scrambled out of bed and raced down to the window of the sitting room directly over the shop, overlooking the empty pavement. More snow had fallen. The surrounding buildings were dark and the crossroads of Coster Street and Station Road were deserted. Below I heard the frantic clang of the shop bell and then my mother and uncle lurched out onto the white street, stage-lit from the open door, their voices ringing off the snow.

She must have attacked first. Already he had dragged her blouse and sweater off one shoulder and was on the retreat, holding a hand to his nose. She waded after him, arms swinging, screaming *On Christmas bloody Eve!*, and cracked him over one ear. He roared, grabbed her hair, and slapped her, pulling her down, and as she screeched and fell she kicked at him and he fell, too. They staggered to their feet and went at each other again, arms and legs flailing; the elongated blue swords of their shadows clashing twenty feet across the snow and up the walls opposite in crisscross mimicry of the duel. Blood appeared from somewhere—his nose, her lip? not much, a few dark drops spattering the white—and maybe it was the sight of that or fear of where it could end that brought them both to a standstill, panting and soaked and staring at each other as clumps of snow dripped off them. Then from my mother came a long, low wailing that rose in pitch until her voice broke into sobs. She turned back to the shop, slamming the door.

I heard her thump up the stairs, and I hid behind the settee while she rampaged around grabbing everything that she recognized as his. Then she clumped back down, and I had taken up my position at the window again just as she flung first the radio and the sweet jars, followed by all the rest of the stuff, including the Christmas presents, straight through the front windows of the shop. My uncle stood swaying in the road as objects and spears of glass crash-landed around him. She managed to throw the things quite a distance but she didn't manage to hit him, perhaps because she was drunk.

As was he. He didn't *walk* out any more than she threw him. In the end he could only stagger away, whimpering excuses back at her, his feet kicking up more snow. It took him a few minutes to collect what he could in his arms and navigate his way up Station Road toward the alley and the footbridge over the railway, and after he had gone, all that remained besides the marks of the brawl—the dropped belongings, the broken glass, and the wrecked parcels—were the ragged, despoiling traces of his zigzag progress up the street, a hundred slips and skids and falls imprinted on the snow. That's my memory of it.

I watched all this standing in my pajamas on the settee, peering over the back of it through the window with my chin resting on my crossed arms, the coal fire dying and the room dark behind me. I watched until long after he was gone and the silence told me that my mother must have got herself as far as her bedroom and passed out. She would be still in her clothes, grunting softly and curled up across the bed; I pictured her with the eiderdown up around her ears against the drafts. I knew that if the noise had woken her up, my grandmother would simply have turned over in bed, smiled into the dark, and gone back to sleep. I felt like the last person left. I knew I ought to be in bed and because I wasn't I was deservedly guilty and forsaken, responsible both for the mess out on the street and for my own solitude. I had already let go of any idea that Santa Claus would be coming now—how could he come near a household like ours?—but I scanned the crossroads and the tops of buildings, clinging to a hope for some kind of timely, redemptive magic; I prayed for some power to appear and make everything all right. Then I started to cry.

Snow came. There was no wind so it floated out of the sky like weightless, frozen rags of wispy white cloth. Some of the school Nativity play propaganda must still have been fresh in my mind; if ever a place was crying out for Peace on Earth Goodwill Toward Men it was here, so I wiped my nose on my sleeve and trusted that someone—if not Santa, then the Baby Jesus or Mary and Joseph or the shepherds, maybe the whole holy caboodle—was watching me from up in the sky, ripping up white tissue paper and dropping the shreds down to cover up the chaos. The amassing snow covered the scars of our disgrace like bandages. The disintegrating red paper and pink ribbons, the dark bulks of my great-uncle's abandoned things, the glinting javelins of glass lost their edges and grew round and safe. The snow went on falling until the tracks of his exit were swabbed away and I could tell myself that he may not have gone because there was no sign that he had ever been. All the bright broken relics, now vanished under a wrapping of whiteness, began to seem as dreamy as a memory that I held of him reaching out, just once, and stroking my hair.

As I watched the snow, my loneliness began to feel like safety.

Nobody could see me, so I must be invisible. And nobody knew what I had seen so I could make that invisible, too. Not by forgetting, but by keeping it for myself, mine to rehearse in my mind until familiarity rendered its violence innocuous, I would make it disappear. The shock of the fight and my uncle's desertion would lap its way over and over through my memory until in time its last waves spent themselves and died in the corners and my mother and uncle as they had appeared to me this night would recede, pulling shadows around themselves, the sounds of their departure faint and ghostly, merely sighs and whispers and a faraway door closing.

And I understood suddenly that I would be able to pretend, and forever if need be, that this night was simply another night separating any two days: neither holy nor enchanted, nor the night my poor uncle left, nor even, necessarily, Christmas Bloody Eve. Another night and then another would come, and another, and each time my memory of this one would lose a little sharpness, and each new night would be its own reliable little spell of quiet between dangers. For a brief time before I fell asleep on the settee, that was nearly enough, to know the glaring colors of our strife were obliterated and to hold in my mind a picture of the street transformed under the black sky and the dense, cleansing whiteness of the snow.

No, there's no similarity at all, none to speak of. Jeremy went quietly. And I was very little then, and frightened.

Dear Ruth

Time passes. We're almost into June. I suppose it's warmed up a bit but by no stretch of the imagination could it be mistaken for warm à la Madeira, which is where we'd be now.

Apologies for silence. Been busy. Getting myself organized you'll be pleased to hear! You're not hearing, of course, but Carole says I shouldn't dwell on that if writing these letters is to be at all useful.

So the upturn in the weather put me in the mood for leafing through the cruise and Australia paperwork. I turned up the brochure and itinerary and that inspired me to check what date we're at today. I lose track of the days, sleep through them when I can. I get more done at night, without the interruptions.

Which is why I know we'd be in Madeira, jewel of the Mediterranean. You always wanted to go.

You were keen to see the mimosa for which Madeira is famed throughout the world. So here's some photos of it from the brochure, sorry they're a bit ragged, I couldn't put my hand on the scissors so I tore them out. Butterflies, too, according to the literature, a feature of the place, some species thought to be unique to the island.

I was looking forward more to the bird spotting, I admit—I had them in the luggage, binoculars, reliable field guide of Mediterranean species, and RSPB spotters' notebook. My motto—never leave home without a notebook! Does that sound familiar or does that sound familiar!?

This notebook still blank, needless to say.

Was walking around most of the night with it in my hands, plus remains of cruise brochure. It's ruined now, but I won't need it again.

Also found this to go with photos. Came across the tape so I'm sticking it all in.

MADEIRA: JEWEL OF THE MEDITERRANEAN

Two carefree days of sampling the delights of seafaring life aboard the *Belle Aurore Atlantis* and then "Land Ho!" What a wonderful land is your first port of call—Madeira, beautiful isle of pure blue skies, warm seas, and floral abundance.

From your very first step on the soil of Madeira the delighted visitor understands why it is known as the Garden Island, as the place is simply awash with color.

Day 1: Stroll at your leisure through the large and colorful flower markets that are one of the most arresting features of Funchal, Madeira's capital. Relax over lunch at one of the quaint bodegas, and while you're at it, why not sample some of the famous Madeira wine? In the afternoon, rendezvous dockside to travel by luxury air-conditioned coach to Camacha to marvel at the local wicker furniture weavers at work, and then on to the island's blissful Botanical Gardens for a breathtaking display of subtropical plants and flowers, most strikingly the luscious golden yellow of the famous mimosa groves.

Day 2: Morning free for shopping in the famous lace- and tapestry-making quarter. After a lunch of traditional Mediterranean fare using the finest local ingredients, we again rendezvous dockside to travel by luxury air-conditioned coach to the enchanting fishing village of Camara de Lobos, where Churchill went to paint. Continue on to the celebrated Levada walks, part of the island's ancient irrigation system, before returning to Funchal for a sumptuous afternoon tea at the worldfamous Reid's Hotel.

Can you imagine it? I can't

Arthur

PS Am unearthing all kinds of things. Seems to me you got a bit carried away with that writing group of yours. Poetry that doesn't rhyme and stories that don't begin or end properly. OK as a hobby I suppose, but the more I try to sort through it all the more there is. I'm tripping over loose pages, folders in every cupboard and drawer I open. I can't make head nor tail. There's reams of it.

PPS Whenever did you find the time? There's REAMS . . .

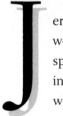eremy telephoned. He said, reading sturdily from a list, that he would be grateful if I would forward his mail using the labels specially printed with his new address that he would send me in a day or two. He proposed to close our bank account but would pay, into my personal account in monthly installments, more than enough money for my purposes. His call had awakened me and when I tried to speak, my mouth felt slow and unchaste and slutty. I struggled to say something that would not sound off-balance and degraded. He told me he had already arranged that the garage bill for the Renault's service would be sent direct to him, and

again my words faltered, snagging in the net of his enunciated, suffocating reasonableness. In the moment's pause, maybe a beat of tenderness passed between us. Then he said if I couldn't be bothered to stick simple address labels on a few envelopes he would drop by for his letters instead.

Out of pride I feigned a little cooperation, but really I was thinking of all the things Jeremy and I had done for so long, ostensibly for the other's sake. What expenditure, what a squandering of spirit, this "working at" our marriage; what a thin and childish pact it was in the first place. If we had ever aspired to a state of marital grace, we had long ago settled instead for efficiency; long after I was weary to extinction at my presence seeming still to be in some way required, I had continued to turn in performances connected with laundry, cleaning, and food. Jeremy had continued to oversee cars, money, and gardening. We had both pretended to be living together in more than the physical sense, wearing for each other the face we supposed the other ought to see because perhaps, behind it, we were guarding a truer, less resolute version of our selves that we feared the other would attack if they knew about it. With slippery expertise we had concealed first the doubt, and then the noiseless, tearing disappointment that life wasn't fuller and brighter than this. Jeremy went on to mention his passport, I think in relation to the coming summer and "grabbing a fortnight somewhere," but my attention had wandered by then. I was wondering when it was, exactly, that we'd started to show each other more tact than kindness.

Since I was awake and it was after four o'clock in the afternoon, I went to my studio—just the smallest bedroom with bare floorboards, an uncurtained window, and a basin in the corner—and tried to think about painting. Illustrated books were open all over the place, reminding me that I had been working on another series of butterfly studies.

Butterflies. I flipped over a few pages trying to remember what I had once found so captivating. I came across notes in my own writing. There were (I read) many species of butterfly—*Lepidoptera*—whose wing patterns mimicked the appearance of other things in the world. I had begun a list. I counted them on my fingers, right hand first, jammed in my dressing gown pocket, tightening each finger in turn, pressing the end of each nail into my palm just enough to get the nip of the edge on flesh. Some butterflies' wings looked like the golden eyes of a certain poisonous lizard. There was one with the blue-green Argus eyes of peacock feathers. Another had wings like a flamenco dancer's pair of fans; another, curling, dead autumn leaves. One resembled the veneer of polished walnut, its wings like little cabinet doors. Then there were some that looked like tropical flowers, one in particular, its wings spattered to resemble the lure of dewdrops marking a pathway down a darkening velvet cave into the deeps of an orchid. Or was it the other way round (I had put a question mark after that one). Was it the orchid that had evolved to look like the butterfly's wings? Whichever was imitating the other, they both looked like something else; here in my writing was another question mark and the word "vagina," followed by two more question marks. I smiled, seeing how I had used the medical word and surrounded it with those perplexed, small, tidy curls of inquiry.

But I no longer wanted to know anything about butterflies. A few days ago I would have said I was fascinated by their sheer variety, the opulence of their colors and patterns, and the "challenge" I felt, as a mere amateur, to "do justice" to such delicacy and brilliance. I would also have said, for I had acquired a few real mounted specimens, pinned and fraying above inked Latin names in display boxes with flakes of broken wing in the corners, that I found something poignant and sacrificial in their labeled entrapment. I picked up one of the boxes from the worktable and looked at it: *Chrysiridia ripheus*—the Madagascar Moth. Not strictly speaking a butterfly at all, but looking like one, its wings open to show a gorgeous twinned miniature sunset. But now I was fascinated not by its classification nor its beauty nor the precise manner of its death. What seemed amazing was the simple cessation of its hair-thin little life, the dry and painless arrest of all the faultless microscopic connections that had joined one beat of its wings, one sweep of its antennae, to the next. I hadn't thought of it before, but it was the single wanton instant of its final coming to stillness that was spread out on display under glass, that one pure extinguishing moment perpetuated by every pair of eyes that gazed at it in the hundred and more years after the creature would anyway be dead.

I thought of the woman no less reduced to a specimen on a mortuary slab, her body pinned open and exposed to the rummaging of a pathologist's latexed hands. Such an obscene curiosity, which could be satisfied by encrypting the end of her life in a series of data entered by a laboratory assistant on a clipboard. But the true, inexcusable obscenity was not the physical progress from being alive to lifelessness, nor the recording of it—it was the manner of her death. I alone was responsible for that. I swept the boxes of butterflies to the floor, where all the papery colored wings fragmented among the splinters of glass and wood. There was nothing poignant about them. They were disgusting.

It was dark when I went out. The night was gray and vapory, rain misting the darkness. I knew I wouldn't see the moon so I walked fast out of the ring of the cul-de-sac, flexed both hands in my coat pockets, and began to run, head down, fixing my attention on the silver reflection of my body dancing off the shining road. Weather is louder at night. The drumroll of raindrops brought cold, pungent spirals of scent up from gardens and pavements. I fisted my hands and pushed them down against the inside of my pockets, squeezed my arms against my sides, and ran on. Walking and running, sometimes stopping for breath, I continued without thinking of where I was going except that I knew I was avoiding anywhere lit.

I turned away from the direction of the town and followed the road until it intersected with two lanes leading into the countryside. Soon I was about two miles from my house, on the edge of woodland that I had only ever driven past. I turned off the lane and crackled and stumbled my way through the bracken. I was grunting and wheezing; in the dark I felt like an animal, but one out of its proper place and unfamiliar with wet roots and ditches and low-hanging branches, and I felt both alone and surrounded, my presence both unsensed and sensed. I was raising enough racket to empty the woods; I liked the idea that from their places among the trees and bracken they might be watching, the badgers and foxes, the voles and hedgehogs. I slowed and stopped, my body aching, my face itching under the heat of the sweat I had worked up. Silence, but for my breathing and the seep and trickle of the rain, drifted through the wood. There was no movement but fronds of bracken swinging back from the trail I had broken behind me and the waft of damp air touching my hair and cooling my skin, the only smells my sweat and the rainy green sap.

Now I could see a white cloudy smudge of moon shining through the trees and white darts of rain spitting out of the sky. From far away came an animal cry, a rising screech of distress that it was impossible to imagine might not be human. It was late and lonely enough for me to let out an answering howl if I wanted to, but I had started to shiver and could not utter a sound. Besides, what answer could I give, and to what? Probably it was a fox. But the call was a kind of refrain; it held no note of urgency and might not even have been real. Perhaps it was the cry of a phantom; it sounded, through the dark, like a wail as old as myth or lamentation, or of suffering itself. It might be not a fox but a ravening beast from a fable, crying out and limping the night lanes with sorrow in its yellow eyes, for it must be by night that creatures from the oldest stories of all are summoned up and stalk the earth, wishing to be remembered. I raised my head and felt the rain pour down on me. Further into the darkness I went, crashing through the wood, branches scratching my face.

Dear Ruth

I'm making a big pile of things for chucking, it's gone on there. Remains of brochure, I mean. Best to get the rubbish all together in one place and do a big blitz and I'm not using the dining room for anything else. Surprising how it mounts up.

Pressure cooker still AWOL.

Later on

Had second thoughts—I took cruise brochure back off the pile and sat there looking at it again, all those photos. Looked for a long time till it was too dark to see.

Wednesday

Am looking at it again now. Mimosa's odd-looking, little cocoons of bright yellow cotton, not like any other flower. I never did like yellow but I shouldn't have forgotten you did. I should have thought of yellow for the flowers instead of going with white.

Bye for now

Arthur

———

THE COLD AND THE BEAUTY AND THE DARK
1932

Chapter 3: Only a Week to Go

Evelyn saw Stan and his mother off from the door herself. It was a dry evening, but foggy. Mrs. Ashworth sniffed and turned up the fur collar on her good coat.

"Nice spread, Evelyn," she said, nodding. "Much obliged to your Mam. Come on, Stan, that train'll be along."

Stan, winding his red scarf around his neck, glanced down at his mother and then at his fiancée.

"Aye, right nice it was, say ta again for us, will you?" he muttered, shuffling toward Evelyn for a kiss. Mrs. Ashworth cleared her throat and stared hard at her son.

She does it on purpose, the old curmudgeon, Evelyn thought. She wasn't letting the two of them have even a minute alone to say good night. She could at least pretend to be busy putting on her gloves or looking up the street. But Evelyn didn't care. They'd got through the ordeal of Stan with his mother in tow meeting all the assembled Leigh family for a special Sunday tea, a week before the wedding. Mrs. Leigh had soaked and braised a whole ham, and she and Evelyn and Auntie Peg had all been baking for days, to say nothing of the sweeping and polishing of the house, which was always spotless, anyway.

But it had all gone off all right, and on top of that there was her lovely new locket. While Stan dithered about kissing

18

her good night in front of his mother, Evelyn fingered it gently at her throat and smiled shyly at him. In less than a week they would be a married couple, and with her help he would start standing up to his mother at last. Mrs. Ashworth had had her own way with him too long, ever since his father cleared off. Everybody said so. It wasn't right. It wasn't right for Stan. In the meantime, Evelyn wouldn't give her the satisfaction.

"You're very welcome I'm sure, Mrs. Ashworth. 'Night, then, Stan," she said brightly. "See you tomorrow, six o'clock sharp. You haven't forgotten you're taking me to the pictures, have you?" She darted forward and pressed her lips to his cheek, kissing him with a loud smacking sound.

"And thank you again for the beautiful locket, Stan," she said, loud enough for his Mam to hear. "Ta-ta, then, Mrs. Ashworth! Mind how you go in the fog."

Mrs. Ashworth's only reply was a pursing of the lips. Evelyn didn't care. Make all the nasty faces you like, she thought. By this time next week I'll be kissing your precious Stan all I please, only right smack on his lips, and right in front of you in your own house. And you won't be able to do a thing about it.

Mrs. Ashworth took Stan's arm decisively, turned him up Roper Street, and marched him away. They made a funny pair of shapes, her as wide as she was high, Stan so tall and rangy. He didn't look back once, but Evelyn hadn't expected him to. In the fog she could only make out the bright red scarf, anyway.

Mam and her aunties Peg and Violet were seeing to the dishes and no doubt gossiping about their visitors, going over the details of Mrs. Ashworth's frock no doubt, and the habit she had of sniffing ever so daintily at her teacup before she sipped from it. How even she hadn't been able to resist Mam's Eccles cakes and how Peg had tried not to stare when she had reached for her third one! How she tried to look down her nose, as if she were doing them a favor letting her Stan marry into the Leighs! And then when Evelyn had shown them all the pretty locket Stan had just given her, how the woman hadn't known whether to bask in the Ashworths' largesse, or tut over her son's extravagance.

The menfolk, Violet's husband, Bill, and Peg's sons, Bradley and Will, were in the front room, also ruminating over the meeting of their future relations by marriage. But they did so more contemplatively, puffing on cigarettes and pipes, their talk interspersed with many a grunt and long stare into the fire. Stanley Ashworth seemed a sound enough lad. On the quiet side, but this was no criticism; the Leigh menfolk weren't big talkers themselves. Anyway, they never got too worked up about such matters. They didn't speculate deeply about a man's character, they waited to see what he was made of. It was better to stay slightly puzzled by it all, and let the lasses get on with unraveling all the ins and outs of courtship and marriage and the uneasy unions of families. It wasn't that the men liked being puzzled by it all, it was just that they liked a quiet life and the best chance of that was not to interfere with woman talk that they could never hope to understand.

That night in her bedroom Evelyn took off her locket and studied it carefully. Stan had given it to her sheepishly, hanging back in the hall as he'd arrived, while Mrs. Leigh had taken charge of his mother and led her away into the front room. He had pressed the box into Evelyn's hand and said, "Hope it's to your liking. Not had much call to go buying jewelry, it's nothing to write home about. Hope it suits."

"Why, Stan!" she had cried, opening the little velvet box. "It's lovely!"

Now she held it up and gazed at the locket in her palm. Really, a locket was more useful than a ring, she told herself. A ring could get in the way if you were doing a dirty job like raking out the fire or scouring the front step. You'd either have to take it off and worry about losing it or you'd worry about scratching it. A locket you could just put on and forget about. There would be a little wedding band for her finger soon, for decency's sake, and that was all anyone needed.

"Oh, and it's got ever such a strong clasp, Stan. No fear I'll be losing it!" she had said to him, watching it spin from its chain. In the dark hall it hadn't caught the eye half as much as it would in a brighter room. In proper sunshine, come the summer, the etched pattern of leaves on the silver surface would surely throw back the light quite beautifully.

"It's only silver," grunted Stan.

"But silver's lovely!" Evelyn had reassured him. "Silver's better on me, with my coloring. Silver's much more flattering than gold, in my opinion. It's much more wearable. In fact I believe I prefer it to gold. Honest, I do."

She had placed the locket against her throat while Stan watched her in silence. Eventually she had turned her back to him and dipped her head.

"Do it up for me, Stan?" she'd said, lifting her hair from the back of her neck.

"I can't be doing with them fiddly things. My hands is too big."

"Oh, go on, do! At least try, Stanley Ashworth!"

Stan, fumbling awkwardly, had managed to secure the clasp. Evelyn twirled around to face him again, smiling radiantly.

"I shall have to get a nice photo of you now," she had said. "To keep in it. A nice one of you, on our wedding day."

"Who'd want my ugly mug in a locket?" Stan had replied. "Wait and get one of this precious baby o' yours, when it turns up. That'd be more like it."

That had caused Evelyn to gasp with excitement. "Oh, Stan!" she had said, her eyes filling with tears. He was as good as saying he wanted her to get a proper baby portrait taken, when the time came. "That's the nicest thing you've said about the baby!"

But Stan hadn't heard. He had already turned and was on his way into the front room where Mrs. Leigh's special tea was waiting.

In the dark of her bedroom Evelyn smiled to herself as she got into bed. Stan was so straightforward, really. A man's hungry so he goes off to get his tea, what could be simpler than that? She was grateful for his good appetite, remembering the sight of him a little later, folding slices of ham and beetroot from his knife into his mouth, face bent low over his plate. That Mrs. Ashworth obviously didn't overfeed him. But she, Evelyn, would try to learn to be as good a cook as her Mam, and everybody knew what satisfying a man's stomach led to, if you were patient.

Dear Ruth

Can't a man sleep undisturbed in his own house at a time of his own choosing?

Mrs. M from across the road barged in again. Said she was worried to see the curtains unopened in daytime—I wanted to say this was to DETER *people like her, not have opposite effect and bring nosy old bags knocking.*

Didn't get the chance though because she came barreling in, took one look at my sorting-out handiwork (another pile started in hall, thinking practically again, nearer the door come time for the final chuck-out) and of course she got the wrong end of the stick. I suppose I can see why, hall's filling up and the dining room also pretty crammed now—but it's only on the surface and did she give me a chance to explain the system?

All these piles are either stuff for a particular purpose, or it's stuff going eventually in a particular place eg: crockery. No need for all the china we managed to accumulate now there's only me, so am streamlining operations in kitchen and dining room. Am considering including flowerpots in with crockery. Those ones in conservatory you've got begonias in. Are they begonias? Have to report all now deceased, therefore pots can go at some point. No real urgency.

But soda bottles. They don't go into same pile as cassettes and records. Obvious, I'd have thought. But Mrs. M's the kind of woman who shouldn't see anything half-finished. She's clearly of limited intelligence and prone to overreacting.

Last time, forgot to mention, she implied I wasn't up to cutting the grass. Understandable to have let it go in the circumstances, she said, and would I like her precious son Tony to get it back to rights next time he comes over to see to hers. I was civil but firm. I'll do it in my own good time. Maybe when this leg trouble has eased off.

I don't recall ever hearing he was a paramedic. She claims you knew. Obviously Tony can Do No Wrong. She subjected me to latest, he's been on some extra training course or other.

By the way—I hadn't noticed till Mrs. M pointed it out, and Carole may have mentioned it, too. It's not like you, but you slipped up this time. These new clothes don't fit. You bought me all that cruise stuff in the wrong size. Everything is way too big—Mrs. M said I need to look for a belt for the slacks or there's going to be a mishap! Didn't like the look on her face when she said that.

Couldn't find a belt but made do with that checked tie we nearly quarreled about. It is too purple but it does the job.

Nothing I can do about the shirt collars, they gape a bit. These days a sweater on the baggy side still passes muster, I suppose.

At least there's plenty of it, the cruise stuff, so I needn't brave the dials on the washing machine just yet. All gobbledy gook to me. I never saw so many clothes. Maybe you had in mind not just the cruise on the Belle Aurore Atlantis but the first couple of months in Oz as well, just in case our shipped crates didn't arrive, or worse, went AWOL. You're good about things like that. I may not have said so.

Bye for now

A

                                                      later

It's raining tonight. Wonder what rain's like when you're out at sea. It's only now we're not cruising the ocean wave I wonder we ever thought we'd get away without mishap, small or great. We had a nerve, thinking we could pull a stunt like that, a six-week cruise and a new life waiting. Got rather upset with this line of thinking so resorted to reading.

I read about the accident in the paper, holding myself tight, my heart bumping against my folded arms.

There was a poetic touch in the way the story of the FATAL HIT AND RUN was told. The paper reported that the scene of the incident was in the heart of idyllic countryside, in an area of outstanding natural beauty. There were two photographs of it: pre-outrage, innocent as a calendar, and afterward, tainted by a cordon of police tape and mounds of flowers in cellophane. "The horror scene" burgeoned treacherously with spring blossom and daffodils, a death trap masquerading as a beauty spot. The implication was that dying

somewhere beautiful might have made a difference to childless, recently retired English teacher Ruth Mitchell (61) of 27 Cardigan
Avenue, Monkwell Down, and her devastated husband, Arthur (68).

The article didn't suggest which way the difference might have
gone, whether death's random visitation upon that particular place
would forever after sully its beauty or whether the place's beauty had
assuaged, if only momentarily, the bane of death. It did not ask what
message about a life might be carried in the very last thing the eye be-
held. I wanted to know, if that final blink closed on one last imprinted
image of beauty rather than of ugliness, would a person reach a conclu-
sion, just as she was leaving it, about the relative aggregations of glory
and squalor in the world? It seemed important.

The *West Wiltshire Gazette* did not speculate. It dwelled instead,
naturally, on what kind of monster was responsible for such a crime. It
seemed almost odd that I did not read my name in the same sentence
as "the perpetrator of this callous and evil criminal act" and I found
myself whispering, *it's me.*

I stared again at the two photographs in the paper. Suddenly I was
back there, on that April afternoon. I retched and started to sweat; I
saw again the hideous colors of the day and the burning sunlight, I felt
the deep heavy jolt as the car struck her, and her fall to the ground. I
heard the silence. I saw her on the road as only I had seen her, blood
pumping from her dead brain and the crows gathering to feast.

I forced myself to read to the end of the article. The police were
appealing for witnesses and "pursuing every lead." Why wouldn't they
come here, and find the Saab locked in the garage? I wanted them to
come. I wouldn't lie. Confession is supposed to relieve everyone, especially the guilt-laden. But even if the next headline on the front page of
the *West Wiltshire Gazette* was FATAL HIT AND RUN: DOCTOR'S WIFE
GUILTY, would it bring relief, would it make any difference at all?

The piece ended with another photograph of the couple as young
teachers: DEDICATED TO YOUTH WELFARE: RUTH AND ARTHUR AT
OVERDALE OUTDOOR EDUCATION CENTER, followed by an unpoetic para-
graph about cycling fatality statistics and safety helmets.

I slept in my clothes, and woke up, before the alarm clock sounded, at nine o'clock in the evening. No drifting around the house tonight; the place was eight miles away, not that the distance meant anything in itself, nor did the rain.

The sky and the cold land together had sunk to an equal darkness, reaching a muffled, stony equilibrium through which I walked with the greatest care. Though the dark was not absolute, the night seemed marginless and I disembodied. I kept close by the hedges. Above the rain and the distant sighing of traffic from the motorway I heard everything: I heard the click of an insect's wings as it landed on a stem by a garden wall and I heard the singing, empty vastness of the sky above me. It occurred to me that I should have been afraid to be out alone on the road at night, but fear didn't come. Rather, what a freedom it was, to walk under this sky instead of the wide, lit gallery of the sun's arc, illuminating every act and failure of a day in its long, sad slide toward nightfall.

Above the high open stretch of road near the place, the moon was a dull ellipse of silver through the thinning cloud, and the houses behind the orchard wore the moonlight coldly, like a sheeting of ice. Under the trees, rainwater trapped in the leaves and blossoms fell on me in slower, wetter drops than on the open road. The traffic cones and cordon of tape had gone, but the bank of piled-up flowers and stuffed toys remained; sodden teddy bears and dripping cuddly dogs presided over a floral shrine almost touching in its pointlessness. Among the flowers lay sheets of waterlogged paper bearing half-obliterated messages, like handkerchiefs drenched in charcoal tears. The huge curling letters of RUTH were turning into watery ghosts of themselves, receding into vagueness. Water plocked down and pooled into little crevices in the cellophane under which the offerings of flowers, trapped in bunches by strings and wires, were already darkening with slime. I knelt down and tore at them, releasing from the crackling of wrappings a shower of cold water and a rank, drainy stench. I pulled some of the rotting blooms off their stems and picked at their petals, tidying and primping what was left of their lolling heads. Slippery black stuff clung to my fingers.

Some of the flower heads were luminous; others seemed soaked in gray. Drifting through the smell of the dead flowers came the smell of the dying ones, cold and peppery: carnations, roses, lilies, clouds of angel breath. I picked out the ones that reflected back the moon's brightness and I discarded the ones that looked dead—they must be, by daylight, the red and orange and purple and blue. All this absorbed me for quite some time. I went through every bunch until I had picked out every pale flower and made a pile of them. The dark ones I threw away over the wall under the trees. When I got to my feet my knees buckled. I was freezing cold; I placed my fingers in my mouth to warm them and the sticky mixture of mud and stalks and crushed petals on my hands tasted bitter, though not poisonous, or at least not yet. It had the tang of something intermediate, something nearly dirty; poised between living sap and the sodden musk of last year's leaves, it was a sharp, growing taste which was nonetheless prognostic of decay and irretrievable rot.

One by one I lifted the pale flower heads from the pile and cast them out across the road which shone and shifted under the moon and swaying trees like a dark river. Then I started to walk away. At the crest of the hill I turned back. I could make out the swirl of flowers on the road, seeming astronomically distant, pale dots of whiteness gleaming in a paradox of a galaxy: infinite yet bordered, its darkness sheltered by a stand of trees. I turned away, and behind me a constellation of water-laden stars rolled across an endless sky, drifting and dispersing over the spot where she had died.

Dear R

*Just as well I'm not venturing out of doors to any extent (legs) be-
cause I'd stick out like a sore thumb in these colors.*

*It's all way too bright, the cruise wear. I said as much to you at the
time but as usual was overruled. And it's a bit lightweight for June but if
I put on enough layers I get by temperature-wise.*

*Not an issue at night, of course, the colors. Everything gets damped
down in the dark. Not just colors. Makes it easier to cope. In the dark
it's not so obvious you're not here. I can imagine that you are and I just
can't see you.*

*And I'm keeping busy. I'm trying to get all the Overdale stuff to-
gether in one place. Ditto your jottings from the writing group*

You never know when plans are going to fall away to nothing.

*People don't think about things falling apart but they should.
People should think about that more. Then they might be more ready
for when they do.*

A

THE COLD AND THE BEAUTY AND THE DARK
1932

Chapter 4: The Wedding Day Dawns

Evelyn breathed carefully on the long mirror and wiped at it with the corner of her bath towel—she wasn't risking her lovely velvet sleeve on a misted-up old mirror! It was kind of Mam to let her get dressed in her own bedroom on her Big Day, in front of the grand old walnut wardrobe with the full-length mirror, but it was such a heavy, old-fashioned thing and the mirror glass wasn't as clear as it used to be. You had to go right up close to get any idea of how you looked.

She stopped rubbing, stepped forward, and peered at herself. She was positively tingling with excitement. Stan might have had a sixth sense, the way the locket matched everything! The silver was just right with the dark green velvet of her suit and the white lace jabot at the neck. She gave a little twirl. She never thought she'd be getting married in bottle green, but it was beautiful velvet, real dress quality. Daphne had seen suits in practically identical velvet on the Ladies' Floor at Kendal Milne in Manchester and at more than three times the price. It would make the day more memorable, wearing an unusual color. Dove gray, lavender, and cream were more common if you weren't in white, but those light colors showed your size and shape and Mam had insisted that come the big day, she wouldn't set a foot out the door, wedding or no wedding, if Evelyn's condition was at all noticeable.

"You've given me heartbreak, young lady. You'll not give me a red face to go with it," she had said. Softening a little, she had gone on, "You'll be all right, lass. Stan's a good enough 'un."

Evelyn frowned a little in the mirror and fingered the cuff of her suit. The moment you felt the velvet in your fingers you could tell it was good stuff. The dark green was more pine than bottle, when you looked closely, and the jacket had a slight flare at the front and a bit of swing in the back, so nothing would show. And she had her pretty lily-of-the-valley posy, waiting downstairs in the cool of the scullery, that she would carry, and the white silk and lace jabot, her "something borrowed" from Auntie Violet, was the real thing. Auntie Violet had always had style. After today Evelyn would have to give it back, but if ever a special occasion came round again, a plain blouse would do quite well under the jacket. She could probably take a panel out of the skirt as well, that's if she needed to, if she got her figure back after the baby. Some women didn't. Anyway, it was hard to imagine the day when she would ever wear the suit again. Evelyn gave herself a little shake. No, how silly of her! Of course! Someday, surely, there would be Daphne's wedding.

Just then Mam disturbed her reverie by knocking on the door. She came in carrying Evelyn's hat. "Here we go, love," she said. "Let's get this on. My, what a hat! It really is the last word, isn't it!"

Evelyn dipped forward and let Mam place the pine green velvet beret-style hat on her head. Standing with her daughter before the mirror, Mrs. Leigh fixed the hat in place with Evelyn's "something old," the pearl pin that had belonged to her own mother, and wiped a tear from her eye. Together they arranged Evelyn's curls around the soft brim and primped the little bunch of white feathers that Mam had sewn onto one side under a white velvet bow.

Evelyn eased her toes into her new, dark green mock-croc shoes, and picked up her white gloves from the bed. Mam tutted and shook her head, and then smiled sadly.

"I know what you're thinking, Mam," Evelyn said. "But don't fret, it don't matter. It would have been a waste of money."

Mam sighed and sat down for a moment on the bed. "Aye, but it were lovely, that little green bag."

She was referring to the beautiful mock-croc clutch bag they had seen in Lewis's that matched the shoes. It was small, elegant, and as Evelyn said, shockingly expensive.

"If your Da was still here there'd be more money," her Mam sighed, "for a proper do. There'd be a bit spare, for the likes of that bag. If he was here, we'd be splashing out a bit," she added, forgetting perhaps that the circumstances of Evelyn and Stan's wedding would have provoked an altogether different reaction in Evelyn's father.

"Now Mam," Evelyn said sensibly, "you can't say that. Look at all them's that been laid off in't last six months, there's nothing you can take for granted these days. And anyway, we agreed. It was a beautiful handbag but there's better ways to spend money, especially when I'll not be working for a while and there's more expense to come."

Mam murmured agreement.

"And a little clutch bag'd be all very well for the Big Day, but what about afterward?" Evelyn said, smoothing down her skirt. "It don't hold hardly anything. Besides, it leaves you just the one free hand."

"Aye, that's true enough." Mam chuckled. "Never thought I'd say it but you're more practical-minded than me, Evelyn Alice Leigh."

"Oh, a little clutch'd be all very well for Lady Muck. But Stan's not exactly the gentleman, opening doors for me wherever I go, is he?" Evelyn went on. "I need both my hands, I do."

"Aye, and your wits about you," Mam said absently. "With a baby on t'way and a husband to look after."

"Exactly!" Evelyn said, sighing happily. "Stan's Mam's not going to be much help to us, neither. She's going to let us fend for ourselves, she says, it's better that way. So there'll be Stan's tea to get, never mind seeing to the baby, and I'll have to rise to more than toast and dripping, won't I, even if he does get his canteen dinner. I can't be lugging shopping and a baby on and off the tram with a clutch bag, can I?".

She laughed. "Anyway, all that's as may be." She fished in the breast pocket of her jacket and drew out a tiny pair of nail scissors. "Here, Mam, take these for me. I'll need them later. Hang on to them till I ask for them, all right? And don't look like that!"

Mam sighed and shook her head. "I won't pretend to

know what you're up to, Evelyn Leigh. But if you say so, love," she said.

"Thanks, Mam. Now I'm all ready, aren't I? I'm wearing my locket and I've got my posy to hold. I'm marrying Stanley Ashworth today and there's nothing more I need. I never wanted a big shindig, anyway. So let's be going."

Dear Ruth

Carole takes the view I should keep these letters going. She says undoubtedly not getting any reply is hard, but coming to terms with that can be part of the process.

Anyway, easier to fit in time for a letter as I'm off my feet, in general. Also have plenty of time for reading.

Your pages made me think of our wedding. You never wanted a big shindig either, or so you said. It seemed quite big enough to me when it came to it, though. Looked out our Order of Service, here it is.

All right, I didn't look it out, it just came to hand, unearthed from bowels of attic. Hadn't seen it for years. It's easier to put my hand on things, now stuff is down from attic and where I can get at it.

Order of Service
Wedding of Arthur and Ruth
St. Mary's Church, Abbotsbourne
14 June 1972

The Procession: A Whiter Shade of Pale

Introduction: The Reverend Geoffrey Greene

Hymn: "Jerusalem"

And did those feet in ancient time
Walk upon England's mountain green?
And was the holy Lamb of God
On England's pleasant pastures seen?
And did the countenance divine
Shine forth upon our clouded hills?
And was Jerusalem builded here
Among those dark satanic mills?

Bring me my bow of burning gold!
Bring me my arrows of desire!
Bring me my spear! O clouds, unfold!
Bring me my chariot of fire!
I will not cease from mental fight,
Nor shall my sword sleep in my hand,
Till we have built Jerusalem
In England's green and pleasant land.

The Marriage

The Lesson and Reading

Hymn: "Lord of the Dance"
(see separate sheet)

The Prayers

The Apache Blessing

Now you will feel no rain, for each of you will be shelter for the other. Now you will feel no cold, for each of you will be warmth to the other. Now there will be no loneliness, for each of you will be companion to the other. Now you are two persons, but there is only one life before you. May beauty surround you both in the journey ahead and through all the years. May happiness be your companion and your days together be good and long upon the earth.

The Signing of the Register

Hymn: "Blowin' in the Wind"
(see separate sheet)

Reminds me what you were like in those days, not that you went the whole hog on the hippie front. But you and your Apache blessings and blowing in the wind and all sorts. Remember the arguments? I'm glad I won the day over Jerusalem. I'm glad you wore white, even if it was a caftan, and at least the daisies in your hair didn't start to wilt till after we were out of the church.

I'm glad I held my own and didn't let you get me in a caftan—I won that argument, thank God, ditto matching daisies for a buttonhole.

A nurse has been. Mrs. M muttered something to the effect she'd called the doctor for me. Not a face I knew, the nurse, but she insisted she knew you. She's attached to the community nursing team. I said oh, attached are you, so where's the strings, but she was looking at my legs and didn't laugh.

Legs very sore. Nurse says they need bandaging. This kind of thing takes time to heal, she says, she'll be popping in to keep an eye, or it might be somebody else, all depends on rota. She left leaflets about support hose and hot meals. I put them with Carole's about loss.

But how long is all this meant to go on for is what I want to know, and of course nobody's got a leaflet about that.

Or about the dreams I get. Maybe dreams are more vivid if you sleep in daytime, I don't know. The latest one was me following a man who's got his back to me and I was following him because I was going to kill him with my bare hands. Quietly and calmly, but quite certainly, I was going to kill him. I couldn't see his face, but it was the driver of the car.

Well that's all

Arthur

Cardigan Avenue was the kind of place I would never have just happened into, even in daytime. It wasn't on the way to anywhere else. The road beneath the moon swayed in shallow intentional curves between trees set at intervals along the pavements, its nonchalance contrived for what would no doubt be labeled residential charm. The houses, set in large competitive gardens, stared out through luminous windows. There was something about them that would deter loiterers, an atmosphere of settlement that was not the same as neighborly. I moved carefully from tree to tree, pausing under each one. Up ahead of me somebody's feet were stopping and scraping on the pavement; a chain clinked and I heard whispers urging a dog to hurry up. I waited in the dark. After a while there was more shuffling and then from farther away more words to the dog and the sound of a door closing, and I moved on.

Number twenty-seven, its number and name, "Overdale," spelled out in looping black wrought iron fixed to the wall, sat quietly among its neighbors. But it didn't quite match up to them and their immodest embellishments; everywhere along the avenue were conservatories, jutting extensions, gazebos, many of them floodlit in the dark. The front windows of Arthur's house were black and all the curtains were closed.

Earlier that evening I had studied a follow-up piece in the paper under the headline TRAGEDY DEEPENS. The report heaped new and wretched detail upon the case, as if the woman's being merely killed would not interest the readers for long. It outlined the hope and waste, the ruined plans. Arthur and Ruth had been about to go on the trip of a lifetime, a world cruise ending in Australia where they were planning to spend at least six months, and possibly settle for good, in order to be close to Ruth's bedridden brother Graham and their nephew and his family. There was a picture of retired engineer and widower Graham (74). He was propped up in bed wearing short-sleeved pajamas. His face was swollen, and he was wincing gamely at a small burning forest of candles on a cake on a trolley, watched by a cluster of people, including some nurses, holding Styrofoam cups. The caption said:

HAPPIER TIMES. *Arthur, Ruth and friends mark Graham's 70th birthday in 2000.*

And there she was: Ruth Mitchell in spectacles and a pale trouser suit, a practical, drip-dry Down Under outfit. Her hair was cut sensibly and a scarf, loosely held in a scarf ring, hung around her neck. Next to her, Arthur stooped toward the camera with his cup in one hand and a bottle in the other, proposing a toast. He was square-shouldered, gaunt, and spoon-jawed. His grin revealed a row of sheeplike teeth that met his upper gum in a row of high arches. His present devastation was analyzed under the subheading DREAMS SHATTERED.

The garden of his house was not as tidy as the others. A garbage can sat out on the middle of the drive near the end, under a tree. The grass was uncut. There were dark stains in the drifts of fallen petals on the front path and the smell that exuded from them was the familiar sweet stench of dying flowers. In the borders, unidentifiable stalks stood skinny and naked as pencils among sparse flower heads, spent and weather-battered.

I made my way up the drive close to the boundary wall. I was intending to wheel the garbage can farther up, nearer the garage doors, where it would be more convenient. Just as I reached it, something made me turn my head. It was something that eyes weren't much use for, not a figure nor quite a shape nor barely a movement, but something under a tree on the other side of the garden, more like a shimmer near the ground. It was the aftershock of a tiny disturbance, the merest righting of the surface after a departure just accomplished, the air closing again around an absence. And while I couldn't tell that it wasn't caused by something quite ordinary and solid and swift such as a cat, I couldn't be sure it was, either. Perhaps it was just the passing moon shadow of a branch lifted by the wind. I waited, shivering, for what might come next.

Then, from deeper in the garden over at the side of the house came sounds actual and unambiguous enough, the *crick-cruck* of a gate latch and the scrape and squeak of hinges. Footsteps sounded on the path, and receded. I stepped silently over the concrete in front of the garage and crossed the front lawn. I trailed through the long wet grass, tugging up strands and soaking my feet. I dared not follow at once into the gully between the house wall and the boundary fence so I paused at the side gate, which stood open. There was a faint, human sourness of sweat and exhaled breath lingering there, I was certain of it. I peered up the gully. Something was moving away from me into the darkness of the back garden. I saw no shape or outline. I knew this presence in the way a bat would; I sensed a greater density, a different dark in the dark, swaying ahead of me. I waited for a while longer and then, making no sound, I followed.

At the corner of the house, I crouched against the wall and that's when I saw him, limping across the lawn, stepping in and out of white light and shadows cast over the grass by the moon. He was tall and rather tottery; in the moonlight his hair and clothes gleamed palely. He was clutching what looked at first like sticks and leaves for the compost heap but was actually a handful of broken flowers picked from the front garden.

Though he was unsteady on his feet and his progress was unhurried, he moved rather fast into the shadow cast by the house, shrugging the light from his back as he would discard a coat. He mounted some shallow steps up to a patio and from there he passed into a long, lean-to conservatory built against the back wall. The interior was unlit and I watched him make his way along it, neither furtive nor afraid, merely discreet, solitary.

I could not bear to see him go. There was a shed set deep in a curve of shrubs against the garden's back wall and I moved toward it across the grass, becoming, like him, only a swift, darker presence in darkness. It was a small wooden pavilion with a window on each side and a shallow porch; I settled myself on the steps and leaned against the low balustrade. A white lilac tree swayed above and all was quiet but for the rasping of its branches on the asphalt roof. The drowsy, creosotey damp mingled with the sharp sweetness of lilac blossom. I sat shivering with cold, and the house before me was still.

Suddenly lights came on in an uncurtained upstairs room. In the glare of four overhead bulbs that beamed into all the corners, I could see him, carrying armfuls of papers to and fro. His mouth was working, talking to his dead wife, Ruth, I supposed, and when he paused near the window I caught glimpses of his face wretchedly pained and channeled with deep lines. Once or twice he stopped and covered his eyes, and his body shook with weeping. But he kept doggedly at his work, his moving shadow split by the angled lights across the yellow wall. Although it was bright, the room seemed colder and bleaker and lonelier than out here where I sat on the damp step.

I realized that all my pointless roaming was at an end. Who better than I to ease the burden of the poor man's distress? My being the cause of it bound me intimately to his suffering; surely an obligation to witness and relieve it must be the reason I was still alive. He needed comfort. He needed me, or he would, eventually, and perhaps with urgency and at a time not of my choosing. And it would be a fitting, if only a small beginning, to keep vigil until I could be of use to him. I would have to be here every night. If I failed to watch, his loneliness would increase; if I ceased watching, I would surely find myself responsible for some new disaster. I would stay here, all night if need be, watching his shadow pass forward and back across the room. I would no longer notice the cold. That would be as much, for the moment, as I could do.

THE COLD AND THE BEAUTY AND THE DARK
1932

Chapter 5: Off to Morecambe

Evelyn got the scissors from Mam, without anyone noticing, after the ceremony, and on the short walk from the registry office to the Co-op Rooms she turned to Stan and told him what she intended to do. He said she was daft but agreed to stand still while she, laughing and with trembling hands, snipped off a few strands of his hair and secured them in the locket. She had already got Daphne to write their initials and the date in minute writing on a tiny piece of paper, and she had set that in the locket, too. She was too excited about getting married to see clearly to do it herself.

It was a grand day, for late February. There was a gleam in the air although the sun didn't quite come out, as Stan's mother grumbled. But as Daphne said, it was shining away up there really, behind the clouds, it just couldn't be bothered with poking through. As one of the witnesses, she had got herself up as fine as you like in an ocher wool dress with matching gloves and her mother's fox fur. She hated wearing hats and had fixed a spray of artificial carnations in her wiry hair. The other witness was Stan's uncle, his mother's brother. He was no end of a swell in his double-breasted suit and spats, with his graying hair slicked down and sliced in a razor-sharp, off-center parting. He owned three shops and had a car and a house in St. Helens. When Evelyn told Daphne this, she giggled and whispered he looked the part, all right. He certainly did, Evelyn thought. He was wearing a generous amount of a heavy cologne that smelled to her like burnt cake and he had pink, immaculate hands. He had come alone. It was known that his wife didn't keep well.

The tea was a wonder. There were sandwiches galore: ham, egg, and tomato, and dainty bridge rolls filled with fish paste. And thanks to Mam and her squad of helpers drawn from family and neighbors, there was an array of cakes and pastries that brought oohs and aahs from everyone. Urns were filled and emptied, the windows steamed up, and by half past three Evelyn was feeling she'd had quite enough excitement for one day.

But there were still the speeches to hear. Stan's uncle went first, addressing the "blushing bride" and saying, with a sly wink that really did make Evelyn blush to the roots of her hair, that he hoped their union would be blessed with a houseful of little Ashworths.

Then Stan made a halting speech, thanking Mrs. Leigh for the grand spread and then, goaded by the assembled company, led by his beaming uncle, he finished hesitantly with, "And we are right pleased you could all come today. Right pleased we are, I and my wife." Afterward he went outside for a smoke. He needed a breath of air after such an ordeal.

Stan's uncle took them all the way in his car to the railway station in Manchester. Daphne came, too, clutching Evelyn's bridal posy that she'd managed to catch, mainly because the bride had thrown it firmly in her direction. Daphne and Stan's uncle seemed to have hit it off and he had invited her along just for the spin and to wave them off.

There were more high jinks at the station. Instead of just leaving them at the entrance, Stan's uncle marched them into the high, echoing ticket hall, poked his nose at the window, and demanded in a very loud voice and waving his arms, "Two first-class tickets to Morecambe for Mr. and Mrs. Stanley Ashworth! And a nice cozy *private* compartment, if you please, for the newlyweds!"

His voice boomed all over the ticket hall. Daphne burst out laughing but Evelyn was so embarrassed she wished the ground would open and swallow her up. Stan looked extremely uncomfortable, too, though he smiled when his uncle drew his wallet from his jacket and with a flourish paid up for their tickets. Not content with that, Stan's uncle turned to Daphne, who, Evelyn noticed for the first time, was holding a brown paper bag, which she handed to him with a smirk.

"Time to do the honors," he announced, and with a loud laugh he pulled from the bag a bottle of whiskey for Stan and for Evelyn a box of Fry's chocolates. Evelyn had never seen, let alone been given, such a splendid box: the "Antony" assortment, it said on the lid.

"That's one of the finest assortments from one of the finest names in the confectionery trade, " Stan's uncle told her. He tapped on the box.

"That's not cardboard. That's a proper lacquered box, that

is. Unique to Fry's. It's meant for keeping your hankies in after. Or your whatnots, your little bits and pieces, eh? You ladies've all got your bits and pieces!"

While Evelyn stammered a thank you, Daphne touched Stan's uncle's arm and said, wide-eyed, "What a lovely box of chocs. That's right generous of you, Mr. Hibbert."

"Oh, there's plenty more where that came from, pet," Stan's uncle said, winking at her, "if you play your cards right. And call me Uncle Les."

Evelyn didn't hear what Daphne had to say to that, because just then Stan announced that they'd miss their train if they didn't hurry.

Evelyn's first thought on arriving at The Haven on the seafront was that it wasn't exactly posh. They had walked from the station and run into trouble finding it, so it was after six o'clock when they knocked on the door. The landlady smelled of lard and talcum powder. She pointed out, sniffing, that they were too late for high tea but she had left them a flask in the parlor. She made it clear that she was doing them a favor and at great inconvenience to herself.

But at least their room overlooked the front. That was what you were paying for, a proper sea view, Evelyn supposed aloud to Stan, who replied that that was a bit rich when there was bugger all to see except the sea. Evelyn laughed and went to the window. Of course it was drafty, being Morecambe with the breeze straight off the sands. It was strong enough to stir the curtain. Maybe Stan had a point about the view. The daylight was fading and the sea was just the same dark gray as the sky.

She shivered. "It is a bit drafty, Stan," she said.

"No good moaning to me, it weren't my idea to come here," he replied.

"Oh, don't be so grumpy, Stan!" Evelyn cried. "Not today!"

Stan grunted. "What d'you expect? There's only a pane of glass between you and the ruddy Atlantic and the ruddy putty's dropping out, by looks of it."

Evelyn laughed. "So you'll just have to cuddle me tighter to keep me warm, then," she said. "Come on, let's go down and see what the old harridan's put out for us' supper, shall we?"

It wasn't much. A flask of tepid tea and a few soft biscuits, most of them broken, in a tin. At bedtime Evelyn was overcome with shyness and went along to the bathroom to change into her new nightgown. Stan was already in bed, sitting up drinking from the whiskey bottle, when she got back. It was considerate of him, really, not to undress in front of her, she thought, though she had hoped he might ask her which side she preferred. She climbed in nervously at the other side. She was cold, but Stan didn't offer her a warming sip of whiskey, or a cuddle.

"I'm not used to this, Stan," she giggled. "It's amazing, in't it? I've never been in a double bed with my husband before."

"Bit late to be bashful, in't it?" Stan said. "Seeing as you're nigh on five months gone. Good night."

But obviously, she reflected later, lying awake in the dark, he hadn't meant any disrespect. He was just stating a fact. Despite the smell of whiskey on him, she had tried to make it clear she wouldn't object if, as she put it, he wanted to "be a husband" to her that night, but he had pretended not to understand. Wedding nerves, perhaps. Or more likely delicacy, because he probably thought she didn't really want to but was pretending she wouldn't mind just for his sake, and what decent man would insist, with his wife in a certain condition? Besides, she was probably bigger than she felt, and that would be off-putting.

In the morning Stan woke complaining of a sore neck because, he said, he had taken the window side and the worst of the draft. Evelyn tried to make light of it. "Oh, well, don't go saying that to the landlady, will you, Stan? She'll only charge you for it. A sore neck's sixpence extra, I bet!" Stan glowered.

Breakfast was adequate. They had porridge and a boiled egg each, both overcooked, and bread and marmalade and tea. At least the dining room was empty and they didn't have to endure the stares of other guests on the morning after their wedding night. After a walk in the drizzle along the seafront and a look round the few gift shops that were open, they had an early lunch of steak and kidney pie in the Red Rose Café, sitting in the window from where, as Evelyn said, they could watch the world go by, even though there didn't seem to be much world that day. Then they made their way slowly to the station. Stan's uncle had given them one-way tickets so they bought third-class seats on the two o'clock back to Manchester. From there they would get the local train to Aldbury.

On the train, Stan read the *Racing Post* while Evelyn lay with her eyes closed. They were stinging again and she hadn't slept well, being unused to sharing a bed with Stan.

She thought back over her Big Day. It had been grand, really. She counted herself lucky. Nobody was having big weddings anymore and only the well-to-do had proper honeymoons. She fingered the slim gold band on her finger and felt the locket at her neck. It wasn't, as she'd reassured Mam, as if she had ever wanted a big shindig, anyway.

I t was the paling of the darkness or the birdsong that woke me. The ground was dusty with a dew like powdered pearls, only a degree away from sugary white frost. Some small creature had paddled across the grass leaving the dark threads of its tracks. I blinked, and tears rushed to the cold surface of my eyes and made them sting. I sneezed and yawned and tried to stretch my back, and then a sudden flash drew my attention to the house.

The sun had just struck the lowest glass panes of the conservatory, and the curtains at every window stood open to the glare. I ached so much I could hardly stand, but I had to get away from the sight of the house so exposed and penetrated. I prayed that Arthur was asleep and would not feel it. I prayed that even though he would have to wake and know again she was gone, he was now asleep and for a while untroubled by thoughts of Ruth. As I crept across the grass I whispered to him that I wouldn't be away for long.

My clothes were soaked and freezing and I was miles from home. I wanted to crawl into the shed and hunker down in a corner until it was dark again, but I didn't dare. It was hard to negotiate my way back; by night I had walked this way easily and freely, now I stumbled and tripped. Buildings and walls and turnings and parked cars loomed out and crowded me. The sky was flaring lilac and orange and pink, and light was shoving in everywhere. It was coming fast, another day of sights I could not bear, a day of breakages, of choking dust and blinding commotion, of futures torn up.

My own house sat in the morning sun, exuding—because it contained—nothing. I barged in and stood gasping for breath in the kitchen. The clock ticked flatly. It was just after six. My heart was hammering with the ecstasy of knowing I'd had a narrow escape. Upstairs, my quiet room waited, where curtains could be drawn against the light until night came again. I started to shake while I was undressing and my damp clothes amassed on the floor where I dropped them.

After a few hours I got up. I looked at myself in the mirror, and in the dimness of the curtained room I was stunned at how marked were the effects of those hours on the shed's steps. I had behaved rather foolishly, I felt, staying out all night and not noticing how late and cold it was getting. I had never spent a night out-of-doors before. I thought then of my great-uncle, and I understood how a man's heart might lose time against the passing minutes of a single night, and wind down beat by beat like a clock, and be discovered in the morning, stopped. My eyes looked young and pale and I couldn't imagine that, were my flesh to be cut and opened, my blood would pulse as fast or be as garish a red as other people's. My body felt hard and small. None of these changes displeased me.

———

Trains didn't run on Christmas Day. And during the winter of 1962, the coldest of the century, they were often canceled anyway because of fresh snowfalls or frozen points or split rails. So they didn't find my great-uncle until early in the afternoon of Boxing Day. By then he had been dead for more than a day and a night, slumped near the middle of the station footbridge and covered in snow, his cheek frozen against a line of riveted bolts on the metal parapet, directly underneath the embossed brass plate that read:

London & North Western Railway
Passengers Crossing Footbridge Do So At Own Risk
No Loitering No Urinating No Spitting
Fine 5/- in accordance with L&NWR Bylaw 5(2).

These details came to me later. My grandmother told me only that he had died of cold. I took this to mean the same as dying of *a* cold, and I clung to her wailing and speechless; I had always understood that nobody died of a cold and my grandmother seemed to be suffering from one, even if it was what she called only a sniffle, a great deal of the time. She had to tell me finally that he had frozen to death, that a night out of doors in such weather was more than flesh and blood could stand. I found this easier to accept. It did not seem so terrible, a mishap rather than a catastrophe. I imagined him lying calmly in a haze of frost and very cold to the touch, waiting, as I was, for something to be done about it. For if he had frozen to death, could he not simply be warmed back to life? Then it might also turn out to be not so terrible that his suspension in the ice was my fault, and forgiveness might be possible.

So I waited, during a succession of days that were bulky and irregular with visitors and discussions in dark voices and the soft sifting of papers. Around this time it was explained to me that in fact he was not my mother's but my long-dead grandfather's uncle, and so was my great-*great*-uncle. The sudden bestowal and its immediate retraction, by his absence, of the extra "great" seemed like another of his unraveling gifts, lost in the snow.

After a while our rooms on the two floors above the shop hung empty and the air seemed muffled, and I realized it was too late for him to come back now. The glass smashed on Christmas Eve was replaced in the boarded-up windows and my mother and grandmother re-opened the shop, which, it turned out, my mother now owned.

We continued in the usual way except of course that my uncle no longer called in on Saturday evenings for the week's earnings and lingered, in a manner tense and jovial, until after dinner on Sunday. In periods of sobriety my mother worked in the shop and kept the books; in her absence my grandmother sat behind the counter knitting, or worked at chores upstairs, keeping an ear open for the sound of the shop bell below. Having memorized the position of every jar on the shelves, she could pick and measure out from any of them the two- and four-ounce bags of sweets that people asked for, just by the feel of the weight in her hand. There was, by law, a set of scales on the counter, but our customers were regulars and knew better than to be skeptical. She also identified and sold by smell several varieties of English, Aromatic, and Virginia loose tobacco, and in the same way she could detect the difference not just between brands of packaged cigarettes but between tipped and untipped. She couldn't, though, stop the thieving of Black Jacks, penny chews, and sweetie cigarettes from the open boxes on the counter, of which crime I was, by collusion, as guilty as any of the older children who peered into the shop every day and came in only if my grandmother was there.

After school I would usually be there, too, swinging my legs from a chair, drawing pictures instead of doing my homework. I dreaded the shop bell. They came in pairs. They ignored me; because my grandmother could not see me any more than she could see them, it seemed I was invisible to them, too. They would fix upon me eyes as apparently sightless and flat with tacit challenge as hers, and in front of me they stole from her with impunity, knowing I would say nothing. One would

go for the sweets while the other would spend a halfpenny on something or other, talking in a voice loud enough to cover any rustling of
the waxed paper lining the boxes. "I'll have a sherbet fountain, please,
missus. All right, kiddo? What're you up to there, then? Oh, that's a
nice picture, look, i'n't she doin' a nice picture?"

And before they left they would sometimes, and always unsmil-
ingly, select a licorice stick or a couple of toffees from their haul and
push them into my waiting hands. I was afraid of them, I suppose, but
I also despised them, the sniggering amateurs. The pilfering of a few
sweets was a villainy almost laughably inferior to that of letting my
great-*great* uncle vanish forever into a freezing cloud of snow.

Dear Ruth

All this writing letters and not getting any replies is no good. I shouldn't even be up reading that story of yours, it's the middle of the night and I need my sleep. You should know that. I catch up in the day but I need my sleep NOW *and you don't seem to understand.*

I get the impression I've made you angry and now you're not speaking. You used to do that. I brought you in a bunch of flowers from the garden to say sorry. I used to do that.

But it's you that gets them in water, I'm no good with that sort of thing, flower arranging. They're in the conservatory.

A funny thing to do, not speaking—funny for you, I mean. You of all people. It was me you were trying to punish when you were not speaking, but it was you it hurt. You hated not talking, you talked about every little thing. There's a story in every minute of every hour of every day, you said. You had all the words for everything, and if you didn't, you knew some poet who did and you'd know where to find them.

The point is, when you withheld words and went around with your mouth locked, I didn't mind. I quite liked it, the quiet. I just never told you that.

This time I do mind. I don't like all the quiet. When it's quiet I get a notion I'm not really alone. The quiet is in the room with me, somehow, and it's not a nice, settled thing, it's an angry kind of quiet. A quiet waiting to explode. I feel like shouting into it but who's to hear? And what would I say?

Because what they don't grasp, all these people who troop through this place asking how I am—is how on earth should I know, since you're not telling me anymore?

Arthur

PS Egg sandwiches do NOT *freeze. Or they do but they're not egg sandwiches when they come out again. They mashed up all right though. I managed to eat them.*

_____

THE COLD AND THE BEAUTY AND THE DARK
1932

Chapter 6: The Ashworths at Bank Street

Evelyn took her coat off quietly and paused in the passage outside the kitchen. She could hear Stan's complaining voice clearly and it was she, as she fully expected, who was the subject of his complaint.

"She's switched off. Half the time she don't even know when I've come in the room," he said. His mother said something Evelyn couldn't hear.

"And she's that bad-tempered," he went on. "Told me she didn't care for my friends and I wasn't to go to any more meetings."

Stan's mother gave a short snort. "Hasn't wasted her time, has she? Six weeks wed and laying down the law. I never liked them Leighs. You have to stand up to her, Stan."

"I did! I says to her I'm not having that, I'll do what I like when I like with who I like. I says to her, what's the ruddy point of sticking round here, anyway? I says, you're as switched off as your ruddy lightbulbs, you. I told her."

Evelyn heard a sharp laugh from her mother-in-law. "Fact is, Stan, you're too soft. Aye, and you're a daft beggar an' all. You let her lead you on, didn't yer? Don't tell me that baby's an accident, she's made a fool out of you. Got you just where she wanted you, up the ruddy aisle. You've only yourself to blame, Stanley Ashworth."

Evelyn set down her parcel of sausages on the floor of the passage, her eyes stinging with tears. She smoothed her hands over her stomach and tried to breathe evenly. She wouldn't raise her voice in this house, she wouldn't give them the satisfaction. But she couldn't just walk in now and cook Stan's tea as if nothing had happened. His mother had probably given him his tea, anyway. She always did if Evelyn's shift hours meant Evelyn didn't get back until after him. A man's tea should be on the table as soon as he got home, according to Mrs. Ashworth. The same rule didn't apply to her tea, of course, so once Stan was off for the evening and Mrs. Ashworth was listening to the wireless, Evelyn would get herself something to eat alone, a cheese and pickle sandwich, maybe an egg. More often than not she would eat her lonely tea standing in the kitchen, and then wash up and go to bed.

She tiptoed away upstairs. She had to get herself under a blanket to cry so they wouldn't hear.

Later, lying curled in bed, she reflected that she probably did seem to be what Stan had called switched off. She either had too much on her mind or she was thinking of nothing at all, and whichever it was, she was just keeping quiet so she could concentrate. If she'd been a big talker he'd have been the first to complain, wouldn't he? If she talked all the time she'd miss all the little noises that kept her in the picture. Her eyes were so tired from the bulb testing work these days, she relied on sounds, and on smells, too, to keep herself from making mistakes. She hadn't noticed it so much at home at Roper Street, it being so familiar to her, how fuzzy things had got. But here in a different house, even though it was just a mile away and practically the same layout as her Mam's, it was taking a bit of time to get the hang of things. She already knew when the kettle was ready or the fire needed coal. She knew who'd come in, Stan or his Mam, before she heard a voice; it was all in the feet. She had also worked out their different smells. Lucky Strikes and Brilliantine was Stan, a sweetness like very old jam mixed with mothballs, Mrs. Ashworth. Even without those signs, their breath was enough to go on. Most days, Stan's was beery. Mrs. Ashworth had taken the pledge years ago and never touched a drop, but she was wheezy and dyspeptic. Evelyn could track her whereabouts easily from the traces of her frequent peppermint belches.

Evelyn reckoned she could even smell the weather, too. She could tell when it was going to rain without so much as a glance at the sky, though Stan said she was talking rubbish because round here it was always *going* to rain if it wasn't already. She smiled, thinking of that. He could be that dry. He was all right, was Stan, if you touched his good side.

But as her Mam said, life was a sea of worries. There was the worry of where this baby was going to go when it arrived, since she and Stan had only the little room next to Stan's Mam's bedroom, small enough even for two and with no space for a cradle. Mrs. Ashworth—Evelyn simply could not call her "Mam"—wouldn't hear of them changing a thing, so they were stuck with Stan's grandfather's big black iron bedstead and a mattress that seemed to have bricks in it, and only the one chest of drawers. Somehow Evelyn would have to make Stan face up to his mother and let them put in a few things for the baby. And they didn't have so much as an inch to call their own outside the bedroom. Even Evelyn's knitting couldn't be left downstairs at the end of the evening.

That wasn't all. It wasn't exactly a worry now, because with her in the family way Stan never laid a finger on her, but what about afterward, with Mrs. Ashworth sleeping next door and the walls so thin? They should be looking to find a place of their own. But Stan wouldn't face that, either. Soon they'd be able to manage the rent on a small place, she kept telling him, but he wouldn't listen, or he'd start spouting rubbish picked up from his daft meetings. He'd showed her a pamphlet written by Alan O'Reilly and a few others. She hadn't understood a word of it, so Stan had explained. All that wanting a house and a few sticks of furniture to call your own was being oppressed, apparently. As long as she allowed herself to be manipulated into aping bourgeois materialist values, especially notions of private ownership, all she was doing was colluding in her own subjugation. It was capitalist forces, whose sole purpose was to bolster the bosses' and the landlords' and the government's profits, that were manipulating her into *thinking* she had to sell her labor in order to acquire personal goods and live according to repressive bourgeois norms, forever yoked to the system. It wasn't what she really wanted.

Well, she really had switched off when he'd come out with all that, but not before saying that in her opinion it was a lot of nonsense, just a lot of big words trying to tell her she didn't know her own mind, and if Stan was falling for all that he was a bigger fool than she'd taken him for. Not that she'd lost her temper. In a quiet voice, just before he had stormed off to the pub, she had added that she didn't recall agreeing to join any ruddy class struggle, least of all on Alan O'Reilly's side of it, and that was her last word on the subject.

She was roused suddenly from her thoughts by noise and shouting, and rushed downstairs.

Mrs. Ashworth was a heavy woman. When her foot had landed on the parcel of sausages on the floor of the passage, she'd skidded and fallen and twisted her ankle. Evelyn helped Stan get her up and seated in the front room, trying to close her ears to the tirade of complaints flowing between the pair of them. Stan went off to get Mrs. Flint four doors down, who worked at the Infirmary, to come and have a look at the injury, while Evelyn, with a sinking heart, went to scrape the squashed raw sausages off the linoleum in the hallway.

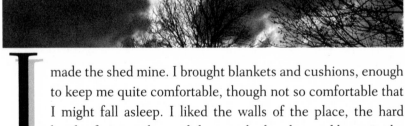

I made the shed mine. I brought blankets and cushions, enough to keep me quite comfortable, though not so comfortable that I might fall asleep. I liked the walls of the place, the hard beads of pine amber and the scorched gashes and knots in the wood, and I liked Ruth's damp floral folding chairs hung on hooks and her spidery gardening gloves discarded and hardened into casts of her tired, curved hands. But the resiny smell of the timbers and the candle-smoky damp that made its way into the peppery blankets felt like mine. There was an outside tap nearby, so I considered getting a little spirit stove and a kettle, and perhaps one of those camping heaters, but then I realized that these would make the place too bright. Sometimes I lit a tea light or two but, like Arthur, I was happiest sitting in the dark.

He never drew a curtain at the back of the house, nor pulled a blind nor closed doors between rooms. He spent a lot of time upstairs, moving clothes and books and bundles of paper around. Then he started going up and down to the attic, too, via a folding ladder hauled down from the ceiling onto the landing. I could see the bottom of it slanting across the doorway of the bedroom that was full of luggage and clothes. That was a worry to me. Whenever I saw his feet, one splayed on the ladder and the other swimming in midair trying to make the next rung, I couldn't tear my eyes away. My heart would pound while I counted the seconds; sometimes it would take him four minutes to manage the first three steps. It was worse when he got higher and disappeared altogether. All I could do then was watch the foot of the ladder, dreading that the next thing I would see would be a flailing bundle of limbs tumbling down into a broken heap. Even if I could have heard him call out I wouldn't have been in time to prevent that.

So I would wait, counting, and there were times I was out of my chair ready to go to him—once I was even setting out across the grass—before I would see a pale blue flash from the attic skylight. Then at least I knew he had made it as far as the light switch. The strip of fluorescent light would tremble and blink and grow steady, and I would settle down to watch.

But that he had got himself up there was all I knew. I had to carry on watching because what I couldn't tell from the shadows as they moved across the skylight was whether he was clambering around on a solid floor or wobbling from joist to joist on those spindly legs of his. I was afraid if I let my attention falter his whole weight might land on some frail partition of gypsum and plaster and he would plunge to the floor below.

I did wonder what was up there that could occupy him for two and three hours at a time. I imagined an Aladdin's cave where he went to gloat every night, but it could hold only a hoarded treasure of sorts; I couldn't believe that any attic of Ruth's would harbor secrets, not of any priceless or desperate kind, anyway. Probably there was just the usual junk: broken furniture, pictures and ornaments out of favor, and the props of outgrown hobbies and earlier lives: books, busted rackets, albums, photographs. Whatever it was, he seemed to be going through it all, though he seemed only to bring down papers and books. Or to be more accurate, threw, from the top of the ladder onto the landing. I was relieved he didn't try to climb down with his arms full.

I would worry that in such a confined space he might have only something precarious to sit on, and what if he fell asleep and slid off his chair and hurt himself that way? Or I worried that he would fatigue himself and set off down the ladder too worn out to be careful, his joints stiff and his eyes dim after reading under that brash light. And what if he was sitting up there hour after hour, crying? What if he fell down the ladder and broke in pieces because his eyes were sore and blinded by tears?

I was always relieved when I saw the attic light go out and his legs appearing at the base of the ladder. He would straighten and steady himself on the floor. Then he would move, shuffling and hesitating in one doorway or another, a silhouette of a man stranded on thresholds he no longer knew. Most often he would wander into the luggage room, lifting a hand to the switch as he entered and turning off the light so that he walked into blackness. Even though I would be expecting it, I always felt abruptly shut out when the house went dark like that. If I had a tea light burning I immediately blew it out so that my darkness was the same as his. I liked the paraffin smell of the first curls of smoke from the snuffed wick.

And I would carry on watching the black window because I knew he would be standing there, looking out. Few sounds reached into the shed from outside, so I would hear my chair creak as I pulled a blanket around myself, and settled. Arthur would be listening, too, I was certain, to his own breathing. His house would be quietly alive with the noises all houses make, and maybe the place seemed to him bigger and emptier, and those distant, lapping sounds from walls and pipes and floors louder, because she was no longer there. Perhaps he talked to

her while he stood at the window. I wondered if he sensed her still in
the house, or beyond it, somewhere out in the darkness. It was possible, of course, that he considered that the burial of her body really was
the end of it. But if she was simply perished, and nowhere at all, would
that mean she was now free, or somehow exiled? I would have liked to
know if he pictured her still as she used to be, or if he imagined a
changed appearance for her in some new existence as a spirit; there's
all the difference in the world.

Why is it easier to imagine that the dead might be waiting for us in
darkness rather than in the light? For a while after my great-uncle died
I cried every bedtime, terrified to go to sleep in case he was now a
ghost and came visiting to take me to task for my part in his death. My
grandmother told me that all you had to do to get rid of a ghost was to
make a loud noise. She would make me cry "Away with you!" and clap
my hands until I laughed. *She* had never been frightened of ghosts, she
said, and I knew from the way she could smile in an empty room that
that was true. But I also knew something she didn't: that the dead
never are quite away, never absolutely gone. They're still there, caught
in the very act of parting from us, betrayed by a swaying curtain of
falling snow, by a movement behind a white sheet, by some trickery of
sunlight and shadow. And imperfectly though their leave-taking may
be enacted, yet it is quiet and quick and you could miss it in the taking
of a breath, and then you wouldn't know the road they took for they
leave no clue where they are going; you would be left staring, hoping
for a single last trace. But I clapped my hands and laughed just the
same, and watched my grandmother smile.

Soon enough, anyway, I was burdened by other knowledge, on top
of the shoplifting and the ghosts, that I couldn't let my grandmother
share. She knitted every afternoon for the Society for the Relief of Blind
Orphans Overseas. I didn't understand why the blind orphans overseas
should find relief in socks and scarves and mittens particularly, though
I worked out for myself that it must be for reasons to do with blindness
or orphanhood that were more compelling than the overseas-ness;
overseas meant a hot climate, surely too hot for hand-knitted woollies.

I also wondered how she knew their sizes, and her telling me the things were sent off to Sales of Work never quite explained it.

One day she finished another baby matinée set—jacket, bonnet, and bootees—in a rather upsetting brown flecked with green, a color difficult to imagine on any baby but since the blind orphan one overseas couldn't mind I supposed the people looking after him wouldn't, either. On my way upstairs a day or two later, I passed my mother's bedroom. The door was ajar; I glanced in and saw, facedown on the bed, a human head. I let out a shriek, but I couldn't drag my eyes away. It couldn't be a head! I stared, and after a moment I could see that it wasn't. It was a wig, an ugly, dark, curly wig. But before I'd begun to ask myself why my mother would have such a thing, I took a step nearer and saw what it really was: a heap of brown wool flecked with green. A single strand snaked out of it and wiggled across the bed into what was left of a forlorn and tiny sleeve.

Why hadn't I noticed? I'd seen the color before; the wool had been socks to begin with, at least twice. My mother was unraveling the orphans' knitting and giving my grandmother the same yarn back to knit up again. I didn't know why, and in the rush of sadness I felt for the orphans (and not for my grandmother, who seemed to blame, somehow) I didn't really wonder. How long had they been going without? was all I could think. What would become of them now, orphaned, blind, overseas, and suddenly without their woollies?

After that I would come home from school to find my grandmother knitting the same thing she had made the week before and the week before that. I said nothing. Not knowing the point of my mother's trickery deprived me of a good reason for exposing it, and as time went on and my curiosity grew, so did my fear of asking for an explanation. At some point I must have concluded that my mother was simply saving herself the cost of new yarn, but by then it was too late. Her deception had become mine also, and I sustained it with fervent and egotistical guilt.

When my grandmother's memory for complicated stitchwork abandoned her and she grew impatient with the intricacies of sleeves and heels and collars, she turned to knitting scarves. My mother would give her the "new" wool in two or three bags, telling her it was red and green and yellow or blue and yellow and pink. Good, everyone likes stripes, my grandmother would say. She would work twenty rows from each bag in turn, smiling as a monotone gray or brown scarf grew from her waggling needles. She would let me choose the color for the fringe, and in a loud, formal voice I would pretend to consider the green, the yellow, or the pink, my heart lopsided with tenderness and shame.

By the time I was nine I was concealing so much that keeping even direr truths from her was routine. I covered my mother's increasingly prolonged absences by mentioning in passing that she was very tired again, just resting in bed. When she sobered up enough to put in bilious and remorseful appearances at mealtimes I unleashed irritating streams of talk to hide the fact that she was too hungover to speak. Sitting between them, I looked from my mother's pouchy, stupefied face to my grandmother's, beaming sightlessly upon her golden girl, and I'd prattle on about nothing. When I came across empty bottles I got them past my grandmother and out to the bin quietly, without one ticking against another. Whatever the weather, every morning I opened windows all over the house hoping that enough new air would freeze out the pall of drink.

After a time the reasons for trying to keep my mother's condition secret didn't cross my mind. Concealment of one kind or another was to me by then a form of good manners, a necessary protective kindness; it progressed from being second nature to becoming my very nature. Because of it, I never could have grown up to be anything other than watchful and cautious. I never could have done otherwise than keep the distance from other people that enabled me to see dangers that they, more engaged in events, might not, and to prevent scenes that would upset them. This was the person I was, or believed myself to be, until that day in April.

Eventually, as I watched, poor Arthur would leave the bedroom window and wander downstairs, through the kitchen and into the conservatory. Once or twice early on he watered the plants there, stroking their leaves and inclining his head to them as if he were petting small living creatures. For a while after that he took to just sitting on a wicker chair, staring, and soon he was bringing papers in with him and would sit reading for hours at a time. I had the impression he read the same things over and over again. Sometimes he wrote.

He ate and drank, although very little. He would swallow milk straight from the carton, and then leave it half-full on the conservatory ledge where the sun would beat down on it all the following day. The next night or two nights later he might stir from his reading, wander across, and down whatever was left. I saw him bring in food and stand there eating with both hands. He seldom used a plate, but if he did he'd leave it behind. If he was forking something into his mouth out of a can, he would drop both can and fork on the floor when he had finished, as if he'd forgotten he was holding them. It mattered to me to know if he was eating canned food cold that should have been heated up, such as baked beans or soup, or if he was not neglecting himself quite so badly and was gorging on something like tuna or sweet corn. Once I saw him, in silhouette, digging with his fingers into something very small and oblong; it must have been a can of sardines. When he'd sucked each finger one by one he lifted the can to his lips and tipped his head back. My stomach heaved at the thought of his tongue questing into the corners. Those edges are lethal. I started to my feet and moaned, feeling the metal slice into his tongue, seeing bright red marbling appear across its coating of thick yellow oil, and run down and stain his lips. I could taste the tinny little plumes of blood mixing with his mouth juices all cloudy with fish scales and crumbs of bone as soft as pumice. I waited to hear him cry out. But all he did was drop the can and calmly wipe his mouth on his sleeve.

I felt a rush of triumph, as if my watching had averted disaster. And I liked the thought that it might have; perhaps something as supposedly intense as the power of prayer was at work in my willing him to keep himself safe.

So I aspired that my watching would be more than watching, and I resolved to surrender myself to it. It was no less than a debt owing to Arthur and Ruth for Ruth's fatal invisibility to me on the road that day, and no less a pact with Arthur for all that he was unaware of it. And I could not hope to repay the debt, or honor the pact, by mere observation; it would call for observance, the keeping of a vigil both devout and penitential.

Dear Ruth

She's a tartar, Stan's mother, that Mrs. Ashworth. Did you base her on somebody we know?

Mrs. M turned up with her son, The Great Tony. He's just as bad. Going on about the grass again, while she's going on about the curtains—the thing is to get the first cut early then stay on top of it—such a shame these nice sunny days to keep them closed blah blah.

Kept them on the doorstep, but then The Great Tony takes it upon himself to have a poke on the pebbledash, says it's cracking where the name's screwed on, insists I have a look. Well, talk about pernickety. Where the L of OVERDALE is attached, yes there's a hairline crack, yes there's a bit of rust stain going down the wall. What business is it of his? I've got it on my list.

What are they up to, the pair of them, do they think I've got money, is that it?

Tony jumps right in, offering his services to fix the wall—I said I thought he'd have enough concerns of his own to keep him busy but apparently not. I told him I'd see to it in my own good time, ditto the grass.

Mrs. M says, Now if I remember rightly you and Ruth came up with the name yourselves, didn't you? It's nice to give a house a name. So much more personal than a number.

I could hardly believe the cheek of the woman. What Overdale means to Ruth and myself, I said to her, is NOBODY ELSE'S BUSINESS BUT OURS.

That got rid of them.

Still waving and smiling at the end of the drive though, they are shameless.

Bye for now

A.

As the nights grew warmer, I drew closer to the house and tracked him from the terrace. I could see into all the downstairs back windows, and I saw him moving slowly to and fro in the kitchen and in and out of the conservatory and dining room. If I didn't see him from the back, I went round to the front of the house and watched from under the tree in the garden. On clear nights, his outline was bright in a wash of quicksilver from the moon and he stumbled through rooms and between objects that shone back upon him the same luminous white.

Often in his wanderings upstairs he would come to the window, sometimes lit and sometimes not, but always uncurtained. He would be holding wads of paper and a pen, and sometimes he would lean on the windowsill to write something down. Sometimes he seemed agitated and sometimes he stood very still, but in either case I could tell he was distressed.

On this particular night, the house looked the same. There were lights on upstairs and no curtains drawn. I crept out of the shed to watch until I had worked out his whereabouts. I waited close in by the shrubs bordering the side of the garden. It had been raining and the air smelled of torn leaves; a dampness lay on my skin and my breathing grew hard and noisy. Then the lights went off upstairs and I imagined him there at the window, peering through the glass trying to see what animal was out there, rasping in the dark. I did and I didn't want him to know it was me.

But suddenly a light snapped on in the kitchen and he appeared in the doorway. His hands, one in an oven glove and the other swathed in a cloth, were holding a covered dish. Smoke rolled out in soft waves above his head. He walked the length of the conservatory and came out onto the terrace, priestlike, bearing the dish before him. I heard a hiss as he set it down on the ground. He dropped the glove and cloth and stepped back. With his bare hand he lifted the lid, yelped, and hurled it hard across the garden. Then he picked up the pot itself and threw that, too. It landed somewhere on the edge of the grass and rolled away into darkness.

Smoke was still pluming out from the kitchen. He stood for a while, sucking on his hand and chewing the insides of his cheeks. I watched, aghast, desperate to know how badly he was hurt. I wanted to call out; only his apparent calm and the realization that I would shatter it by emerging out of the dark and running to him kept me quiet and invisible. For he seemed to be considering the matter, trying to puzzle out the reasons for this, why certain things had gone wrong: why had this scorching hot object been in his hand, and what did it have to do with him that he had burned himself? He picked up the cloth from the ground and wrapped his hand in it. Then, by the light escaping from the house, I saw the line of his face as he tilted his head to the sky, his mouth open in a voiceless howl. If he had stood there another moment I would have had to go to his side and lead him back to the kitchen, draw his burning hand under cold water, talking to him all the while, soothing and reassuring him. I would have heard him whimper and I would have smelled burnt smoking meat mixed with his old man smell, both rank and dry, like rotten wood. I would have begged him to be comforted, and unafraid.

But just then he cried out, in a yowling moan. It was a cry of defeat, as if the burning of his hand betrayed to him the futility of a simple attempt to heat up something for his supper. His head drooped. I couldn't go to him yet. He wiped his face with his good hand, turned away, and shuffled into the house.

The kitchen light went out. I watched the smoke disperse across the terrace in pale waving strings. Then I stepped out from the shelter of the shrubs, and feeling my way and still keeping an eye on the house, I began searching. I found the lid at once; it had rolled a track through the uncut grass that was easy to follow. It took longer to locate the dish, which had spun away and landed deep in the border at the other side of the garden.

It was one of those expensive enameled casserole dishes, and still warm to the touch. Whatever had been in it was now a bumpy carbonized heap fused to the base, a tiny burned-out pyre sitting in a lake of tar. On the side of the lid there was a big, fresh-looking chip. I was a little careless; walking back to the house I set the lid back on the dish and there was a loud clang and scrape that echoed across the garden. I stopped dead, expecting the noise to bring Arthur back out, but it didn't. I walked into the smoky kitchen clutching the dish tight against my chest.

First, I switched off the oven. Next I found scouring pads under the sink and I got to work in the dark. I scraped and scrubbed and after a while I could feel my fingers gliding on the enamel as the burnt flakes loosened and liquefied. The surface was too far gone for a perfect result but the dish would be at least usable again. I left it out on the draining board with the lid next to it so he might see how well I had done. I would have given a lot to see a look of pleasure on his face, the corners of his mouth tipping upward into even the faintest smile.

Then I went back to the conservatory. Litter had amassed all over the shelves and floor. Torn cartons and banana skins, discarded cups and bottles, newspaper cuttings, photographs and piles of papers, dirty dishes and cutlery were strewn among a crowd of indoor plants and clusters of rotting garden flowers. I shifted some dead geraniums along so that I could lean against the window ledge for a moment while I decided what to do first; they were desiccated in their plastic pots and top-heavy, and the movement tipped them straight onto the floor. I kicked at them. The pots rolled and scraped on the tiles, scattering mulch and fingery white plant roots among the litter and dry leaves. Clearing up the mess I had made myself seemed as good a place as any to start, and I went back to the kitchen to look for a dustpan and brush.

Arthur, I felt, was aware of my presence and stayed away out of politeness. Yet as I worked, I was not entirely alone. In her conservatory, with her dustpan and brush in my hands, sweeping up the relics of plants she had tended and maybe even grown from seeds she had sown herself, I knew myself to be under an authoritative and assessing gaze that could only be Ruth's. I lifted the broken stems and roots tenderly, feeling regretful and self-conscious. I murmured the words that would come from any clumsy and embarrassed visitor after such a mishap, putting off the moment when I would have to broach, somehow, the real matter that stood between us.

And so I found myself in a rather one-sided conversation. Though she seemed to have nothing to ask me, I had questions for her, to which her replies came swift and unfiltered to my mind, and rather dismissive. I asked her several times if there really could be such a thing as dying without minding it. Of course there couldn't. I wondered if there had been a second or two after she landed on the road when dying sooner rather than later seemed preferable, less dismaying than surviving long enough to find out in detail how irreversibly she was damaged. You tell me. What is it to you, anyway?

I didn't manage to apologize to her, quite. No expression of shame could be adequate, and all the words I tried to construct into an entreaty that she might forgive me seemed threaded together with a wholly unintentional defiance, even levity, as when a contrite child—a pupil of Ruth's, say—trying genuinely to apologize realizes that the teacher will never believe her sorry enough, and so is unable to sound quite serious. Nor did I come even close to completing the tidying and cleaning. Long before I had finished I heard the first birds and saw the glowing of light low in the sky. I went quietly and quickly from the house.

THE COLD AND THE BEAUTY AND THE DARK
1932

Chapter 7: Evelyn Confides

On a bright Saturday afternoon in April, Evelyn knocked on Daphne's door in Chadderton Street. To her relief it opened almost immediately. The walk from Stan's Mam's round to Daphne's was a long one. Her back ached and her ankles were swollen. Still nearly three months to go and already she was getting so tired. Daphne drew her into the chair nearest the fire.

"The boys and my Dad have all gone off t'match," she said, "and Mam's round at Gran's. So we can just be cozy, eh? Eh, but you're looking tired, lass. You're carrying heavy."

Evelyn sighed. "Aye, the Leighs all carry the first heavy," she said. "I suppose that's all there is to it."

"Aye, perhaps. I'll get kettle on."

Evelyn smiled gratefully and leaned back in her chair. You didn't have to spell things out to Daphne, she seemed to know. Now that Daphne had switched to the day shift they didn't see so much of each other. A Saturday afternoon knitting by a nice fire and chatting with her friend was the one good thing to come out of Stan's latest habit of staying away from home from Friday till Sunday. Her eyes filled with tears and she wiped them away fiercely, staring into the glowing yellow of the flames.

"I've not seen your Stan in a while," Daphne said when they were sipping their tea, as if reading her mind. "Behaving, is he? How's that mother of his?"

Evelyn hesitated, considering. There could be no harm in telling Daphne. What else were friends for?

"Oh, Daphne, I hardly see him myself. He stops over Fridays and Saturdays in Manchester these days. On Alan O'Reilly's floor. Or so he says. O'Reilly's only got the one room. On Reuben Street, over the pawnbroker's."

"He does *what?*"

"He says it's the meetings," Evelyn said quickly. "They're going on later now, till after t'last bus on Friday night. Then they're back at it all day Saturday an' all, and Sundays. They're up to something, I don't know what."

"Getting drunk, like as not. Or worse. Stirring up trouble."

"Maybe. Wouldn't be surprised, knowing O'Reilly."

"Knowing Stan," Daphne said, not too unkindly.

"Aye, I know." Evelyn sighed and took up the little baby's jacket she was knitting. "But at least he's not coming home drunk. At least he's not getting a name for himself round here. Oh, it is a difficult shade, this lemon. Fiddly." She rubbed her eyes and went on to the end of the row.

"Give it here," Daphne said. "Three-ply's always hard going." She took the work from Evelyn's lap and examined it thoughtfully, then handed it back. "Plain enough, though. You could do it with your eyes shut."

She took up her own work, bed socks for her gran in pale green. "I reckon I know what they're up to, your Stan's lot," she said. "Our Paul's been going on about it. You know Paul, can't keep his mouth shut. Only it's unofficial and he says I'm not to gab or they'll put a stop to it. But there's this big walk planned. They're all going. It's tomorrow."

"Big walk? What big walk, where to? What on earth for?"

"Mind you, he's not one of them agitators, Paul," Daphne said quickly. "He's not like some others. He's harmless, just keen on his rambling. He's going for the principle."

Evelyn was perplexed. As they knitted, Daphne explained everything she'd heard from her brother. Paul regularly went out on Sunday hikes with a group of other young people, taking the bus out of the town and into the surrounding countryside. The trouble was that strictly speaking there weren't many places they were allowed to go, even though they did no harm. Some landowners turned a blind eye to the ramblers but others put up fences to stop them. Sometimes the innocent walkers were threatened or even attacked by gamekeepers when all they wanted to do was go across empty land that was no good for livestock or crops. The landlords were within their rights to prevent them, but there was a rising swell of people, according to Paul, calling for a change in the law. Now things had come to a head. Hundreds if not thousands of people would be converging to join in a big walk planned for the next day. It would be no less than a mass trespass over Derbyshire's most famous peak, Kinder Scout. At present ordinary folk were turned away from there and only a few snooty walking clubs got the necessary "prior permission in writing" from the landowner, the Duke of Devonshire, to go to the summit. Paul told Daphne that a gesture by ordinary folk walking up there peacefully would help get the law changed. If that happened, you wouldn't have to be in with the toffs to enjoy a country walk. Sure enough there were folk spouting political nonsense about the rights of the working man but all Paul wanted was to be able to go on a harmless walk without getting accosted by a gamekeeper.

"He wants me to go as well," Daphne said. "It'll be a bit o' fun, he says. We're taking a picnic. There'll be more folk up there tomorrow than you'll ever see in your life."

"But it's breaking the law!" Evelyn exclaimed.

"That's what I said," Daphne replied. "But Paul says that's the point. The point is there'll be hundreds doing it, and it's not the same as committing a crime when it's the law that's wrong and wants changing. I'm not bothered either way, it's a day out. I reckon on going and I reckon you're coming an' all, Evelyn Ashworth. It'll put the roses back in your cheeks."

"But there might be trouble. What if something happens?"

"Don't talk daft," Daphne said. "We'll be with Paul, and anyway it's all to be peaceful. We'll keep ourselves to ourselves and just have a nice day out."

"I shouldn't," Evelyn said, shaking her head. "It'll be ruddy freezing for one thing. Anyway, I've been. I was out Kinder Scout way years ago, on the Chapel Whitsun outing. And anyway," she went on, "I'm not going climbing mountains in my condition."

"No fear, no more am I!" laughed Daphne. "It's only a hill, not a proper mountain. We'll wrap up warm. It's only for a walk. We'll just go as far as we fancy, find a nice spot, and watch the fun."

"I'm not getting caught up in any monkey business," Evelyn sniffed.

" 'Course not," Daphne said. "It's just summat to watch. It's a good spin out to Hayfield on the bus and it'll be nice round there at daffodil time." She picked up Evelyn's knitting and began working a row. "You can bet your Stan'll be going. You can bet tomorrow night he'll saunter back to his Mam's expecting you there with his tea ready. You surprise him. Show him if he can go marching up Kinder Scout, so can you."

The needles clicked. "He takes you for granted, does your Stan."

Evelyn sighed again. "All right," she said. "I'll catch my death like as not, but I'm going."

Dear Ruth

I know it's been a while but I'm not myself in some ways. Hand bandaged. Plus I'm very busy plus leg ulcers—no fun I can tell you.

Also no fun—bloody nurse, two of them now and you never know which, meddling with legs, now interfering with hand on almost daily basis and they don't care how much they hurt me. Plus Carole and Mrs. M barging in.

And NOW *that woman from your little writing group keeps coming. They're working on a memorial, she says. Della, that's her name—she seems to be the ringleader.*

I haven't mentioned your story to her, that's between you and me. You put in Kinder Scout! I have to correct you though, on that bit about it being cold up there. Don't tell me you've forgotten. You get the shelter of the hill if the wind's in the right direction. Overdale Lodge itself I grant you could be on the Spartan side but you have to admit it was quite cozy after the storage heaters went in. 1978 or thereabouts.

Had a few photos down to look at. Happy days.

Anyway back to these women turning up on doorstep. They've all got a look in their eye. They're all in it together, they think I can't see that. Usually they wake me up—on top of that they bully me about my clothes, too.

EG—Mrs. M appeared uninvited with what she called a complete hot dinner and without so much as a by-your-leave sticks it in oven, fusses about setting the timer but she didn't know how to work it, neither did I. She said it'd take 30 minutes and that was just enough time for a bath, wouldn't it be a good idea if she popped up and ran me one. I spoke quite sharply.

I think she's definitely after me.

She said she'd be calling back for the dish and she'd better find it empty, wag wag goes the finger, she thinks she's funny. Well, forewarned—I just won't answer the door.

Though the dish is empty because I flung the whole lot into the back hedge.

Gave me an idea though. If you ask me the bloody council's messing about with the trash day and not telling me so I'm not bothering putting ours out now. Anything for chucking can go in the hedge. Or it can stay here, plenty space in the hall—I'll get round to a big sort out when it suits me.

All these people. They all still ask how I am and I say nothing and I have nothing much to contribute on other subjects either. What difference does it make if I agree it's a nice day or not? It's not long before I see their mouths squirming around for something to say. Throats get cleared and looks flit from one pair of eyes to another. No wonder I lose my temper.

Mrs. M: Am I sure I'm not a big casserole fan? It's just good plain English food—no garlic!

Della: She'd be only too pleased to make me a cup of tea to have with the cake she's brought. Ruth liked Earl Grey, didn't she? Della likes camomile of an evening but she can't get along with peppermint, it repeats on her.

Nurse: Isn't Arthur a naughty old lazybones, not cutting his nails, she's got people who'd love to be able to cut their nails for themselves.

Carole: Is the pressure cooker perhaps standing for something else? Is the pressure cooker maybe not really about the pressure cooker? Is it symbolic of earlier times?

See what's going on? They think they can get me via toenails and tea and tributes.

And not a word these days about how it's all right for me to be angry.

Example—I told Carole in no uncertain terms what I'd do to that bastard driver if I got my hands on him.

Oh, she pretended to understand, but I wasn't fooled. "Oh. Oh, Arthur, yes I see, well, but, oh dear, you don't think maybe justice is best left to the police? Of course it's understandable . . ."

The police are useless! Fucking useless! I told her. Scared her, I think. Obviously she doesn't think the anger's all right at all—first sign *of it and she wants it all bottled up again. Stupid bitch in my opinion (as I pointed out).*

> *Relieved to see the back of them all*
> *What makes these people tick?*
> *I don't even know them.*
> *And I like garlic, as you know.*

NO WONDER I LOSE MY TEMPER.

Arthur

Inside the house, Arthur was roaming upstairs. But there was a change. He wasn't properly dressed. He was wearing only a raincoat that wasn't completely buttoned and I could see he was naked under it. His wandering seemed more urgent and erratic. He would pause, then suddenly stir and start up to another room and once there, stand and do nothing. Or he would conduct frantic searches in this room or that, and abandon them without finding anything. He walked about with a tea towel over his shoulder and a pen and a bundle of papers in his hands. There were papers stuffed in the coat pockets, too. When he made his way up the ladder to the attic

I shuddered to see that his feet were bare on the sharp metal rungs. When the attic light came on I made my way straight into the house, impatient to get started.

I worked by the light set into the hood over the cooker, as golden and soft as candlelight. There was plenty of hot water, at least. The washing up didn't take so very long and once I'd scrubbed the grill and stovetop and found garbage bags and bagged the rotten scraps I began to see my way. The stink subsided. The countertops polished up nicely. I found bleach and cleaning spray and went around again twice, both in the kitchen and the conservatory, and the smell disappeared altogether, or rather was replaced by a much better one not unlike the smell of the house in Beaulieu Gardens.

Ruth would be a fiend of a housekeeper, I was sure of that. She would be pleased to have her place put back to rights, and I worked with some notion of carrying out her wishes and surpassing even her standards; I scrubbed with a desire for reparation and praise. Resting for a moment, I looked around, not with satisfaction—that was for Ruth to accord or deny me—but with a wish that she should see and judge. Quickly I told myself—no, I told *her*—that of course this was only a quick cleanup. After so many weeks' neglect there would be, I explained, deeper layers of filth and chaos than I could erase in one go. By now there would be dirt settling in here, there, and everywhere, feeling its dark way into the house's fabric rather than merely across its surfaces, and that would take more time and effort to penetrate and correct. As I measured out another capful of detergent, I assured Ruth that I had only just begun. I extinguished the light over the cooker and, starting at the conservatory door, I set about the washing of the kitchen floor in the manner of my grandmother, on my hands and knees with a coarse cloth and a bucket of soapy water, in darkness.

I worked my way across the floor to the door that led into the hall. I stood up and opened it, and borne in with the silence from the rest of the house came also another, even worse smell. I shouldn't have been surprised, I suppose. If he had let the kitchen get into such a state, why would he have been any more careful about the bathroom? I shuddered, for Ruth. She would be mortified.

The hall was littered with papers and piles of rubbish but I didn't take time to look at them closely. The downstairs lavatory was next to the front door. I didn't need to see any more than I was shown by the glow of orange through the window from the street lamps of Cardigan Avenue. I felt rather sick before I had improved matters to an acceptable standard. It did not occur to me not to flush the lavatory as I was finishing with the bleach. So ordinary a sound in a daytime way, in the darkness it roared, and I was afraid it would bring Arthur hurrying down the stairs, calling out. But the torrent of noise had already begun to subside, and then it stopped altogether, and still from upstairs nothing stirred. I walked calmly back into the kitchen. I was surprised by how slippery the floor felt under my shoes, and how the newly clean smell sprang to my nose. I wanted to clap my hands but instead I put on the kettle, humming a tune.

I scraped a foot here and there across the floor as I waited for the water to boil. I like a task with visible results, achieved by straightforward means. I like not just the fruits of my labors but also evidence of the expenditure of that labor. Here was a lovely clean floor and not only that, a bucket of filthy water to show for it as well.

And soon the floor would need its next wash, and once it got it, all it would be was clean again, and that was all: a floor neither more nor less clean than it always was after a good scrub. It was reassuring, this act of maintenance with no expectation of development. Nobody was waiting for the floor eventually to advance and blossom under my care, nobody hoped for any conceptual, breaking insight from me into the cleanliness of floors in general. I liked the certainty of the repetition that would never produce anything more surprising than a clean floor, a pleasing smell, and a gallon of water swooshing down the sink.

In that sense Arthur would be a bit like a floor; it would soothe me just to keep him nice, and judging by what I had so far seen, that would be a not entirely trivial achievement. And apart from any advantage to him, there was Ruth to consider. She was distressed by the state he had got himself into; she conveyed that loud and clear. I would henceforth enter Arthur's house with ease. I had Ruth's approval; more than that I was, quite possibly, acting under her instruction. All three of us would benefit.

Moreover, I had already found in myself a dedication to the task quite independent of any consideration for Arthur and Ruth, though I didn't like to think of either of them knowing this.

But we would all see eye-to-eye. Already I detected something habitual and self-preserving in Arthur's absence from the scene of any domestic operations. Once he was safely up in the attic, I sensed that by silent and mutual agreement he would stay there, leaving me to get on elsewhere in the house. And while we were both occupied we would be respectful of each other's need for peace and quiet. Neither of us would make any unnecessary noise.

I made tea and drank mine in silence. Then I poured out a cup for Arthur and carried it upstairs. Shadows from the open hatch to the attic crossed the landing carpet like tiny patches of rapid, passing cloud. From the foot of the ladder I could hear, among the thudding of objects, Arthur's voice rising in a muttering, plaintive monologue. I took the teaspoon from the saucer and tapped it against the cup, five times. The sounds from the attic stopped. I tapped another five times, and placed the cup and saucer gently on the floor. I went downstairs and into the conservatory. Already there was the merest threat of light in the sky and the garden walls and chimneys and roofs of Arthur's neighbors' houses were beginning to emerge out of darkness. Again it was time for me to go.

Dear Ruth

Been thinking and thinking.
It was you.
I know that doesn't make sense, but it doesn't make sense that it wasn't you, either.
Can't have been anyone else, can it? Nobody else tings on the cup like that.
Tried to tell leg nurse about it—there's a new one, foreign, name's full of sounds like "brushes" or "shooshes"'all strung together. English not up to scratch, she didn't have a clue what I was talking about.
Better kept to myself, anyway—to ourselves, rather.
Thank you, dear.

Arthur

Ps I'm leaving this where it'll be easy to find. Hope you get it.

THE COLD AND THE BEAUTY AND THE DARK
1932

Chapter 8: The Walk

The day following, Evelyn was up long before Stan's Mam and was knocking on Daphne's door at half past seven. She had popped into Woolworth's on her way home from Daphne's after their comfortable Saturday afternoon the day before and bought a bag of biscuits, her contribution to the picnic, even though Daphne had told her not to bother. On arrival, Evelyn could see why! There were enough sandwiches for a dozen, packed in an enormous basket.

"We'll never eat all that! We'll never *carry* all that!" she exclaimed, aghast.

Daphne hooted with laughter. "You don't know Paul! Besides, everybody gets hungry out of doors. It's the fresh air."

But the basket was very heavy. Daphne's mother sided with Evelyn and sent Daphne to fetch another basket. They unpacked the first and divided its contents between the two, while Daphne's mother clucked around them.

"It's a shame you've not got your pram yet," she said to Evelyn, "or you could've pushed your picnic along in that and saved your arms."

Evelyn nodded. She didn't like to say that she couldn't see how she was going to get a pram at all unless Stan started saving a bit more. At this rate she'd be carrying that baby in a shawl on her back until it was ready to walk.

The three of them set off happily. Paul was dressed in a strange but practical getup of knickerbockers and thick boots that brought hoots of laughter from the girls. Evelyn and Daphne took a basket each and Paul carried, slung over one shoulder, a special case containing a spirit stove, paraffin, kettle, and all the tea things. He wasn't going up Kinder Scout without getting a hot brew at the top, he said. He also carried a stout walking stick and a pair of binoculars.

They walked down to Aldbury High Street and caught the tram into Stockport, from where they had to catch the bus out to Hayfield. The tram had run a little late and now they were cutting it fine, and the bus station was milling with people. Paul said he'd never seen such a crowd on a Sunday. There were several extra buses laid on as well as hired charabancs and in the confusion Paul took off into the melée to find out where their bus was leaving from. After a minute he reappeared to say it was way over at the other side and they would have to run. Then he was off again, followed by Daphne, and Evelyn had a hard time keeping up. Puffing after them with the heavy basket, she fixed her eyes on Daphne's bright green headscarf, bobbing ahead of her. It was lucky Daphne was so big and liked bright colors, she thought, or she'd have lost her by now. Just then she saw a frowning Paul coming toward her through the sea of people. When he caught sight of her his face broke into a grin.

"Eh, lass, you're struggling! Give us that here." So saying he took the basket from Evelyn's aching arm and steered her toward the bus. She could have cried with gratitude.

They clambered aboard and got the last seats. The bus would wind its way through Stockport and on out toward

New Mills before going on to Hayfield. From there it would go down to Chapel-en-le-Frith and on to Castleton and end up in Sheffield. Along the way it picked up more passengers and soon it was crammed with people, many of them standing, some with rucksacks and sticks, others in working jackets and caps. There were children, dogs, and numerous picnic baskets. A group of five men tried to board with a furled banner mounted on two tall poles, but the conductor refused to let them on.

As the bus rolled away, leaving them behind, Paul gazed after them and said, "Never seen the like. Going to be a big do, this."

With its full load the bus went slowly. Sometimes a hired charabanc overtook them, with flags flying from the windows. Evelyn was not quick enough to read what they said, but Daphne reported excitedly, "Ooh! Workers for something or other! Anti-fascist Federation of—oh, it's flapping, I can't see what! Oh, Paul, that one's got 'Communist' on it!"

She turned to Evelyn, wide-eyed. "Is that the sort of thing your Stan's getting up to these days?" Evelyn shrugged. She didn't know and she didn't want to know. Daphne pulled at Paul's sleeve. "Paul, Evelyn's Stan might be one o' them! He's forever at meetings. "

"More fool him, then," Paul said tersely, "and you still newlyweds."

"He's one of the regulars," Evelyn said. "He tires himself out on it."

"Plain daft if you ask me," Paul said. "Plain bloody daft."

Evelyn wasn't sure if he meant Stan was daft to go to all

the meetings, or daft to stay away from her, but she flushed with pleasure.

"It's that Alan O'Reilly's doing, really," she said demurely.

Daphne hooted with scorn. "Ho! I wonder if he's brought a picnic, your famous Comrade O'Reilly? Bet they won't! Well, they're not cadging off us, that's for sure!"

"No fear!" Paul cried, making them all laugh.

After that they settled down to the bus ride. Paul got into conversation with others on board, chatting about other walking routes and scenic paths that Evelyn had never heard of. She was content to watch out the window. Trees and buildings looked different on Sundays, especially around Eastertime, cleaner than on weekdays. She had said that to Stan once and he hadn't had a clue what she was going on about. She was looking out, trying to explain it again to herself but at the same time thinking Paul would understand what she meant. She wouldn't have to explain it to him. She gave herself a shake. What funny thoughts she was getting, now she was pregnant! Why, Paul was at least eight years younger than she was, just a nice decent lad. She turned her thoughts to Stan and wondered if she would see him later. It seemed unlikely, she'd never find him among so many people. She nearly cried right there and then, and that too must be because she was pregnant. Things could come over her so suddenly these days.

There was a cold wind blowing when they got off the bus, Paul said, on account of Hayfield being that much higher. Evelyn didn't mind once she had got her jerkin buttoned and a scarf on. Daphne had packed a couple of spare cardigans, at her mother's insistence. Paul met up with some of his regular walking companions and so they all went along together in a friendly, loose straggle up the main street. There were lots of people, mainly young folk, and a lot more men and boys than women and girls. For a moment Evelyn felt awkward, surrounded by the laughing Daphne and Paul and his band of high-spirited lads. What was she doing here? Maybe Daphne's mother had only let Daphne go on condition Evelyn went, too. Maybe she thought if there was a respectable married woman in tow, expecting a baby what's more, it would keep Daphne and Paul from getting too giddy.

Hayfield people stood out at their doors, watching the procession go past. Evelyn couldn't make out faces but she could tell by the shapes they made, standing tall with their arms folded, filling up their doorways and hardly moving, that they were wary of this invasion of their quiet village.

Just then, somewhere ahead of them, there was a holdup. It was impossible to see what was causing it but the whole procession ground to a halt and then came sounds of a bit of commotion up ahead, snatches of shouting and even some singing. A few people round about them joined in the song. Paul said in a loud growl, glaring round, "Manchester riffraff, Jews and communists. Stirring up the apprentices from Mather & Platt and the other big factories. They've been at it for months."

"Well," quipped Daphne, "what were you expecting? The Salvation Army?"

This broke the tension and several people laughed along with them. Evelyn began to long to sit down. Policemen were going up and down at the edge of the procession, holding truncheons. But they were addressing the crowds with civility, instructing people to make their way without hurrying up the main street. At the end of the village and once over the river at Bowden Bridge, they were to go as far as the quarry and wait there. A policeman asked Evelyn if she was feeling all right, which she thought very nice of him and, encouraged, she asked if he had seen the Northwest Federation of Free Working Men because she was looking for her husband. The policeman shook his head. He told her there were six hundred people here and more arriving, God only knew where from.

They got as far as the quarry only just in time to hear the tail end of the speeches and, as Paul called it, "that bloody daft political carry-on." Most of the speakers and leaders had moved off already and the platform was being dismantled and two or three bands were packing up. Evelyn's basket was already weighing very heavy on her arm and she didn't feel much in the way of a walk, but after a breather they pressed on toward the reservoir, following the line of people already heading that way.

The sun came out, and cheering though it was, Evelyn could have done without it. The combination of a cold breeze and the bright light made her eyes water so badly she hardly knew where she was going. But it was lovely being in the country, she told herself. The air smelled sweet and in the fields next to the road there were lambs bleating away and the big ewes were all bunched right up at the wall, watching the people troop past. The big daft things stood like soft gray boulders. Evelyn went up to one and it didn't budge. As she stared at it, all the while the wind and sunlight were sweeping over it, changing the colors on its back from silver to mucky gray to nearly dark as soot, like a smudge in the middle of a picture. She must have been dawdling, because Daphne called out.

"Come on, Evelyn! You ha'n't got all day to waste chatting to your cousins!"

Evelyn laughed and called back that Daphne was a cheeky so-and-so. They walked on amid more laughter. Daffodils were out and the wind blew straight down the lane off the hill and tipped the flowers right to the ground, turning their leaves inside out and parting the shiny new grass like a comb.

Soon they left the road and struck out on a level track that led first between fields and then up into the hills. The track wound along beside a wide rushing stream, and as they went closer the hills loomed at them and seemed to close in. After a mile or so the stream and the track diverged. The track swerved deeply and suddenly they came across, around a long curve and nestling into the lower reaches of the hill, the last thing Evelyn had expected to see. It was a large house, built of red brick with a steep slate roof and a grand porch, with all manner of elaborate turrets and tall windows and high gables. A stunted windbreak of trees and clusters of thick evergreen shrubs surrounded it. Though it was too solid to be magical or even romantic, the house had a storybook quality, and though well maintained, it looked shut up and forlorn.

"That's Overdale," Paul said a little grimly. "Overdale Lodge. Bloody eyesore."

"Who lives there?" Evelyn asked.

"Nobody," Paul said. "Not anymore. It was just for shooting parties, for rich folks coming out from Manchester. All that's long gone now so it's shut up. It was them Braddocks as had it built, must be nigh on forty, fifty year ago. You know, the family as owns Braddock Mills."

"Seems a shame, a grand place like that and nobody stopping there no more," Evelyn murmured.

"Well, times has changed," Paul grunted. "Built in Braddock senior's day, before the War. Godfrey Braddock the son, he owns Braddock Mills now. He's still rolling in money, I daresay."

"Eh, it's grand enough. All right for some," Daphne said. "Mind you, I wouldn't fancy it. Bet it's freezing, imagine trying to heat a place that size!"

"Aye, and it's a flaming long way to fetch in t'coal!" Evelyn said, laughing.

On they went, up Kinder Bank. The going was steadily uphill and Evelyn got more and more winded. She couldn't find the breath for walking as well as chatting with her companions, and it was single file in places, anyway. She fell behind and began to feel lonely, walking with her eyes on the fuzzy outlines of their backs, not hearing what they were talking about and too tired to call for them to wait. Most people, including her, stayed on the path, though some were fanning out across the slope, Paul among them. It must have been tougher going up there, off the path. People were using their sticks and trudging along slantwise, bending into the hillside.

There were streams to cross, or the same one several times; several little channels of water ran through the tussocks of moor grass and over the path. Evelyn managed it fine to begin with. She had on her stout shoes, not long resoled, and also, acting on Paul's advice, she had put on a thick pair of socks. But there was a lot of wet and mud to be gone through, and Evelyn had a sudden memory of her Big Day and her green mock-croc shoes, which she had not thought about for weeks. They were still like new in a box under the bed, as she hadn't had them on again. They wouldn't have lasted five minutes in this!

She struggled on, her feet damp but not soaked through. She was far too hot now, what with the walking and carrying the basket, never mind Daphne's extra cardigan. Sweat was running all down her body and her eyes and nose were pouring, too. She must look a sight, she was sure, so in a way she was pleased the others had gone ahead. She wished she had slacks on, like some of the real walking girls. They had proper boots, too. Expensive they looked, the slacks, and flattering; the girls looked very comfortable in them. Best of all, they didn't have the worry of the wind blowing their skirts up, because Evelyn had that to manage on top of all her other woes, keeping one hand free to hold her skirt firmly against her legs, for modesty's sake. But then, she thought, even if she had had the money for them, there wouldn't be a pair of slacks she could get into, not at the stage she was at now.

Now and then when she stopped for a rest the wind felt colder, and it was lovely for a moment, feeling the sweat dry off on her skin, but after a few minutes the wind would start to bite. If she didn't keep moving she got chilled to the bone, and she was getting so tired. The wind was cutting right through her jerkin and freezing her legs. The others were too far ahead for her to shout and tell them she was heading back down and she didn't want to make a fuss by having them fret that she had got lost. Anyway, she was carrying half the picnic. She gave herself a talking-to and moved on.

She caught up with the others by the sheep gate at the top of the dam. There was shelter out of the wind if you tucked in under White Brow, with the reservoir stretching away to your right, so that was a blessing. Daphne, Paul, and Evelyn found themselves a spot not far off the path with some flat stones for them to sit on and one on which they could set up the stove. Paul got it lit after several attempts. Evelyn was heartily glad to stop. After a while she could breathe more easily and she could even say, by the time she had a hot brew warming her hands and was munching on a sandwich, that she was enjoying herself again.

They ate and drank gratefully. Sometimes the sun came out strong and warm on their faces and raised the flat, reedy smell of grass and rocks. Evelyn could hear birds, miles above them it seemed. The other two were going on and on about the view and passing the binoculars between them, but she was more interested in the sky, lying back on the blanket and sensing the vastness of it above her and all that lovely emptiness. The wind was high and gusting, and though she didn't feel it in the shelter of the Brow she could hear it, a high-up rushing like a faraway waterfall, washing and washing the air clean, sweeping gray and white plumes of cloud over the sun as if it was chasing swirls of dust out of the corners of the sky.

Maybe it was because of the baby and all the extra weight, or maybe it was simple fatigue, but when they were packed up and ready to move off Evelyn had stiffened up so much she could hardly stand straight.

"Oh, wait, let's not go yet!" she said, rubbing her back, trying to make light of it.

Daphne understood. "Oh, all right, let's have another ciggie," she said, passing round her packet while Evelyn sank back onto the ground.

"I should've brought a hip flask," Paul said, clicking his tongue. "A nip in you would do the trick."

Evelyn immediately thought of Stan. Was he up here on the hill, too, taking nips from a flask? Would he be content with just nips?

Now, down below them on the path, folk were filing through the sheep gate and on up to William Clough. It was boggy either side of the path, so everybody slowed up and went through single file, and Evelyn thought to herself that even though it was too far away for her to make out faces, she would know Stan if she saw him. He always had on his red scarf these days and he was a big, tall devil. What with that and his way of stooping so his head poked forward, she'd know him even from that distance.

She explained to Daphne and Paul that she would only hold them up if she went any farther. They were content enough to go on without her once she had reassured them that she would be fine on her own. All she knew, she told them, was that she couldn't go back into that wind stinging her eyes the way it did. She would stop here and mind the picnic things. They would get on faster with nothing to carry, and if Paul left her enough matches she would have tea waiting for them when they got back.

Dusting, because it was the quietest, became my favorite task. While the floor was creaking softly above me I would sweep a cloth over surfaces, lifting and setting down Ruth's things, reaching behind objects and into crevices. I drew my hand across the veneers and ornaments and slipcovers of her life, and by their contours learned her ways. At 27 Cardigan Avenue she was both visionary and manager: Capability Ruth, the romantic yet practical arranger of all the miniature landscapes of her house. I could hear her scolding Arthur, telling him how upset she was about the mess everywhere. She imposed a kind of foursquare, insistent balance; she liked a vista of furniture receding into well-angled, decorous forms against warm-hued walls, she liked to frame windows in drapes tied back like garlands. Her taste veered toward the chintzy: nature improved upon and improbably floral so as to invoke stasis and order. Her cushions lay on the sofa as plump and peaceful as solid little cherubs from a pastorale, asleep on a bank. Her floors were predominantly green and gold, somewhat bleached and shady in the light of the moon. I imagined she liked carpets to remind her of moss and sand.

When I cleaned the composed and satisfied arrangements of Ruth's downstairs rooms I moved carefully and quickly among the lamps and vases and dishes on side tables. Their settled roundness seemed slightly to reproach me for my angular, darting manner. And when my work was accomplished I took my leave like a verger, turning at the threshold for a last look, to watch emptiness flow back into the space I had disturbed. Knowing I had done all I could, I was content to leave the room to guard its own frail shadows, as though my parting gift were to stop the clocks and arrest Ruth's hazy idyll in the dark where it could rest undisturbed. No new stark encounter on a deserted road under windblown trees could violate it now; I was keeping it safe from any further brash and irreverent tests of its flimsiness.

And oh, the repetition! Arthur would undo all my work in minutes and not even notice. Whenever I put a room to rights after one of his foraging raids on cupboards or drawers or shelves, I knew that I would probably find it all upside down again the next night. Sometimes I would stifle a sigh when I came across the kitchen or bathroom filthy again, but I didn't really mind. The endless round of these tasks released me into a ritual both seemly and devotional, and as elevating as meditation.

I think that my grandmother found a similar, steadying comfort in housework and the mild tyranny of its routines. Perhaps housekeeping, for her, was a mundane anchoring force in a life made unstable by my mother's erratic ways, though my grandmother herself would never have expressed it like that. All she might have said, with a sigh and a smile, was that she didn't suppose the floor was going to wash itself.

She rolled her two main responsibilities—housekeeping and me—into one, setting about chores with her face tipped up smiling and her hands going like feelers around her, chivvying me along in the role of little helper. By touch and with great care she washed and rinsed and wrung laundry through the mangle; she hung out, folded, smoothed, and ironed our clothes and linen, and sorted it into piles for me to put away. She scrubbed floors and sinks, she dusted and polished. She timed an egg by singing four verses of "Abide With Me" while I, sometimes singing along, watched the trickle of colored sand slip through the neck of the timer; she was never off by more than a few seconds. The rising gurgle of boiling water going into the teapot told her when she had filled it to its limit. She kept her white stick by the top of the stairs leading down to the shop; indoors she measured the distances between obstacles in counted steps.

By the scent and slant of the wind on Mondays she could judge how long to leave the washing to hang out in the backyard, and if I was good and quick and pegged up the handkerchiefs for her before I left for school, she might play our wet ghosts game, tiptoeing invisibly along on the other side of the line and keeping me guessing which of the vast, obscuring sheets she was hiding behind. No matter how I gazed I was never able to tell if this one or that twitched from a touch of the breeze, from a flick of her hand, or from the breathy sigh of a ghost. I hardly dared peep underneath for a glimpse of her splayed feet in the black shoes, for what if they were elsewhere and *not* planted behind the sheet that at any moment would suddenly balloon out at me? And what did it mean, the thrill and horror of the sheet's absolute stillness; had she, like my great-uncle, gone with the ghosts at last, and become one herself? She kept me waiting, and waiting. And when I would be almost faint with dread, a wail would float from the other side of the sheet and one whole wet square would swell with the dome of her head and flap forward against her outstretched arms. Then I would lunge at her, squealing to be caught in a damp cottony hug.

One Monday she didn't put the washing out at all. When I got home from school she told me there was grit in the wind that day. The wind was blowing from the wrong direction, carrying smoke and dust from the railway and bringing soot down the chimney. She said this as if she didn't care. The weather, it seemed, had blown away all her briskness and left her dreamy and vague, or perhaps it was rather that the wind had brought something else to her attention. She closed the windows and told me to find the tin of polish and a duster and give the sitting room an extra going-round while she washed the kitchen floor.

I heard her sighing as she reached for a bucket and ran the tap. The wind had made me contrary, too, in the way that the wrong weather upsets young animals; suddenly I was full of a skittish, supple anger. I dug my thumb into the tin, climbed on a stool, and smeared a lump of polish along the top of the picture rail. When I got down I waved the duster a few times, then I wandered away, past the room where my mother was spending a second day in bed with a stash of bottles under the covers, up to the dull quiet of my room in the attic. I sat on my bed until I felt blank. When I came down my grandmother was smiling but her eyes were as cold as pearls. The spell of dreaminess brought on by the weather was broken. Whatever the wind had brought, she had washed it along and out of the day.

"I gave you a job to do."

Anger gusted inside me again. "I did it."

"It's still dusty in here."

"How do you know?" She didn't reply. The lavender and beeswax air lay over us like a coat. "You can smell I've done it!"

She moved across to her chair and sat down. "I can see you didn't."

"No, you can't! How can you?"

She was still smiling. "Aye, well, miss. I see what I see."

"But you *can't* see!"

"Even so. There are colors. Everything's got its color."

"But *you* can't see them," I told her. "You can't see anything."

"Maybe, aye. Maybe not things. Not as such. But I get the colors for things. They go roaming about," she said, drawing her palm across the side of her head, "in here."

"How you can see the colors of things but not the things? That's daft!"

"Don't you be cheeky. Colors *for* things, I said, not *of* things. There are colors for things. And you did not dust this room."

"All right then, what's the color for dust? There isn't one!" I took a deep, brave breath and announced, "You're just talking *daft*!"

"Maybe there isn't," she said matter-of-factly, "but there's a color for big fibs." She fished with one hand for the bag of knitting on the floor under her chair and pulled it onto her lap. "Yes, and there's a color for a girl who cheeks her grandma. Now be a good girl and get us a cup of tea. And don't bang the kettle."

Dear Ruth

I'm angry, if you want to know.

You might have replied. Just a few words would have done. What's the matter, run out of words?

Bloody words. That woman Della from your writing group. She brought the tribute. Her eyebrows shoot up and down a lot, don't they? She says the whole bunch of them contributed but she came on her own in case presence of the others was too much. They don't want to over-whelm me.

She's had it written out in fancy writing and framed. Stayed ages pretending the visit was for my sake not hers, for example did I want to "'talk about dear Ruth"? There's no reply to that, I said nothing, just cracked my knuckles. So just to kick us off she brings down her eye-brows and says, "Oh! Didn't Ruth have such a sensitivity for words?!'"

They stick around, don't they, words. They're all over the place, only not a one from you to me.

I told her, And well she might've, she was still an English teacher this time two years ago. And very highly regarded, did I have to remind her how many former pupils turned up at the funeral?

At which she said "Awwwww, Arthur. Awwww, I know ..."

Imbecile. I said, Mr. Mitchell to you, thank you very much, Della, but she ignored me.

She said she was glad I was managing to talk about you "a little," "at last," and she'd "hardly dared hope" the group's tribute would help me "make the breakthrough" but she was thrilled it had. What on earth is she talking about? If I have something to say I say it, and if I don't I don't. Why should it bother anyone that I haven't got things to say to the people who turn up here?

I honestly think they show up for entertainment. And I shan't oblige.

Nobody including Della wants to hear about what's important, ie what the driver of that car's got coming to him.

She insisted on reading the tribute out loud, because she said it was quite powerful and she didn't want me to be alone the first time I read it, after she'd gone. Also poetry can be such a comfort at a time like this, etc etc.

Well, prepare to be amazed, here it is:

Tribute to Ruth
Friend, knocked off your bike:
Cut down
And who's to say not in your prime?
For sixty-one is only the counting of the years
The measuring of Time,
Time allotted by a Higher Power
That dispenses Life's green springs and verdant summers,
Its mellow autumns and fading winters.
Friend, your gifts were many
And freely given: spread around
For the benefit of friends and family
And members of the wider community.
Neighbor, teacher, wife, friend.
Your generosity was without end.
Ruth, your name's meaning is obscure
But your life was crystal clear, like pure
Running water.
Wise proud warrior!
Woman! Of flesh and spirit, earth and sky!
A Writer, and in this a Mother to boot——
For your poems and short stories
Are your children: the fruit
Of your creativity, given birth through
Life's long labor in the orchard of womanhood.
As roses ramble upward through a tree, hold fast to the trunk
And blossom, so your work holds, clings to the memory of you.
Ruth, cut down like a reed,
We whom you leave behind

Can only hope it was quick, a swift
Release without pain.
Your poems and short stories full of humor and wisdom
You leave them behind, a legacy to keep
For those who stand by the grave and weep.
We will do our best without you.
And it will be hard, for friendship
Is precious, your loss so sudden.
All Death
Is cruel but Ruth, yours more than most.
So long, Writer, Woman, Friend.
Our love for you will never end.
Your inspiration will not cease.
Ruth, may you rest in peace.

From Della, Pam, Maggie, Kate, Linda, and Trish
Monkswell & District Women Writers Group

I don't think the Poet Laureate needs to be looking over his shoulder just yet, do you? Who is the Poet Laureate these days, anyway? You'd know.

When she'd read it Della hung around waiting for me to tell her I thought they were all geniuses, eyebrows on the move again and eyes brimming.

It only rhymes, I said, here and there. We didn't think that mattered, she says. We just wanted to express something about Ruth. After some discussion we agreed that being restricted to any particular rhyme scheme might stifle creativity.

I'm trying to get her to go when she produces the hammer.

Next she fishes in her bag and brings out a picture hook. She didn't want to trouble me to go looking for mine, easier to bring hers from home, she says, and where would I like it? Didn't reply, so then she says, Never mind, I expect you'd like me to decide. Most men don't know a suitable wall from the side of an elephant when it comes to getting the right hang, most men wouldn't notice if the Mona Lisa was upside down!

I let her stick it up under the clock on the wall behind the TV. It won't catch my eye there, as I'm not watching TV anymore.

Arthur.

PS Fucking tribute, pardon my French.

It got to me, just knowing it was there. I took it down, couldn't find claw hammer so pulled out hook with kitchen scissors, tore wallpaper, and left a hole. Tore a bit more paper off to see state of plaster generally, was wondering if that wall could do with a once-over. It could now. Plaster came with it. May get round to it, I like to have a job or two in the offing. Keeping it in the pipeline for now—there's enough going on.

PPS If I hadn't let the bloody woman in there wouldn't be all this mess and need for redecoration, not an inconsiderable task at my age.

PPPS She said (parting shot)—Now don't hesitate if there's a single thing I can do. So I'm going to ask her for a contribution toward materials.

THE COLD AND THE BEAUTY AND THE DARK
1932

Chapter 9: One Last Look

All over the hillside people were packing up and heading down to the path to file through the sheep gate. Evelyn watched the line of walkers. She couldn't make them out clearly but she gazed at them as they went on into the distance, thinking that they looked liked a long dark snake sliding ahead along the path. She could see well enough the side of the hill against the sky where it suddenly steepened above the path, and soon enough the snake of people slithered away completely, leaving Evelyn alone, aware of no other living thing except the birds. Those must be skylarks, she thought, though she could also hear familiar town birds, crows and gulls and some other sort, too, making a cry of "sweek-sweek" that mixed with the wailing of the wind.

As Evelyn was gazing into the distance, the sun broke unexpectedly through the clouds, turning the surface of the reservoir into a flat mirror, like a sheet of steel. Then a squall of wind blew across it and broke the sheet into sparkling, brittle splinters. Evelyn shivered and settled herself for a rest. She used Paul's sweater as a pillow and was glad of a couple of cardigans to tuck around her legs. She found herself another biscuit to nibble, just to keep the chill away, and then she lay back, looking up at the sky and thinking how beautiful it all was. Then she fell asleep.

And because she had been asleep, she was never able to say with certainty afterward how long she had spent alone there on the hill. They told her it had been the best part of three hours, but if someone else had said it had been no more than ten minutes, she might have believed that just as easily. She would never know how much, in hours and minutes, that patch of her life up there on the hillside had taken out of the whole. She knew only that it marked the difference between Before and After, and changed everything, forever.

She did know, however, that in some drowsy state, she heard the birds again and they seemed to be much louder. She sat up and looked again at the reservoir and had to put a hand up against the flash of the sun coming off it, but she was too late, and she was left with a burning, ripped feeling across her eyes. She lay back again to wait for the stinging to die down, and then the birds began to sound friendly again and she turned her head on the pillow of Paul's sweater so the wool tickled her face, and her baby lay like a warm, thick stone in her belly. With her eyes closed she felt Stan's locket between her fingers and ran it along the chain close to the side of her neck next to her ear because she liked the silky, buzzing sound it made. Then she must have fallen asleep again.

She woke to the noise of shouting. She sat up, blinking, and waited for the dazzle to fade. Through the grainy darkness of her vision the reservoir was now a blot of lavender blue and the sky was heavy with clouds that lightened to whiteness where they met the water. Evelyn felt as if she were rocking about on a raft, for the hillside grass was rippling around her under wavy stripes of sunlight and shadow.

Over to her left where the shouting was coming from, where the path from its highest point dipped sharply into William Clough, she caught a movement. Some people were making their way back toward the sheep gate. She saw at once the gash of bright red around the neck and the dark, hunched figure of Stan, walking alone. Then she saw, moving ahead of him, a smaller figure, a bright, drifting smear of color against the path. It was a girl in a yellow skirt and a blue jacket, with a yellow hat or scarf. Behind them some more figures came along, dark and moving urgently so Evelyn supposed they were men. They were shoving at one another and running and shouting. There was laughter, too, and voices chanting something.

She turned her attention back to the figure that was unmistakably Stan. The girl in blue and yellow was now waiting for him at the sheep gate, watching him walk toward her. She stood with her hands in her pockets. Evelyn could tell she was saving up the look of him to keep for herself. She had done the same thing herself and she knew you only did that when you felt a certain way. But just before he reached her, there was another shout, this time from a way farther down in the clough, and Stan stopped and turned to the men coming from behind him. He set one hand into the back of his waist and lifted the other hand and clasped the back of his neck. Then he tipped his head back as if he were letting the weight of it rest in his cupped hand. Evelyn knew it so well, that way he had of gripping his neck, and with a rush of simple tenderness opened her mouth to call out to him. But just then the girl moved forward, skipping along from the sheep gate. She put her arms around him and pressed her face into his back. Stan turned to her. He was much taller than she was. Evelyn saw him dip his head to her, saying something, and then he loosened the red scarf Evelyn had knitted for him and drew it around the girl's neck and pulled her close. Then he brought his face down to hers and kissed her. Evelyn saw the red scarf around both their necks and the girl's blue arms up around his shoulders, and the two heads meeting. A couple of whistles came their way from the men down the path and they separated.

All at once Evelyn's eyes began to run with sore, gluey tears and the baby heaved inside her stomach with a kick that she felt almost in her throat. She would have cried out but the kick startled her, and then suddenly she started to shake uncontrollably. She went on staring and staring down the hillside but now it was like gazing through a dirty window and she couldn't see anything. It began to rain, in hard, spitting drops that felt like hail or grit, and Evelyn went on gazing. She tipped her face up to the sky wishing it would pull her up into itself until she disappeared, or that it would rain down hard enough for her to be dissolved. She was so breathless she felt faint. The world seemed to be turning dark, as if the rainstorm were blowing her before it, sweeping her westward to the very end of this bright day on the hillside and straight down into the night, where she would be left alone and lost in complete darkness, with the wind howling and the rain pouring down. She squeezed her eyes tight shut and sobbed, and it seemed her crying would never, ever stop. She was frightened of looking again at the sheep gate for fear of seeing them kissing once more, their colors entwining and blending, but when she opened her eyes there was nothing to see at all.

It was much later when they led her off the hillside. They found her quite some way from their picnic spot, huddled and shaking and soaked through. Paul and Daphne each took one of her arms and there were other people around, all trying to help, though Evelyn was so dazed she could not take in very much or answer all the questions she was being asked. She was chilled to the bone. They led her down slowly, their voices gentle and with none of their usual bantering and teasing, so that she could sense their deep, unspoken concern. Daphne and Paul got her to the pub, where the landlord and his wife could not have been kinder. They were found a quiet room and blankets were fetched, as well as a cup of tea to go with the glass of brandy that the landlord said would be very warming. After a while a doctor arrived and announced that she was suffering from shock and mild exposure. He wasn't qualified to comment on the sightless eyes but shock could do strange things especially to pregnant women, he said, and they would probably be as right as rain after a good night's sleep. The baby would come to no harm, babies were tough little creatures, and that was the main thing, wasn't it?

Months later Evelyn heard from Daphne, who got it from Paul, that everybody was saying the Kinder Scout Mass Trespass had gone down as a great day by all accounts, even a historic one. And I was there, she thought to herself. I was there, but really, I missed it. The violent confrontation between the walkers and the keepers had occurred farther away, past Kinder Downfall and deeper into William Clough, and all up along the top of Ashop Head. People had been swarming all over the place, charging around and knocking one another about with sticks and what have you. And all, Evelyn thought privately, all for a few acres of heathland.

For her the day had drawn to a confusing and unhappy close with the bus ride home. She sat shivering and exhausted in blankets while excited singing and shouting went on around her. Daphne sat next to her and patted her hand from time to time and asked if she was all right. She nodded and kept her eyes shut. No looking out the window this time. Instead she let her mind's eye wander over the images of the day. She tried to memorize its details, knowing they were now no more than things she had seen once but never would again, except as mementos in an album, memories of a day on Kinder Scout etched deep on her heart, that would devour the rest of her life. All she had left now was what she brought with her down from the hillside: the cold and the beauty and the dark, one present, one vanished, and one waiting up ahead for her.

Dear Ruth

Re: legs.

Nurse whats-her-name and the other one came together today, ominous in itself and that was before I saw their faces. One came to the front door, the other was prying round the back. It doesn't do anybody any good getting woken up like that, all in a fright. I'd nodded off in conservatory. They startled me, and that floor's more slippery now. What are you using on it, they demanded to know. One of them was sliding her foot along it. You must be using something on it.

Told them to ask you, cleaning products being your department, and got the pursed lips. One wanted to go into the soft talk but I wasn't having any. Treating me as if I was demented, I won't have it. Mutterings about Community Psychiatric Services again, which I ignored as per.

The other one sits down and starts making notes. Home care review, she says. Goals, paperwork, drives them all mad. The first one gets me back in my chair and pinned down and does the legs. She launches into a lecture. Polishing the floor may be "unadvisable" as combo of wax and ceramic tiles can be extremely slippery. And there is such a thing as overdoing housework and would I please heed earlier advice about resting with legs up, and bear in mind risk of breaking skin on shins and infecting the ulcers if I'm charging around the place. Obviously a waste of breath on my part to try and explain again about you and the housework, they just don't want to hear the facts.

Pigheaded young woman, actually—she didn't take kindly to being corrected. The word is Inadvisable not Unadvisable, I took some pleasure in pointing out, and she gave me one of those "who's a naughty boy" looks and said there was no need to shout. I wasn't shouting, which I also pointed out.

Actually the IN not UN business is more your kind of remark than mine, though you generally saved that kind of thing for later instead of coming out with it at the time. But it felt like it was you in my brain, and you talking. Don't recall you ever tripping anyone up on this particular example, but it was you, all right.

I'm glad you're speaking to them. I suppose you have to do it through me, at least for now. I wish you'd speak to them more. I wish you'd speak to them about my legs. Wouldn't you think in this day and age they'd be able to do something? Other than squeezing them into elastic bandages, I mean, and that gunk they smear on.

You could get them to understand. You could get them to see I can't be doing with the discomfort 24 hours a day and if I take the bandages off it's only because I need a respite. They should try it for themselves, they'd soon see what I'm talking about. And if I forget to put the bandages back on I can't see that affects anyone but me so why the bullying. I don't care for the tone they're taking. Oh yes they've got a job to do but I'm more than twice their age.

They've no right using words like uncooperative and threatening me with hospital.

Arthur

OK—trying to obey orders of Bossyboots and Co. went to sleep at some point once they'd gone and after I woke I just lay there, still resting. Keeping legs up. Thinking and thinking thoughts of Overdale. I tried talking to you but I don't think you were in the vicinity, quite. It was on the early side for you. Still light.

So instead I read some more of your story about Overdale. You take me right back there. I had some pictures fished out over the floor already, hadn't looked at them in years.

And I found this, your poem with the photograph.

Overdale
I remember the white waterfall,
a liquid horsetail spilling over white rocks,
wires of spray silvering the white air,
making rainbows and wetting our faces.

I suppose you meant to finish it someday. Was that all you remembered, the waterfall?

I've taken the liberty and come up with a second verse. Here goes:

We ate lunch out of flapping paper bags.
We tried to open cheese triangles with gloves on
and the girls' hair stuck to their noses.
One boy's juice carton waltzed off with the wind
And you gave him hell about the environment.

Does that scan or whatever it's meant to do? Della says poems don't have to rhyme, just as well, I haven't the talent, don't claim to. In fact if it's a poem at all, I don't see why.

But A for effort?

Here's the photograph. Taken by that lad mad about cameras, came two years running. Forget his name, was it Lee, he got us the prints, wouldn't take the money, it was to say thank you, he said.

Now, not sure if I'm remembering the day from itself or from the photo. Or remembering a bundle of days like that. There were countless of them, those hiking days, the stiles and sheep gates and views and resting places and bogs and rocks. Different kids of course, give or take, but the same complaints: blisters, hunger, thirst, boredom, wet, cold. Same smiles, too, even if just for a photo. Same lunches in paper bags, wolfed down somewhere out of the wind if we were lucky—roll with luncheon meat or similar, choice of cheese triangle (see poem above) OR hard-boiled egg, Yo-Yo OR KitKat, an apple, and a carton of orange squash. All litter including apple cores and eggshell to be carried home.

What became of luncheon meat? It wasn't that bad if you were hungry and freezing. I have clearer recollection of the luncheon meat than of the waterfall. Has anybody ever put luncheon meat in a poem?

Bye for now

A.

In the end, only my grandmother's smile proved inexhaustible. Her hips gave up and her hands also became arthritic but she continued to smile, working her knitting on her lap a little more slowly. She took painkillers smiling over the rim of her glass; when she got too crippled to get in and out of the bath I brought basins of water and washed her in her chair, and she would smile. Afterward I would take her compact and lipstick and dab her face and lips and leave her smiling in a sugary-scented haze. She found these washing rituals exhausting; almost at once she would doze off, vacating the smile that would somehow wait on her pink frosted mouth until she returned from sleep and reentered it.

By then I was suspicious of it, that smile. It seemed to me implausibly rapturous. It could mean only that she had decided to see in her darkness certain things and not others. She talked about the view from a hill somewhere in the north one April day when she was young, and I could tell from her face that she had gone back in her mind to gaze at it again, seeing from her chair next to the sweating gas fire and the liverish wallpaper patterned with brown lozenges, skylarks' wings brushing against the clouds over a sparkling reservoir half a mile away and stiff stripes of sun and shadow rippling deep violet water. I think she returned there easily, to this place whose name escaped her, to that bright cold day more than half her lifetime ago. Her mind was not so much failing, as obscuring the importance of knowing precisely where or when a thing occurred; she spoke of her gratitude at being able to remember it at all, and smiled.

As the walls between the years and decades came down, she began to think that life had a way of turning out all right in the end; there were ways back, after all, from disaster, and the old cruelties, even her husband's, had seldom been deliberate and so perhaps had hardly been cruel. Just who had inflicted them anyway, and upon whom, exactly? The smell of alcohol, the sounds of someone falling against furniture and crying out, furious words, the swipe of a hand or a fist came out of darkness and at random whether from her husband or from anyone else. And it was either now, or it was all a long time ago, she didn't remember. Time had lessened the sting; time reduced all wrongs because misdeeds died just as people did. Records faded and got muddled and generation melded into blurry generation the way photographs piled on a windowsill imprint shadows of themselves on the image below, one upon another. So my grandmother settled into her smiling contemplations and let her fragile and partial visions illustrate a whimsical philosophy of all things being for the best. Her memories, freed from sequentiality and filtered clean of bitterness, ceased to add up to her true history and so ceased to trouble her.

To conjure these flimsy apparitions from the past was work that kept her no less busy than her knitting did; she knitted, I now think, for more than the comfort of repetition. I think she knitted so that her skipping fingers might somehow impart some of their agility to her mind, to help it go on sifting through its gallery of imperfect and far-off images. There was perhaps something of a grimace of concentration about her smile.

Because how unimaginably tiring it must have been for her, every day, to summon from the dark a faith that the world though invisible to her was benign, finally, and had been all this while busily fashioning out of the uncolored fragments of everyone's defeats and little pleasures, not just consequences, but parables. Or perhaps, spared every smear and crease on the surface of events, every blank glare on her daughter's devastated face, my grandmother found it easier than I did to believe that nobody's life was ever so blighted as to be wholly without point, that memories were never thin and useless but bloomed out of experience to some good end, to become stories that would stand for something greater than themselves.

Dear Ruth

I remember that story of yours in the Save Overdale Campaign Newsletter but that was back in the Eighties, when we were trying to stop them from closing it. I knew you had your writers group, Della & her cohorts, and there was that booklet of poetry and whatnot you got printed up that one time. All well and good.

But I never saw anything you wrote. You never showed me a word. You called it all "work in progress." You always made it sound as if you were just practicing. You most certainly did not mention a novel and here it is popping up all over the house.

The Overdale photo, I keep it on me now. I don't remember if it was taken before or after the juice-carton incident but we all look well, if not cheerful. You can't smile nicely into a force five gale, not even for some lad's Duke of Edinburgh Award Special Photography Project.

But Ruth, see, the picture. It's what's not in it. It's got 1969 on the back. It looks about late April so it must have been Easter. You can just see lambs there with the ewes in the field miles away on the right, little white blobs close to the big dark ones, and look at the state of the bracken, it's certainly not October. Which means it must have been just after. Might even have been the very morning after! Funny how you can't tell from our faces. You'd think it would show.

Remember, Ruth? 1969 Easter at Overdale, only a few weeks after the February half-term when we first met there. The night we arrived, the Thursday before Good Friday, when we sneaked out and we talked in the dark? You told me you'd been the first person at your school to put your name down to bring the Easter party to Overdale. You'd made yourself a bit unpopular in the staff room because you'd just been at half-term, but it was first come first served. And that was all because I'd happened to mention at half-term that I'd likely be back at Easter with another of my lot?

I was pleased when you told me that, Ruth, but I couldn't say so. I couldn't tell you I hadn't "happened to mention" coming back at Easter. I'd worked it into the conversation just so you'd know. Shaking with fear in case I was making it obvious. It seemed important I wasn't obvious, can't think why now. Not able to do the direct thing and just tell you I had to see you again. Dropping a hint instead of saying what I wanted and then making it happen. Calling it being shy when all it was was weakness. Weak with words.

I'd spent that Thursday traveling with the kids on the bus. The usual mayhem—three vomit stops—and my insides lurching, wondering if I'd see you. Getting ready for a big letdown in case you weren't there.

But you were. Your brown hair in a single long pigtail right down your back and some pendant made of pottery on a leather thong— you looked like a squaw. I couldn't wait to get the kids' tea and the first round of the darts and table tennis tournaments over. We postponed picking the Snakes & Ladders teams, and let them skip showers, remember? Thought we'd never get them settled. The first night's always the worst, they're high as kites, been cooped up on the bus half the day. And first night there's always one or two feeling lost and homesick, the silent weepers you have to watch out for. The dorms didn't go quiet till nearly eleven, and by then it was well after dark.

That stumped me! I'd thought of asking you to come out to see the sunset to get you away from the others, and it was already pitch dark and I didn't know what to do.

But you said, So, Arthur, you're the ornithologist, do you get nightingales hereabouts? I've always wanted to hear a nightingale.

And I nearly said, Nope, no chance this high up, or this far north, or this time of year.

Then I saw your eyes, and I said, Oh, uh ... well maybe, and it's a fine clear night. Care to venture out?

So out we went to listen for a nightingale. I saw the others, Bill What's-his-name and Mary Dixon, smirking, didn't care. All they cared *about was getting a few beers open and the ciggies out. Who else was there that year, I can't remember, can you?*

I remember I initiated you to the unofficial spare key system that night—the set Bill had made and we kept hidden outside in the porch so any of the staff could slip out after lockup? With Bill and the others it was most often down to the pub or the fish and chip shop. In our case, into the hills, to be alone.

Ruth. The way the wind dropped, and we lay in the shelter of a rock under the hill's curve. The stars—candles seen through pinpricks in a black velvet curtain according to you (you see, I remembered!) and the moon over the reservoir and not a sound except the wind higher up on the peak, a sighing sound. No nightingale, no night birds at all. My parka on the ground and the smell of the reeds and heather. Like old vines and honey you said, this must be what ancient Greece smells like. I didn't comment, to me it was just dried and rooty, plus that muddy smell off the parka.

I'll never forget that time, Ruth. We never did talk about it. You were lovely that night.

And here's another thing I never said. Thank you. What happened was heaven on earth. Never mind ancient Greece, heaven on earth. I was thirty-two years of age and it was my first time. You told me about your ex-fiancé and you asked did I mind I wasn't the first. And all I said was, no I don't mind. Did I add something like, well, this is 1969 after all?

Why didn't I say I already loved you so much you could have come to me with the smell of a hundred men in your hair and I wouldn't have cared, as long as you stayed with me?

With love

Arthur

PS Did it mean as much to you?

PPS I ask because I think you forgot about the parka, significance of—you didn't understand why I held on to it, "Oh, THAT smelly aw- ful old thing" you called it, the first time I looked for it after you'd put it in the garbage. Must have been twenty years later.

J eremy had taken to telephoning me when it was not convenient for me to speak to him. I didn't want to leave the receiver
off the hook because he might then have reported the line as
faulty or even come to the house, and either of those events
would have meant intrusion. It was easy enough after the first
few times just to ignore the ringing.

It was more important that I got adequate rest. I would arrive back
at the cul-de-sac at daybreak and go to bed at once, though I couldn't
sleep straightaway. I would lie feverish in the way I remembered being
as a child once or twice, in bed and missing school, and secretly happy

to be so still and separate. After what seemed a long time, sounds would bob in on the surface of the day outside: motors running, children's feet on gravel, doors opening and closing. My mind played out the scenes whose sounds I heard: my neighbor Gail shepherding her daughters Thomasina and Jessica from their mock-Tudor house into the station wagon, big and small hands clicking seat belts, her slavering dogs, Bertie and Maisie, jumping in the back, leashes thrown in after them. Later would come the *cruck* of letterboxes in between the revving and halting of the post van at its usual two stopping points in the cul-de-sac.

Eventually, silence would come and embed itself. No, not silence. It was more like sound loitering in the shade while the day outside swelled with light, and the morning hours, burdened with heat, struggled to pass and expired, inevitably, in the end; then it would be afternoon, when the day seemed to sigh and slacken and give in to an indolent winding down toward evening. Languorous and minimal as a cat, I barely moved from hour to hour except, in my sleep, to yawn and stretch, as if testing some notion of elasticity in my lungs and limbs. I would sleep, and wake, and sleep, dreaming that I was not in my white nest of a bed but outside, under a warm sky. At intervals I would find myself half roused as if I had been dreaming in a hammock under white trees in a white garden somewhere, or lying on a pillowy bank of white grass like rough toweling, lulled by the prinking of distant radio tunes, a barking dog. Then I would lie very still in case I really was in a garden and the neighbors might be walking by, talking about me, and might see me and cast worried smiles and call out with questions. Only half awake, I would wonder if I had just missed the ringing of a telephone, or I might think that I could hear one but that it didn't matter. It soothed me to lie still and not even try to get to it, for surely it was too far away.

Then I would let myself slip farther away, deeper into my whiteness, and the whisper of the sheets as I drew them up around my ears and over my head was the same sighing as the wind in the pink blossom branches overhanging the narrow road in April, and the beat of my pulse on the pillow under my throat the same sad faraway sound as the drip of rain on the colorless flowers under the trees and on the messages of loss and regret, washing them all away.

Later a telephone or a doorbell would ring again, but not here, nor anywhere very near. All sounds came from the faraway "out there" of a warm cul-de-sac afternoon of opened windows and summery gardens and neighbor greeting neighbor: dreamy calling voices, the tap of claws as dogs trailed along the sun-soft tarmac of the road, the tick of a pram or a child's tricycle wheeled by under the shade of the hedge. I had to burrow away from the sounds of innocuous, innocent lives. A telephone would go on ringing, in another room or maybe in another house, maybe the one against whose wall a pruning ladder had just struck with a soft, wooden *tock* that traveled across the way and flicked off the side of the house opposite, then bounced back, the sound mingling with the clip of shears slicing high up under the eaves and an exuberant fluster of clematis fronds falling in clouds of black and green against the brittle blue of a July sky. It was bitter and pleasant to lie immersed in whiteness with eyes closed against the sight of any more events beyond my window. The police were still hunting for a killer. There was so much more than glass, now, between me and what went on out there.

Eventually, of course, I had to answer the telephone. I told Jeremy I hadn't got more than a few minutes because I was already late, and he asked me what I could be late for at nine o'clock in the evening. I was startled by this question. I hadn't been awake long. As usual I had waited until it was dark so that when I got up I didn't feel I was leaving my bed behind so much as entering another embrace. I stepped out of my bedroom not to confront a darkening house merely unlit, but to encounter the night. It breathed on me as I walked downstairs, and it floated behind, lifting the hairs on my neck, swirling around my feet, hanging on my clothes. It swept ahead and spread into the spaces before me. I had lit some candles for the pleasure of the counterpoising dots of gold in the blanketing darkness, just enough light by which to watch the night filling my empty rooms. The telephone had rung as I was putting down the box of matches.

Jeremy said he wanted to know if I was all right and then began to tell me why he knew I wasn't. As I listened, I nipped out the flame of a candle and dabbed the escaping drop of wax between my thumb and forefinger until it was a cool, curved disk with brittle edges, like a fingernail detached from a corpse. I nibbled it while I waited. It tasted of oil and smoke.

"Are you there? Hello? This is the whole problem. This is pure emotional blackmail."

I didn't speak.

"All right. But since you have at least answered the telephone, perhaps you would tell me how you are?"

"I am here. I'm the same."

"Are you? . . . I mean, have you . . . how are . . . have things . . ." He couldn't flatten down the brisk interrogative breeze fluttering through his voice, lifting the edges of words and sniffing underneath. *What things?* "Are you coping with the heat, for instance? It's terribly hot."

"I told you, I'm the same." As I said that an ache was rising in my chest and my heart began a kind of bumpy climb up my ribs. I tried to concentrate on how safe I was, to remember that I was alone in a dark room and that although his voice was present, he wasn't.

"I know you're shutting yourself away in the house," he insisted. "Gail says she and Hector haven't seen you for weeks, she thought you were away. She's been trying to rouse you."

I nipped out the flame of another candle. Smoke from the sooty wick trickled up my nose and I coughed. "I'm all right."

"Look, I'm concerned. I think you may be at risk of going into a depression. I know just the person you should see; I think I should fix you up with an appointment."

I swallowed the fragments of wax nail. "There's no need for that."

"But you are reacting very extremely to this. I'd like you to see him."

"I don't want to see anyone."

"I think you should. I'm worried. In fact, I think I'll come round this weekend."

"Don't. You can't. The thing is—I'm going away."

"Going away? Where? What for?"

"I haven't decided. But definitely somewhere. Possibly for the rest of the summer. Maybe longer."

"Well, maybe a holiday's not such a bad idea. Actually it's a good idea. France, I suppose? Make sure I have the details before you go, all right?"

"All right."

"Good. Well done. A long break, how I envy you. By the way, the weather! Have you been remembering about the basil?"

"The basil?"

"Don't tell me you haven't watered the pots? They'll be bone dry! The parsley's probably had it already!"

"You're worried about the *herbs*?"

"Well, I don't see why everything has to go to the dogs. I did a lot of work on those pots. You said you wanted to make pesto."

I hung up. I couldn't draw the breath for a reply in case it encouraged any more; before I could stop him we would be on to greenfly and the lawn sprinkler. But in the end, Jeremy proved helpful. A conversation with him that I hadn't wanted to have at all had shown me my way forward. I had not realized before I said it that I even wanted to go away, let alone that I intended to. But of course I did. It was the natural and only possible next step.

Dear Ruth

Developments. As I'd got it off the wall and had no further use for it, I was aiming to put Della's memorial effort out for the garbagemen. That should have been that. Only did I stumble or did I drop it (or was it shoddy goods to start with) but the glass in the frame broke. I managed to nick my hand and I've written a note to remind myself to avoid the hall in bare feet from now on. You never get every last shard up. Less floor room in hall now, anyway, as I've got a lot of stuff stored there, got it down from the attic where it's no use to anyone, and I'm not undoing all my good work just because of a little broken glass.

*But mindful that it was broken glass, I didn't stick the memorial in the actual garbage can. I can just imagine the hoo-hah if one of the bloody garbagemen got so much as a scratch. They don't seem to wear gloves anymore. So I just placed it carefully against the wall next to can. Next day, can's been emptied, a minor miracle—*AND *left on its side halfway up the drive. That's happened before, they just* FLING *it down and seem to expect thanks for it. Anyway, damn tribute's still there against the wall, not even touched. That's willful dereliction. No doubt they'll find some red tape or small print to justify yet more atrocious service, as per.*

Damned if I'm giving in was my first thought, you'll be pleased to hear. A sure sign I'm getting back to normal. Standing up for myself vis-à-vis obstinacy of garbage men instead of going down in welter of self-pity. They are NOT *getting away with it and I'll damn well leave it there till they* DO *pick it up, we'll see who prevails. I'm the taxpayer, as I'll remind them. I'm staying at home these days, as it suits me to, but I certainly intend to be on the lookout and I'll make my feelings known next time they deign to call.*

So I left the bloody thing—and left also garbage can on its side because there's a principle involved. Next thing is Mrs. M's at the door with a bunch of freesias. She starts spouting some notion that you were fond of them. I couldn't shed any light on that possibility, I said.

Then she asks, did she get me out of the bath and have I mislaid dressing gown—did I grab raincoat as first thing to come to hand? Mind your own business, I said.

Then she waved freesias and said she thought she should ask first, was it all right with me. Floral expressions of sympathy are all very well, she goes on, but she's sensitive to the fact that somebody's got to clear up in the end and she'll never forget those sordid scenes at Kensington Palace post-Diana. They had to bring in those diggers you use after avalanches.

And they're piling up already, she said, waving down the drive. Give it a week and it'll be a nasty heap of compost obstructing the thoroughfare and encroaching onto the sidewalk (her very words). Not at all welcome, not very Cardigan Avenue. She says, if somebody slipped you could be liable. Maybe she should ask The Great Tony to tidy it up. I stood and let her go on. Maybe she thought she was making sense or she was expecting me to say something back. I was completely at sea.

Though clearly, she said, sniffing the freesias, others haven't had the courtesy to check first. I was still baffled and said so. Then she said, you know, your poem out on the drive, the poem you left out for people to read. She's got an excited look about her now.

So out we go (she insisted I get my slippers on first) and there at the end of the drive in front of Della's tribute there are at least a dozen bunches of flowers including a handful of dead daisies tied with a bit of tinsel, "From Amy Watson (aged 5) at No. 48." Just lying there where the wall of the drive curves out. Still baffled. Mrs. M says people like to leave a marker. She says people are just showing support in the best way they know. Showing support.

Ruth, you're the one with the words—what does that mean? SHOW-ING SUPPORT? *I'm not talking about the word itself, that's plain enough,*

I mean, what does it MEAN? SUPPORT? A prop for a leaning wall? What's the use of that if bricks have been pulled out from the bottom? It's collapsing anyhow. Support will only put off the inevitable, it'll end up a pile of rubble eventually.

So Mrs. M puts her flowers down with the rest and blows her nose, peers at my face and says now she sees me in daylight she wonders if I need a dermatologist. Then she launches into the usual—importance of eating properly etc and it's no bother at all if she's cooking for herself anyway, and later on she'll just pop over with something.

See what's going on? Freesia business was a ruse to get me out of the house and agreeing to all kinds of things, more hot dinners etc.

I am beginning to understand her motives. Probably been waiting to pounce for years and now with you gone she's making her move. Think of the kerfuffle that would create. There's no way to deal with that sort of thing except walk away, it's the only language her kind understand. Which is exactly what I did.

Wish you were here.

Won't you come again?

That's all.

Arthur.

THE COLD AND THE BEAUTY AND THE DARK
1940–1941

Chapter 10: The Ravages of War

Little Grace Ashworth had her mother's dimples and her father's dark hair, and at the age of eight was by all accounts a strikingly pretty girl. Evelyn brushed and plaited her soft hair every morning, marveling at its silkiness, and she stroked her daughter's smooth face and gave a gentle prod where the dimples would appear on each cheek. "Let's be putting those dimples on show today, eh?" she would say. "Be a happy good lass for your Mam."

But she herself would never see those dimples. And Grace had already acquired something of her father's brooding and taciturn nature, so that for days on end very few other people did, either. Sometimes Evelyn worried that in her daughter's silences there was a reproach meant for her, as if it were Evelyn's own fault that she was blind. A mood would settle on the little girl for days at a time and Evelyn would fret to herself that she would never be forgiven for the fact that Grace had been born to a mother who was unable to see her.

If only Stan had taken more trouble and time with his daughter, but he only noticed Grace on the very few occasions on which she was naughty. He had as little to do with her, or with Evelyn, as possible. She never had found out any more about the girl in blue and yellow. When it occurred to her, weeks after the day on Kinder Scout, that she would be quite within her rights as a wife to insist on knowing, it had no longer seemed important. Then Grace had been born and it seemed less important still.

Now, whenever he wasn't at work he would be out somewhere. He had long since stopped saying where he was going and Evelyn had long ago stopped asking. After all these years, whether Stan was at a meeting or drinking with Alan O'Reilly, or carrying on with some girl or another, it made little difference to her. All she knew was that with the passing of time her own heart seemed to grow smaller.

In the house, he and his mother continued in their old ways, ignoring his wife and daughter as much as they could. It seemed to Evelyn that she only really existed when her mother-in-law was laying down the law to her about some detail of their arrangements. Would Evelyn kindly oblige her by not taking up more than half of a rail of the drying pulley in the scullery. Would Evelyn point out to Grace that shoes must not be left on the stairs. Life under old Mrs. Ashworth's roof was uneasy to say the least.

When war came again in 1939 Stan was among the first to join up, to everyone's surprise except Evelyn's. For years now he had been using his meetings mainly as an excuse to spend hours out of the house, and Evelyn had guessed at once that no lingering left-wing political ideals would withstand the temptation presented by the chance to join the army and get away for months or maybe years, even if it meant going into danger.

For her, life went on much as usual. It was certainly no better with him gone. If anything Mrs. Ashworth went even further out of her way to be difficult. She was no help with Grace, even though Grace was an unnaturally quiet and un-demanding child. She was "living on a knife edge" with her only son away, fighting for his country, and she couldn't do with a child stampeding around, added to which, she claimed, she was an old lady now and too nervy to leave the house.

When everyone was issued gas masks in March 1940, the war had come suddenly much closer to home. And when, only a few weeks later, Grace was evacuated to the Cheshire countryside, Evelyn thought her heart would break. She now had an intimate knowledge of every quirk and pit-fall of the house in Bank Street and could look after herself well enough, and she tried to draw comfort from knowing that Grace was out of danger and away from her irritable grandmother, and in the country, where surely fresh air and homegrown vegetables would be in greater supply than in smoky old Aldbury. Her own wants were few, and Stan's army pay was regular.

The local shopkeepers knew her and her white stick, and were all friendly, and neighbors went out of their way to pass the time of day with her, perhaps sensing that she would be lonely with her little girl gone. Everybody respected her for her cheerfulness and her way of dressing her shy, polite daughter so beautifully, in expertly hand-knitted garments, every stitch made by herself. Just as important, they knew old Mrs. Ashworth and the kind of woman she was. Most of them had felt the rough side of her tongue at one time or an-other.

So the butcher took special care that bacon for young

Mrs. Ashworth was sliced from the lean end of the slab, and that she wasn't left out if, for example, some nice rabbits came his way, delivered after dark to the back of the shop. The grocer next door might whisper that he'd had a special delivery, nothing official, mind, but maybe she could find room for an extra egg in the bottom of her shopping bag and mum's the word?

It was months later, toward the end of a day's shopping in preparation for a bleak Christmas, on December 23, that the raid came. London and the other big cities in the south of England had been taking the brunt of the Luftwaffe's attention for months, yet the first raid on Manchester still came as a shock. For one thing, though the raid went on for a number of days and nights, nobody had expected it to begin in broad daylight. A still bigger shock, and a puzzle, was the apparently random dropping of bombs on Aldbury, several miles away. Theories abounded: simple incompetent targeting by a plane aiming for the Ship Canal or the docks, or a navigational error, or a pilot getting rid of bombs too heavy for the hazardous daylight flight back to a base in Norway. But whatever the reason, the line of bombs blasted away several buildings over four Aldbury streets and left a burning scar a mile long. People said it was a miracle more damage wasn't done and more people weren't killed, it being so near to Christmas and folk out and about. But 43 Bank Street was among the eight houses destroyed, and old Mrs. Ashworth was among the five people who died.

Daphne's brother Paul, like Stan, had enlisted, so with the help of Colin and Jem, the two other Baker brothers, Evelyn salvaged a few possessions and moved in gratefully with

Daphne and her family. Mrs. Baker, on Evelyn's behalf, contacted Stan's regiment. She was told that Private Stanley Ashworth was serving somewhere in North Africa and was instructed that if she wrote with the details of Mrs. Ashworth's death, her letter would be forwarded to Stan's commanding officer and the sad news conveyed to Stan. They were not to expect a quick reply. Compassionate leave could be not granted in the circumstances and the old lady's funeral should not be delayed.

The first communication from North Africa came early in the New Year. It was not what Evelyn had been expecting. It was not from Stan. His unit had been engaged in heavy combat against the Italians in Egypt and Stan had been declared missing, presumed killed, after a desert battle lasting several days that had begun on December 14.

So Mrs. Ashworth had been spared the knowledge that Stan had been killed. That was Evelyn's chief thought when she heard the news. The same numbness that she had felt on hearing of her own father's death when she was twelve came over her again. She tried to shed tears for Stan but none came. Perhaps that was just as well, she thought; it wouldn't do Grace any good to see her mother break down when she traveled out to Cheshire to tell her she had lost her father.

It was in times of adversity, Daphne's mother said, that you found out who your true friends were. Sometimes contrary to appearances, she added darkly. For although he had been a most infrequent visitor to his sister and nephew in Bank Street, it was Stan's uncle, who now owned five shops, who stepped in and insisted that Evelyn would not make the journey by bus and train by herself to visit Grace and break the news. He would drive her there and back, he said, waving aside Evelyn's concern about the gasoline ration.

Grace seemed to take the news very calmly, but on that frosty day, walking across the village green while Stan's uncle waited in the car, Evelyn would never again in her life wish more fervently that she could see her little girl's face. If only Grace would speak her thoughts and feelings, but she said very little, and although she did not snatch away her hand when Evelyn squeezed it tightly in hers, she consented rather stiffly to her mother's hug and seemed impatient when Evelyn stroked her hair. She began to fidget when Evelyn drew her close and cradled her head in her arms. Neither of them cried.

Evelyn was glad for Stan's uncle's cheerful presence, and overawed by his generosity. He treated them to a luncheon in the somber dining room of the Victoria Arms in Warrington. It was a meal of Brown Windsor soup, mock lamb cutlets, and vegetables, followed by tapioca pudding. He ordered for himself and Evelyn large glasses of port to keep out the cold, and insisted throughout the meal that Grace take nips from his glass as well, until he saw the roses in her cheeks again. Grace was quiet and ate solidly, while Evelyn answered for her the many kind questions that Stan's uncle asked her. When they took her back to the elderly couple with whom she was staying, Stan's uncle pressed half a crown into Grace's hand and told her she was a bonny girl and he'd tip her again next time if he heard that she'd been good and brave while he was away.

On the journey back, Evelyn grew thoughtful. In a matter

of a few weeks her life had changed completely. She was now solely responsible for her strange, aloof little daughter, and however difficult life had been with her mother-in-law and husband in Bank Street, she no longer had either of them. Her own mother was very frail now and had moved in with Aunt Violet and Uncle Bill after Auntie Peg's death in 1937. There simply was not enough room in their already cramped house for her and Grace. It was only through the charity of friends that she even had a roof over her head, but she couldn't stay with the Bakers forever.

But she couldn't get a place of her own, with no way of paying the rent. There was no factory work she could do, and her widow's pension would cover only the essentials of life. She made a bit knitting this and that for people and getting paid a little for it, but it wasn't anything like a living. What would become of Grace? Who would believe any blind woman capable of bringing up a child, let alone a blind woman living alone in poverty? Evelyn had not until now faced the stark truth. The child of a poor, blind, widowed mother would be taken away and put in a children's home. It was then that she began to cry.

Stan's uncle revved the engine and cast an anxious look at his passenger.

" 'Course you're upset, love," he said, patting her knee. "You just let it all out. People may have their faults but when all's said and done it's a terrible business, war."

Evelyn blew her nose and nodded.

"Now, young lady, I've been thinking," Stan's uncle went on. "As you know, I am Leslie Hibbert, Purveyor of Confectionery & Tobacco, sole owner and proprietor of five premises of that name across the northwest from Blackpool to Bakewell. I am a man as has always stood on his own two feet. I am a man as likes to see other folk standing on *their* own two feet."

"I know. And that's only right and proper, Mr. Hibbert," Evelyn said a little uncertainly.

Stan's uncle cleared his throat. "Call me Uncle Les. Now, here's the gist. I am, furthermore, a man as is placed to give a helping hand to those as tries to stand on their own two feet. I like to see folk try to make a go of it. And you've tried to make a right good go of it, what with your handicap. Stanley was never easy. You're a right clever lass, handicapped or not, and there's nobody can tell me otherwise."

"Well, you can only do your best, can't you?" Evelyn said, puzzled.

"Aye. Now, it so happens I'm getting rid of a bad 'un. Beggar that's running the Irlam shop, he's had his fingers in't till. He'll be out on his ear come Friday. There's rooms on the two floors over't shop and I'll not take any rent off you. I'll get you in some help behind the counter but you're manageress. You'll do the books and the orders and answer to me for the profits. Daresay little Grace will be a help to you, she'll know her figures by this time and the stock's not heavy to lift. You'll find me a reasonable man."

"Mr. Hibb—, Uncle Les, I don't know what to say. Me and Grace, you mean we'd live over the shop? For nowt?"

"Aye, but I'm expecting you to keep an—" Uncle Les's voice stumbled on the word "eye." "I'm expecting you to keep it all running smoothly. Make sure we're open prompt, keep the stock turning over, keep the hired girl in line. You'll get the hang of the ordering and doing the books, you're a clever lass. That hasn't escaped my notice."

Evelyn tried to stammer out some words of gratitude but Uncle Les interrupted her.

He cleared his throat. "Nay, don't thank me. All I ask is I'll trouble you for your company now and then, you and little Gracie. I'm a lonely man since Mrs. Hibbert passed on and family's family, when all's said and done. I like to see a kiddie about the place and I've none of my own. Mrs. Hibbert wasn't able. And a home's not a home without a kiddie."

The night following was thick and humid, the sky as heavy as wax. The matches had gone soft and when I finally got one to light, the shed glowed a thundery yellow and smelled wormy and sulfur warm. Though the weather was not ideal for it, I had a particular plan. I had not attempted it until then because of the noise it would make, but that was no longer a consideration. We had an understanding. He was ready to let me do more for him; I could tell that even before I had read his letters to me.

Once he was in the attic I made my way upstairs. I went straight to the spare room where I knew he had been leaving his dirty clothes.

The place was strewn with them, banked up on the bed and across the floor in a jumble of turquoise, lime, orange, purple, plain, checked, patterned. I had seen him ransack the heaps time after time, although less often since he had taken to wearing the raincoat. There was not a clean stitch left. Everything had been worn until it stank, then dropped on the floor and most probably worn again.

Back in the kitchen, I didn't need any light. The feel of the materials told me that most of his things were synthetic. I shoved the first load in and started the machine. Pretty they were, the lights on the dials in the dark, and the machine shook and winked and juddered in a way that was businesslike, and somehow energizing. I ran upstairs and brought down more clothes and waited for the first load to finish. I hauled it out and started the second. If I worked fast then I could get all of it done and out on the line and it might even be dry before I had to leave. Even though there was not a breath of wind, I might get everything in, folded and ready. He would come down to a house smelling of clean clothes.

There is something robust and proper about a good wash day. Whether on a Monday morning, as happened in my grandmother's time, or on a warm summer's night, laundry needs to be tackled, not picked at. It isn't a job to be slipped through at odd moments so nobody notices it's happened at all except when, one by one, garments reemerge clean from somewhere; a full, wet clothesline deserves notice as the small statement of competence it is. I believe that the washing of clothes ought to raise the temperature, make the walls run, fill the air as it did that night. So if I had a criticism of Ruth it was this: her arrangements suggested that she laundered on the quiet. I don't think she even dried things in the proper way, hung outside on a line, because there was only a short length of rope on a hook, coiled against the house wall, that stretched a few feet across the terrace. I guessed her habit was to put things on hangers and leave them dripping in the conservatory or over the bath. I searched the shed and found a decent length of line. I fixed it to the neck of the downpipe at one corner of the conservatory and took it down across the grass and tied it off round the top of the pergola at the far side of the garden.

It was still dark by the time the first three washes were hung. I walked along the line for a while, smoothing and squeezing garments as I went: his pegged-up slacks and shirts and sweaters, the under-pants and socks, a row of shapes so soft and indistinct as to have al-most no dimension at all, pasted on the night air like the afterimages of a departed procession of dismembered torsos and limbs. But there was nothing sinister about it. They looked too much like bits of giant pup-pet to be anything but faintly comical; there was also something amus-ing, touching even, about masculine clothes separated from their wearer.

I brought in the first load, chilly to the touch, and ran a warm iron over everything to drive off the damp. The kitchen filled with the wa-tery, cold sweetness of grass and the almost melting tang of hot poly-ester; it was absurdly thrilling. I went back upstairs and picked up towels and bed linen and put those in the wash, too. Back and forth I went from the machine to the garden, ironing things as they came in. There wasn't a lot of space left in the kitchen with the ironing board up and mounds of clothing, but during a lull around two o'clock I dragged in one of the conservatory chairs. I made myself tea and sat watching the machine as it shuddered and droned from its corner in the dark.

I woke up to a stillness inside the house. The machine had stopped. The only sounds were a lashing wind and the rattle of rain coming down against the windows and roof. Outside, the whole line of washing was swaying and the empty laundry basket I'd left out was rolling around on the terrace. I dashed into the conservatory.

The storm had come on so fast. His clothes and towels were al-ready soaked and being whipped around by the weather, and they were getting muddy too; rain was spiking into the grass and sparking straight back up. All I could see was a squally swirl of shapes and dripping shadows, like dark and darker paint running down the glass.

I ran outside to the far end of the line and started working my way along, unpegging. Cold sprays of rain bit my face. I slung some of the clothes over my shoulder and dragged other things down into the crook of my arm, but it was like hauling waterlogged creatures in from the sea; I started to go numb under the weight of them and their icy cling. I couldn't make out anything much; as well as the rain and my running eyes, the drenched washing still on the line cracked around me like flags.

He didn't make a sound, so I don't know what made me turn when I did, but there he was, not six feet away, sidling toward me on the other side of the line, his face set grim against the rain, hair flattened and dark over his skull, and his raised arms draped in laundry. Maybe he didn't call out because his lips were clamped tight on a row of clothes pegs. They arced out of his mouth like the struts of a stubby, naked fan. I hadn't thought about the pegs, I'd just yanked them out and let them fall on the ground. I made a movement toward him and then he started, let the pegs fall from his mouth, flipped the wet bundle from his arms onto the grass, and hurried, limping, back to the house.

Dear Ruth

> *Wish you'd write.*
> *But thank you, dear. Clean togs welcome.*
> *Can't get far on the legs, down to bottom of drive two or three times a day to read Della's poem is about it.*
> *I sat on the stairs for a long time today.*
> *Have had to submit to soup from across the road. Mrs. M's son The Great Tony the paramedic came over with it—bossy bugger, like mother like son. He also had a shopping list. He said Mrs. M had jotted down some basics and would I run my eye over it and add anything else I could think of. He got my debit card number off me and said he'd get the whole thing fixed up online and I wouldn't even have to sign for it—Mrs. M would take delivery and drop it all over regular as clock-work, I wouldn't need to stir.* BUT *it would do me good to get out and he'd take me shopping anytime I cared to go.*
> *I scratched my head over that—can't recall what I agreed to, list is still here somewhere. Maybe it's all written down. Could you deal with it?*
> *Later on was rootling around in some of your heaps and found something on mimosa!* WAS *it necessary however to hang on to so much paper? Here's the bit:*

All I Want (Mimosas)
Maria G. Bracci-Cambini
to Joan
May 20, 1983
From "your Tosca"

A farmhouse
that's all I want
out of Life.

A farmhouse,
and Sun,
and
Mimosas
    In a willow-y tree.

Where, when shadows fall
and seasons pass,
an echo of long ago
will speak to me
    And the mimosa sighing
    On the willow-y tree.

Who was Maria Bracci-Cambini? And who was Joan? I knew you were fond of mimosa and we both liked a bit of sun now and then, but did you want a farmhouse too, Ruth? You never mentioned it.

All these words everywhere. I keep coming across things you never talked about.

I never knew there was such a word as willow-y—willowy, yes. It looks nice, though—willow-y.

There's a book out now about punctuation. I expect you'd have bought it.

Arthur

———

THE COLD AND THE BEAUTY AND THE DARK
1947

Chapter 11: For the Love of Grace

"Grace, come and sit next to your uncle," Evelyn said. "We'll tackle t'washing up in a bit."

Grace was still sitting on her chair at the dining table in the window, scowling. Uncle Les, enjoying his second cigarette after Sunday dinner, downed his glass of port and inspected his fingernails, buffing them absentmindedly against his lapel.

"Aye, come on over here, lass," he said for the third or fourth time, patting the space next to him. "You know your old uncle doesn't like you to sulk. Here, I've a bag o' chocolate éclairs somewhere."

Grace sighed heavily but then obeyed, slipping off her chair silently. Evelyn frowned and carried on knitting. She knew Grace moved quietly on purpose, so that Evelyn wouldn't know where she was. It was two or three years since she had allowed her mother to hug her. Grace had always been a private, reticent child, but why had she, at fifteen, grown so distant and secretive?

The settee creaked a little as Grace sat down. Uncle Les cleared his throat. The clock ticked on the mantelpiece and Evelyn's needles clicked. Evelyn heard the whisper of clothing, then a soft squirming sound, followed by a sigh.

Grace must be settling herself and relaxing. Maybe her mood would improve. She smiled.

"Anybody fancy having the wireless on?" she asked.

Uncle Les coughed and the settee creaked again. "Nay, never mind for Grace and me," he said. "Gracie's got her homework to do, hasn't she?"

"I needn't do it now," Grace said in a low voice. "Later will do."

Uncle Les tutted. "Now, now, lass," he said, "if it's there to be done, it's best tackled, eh? While I'm here to help."

Evelyn frowned. Grace *was* ungrateful. It was kind of Uncle Les to take such an interest in her education. He had bought her a desk and chair for her little bedroom, and every Sunday he would spend at least an hour with her there, going over her homework. He admitted that history and science were not his forte, but anything to do with figures and he was a dab hand.

"I don't want to," Grace said petulantly. "I don't feel well. My stomach hurts. Here."

"Eh?" Uncle Les said sharply. "What's up?"

"You've had a bit too much dinner, I expect," Evelyn said brightly. "Best ignore it, it'll pass."

"Mother, I've hardly ate anything," Grace said, her voice tightening. "I feel sick an' all." She suddenly burst into tears.

"Why, Grace, whatever is the matter, love?" Evelyn cried.

"There's something bad in my stomach!"

Uncle Les stood up. "Come on, Gracie," he said with authority. "Give over, now, you're upsetting your mother. That's enough excuses. Homework's got to be done. No, Evelyn, you leave this to me. Gracie, upstairs with you. Now."

Later, Uncle Les came down alone. He stood in front of the fire as he spoke, a sure sign that he meant to be taken seriously.

"Evelyn, love, I've had words with little Gracie. She is a bit under the weather."

"Under the weather? She's only a young lass! Maybe she could do with an iron tonic."

"An iron tonic won't do owt," Uncle Les said. "Iron tonic's not what's called for."

"I'll have to get t'doctor to her, then."

"Nay, there's no call for that! There's nowt wrong with her a rest won't put right. Now, I know a nice little place just out of Blackpool. Quiet, family run. Folk go there for all sorts, you get a proper pick-me-up—a sea cure plus all your home comforts. Mrs. Hibbert used to swear by it. A week there'll do Grace a power o'good. And it's on me, it'll not set you back a penny."

Evelyn bit her lip. "But if she's poorly she needs the doctor. And a whole week off school?"

"Well, she's leaving anyroad come Whitsun, i'n't she? A week won't make a scrap of difference. Fresh air, all mod cons. Do her good."

Evelyn considered. "Well, it does sound nice. These young girls, they do go at everthing so, these days. They outgrow their strength. Maybe she could do with a rest."

"Aye, that's the way to look at it. 'Course, goes wi'out saying I'd like for you to go with her, like, the both of you, treat yourselves." Evelyn gasped with astonishment. "But another time, eh? With t'shop to mind," Uncle Les went on, "it can't be done."

"Oh, well, no!" Evelyn exclaimed. "It's right kind of you to treat our Grace. I'm ever so grateful, Uncle Les."

Les took his leave soon afterward instead of staying on for tea. Evelyn was touched at how concerned he was about Grace and told herself again what a blessing he was. He contiued to provide them with a home even when their shop earnings were, as he told them, the poorest of all his five concerns. It worried Evelyn that Grace seemed to resent his generosity. In fact, she couldn't get a civil word out of the girl on the subject of Uncle Les. Her shyness of him had deepened into a kind of sullen dislike, if not actual fear. Evelyn would have to talk to her about it, when she was back from Blackpool and feeling better. Grace was becoming a young woman, far too old for such bad manners.

Evelyn knitted on alone by the fire, worrying about Grace and wishing she were the kind of mother to whom a young girl would bring her troubles, as she always had to her own dearly remembered Mam.

The following Saturday evening when Uncle Les called for the earnings, Grace was no less sullen but she was ready with her case packed. Evelyn hadn't known what to put in, not that Grace owned anything in the way of clothes for a seaside holiday, anyway. Les bundled her into the car and reassured Evelyn that she needn't worry, Grace wouldn't want for anything. This place in Blackpool laid on everything and at the end of the week she'd be right as rain again.

Dear Ruth

Well—couldn't help letting Mrs. M and the nurse in on it, when they made reference to clean clothes—blank stares all round, they just can't grasp it. Legs no bundle of laughs, by the way.

Anyway, on the face of it of course it is quite unbelievable. But I've got the evidence of my own eyes. Not to mention the clothes. Never thought it possible, I always was the skeptic where any kind of hocus-pocus was concerned.

You were the one for all that—airy-fairy, I called you, remember? Then you'd say, We don't know what lies beyond, can't you just keep an open mind, Arthur?

I don't remember you ever saying you would definitely come back if it so happened you went before me, but I don't remember you didn't, either. We didn't dwell on that sort of thing, did we? I suppose I thought there would be time for that kind of talk when we got older.

Anyway there's something in it, obviously, all this "other side" stuff. I don't pretend to know what. Don't need to, seeing's believing and it improves things no end.

Thank you.

Not that I wouldn't appreciate you leaving me a line or two, just to confirm the above.

By the way—that story of yours, it's taken an odd turn, hasn't it? The young girl and that old uncle (filthy animal), that's a bit off-color surely, or am I reading too much into it?

That's not a criticism, I just didn't think your mind worked that way. Also, no mention of Overdale since Chapter 8, and that does seem a pity. I've found the whole albums of Overdale, why did they go up to the attic in the first place?

Is that all there's to be of Overdale in the whole story? I always thought Overdale would make a very interesting setting. Still, up to you. What's going to happen next is what I want to know.

Read on, you'd be saying... in fact I can just hear you. I can hear you.

Arthur

The next night was quite different, cloudy but dry and calm. When I took out the muddy clothes and sheets I'd had to wash again and put them on the line, I heard some night bird croaking not far away, a round throaty call that opened out as if it were sounding across a long, empty lake, though there was no such expanse of water anywhere nearby. That's how still it was.

The other difference was that I entered the house knowing that I was expected. I didn't watch from the shed or garden and wait until he was occupied upstairs. That seemed an unnecessary formality now.

Besides, I had a lot to do. There was enough washing and ironing to keep me occupied and of course I was behind with the general cleaning after my blitz on the laundry. Whenever I could, I paused at the foot of the stairs from time to time and caught sometimes a moving shadow from above. I longed to be shown more. Should I be afraid for him? All that talk in the letters about his legs, and the night before there had been something abject in the set of his shoulders as he walked in pain away from me. I was desperate to know he was all right.

But the darkness that surrounded us would, in time, open other channels by which I would learn all I needed to know. In darkness I was tuned to him in ways impossible in the light. As I went about my work, I detected echoes in the rest of the house; he, too, was allowing himself the wish to find out more, to see me again, even to pine a little. As the hours passed, this desire to understand each other formed itself into a certain shy and rhythmic etiquette. The creaking above me meant that Arthur was walking the floors with consideration for what I could hear. I hummed under my breath when he was within earshot and he sighed when he sensed I was listening. When I was tired from bending to unload the washing machine and paused to stretch for a moment, I could tell he was turning from a window and inclining his head toward me in a soft gesture of thanks.

I felt no need to hurry through my tasks, so when I came across the letters I stopped and reread them carefully before tidying them into some order, which I knew would anyway be short-lived. They would be scattered everywhere again in no time, not that I minded. Parts of them seemed written by a different Arthur from mine, not my dreamy, considerate, placid Arthur. It was obvious that daylight made him crazy, too, and at the core of our night companionship was a silent agreement that all we were doing was taking sensible steps to avoid it.

Neither of us felt quite the same need for silence anymore. He was shutting and opening cupboards. If I closed a door, he closed one, too. When I started work in the hall I knew he would be loitering around the top of the stairs and picking up the forward-backward drone of the vacuum cleaner. Maybe he was able to imagine its little winking darts of green and red light sweeping across my feet, and the stiff to-and-fro reflection of my moving body, snipped into hundreds of diamonds breaking and merging in the pattern of the front door glass. Sometimes as I went about I sang, and I knew he would be catching the melody and trying to memorize it, so that one night soon he could whistle it back.

In this manner we passed through and around the house all night. He never came very close nor did I go upstairs to him, yet each of us knew the maneuvers of the other. We had become partners in a dance that kept us wordlessly apart and yearning, yet we could not keep from its magnetically sad and restive oscillations. All those imagined movements of the other, turning and returning through every mesmeric step and measure though never joining, were part of us now.

Dear Ruth

A new complexion on things altogether!

Woke up today and actually felt myself smile. Could tell by how it felt that I hadn't done that in a long while, so went to bathroom mirror just to check I really was smiling. A test, if you like, to see if I was really here. Face quite a surprise! Who's that old thin hairy man? Then I heard you say, It's you, Arthur. Heard your voice clear as anything. In a manner of speaking, I mean.

You said, It's you, dear. Don't worry.

Don't worry! It's a bit late for that, I thought. Though I must have said it, because the lips in the face on the mirror were moving.

I hadn't appreciated how long I'd let slide between shaves. But I got your message, looking in the mirror there.

A beard quite suits you, that's what you were saying, wasn't it? Never saw you with a beard in all these years and it's quite a novelty, but no need to get rid of it on my account, I don't mind it at all, dear. You had longish hair when I met you. And the sideburns! You wore them as long as the Education Authority would allow its staff to have them in those days.

I admit that just then I laughed at the mirror and wondered if I was going crazy—because wouldn't a madman hearing voices look exactly like me? But I was wise to that in a flash—that was just me, trying to trip myself up. That old face in the mirror was having a bit of a joke with me, I could see it in HIS eyes. I could see myself clearly. My Self. Besides which, I'm sure I heard your voice. And why would you say you didn't mind the beard unless that was what you meant?

I know you meant it!! I'm just double-checking.

I plan to go more carefully from now on. About how much I say about all of this. Not everybody could deal with it, could they? I do see that. To a certain kind of person it seems rather nutty—for instance the Mrs. M's of this world. She's not a sensible woman under that surface.

She goes jumping to all the wrong conclusions—she specializes in wrong conclusions, two and two always making five.

So I'll try harder to keep a wide berth. She seems to have got the message I'm catching up on my sleep in the daytime. None of her business if I choose to get on with things at night, I told her to her face. It's still a free country. I've stood at the window often enough and watched her watching the house, though. One of these days I'll stick my tongue out. Or worse.

Things are changing for the better. I'm feeling much more like my old self, thanks to you, dear.

Or maybe that should be new self.

Arthur

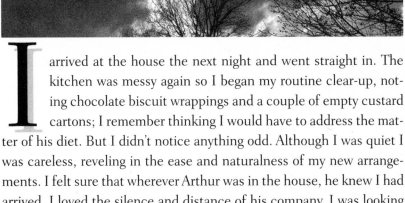

I arrived at the house the next night and went straight in. The kitchen was messy again so I began my routine clear-up, noting chocolate biscuit wrappings and a couple of empty custard cartons; I remember thinking I would have to address the matter of his diet. But I didn't notice anything odd. Although I was quiet I was careless, reveling in the ease and naturalness of my new arrangements. I felt sure that wherever Arthur was in the house, he knew I had arrived. I loved the silence and distance of his company. I was looking forward to my next task; I planned to go upstairs and tackle the rooms there, knowing I might hear a murmur in the dark, catch a glimpse of his back through a doorway or feel the warmth of his breath at a spot where he had lingered for a moment. So the first thing I did was put on the kettle to make him some tea and then I began to go through the clean linen, sorting it into piles for the airing cupboard that I expected would be on the landing or in the upstairs bathroom. What was it that penetrated my optimistic mood? I didn't hear a sound. But suddenly the hairs on the back of my neck rose, and I knew something was wrong.

I found him on the hall floor surrounded by the papers he must have dropped when he tripped on the stairs. He had dragged himself to the wall and lay propped against it, his head back and eyes closed. I must have cried out. I heard him groan in reply, so at least then I knew he was alive. There were no obvious signs of injury, but how could I tell how badly he was hurt? I couldn't tell if he had fallen from the top of the stairs or slipped on the last tread. Worst of all, how long had he been lying there? Should I give him water? Ask him to move his limbs, wiggle his toes and fingers? It was fourteen hours since I had left the house. Even in my consternation for him I was swamped with shame at my own negligence.

I crouched down and took his hand, and whispered, "Arthur, I'm here now. I'm so sorry. Don't worry, Arthur. You're going to be all right." My voice was remarkably calm. "Don't worry, dear," I said, stroking his head. "Stay calm. I'm going to get help."

He didn't open his eyes but he groaned again and raised a hand to my arm and patted it gently as if, whatever the effort, it were important to him that I should be reassured.

I got to my feet and dialed from the telephone in the hall. My voice began to shake, but after I had asked for an ambulance and given his name and address, I managed to give all the other information I was asked: was he conscious, was he having difficulty breathing, had he vomited, could he move unaided. Was anyone else there?

"No. There's just the two of us."

"Right. Can I take your name, please?"

"*My* name?"

"Yes, please. I need your name to log the call and activate an ambulance request. Can you give me your name?"

"*My* name . . . it's . . ."

"Are you all right, dear?"

"It's Ruth. Ruth Mitchell."

"OK, thank you, Ruth. Are you a relative? Ruth, are you Arthur's wife?"

"Yes."

"All right, Ruth, thank you. Ruth, your request for an ambulance is now in the system, and the ambulance should be with you within seven minutes. All right? You're able to stay with Arthur until then, are you, Ruth?"

"Of course."

I got some blankets and pillows and tried to make him more comfortable. Still he didn't open his eyes. I opened the front door a little and then I sat down close to him, holding his hand, and waited. I heard the siren long before I saw the lights.

"Arthur, they're here now," I told him gently. "I can't stay, dear. You know why. They wouldn't understand, would they?"

He squeezed my hand. I kissed his forehead and left.

I made it with only a moment to spare, out through the conservatory and into the shed. I watched the sky above the roof of the house flicker with pale blue flashes but of course I couldn't see what was happening inside. I sensed some commotion but I prayed they wouldn't waste time trying to find the person who had called for the ambulance when the important thing was to get him to hospital. After a while the siren started up again. The lights bobbed and moved and then disappeared. As the wailing faded to silence, a stout woman appeared in the kitchen; it was the neighbor, I supposed, alerted by the ambulance. I could imagine her waving Arthur off and telling the paramedics that she would lock up the house. She began searching through the cupboards. After a few minutes she brought out the enameled casserole dish that I'd scrubbed clean, put it under her arm, and left, leaving the house dark.

I let myself back in and stood quite still for while, shocked. In the space of a few minutes he had been taken from me. All I had wanted, entering the house half an hour ago, was to take care of him. I had been folding his clothes, thinking about what to do about his weight, wondering what he liked to eat, and picturing nourishing little suppers laid out for him in the dining room, but this seemed now to be over-weeningly ambitious and vain of me. From now on I would have to be much more protective. I would get him out of the hospital somehow, and after that I would never leave his side. I had been slow-minded not to realize that this must have been what I meant when I had told Jeremy I was planning to be away for a long time.

I had been slow-minded, too, in failing to see that I was repeat-ing my old mistake, concentrating again on the wrong things and allow-ing my attention to drift away from where it most properly should have been turned. All the time I had been fretting about his weight I had forgotten how unsteady he was on his feet; what notice had I taken of that, what safeguarding instinct had alerted me to the danger of a fall?

Would I never learn, was there to be no end to this accretion of guilt and the amassing of secrets I had to keep? A meaningless spillage of fruit and eggs on a bright day had blinded me to the presence of a living woman. Putting my faith in miracles and magic, I had let my un-cle walk through the snow to his death. In the same hour that I had been concocting a ridiculously Gothic explanation for the torments of my mother's life, my grandmother's had slipped away.

It was in a biology lesson on the tapeworm when I was twelve that I saw for the first time the point of school. I was aghast to learn of the peril I was in. We were told how the tapeworm's eggs lurked on dogs and cats and how a single lick from a pet (already less fluffy and harm-less, already a little less beloved) might be all it took. One touch of a finger on the lips could do it. Disgust made monuments of us. We sat like stones while The Life Cycle of The Parasite spilled from Miss

Lawson's mouth and reeled through our heads like a horror film. Once the eggs were in you, you'd had it. This worm went to work in your gut, gobbling up whatever you put in your stomach. Its ribbon body elongated segment by segment until it wriggled a way right through you, and it just went on eating. You'd gorge on quantities that would make normal people sick, and never be satisfied. You'd be twitchy and gaunt and unable to smile, but you wouldn't die, you'd just look as if you were about to. In civilized countries (lucky us) the tapeworm was rare, but in certain parts of the world people went around like that for years. Then Miss Lawson rescued us. There was a cure.

I danced home. At last I knew what was wrong with my mother. When she fell unconscious it wasn't because she was drunk, it was from sheer fatigue and desperation because there was a tapeworm inside her, soaking up every last drop. It wasn't really *her* drinking at all, it was the tapeworm. Now I could explain the slow-drowning look on her face; something deep in the lakes of drink she swallowed down was dragging her under. That must be why her thinness was not like other people's thinness but seemed like something at work in her, using her up before my eyes. She was perishing from the inside, and now that I knew why I could tell my grandmother. It could be spoken of at last. My grandmother would speak to the doctor and everything would be put right.

She wasn't there. She had died in her chair that morning, probably quite soon after I had left her, newly washed and talcum-powdered. My mother hadn't thought to bring me back early from school because what would be the point? She was dead and that was enough to be going on with.

So even before the biology lesson it had been too late. Maybe at the very moment I was putting two and two together about the tapeworm, they were pulling her knitting from her lap, folding her hands, and lifting her from her chair. I imagined her smiling under a layer of scented white dust as they took her away. That evening, looking at my mother's stone eyes, I thought about the tapeworm again, but I felt much too guilty to mention it.

———

I wandered around downstairs for a while longer. Earlier at Beaulieu Gardens I had found it difficult to sleep; it had been one of those days of hard weather when the sky was white and gray and shone like tin. Now darkness lay across the furniture in Arthur's house and reached into the velvety corners of every room, and all the doors stood open. I walked around and closed them, and the sound that made seemed distant and dull and furtive as if I were hearing from elsewhere in the house a gentle wind blowing through its spaces, nudging the doors shut.

But everywhere was utterly still, as if nobody had lived here for years. The house smelled different, like powder or ash; I should not have been surprised to find dry leaves or bones lying in forgotten rooms. It seemed I had been away for ages, it seemed I had never left. Maybe I had been preparing myself for this, for a night that was bound to come, when I'd understand that whatever I needed it was not to be found in the world Jeremy lived in and where I had found myself stranded for a while, waiting on the vaguest of terms, becalmed by the painting of butterflies and my many other narcotic and listless habits. Unbearably empty though the house was, I knew I had come home. I could be no more nor less in possession of this house if it so happened I were roaming around on the other side of its walls. I could be no more nor less in possession of myself if I were adrift on an ocean.

I made my way upstairs. I had never been in the house alone before and now its gloating darkness was mine; even while Arthur's absence was growing like an ache in my body, I felt safe. I could tell that Ruth had felt this, too, sometimes, in the moment following the closing of the door. She would pause while a shiver of solitude ran through her and she thought of the lightless rooms proffering their spaces for her alone, and anticipated her body alone disturbing the cool, resting air. Like me, she thought of the dark not as dark but as an element, pure, neutral, white—yet miscible, were she but to enter it and let herself dissolve into its shadows. I wondered if she had been tempted, as I now was, to go naked through the house touching nothing and feeling nothing, guilt shed like clothing, aware only of the changing textures of floors underfoot and the tingle, as doors opened, of the air of each room releasing a sigh over bare skin.

I went into Arthur and Ruth's bedroom, into the faint oily damp of fingertip sweat and the aroma of hair and skin-softened bed linen and worn clothes. I undressed. I tried to remember undressing for Jeremy, as distinct from merely taking off my clothes while he happened to be present, and couldn't. I could not remember a single occasion when he had looked at me in a way that made me conscious I was becoming naked rather than just removing garments, but nor did I remember grieving for the want of his scrutiny. I could not remember, even once, when the notion of his contemplating my body occurred to me at all.

I walked naked to the bathroom and showered under a flow of water that felt astringent, sharpened by the darkness. Ruth liked her soaps and lotions to be leafy-scented but with a cut of something spicy and medicinal: calendula, lavender, clove. I used two or three. Arthur's towels were in the wash, so I took her robe from its peg behind the door and wrapped my wet body in its clothy smell of dried perfume. In the pocket I found a fluffy throat pastille.

With Arthur gone, it was hard to believe there was anything much to do. I lit candles and tidied up a little, but I had no heart to tackle the chaos of paper littering the place. I picked up a few pages here and there and read them, going over and over bits of his letters to me. Then I thought maybe I should try to rest, to refresh myself for his return, but when I lay down I would suddenly be certain I should keep busy, and I would get up again. I would start toward the stairs with something to carry up or I would begin to fold a tea towel or put away spoons, but come to a standstill, staring at what was in my hands. I turned over plates and cups as if I had to memorize something about them, in case I might never in my life see their like again. I stopped at windows and thought how wrong it was that I should be here and Arthur not, and how like and unlike an earlier time this had been, waiting for an ambulance, sedated by my own helplessness.

THE COLD AND THE BEAUTY AND THE DARK
1950

Chapter 12: Grace Tries to Take a Stand

It was Grace's eighteenth birthday, and a Saturday in July. Summer lay like a warm haze over the sleepy little corner shop. The blinds had been drawn half down over the windows to protect the contents from the sun, but still the heat burned through, sending the warm sickly smells of powdered sugar and tobacco mixed with dust into the dark stuffy air. Grace had slipped into a doze in her chair behind the counter. There had been few customers all day, perhaps because the shop did not sell ices. There was an ice-cream kiosk a few yards up past the station and Uncle Les said they couldn't compete on price. They moved quite a few bottles of pop in this kind of weather, but in general business was slack. Nobody wanted melting chocolate, bags of sweating barley sugar, or warm, prickly twists of sherbet.

Grace didn't care. She despised the shop and that extended to its customers, too. Three years ago she had left school and come to work in the shop full-time. Her mother very seldom served behind the counter anymore, and many of the regular customers had dropped away. Only a handful of the old gents came in for their pipe tobacco anymore and Grace was none too pleased to see even them. To her they were a bunch of stinky old men and she couldn't be bothered making herself pleasant. She hated their wavery voices and their coughing and their shuffling feet. She hated their lips clamped over their rotten pipes, and most of all she was repelled by their hands. She couldn't bear to take money from them in case there was an accidental brushing of their skin against hers. She placed a plate on the counter for them to drop their money into, and she paid out their change in the same way.

The women and children who came in for sweets were scarcely less offensive. Grace had strict rules about finger marks and shopping baskets on the counter, and about children taking gobstoppers out of their mouths on the premises. She put up a sign threatening the direst consequences if bicycles were left against the window or if chewing gum was dropped on the pavement.

The ringing of the shop bell woke Grace up. Uncle Les strode in, rubbing his hands. "What, not cashed up yet, young lady? Resting on our laurels, are we, and on our birthday?"

Grace glared at him, made her way over to the till, and stabbed down hard on the keys to make it open. "Won't take long, there's little enough to count," she said with bitter satisfaction.

Uncle Les leaned across the counter and seized her by the wrist. "Giving me cheek, are you?" he said in a rough whisper. "Eh, but you've ruined me. You're a minx and a madam," he said through clenched teeth. "Always were."

"You ruined *me*. I hate you. You're a pig."

"Keep your voice down, your Mam'll hear. Is that what you want? You want me to tell her her daughter was born bad and she's been a dirty little minx since she was eight years old? I could put the pair of you out on the street, and don't you forget it."

"I *hate* you. Anyway, Mam's round the baker's getting me a birthday cake," she said. With a wail of despair in her voice, she added, "A birthday cake! Oh, happy birthday, Grace!"

Uncle Les let go of her wrist and slapped her across the face. "Your Mam doesn't know what you are, thanks to me. It's a mercy she can't see you, it's a mercy your father never had to lay eyes on you. There's bad blood in you. So get yourself round here where I can get at you."

"Why should I? I won't."

"Oh, but you will." Uncle Les's voice was quiet and slow. "You will, miss. Birthday or no birthday, because I say so. And don't forget I'm doing you a favor. You're getting past it. You're getting too old for my tastes. Now do as you're told."

Grace stared at him, biting her lip, but obeyed. Uncle Les pulled down the shop blinds and locked the door. He turned back, unbuttoning his trousers, and moved toward Grace, who had seated herself up on the edge of the counter.

"Aye, you know what you are. You know what I want. And I get what I want. So let's be having you, you hussy," he said.

Grace parted her legs and looked away as Uncle Les pushed a hand roughly up between them.

"I'm late," she said. Then she slapped his face, hard.

"What?" Uncle Les drew his hand away and fisted it, ready to strike her. "You bitch!"

Grace flinched for a split second and then squared up to him. "You heard. And don't you dare lift another finger to me or I won't care who knows. I'll tell the whole world what you done to me."

Uncle Les buttoned himself up, staring at her. "But I'm careful. I've been careful since that last time, three years ago that were. Who else have you gone with, you bitch?"

Grace smoothed down her dress and slipped off the counter with a sideways look. "I'm late. Do you want to tell my Mam I'm in the family way," she said, "and not for the first time, neither? Or are you going to help me out?"

Uncle Les pulled her round to face him. "Are you trying to get money out of me?"

Grace gave a sour laugh. "Money? I wouldn't touch your rotten money. No, you just have to cough up for another week outside Blackpool, that'll do it. Call it a birthday present. Still there, is it, your nice quiet place, family run? I'm sure if it isn't you'll find another. Somewhere discreet. Only be quick about it."

She twisted her arm away and picked up her purse from the corner of the counter. Quickly she pulled out a compact and dabbed her face with powder. She slung the purse over her arm, marched to the door, and unlocked it.

"Oy, where do you think you're going? Your mother'll be back any minute."

"Say ta-ta for me, then," Grace said, opening the door. "Tell her I'm not staying for tea. I'm going to the Red Lion. I've got friends that want to buy me a drink and wish me happy birthday. Enjoy the cake, won't you?"

Soon after my grandmother died, my mother closed the shop and sold it to a firm of bookmakers. They bought only the ground floor and we kept the rooms above. First of all they demolished the shop front and replaced it with mysterious, opaque glass, and a flat illuminated sign. There were laws against children setting foot on premises licensed for gaming, so the bookies made us a separate door from the street, opening onto a passageway newly partitioned from the rest of the ground floor, that led to our stairs at the back. In the space of two or three days the old shop ceased to exist and the new betting shop became, to me, forbidden ground.

My mother liked it, though. When I got back from school that's where she would usually be. I asked her once if she won money every day and she told me scathingly she didn't go there to *gamble*. That would be common. She only went for a bit of company, which was the least anyone was entitled to. I found out later that in fact from time to time and for a few discreet shillings she kept the floor swept clean of discarded betting slips. She also became adept at attaching herself to the day's winners; if she could persuade them she'd brought them their luck, as often as not she could also persuade them to take her to celebrate at the Calypso Lounge of the Commercial Hotel up the street.

The betting shop and the Calypso Lounge were within a few hundred yards of each other and I walked past them nearly every day, but I could never picture my mother actually in them. I didn't know if that was because I never saw inside them for myself, or if I had some notion of keeping alive my grandmother's disdain for drinking and gambling. Whatever the reason, my mother grew ever more insubstantial and puzzling. She seldom went more than half a mile beyond the radius of home, but still her life seemed conducted at too vast a distance for me to make it out clearly, like something mimed on a rickety stage very far away, tawdry and mercifully unclear.

I left school when I was fifteen and got a job in a shop selling artists' supplies. I went to night classes in painting and drawing, starting with still lifes of fruit and the more picturesque vegetables. All my attempts were misbegotten, deformed; not once did I not regret my despoliation of the white paper, not once did I prefer what I had done to its insensate purity before a mark had been laid upon it. Yet even as my efforts failed, images poured into my mind's eye and I tried to catch them and set them down with watery brushstrokes or with wiry, silvered turns of my pencil. I filled sheets and sheets with seashells, feathers, bark, clouds, grasses. Some were painted from life, and others were either remembered or dreamed, I do not know; all were phantoms, lit by the gleam of white paper beneath. One tutor described my work as uncommitted and dismissive of basic tonal values, but I didn't see those as faults. Another graded me poorly for putting both the observed and the imagined together in the same pictures, but I couldn't see that there was a difference. Even if there was, was one more real than the other? Nor could I be persuaded to paint anything alive or moving.

So my mother and I continued for a time, living not together but side by side, doing all that we could, through some sort of kindness, to erase each other. By the time I was nineteen she was often drunk for days at a time, venturing no farther than across the rolling seas of her own floors and negotiating her way with arms outstretched for the next anchor post of furniture. One day she fell against a small table, hit her head on the edge of the fireplace, and gashed her leg on a metal ashtray that was knocked off in the crash. I came back from the art shop to find her lying in her dressing gown on the yellow linoleum in the passageway. A ragged red trail of smears and drips reached behind her all the way back up the stairs. She had tried to drag herself as far as the street and given up, and when she'd thumped on the partition wall nobody in the betting shop had heard her above the television's live relay of the afternoon's racing from Sandown.

The ambulance took a long time. While we waited I cradled her in my lap and pressed my scarf, the only thing to hand, against the wound on her head. I wasn't alarmed when she lost consciousness. I was too alert, all my attention taken by the sound of the racing commentary that floated on through the wall in an absurd, unvarying cycle, dignity ending in indignity, the man's voice starting so measured, and then losing control and rising finally to that nervy, screaming finish. Was he not ashamed of his hysteria, did he not know that there was something ridiculous in such public, repetitive, and climactic excesses?

My mother's hip and a number of ribs were broken and her bones were slow to heal. In the hospital her feet and hands turned blue and she stopped speaking. Bruises burst out in purple plumes all over her. She got a lung infection and then she died. Her absence joined my grandmother's as a kind of added weight inside me that I was afraid I would carry for the rest of my life. My pictures grew paler and more ghostly still, and I got married.

Dear Ruth

I'm rather disturbed by the last bit of your story, I must say. How could you think up that kind of thing? I had no idea your mind worked that way. It's not going to get any closer to the bone, is it? You weren't going to publish it under your own name, were you?

There must have been many times before now, times in the old way I mean, when I heard you about the place, downstairs or in the next room, but it was different then. I could hear where you were, and usually I could tell what you were doing, but it meant nothing. Not then. Why is it so different now?

And there's another thing about this new way of ours. In the old way I actually saw you, every day I actually saw you for real. Now in the new way I don't, not actually—yet you are clearer and more real to me than ever you were.

Now I see you, Ruth. I do see you. In my way.

Fondly

Arthur

PS Ruth I remember you at Overdale Lodge, the first time, the first evening, the first year. How you looked then is how I see you now.

Did it really happen as neatly as that, my mother died and I got married? Of course not. Her dying was lurid and protracted. For those weeks in the hospital I was her only visitor, after the manager and a couple of the punters from the betting shop had dropped in, and day by day I sat studying her decline and hoping to get from her—exactly how I did not know, since she had given up on speech—some admission that it was unreasonable to expect me to bear so great a strain alone. I brought fruit she would not eat. I brought magazines to read aloud to her in which she took not the slightest interest. Soon, rather than just sit staring at her, I ate the grapes and read the magazines myself at the bedside while she lay with her eyes either blank and open, or closed, probably more to escape me than to invite sleep. After a few weeks of this my vigil began to feel like an effort that should be rewarded by her consenting to be dead by the next time I looked up. It wasn't absolutely that I wanted her to die, I just felt that for both our sakes she ought to, before I could be found even more wanting.

It went on. Every day I agreed with the nurses that she was turning out to be "quite a fighter," while privately I thought her remaining alive had nothing to do with tenacity or strength but was more a failure of skill and application. She hated life, so surely it was obtuse of her to be quite so lacking in ambition to get it over with? She deteriorated, but lingered. For another month, death loomed just beyond her reach like an accomplishment she had yet to acquire.

It was after she finally died that I met Jeremy—or, to be more ac-curate, that he noticed me. He was an intern then. While she was alive he hadn't taken any particular interest in either of us. We had met once over a brief assessment of her condition, conducted at the end of her bed, during which his eyes had been fixed either on her feet or on his notes. He spoke in my hearing, not to me, with no apparent concern about whether or not I was listening. I only came to his attention after-ward, when I was having trouble leaving the hospital.

On the day after my mother's funeral I went back to the ward to give the nurses some of the flowers. The moment I walked back into its high white space and pungent smell, I realized how much I missed the routine of my daily visits: greeting the nurses, reporting to my mother on the weather, removing fruit too far gone, tidying her hair. I missed the sense of purpose I'd felt witnessing her descent, however starkly it had revealed my own shortcomings; what was I supposed to do now? I missed not so much my mother as the care that had been taken of her: the nurses' firmly timetabled administrations of drugs and fluids, and toward the end, their optimistic, hour-by-hour regime for her comfort in the absence of any hope of her recovery. The ward was the only place I knew where kindness had not failed, and I did not belong there anymore.

Everyone said it was good of me to drop in with the flowers, everyone said they were lovely but they were a bit too busy to see to them straightaway. I volunteered to put them in water myself—goodness, didn't I know where the vases were kept by this time!—and when I had done that I saw two or three patients without visitors whose flowers also needed freshening up. I stayed two hours. I had noticed how short of vases the ward was so the next day I took some in, along with a bottle of hand lotion that one of the patients had mentioned her sister had forgotten to get for her. I popped out on an errand for another, to buy a hair net, and then stayed to chat for a while. Over the next two or three weeks I found the nurses too busy to take much notice of me, but the patients seemed glad to see me. I listened to medical sagas of endurance and suffering, I listened to complaints about their visitors and those who failed to visit. I changed library books, peeled apples, wrote in crossword clues, posted letters; nothing was too much trouble. Next to the patients I appeared perfectly cheerful and somehow whole, and they didn't seem to realize that I wasn't really a kind person at all.

One day as I was leaving, Jeremy was also waiting for the elevator. I was pleased he was there because its sequence of hums and clicks and whines, the little mechanical fanfare announcing my ejection from the ward for the night, sounded less lonely with someone beside me. Already I was missing the lulling hospital sounds: trolleys, soft treading feet, the swish of curtains drawn around beds. He stared at the elevator doors, I studied him. His shoulders, but also something in his face, gave him a burdened air.

"Hi. Just off?" he said.

I nodded. He nodded back. "People often do find it difficult," he said rather nicely. "I mean after."

"After what?" I said, and he blushed.

The elevator arrived and we traveled down. At the bottom he asked for my telephone number. Three days later he took me out for a drink

and talked about himself. As I listened, I was thinking that even if burdened he looked, in the way doctors can, becalmed by responsibility.
Despite the junior-doctor pallor and slumped shoulders, he exuded
enough certainty about life to deal with whatever might be waiting for
me "after," beyond the ward; he had a forward-going force that I knew
I lacked. And he seemed an intrepid person—indeed the very practice
of medicine was to me intrepid in itself: all those intimate, dreadful in-
cursions into other people's bodies, how did he ever *dare?* When he
said that he intended to specialize in anesthesia, I knew he wouldn't let
me feel a thing. It was the most seductive promise he could have
made, to keep me benumbed.

What did I offer in return? Nothing really, of any visible value, perhaps nothing at all beyond my self as a prepared and willing surface for
the marital textures of stasis and familiarity, an implicit pledge that I
would spring no surprises. Two years later I entered marriage gratefully. It was like stepping into a clean white room whose door Jeremy
held open and then closed quietly behind us.

For most of the rest of that night I drifted through Arthur's house.
Eventually I lay down on the sofa and drew in a long, stifling breath
that made me wonder if I was taking in water rather than air, and indeed if I should not prefer to be drowning rather than falling asleep. It
seemed that I was staring into dark water from a raft, alive but not
quite rescued, and afloat slightly reluctantly. My eyes began to sting. I
wanted Arthur with me.

———

THE COLD AND THE BEAUTY AND THE DARK
1956

Chapter 13: Hospital Visiting

It seemed to Evelyn that Grace hardly spoke to her anymore. They had never found it easy to communicate but for the past four months, since Uncle Les had been in and out of hospital, first with a collapsed lung and pneumonia and then with what the doctors called "complications," it had got worse. She could sense Grace turning away from her whenever she came into a room, she could feel how wide a berth she was given whenever she got up from her chair. If Grace was in the kitchen and Evelyn entered, Grace would leave. If Evelyn was there, Grace wouldn't come in. It was if she could not have borne so much as an accidental brush of her mother's hand. Evelyn longed for her hand to be touched, or to be allowed the lightest caress of her daughter's hair or her shoulder. It would have helped her to "see" her, perhaps.

But it was many years since they had embraced each other. That was fair enough, there was no call for grown women to go around hugging and kissing each other all day, but Evelyn and her Mam had occasionally given each other a peck and a pat and it had probably done them good. But Grace had never been that kind of child.

Evelyn sighed and put down her knitting. Uncle Les looked forward to their weekly visits to him in hospital on Wednesdays, the shop's half-day, and Grace should have shut up below and come up by now. If they had a quick early dinner they could make it to the half-past-one bus and that meant an hour and a quarter with him before all visitors had to leave at half past three. If they missed the bus going, they had barely half an hour. But more and more often Grace would slip away after shutting the shop and not come up for her dinner until it was past quarter to one. When Evelyn had asked her where she got to, all she would say was she hadn't noticed the time. Any further questions were met with a sullen silence, not that Evelyn really needed to ask any; the smell of cigarette smoke and strong drink on her were explanation enough.

The other thing that worried Evelyn constantly was Grace's attitude to Uncle Les. When he had first been taken ill, Grace had made it clear she didn't care. He's as tough as an old boot, that one. Don't let him fool you, he'll see *you* buried, she had said harshly. It was only after that first month, when he suddenly relapsed and then deteriorated, that she had begun to take any interest in how he was, wanting to know from day to day if he was out of danger or not. For about three weeks it had seemed to matter to her whether he lived or died. But then when he had been declared on the mend but facing a long, slow recovery, she lost interest again.

In fact, for the past four or five visits, she had spent at the most a few minutes at the bedside, keeping her coat on and refusing to sit down, before announcing that she was off for a walk and would come back for Evelyn at the end of the visiting hour. It was a blessing that Uncle Les had been too ill to take offense, but he was getting stronger now and Evelyn did not want him upset by Grace's attitude. Grace just didn't seem to recognize how much they owed to Uncle Les, and how much they still relied on his goodwill.

Just then she heard Grace's solid tread on the stairs. Evelyn sighed again, got up, and went to the kitchen. There were potatoes to mash, and with a bit of luck the sausages in the oven wouldn't be burnt quite to cinders.

On the bus, Evelyn squeezed into the window seat and Grace planted herself beside her, breathing hard. She sounded hot and heavy, but it was only May and there was a cool, fresh wind. Grace pulled in her breath and held it. Evelyn felt the tension in her and reached out to place a hand on her arm.

"Are you all right, love?" she said. "You sound a bit puffed."

"I'm all right," Grace said, shifting away from Evelyn's touch. "Indigestion."

"I'm not surprised," Evelyn said with a forced chuckle. "By the time you were sat down to your dinner you'd barely five minutes to eat it."

Grace had no reply to that and they traveled on in silence. The bus dropped them at the hospital gates. It was at least another five minutes' brisk walk across the hospital grounds and down several echoing corridors to the Respiratory Diseases ward. Evelyn knew better than to take Grace's arm so as usual she kept at her side by concentrating on the sound of Grace's feet, waving her white stick to and fro ahead of her as she went. Today, Grace's loud breathing mixed with the sound of her footfall. Her indigestion did seem to be troublesome. Maybe this would teach her not to cut it so fine on Wednesdays in future. Evelyn was about to suggest that she really needed to give herself a bit longer to digest her meal when Grace stopped dead.

Evelyn was alarmed. "Grace, what's up? Are you all right?"

There was silence for a moment. "Aye, stop fussing, it'll pass," Grace growled. From the direction of her voice Evelyn knew she was either crouching on the ground or doubled over. "It's just a stitch in my side."

Sure enough after a short while Grace said brightly, "Come on, then. Let's get it over with."

"Oh, Grace, you are unkind about your uncle," Evelyn murmured. But she was pleased that Grace sounded more like herself, even if it had to be a rather short-tempered self.

They reached the ward after the usual squeaky walk along the polished linoleum floors and brick-lined corridors. When they got to the bedside Grace muttered that Uncle Les was asleep. She almost pushed her mother into a chair and said she would be back at half past three. Evelyn opened her mouth to protest, but changed her mind. It might not be such a bad idea if Grace took herself off, since she was clearly in a nasty mood. She didn't quite trust her not to make a scene and that was the last thing anyone wanted, especially around sick folk lying in a hospital ward.

After a minute or two, Uncle Les woke up. Evelyn knitted away, addressing remarks to him, which he answered sleepily. She was quite content not to have to make too much conversation, and she wondered to herself how many more Wednesday visits would be required. She noticed that his voice sounded stronger and he hardly coughed at all. There had been mention of a convalescent home in the countryside for a month's recuperation, which would certainly be a difficult journey for her and Grace by bus.

When Uncle Les drifted off to sleep again she tap-tapped her way with her white stick to the end of the ward where, as she expected, a nurse came out and greeted her. Yes, she confirmed, Doctor was very pleased with Mr. Hibbert and fully expected that another week should see him strong enough to leave hospital. A spell of convalescence in a well-run establishment such as the Maud Braddock Memorial Home for Invalids would be just the thing. A few more weeks of fresh air and not overdoing things would put him properly back on his feet. Evelyn nodded and turned to go back, waving her stick in front of her.

"I'm just due to do my rounds," the nurse said. "Here's my arm, if you'll allow me?"

Without waiting for a reply she took Evelyn's arm and tucked it cozily under her own, and led her slowly back up the ward. As they went, she spoke in a gentle voice to Evelyn about the flowers placed here and there. Mr. Crowe had orange chrysanthemums, but the lovely scent came from the simple lilies of the valley in a little vase on Mr. McIntyre's bedside table. His wife had brought them from the garden. Evelyn squeezed the nurse's arm.

"I had lilies of the valley for my wedding posy. Over twenty years ago. Oh, I can see that posy now! Lovely, it was."

The nurse murmured sympathetically.

"Aye, and the wallflowers in the gardens out yonder," Evelyn went on, "they've a grand smell, too. I walked past them from the gate."

"Yes, I saw they were out. Lovely colors."

"Aye, they're bonny-lookin'. As I remember." She turned and smiled at the nurse, her eyes brimming with tears.

"Oh, dear, I am sorry!" the young nurse said. "I'm so thoughtless. Only with you coming every Wednesday, I got to thinking if *I* couldn't see, what I'd want would be somebody letting me know what there *was* to see. Then I might sort of see it in my head. Only maybe it's not like that at all. Oh, I'm ever so sorry if I've offended—"

"Nay! Nay, go on with you! You've got it spot-on. I'm not used to it, that's all, somebody thinking about it that way. My Grace, now, she . . ." Evelyn fished her handkerchief from her sleeve and wiped her eyes. "She's just not a big talker, I suppose. Well, thank you, lass," she said. "Thank you ever so."

They had arrived back at Uncle Les's bed and the nurse helped Evelyn back into her chair. "You're right welcome. You've another fifteen minutes," she said. "We'll miss you when Mr. Hibbert goes."

Evelyn beamed. Then the nurse leaned in close and whispered in her ear. "Sister was saying your smile lights up the whole ward. You're an inspiration, you are. Take care now."

It seemed impossible to Evelyn that she might inspire anyone, but she went on smiling at the compliment, and turned her attention again to entertaining Uncle Les with snippets of news.

When Grace arrived back sullenly at a quarter to four, Evelyn was waiting for her under the porch of the entrance to the ward. It had begun to rain. Grace marched back to the bus stop so fast that Evelyn had to call out to her to slow down. Not a word was exchanged on the journey home. On the bus, Evelyn pondered the words of the nurse, wondering about the sympathy that had come from the young woman so naturally, as if she were filled with it and it overflowed. Where did it all come from? She knew it was wrong of her, but she couldn't help hoping that even a little of something similar was lodging somewhere deep in Grace's heart, and would come out one day. Then she immediately felt guilty. The nurse probably had a mother waiting at home ready to notice that her young daughter looked tired or troubled, or had done her hair a new way, or had a new glow about her. It wasn't Grace's fault.

Sleep came in the end. It always does. It's not sleep itself that's the problem, it's when you sleep; Arthur and I both knew well enough by now how determined people were to prevent us from sleeping at times it was inconvenient to them. But of course they couldn't stop us any more than we could stop the dreams that came when we did.

That first night alone and waiting for him, I had a dream that began in water, dark water flickering with iridescent, darting fish, though on reflection it might have been a dark sky alive with butterflies. Whether air or water it was warm, and in it my breath softened and slowed and I swam or floated toward a bumpy-looking ledge that turned out to be the distant line between a lake and a sky just beginning to blaze with light; as I came nearer, the horizon split against the rising dome of the sun.

The dream woke me as if a torch had been shone into my eyes. I got up to get a drink of water and I stood in the kitchen listening to the kind of low noise all kitchens make, not really a sound at all. Every kitchen's undercurrents are the same and different, and kitchens smell the same and different. Here it was milky, sweetish. I wandered out to the back garden. The fresh air rushed at me and I plonked myself down on the terrace steps. It was so cold and lovely.

I was shivering. I was in need of food, too, I realized; my stomach began to grumble. Though I knew I should go in and get warm and find something to eat, I went on sitting there, looking up at the sky. I wondered what it would be like to be in a house near running water and surrounded by mountains so that every night would be filled with flows and echoes. I could hear the emptiness up there, and it made me think of flying, not with great flapping wings but in the way the gift of flight is bestowed in a dream or by magic, when the wind streams under you and you soar without effort simply because you have been granted the belief that you can. I closed my eyes and felt myself flying close to the top of a hillside invisible in the dark but there all the same, rising from a gleaming stretch of water.

Before it grew light, and now thinking practically of Arthur's return, I went back upstairs. I chose quickly from the closet, not taking time to assess its contents carefully. The clothes were obvious, anyway: sensible, not ugly but certainly not alluring or attractive. There was something so habitual and plain about them it seemed impossible they had ever been bought new, or chosen at all, never mind with pleasure; it was difficult to discern anything in them that would cause them to be selected from among others. I put on olive green slacks, a cream sweater, and some slip-on shoes. I looked like nobody, or anybody. I didn't mind. For years I had been heading the same way myself, toward a capitulation to the expectation that women past a certain age dress only for weather, convenience, and disguise. It was obvious to me that it had been decades since Arthur had either been asked for or offered an opinion of Ruth's appearance.

I didn't know when to expect him, of course. My safest course was to wait out each day in my usual way, but with extra caution; probably he would not return alone and they might barge in while I was asleep. So when dawn came, I made my way up to the attic. The air was pleasantly thick and warm. I was so tired I could have bedded down on the bare boards but I was pleased to find a pile of curtains and some rolled-up rugs. I arranged them into a kind of nest and settled down, dragging a dusty white net curtain around myself so that it covered me completely. I held it to my face until it was wet and salty. Then I opened my eyes and pulled the cloth right around my head and held it taut so I couldn't blink. I stared through its gauzy whiteness. The sun from the skylight glimmered through, a cloudy bright rectangle in the flat, milky shadow of the sloping ceiling. I breathed in and pretended I was in the countryside in a field full of flowers, looking up at the sun just after it has rained. Over the white nylon I ran a finger down my nose and over my cheeks and across my lips, which were smiling now. My musty smooth curtain was a new white skin come to cover me up so nobody would know what I was like underneath. I fell asleep, and the day passed.

When I got up again I was restless and could not settle to anything. I knew he would not come at night, but still I tried to kill time by measuring my every move in little units of anticipation, awaiting his return. I stripped his bed and changed the sheets, smoothing my hands over the pillow just where his head would, very soon I prayed, leave a soft dent. I opened the bedroom window with some funny idea that he had flown away and now he'd be able to get back in, like Peter Pan; if I was to go down to make tea, he would alight on the floor above me in the moment between my filling the kettle and opening a bottle of milk. If I counted the strokes as I brushed my hair, he would be here before I reached a hundred. If I started to sing to myself in a low voice, affecting a nonchalance I didn't feel, it would summon him back, and the opening of the door would be the first sound to interrupt this meandering, patient song of mine.

By the next morning I was worried. I spent all day in the attic, unable to sleep. So I heard everything as I lay there: the arrival of a car, the front door opening, people talking, and after a few minutes a woman's voice more insistent than the rest. In all the noise and movement I could not make out a sound from Arthur himself. After a while the house grew quiet again, and I slept. When I woke, I guessed it was around three o'clock in the afternoon. Maybe they had put him to bed. I thought of him in his room, wakeful, curious, perhaps still afraid. I willed him to turn over and close his eyes, not to fight sleep, and I fancied I heard a little whine, the kind an animal makes when it knows that the time for choosing to fight or to give in has passed, because either it is already defeated, or it is safe. Then I fell asleep again.

Dear Ruth

I'm back. I couldn't wait to get back.

I'd forgive you for thinking me slow to catch on—well, I have been slow—but I've got it now. I'm getting to the crux of it now. I can think clearly here. You're here, but only here. You're nowhere else. Not in the hospital. I missed you terribly.

The hospital—it's a zoo in there.

The ward was hellish. I came to thinking how could this get any worse—then it did. Mrs. M swooped in and perched like buzzard refusing to budge because, she said, somebody had to catch the doctor and explain the situation. She said the nurses don't pay attention to anything these days much less pass it on to the doctors—all this according to The Great Tony. I was lucky, she said, to have an NHS insider like Tony on my case. You need somebody who can get to the right people, knows their way around the system.

She brought a book for me, something somebody had given her but it wasn't her kind of thing. An anthology. She didn't know till recently I was a poetry fan, she was surprised to find the house swimming in it or she'd have passed it on before.

Doctor didn't come all morning, so finally she went. I had a squint at the book, it didn't do anything for me either.

Poetry isn't like water or air. You actually don't need it to live. I can hear you disagreeing, but it's a fact. Poetry's more like the wine or perfume in a life. It's nice to have, but you can get along all right without. You can manage with just having everything plain, or at least you can until you've acquired the taste for the more rarefied, then it's harder. But as long as you're getting along without anything fancy, you don't see that you're missing much.

All right, you're frowning at that. But that's me. Ordinary and plain. It's my history, I suppose. There are some histories you couldn't squeeze a poem into sideways and that was mine, not that I'm complaining. Good people, my parents, though of course you only knew Dad and he wasn't the same man after Mum died. All that's history, too, in the background—nobody really remembers.

Funny word—I'm thinking about words—the background. My background—when was it? Where is it now? Overdale Lodge? Or before we met? Or after? When does anyone's background stop and their foreground begin? We were married all those years, isn't that a background in itself, does it blank out what came earlier, does whatever comes after meld into it and get lost, or does it stand out sharper? Maybe we're just a fuzzy pair of figures somewhere in a painting, so small and on the edge that only we know we're there at all. Nobody else really sees us.

But it's still ours, our life—no matter it's just a collection of dots in one corner of a picture, no matter we're background figures, no matter how many people miss that we're even there.

But you can't set it down, not even our little life, nobody can—not in a picture, not in words.

I just wish I could.

I remember the kind of pictures you liked. The ones you said were like film sets if only they'd known how to make films then. In the Renaissance. We watched that thing on TV, remember, about how they painted them to make your eye go straight to the little golden figures cavorting about in flowers without a stitch on, and next onto the tumbling green cascades and ruins and peacocks, and then to the blue distant forests and mountains and sky. Was the order of the colors meant to calm you down or something, make you think deep thoughts? Maybe that's the kind of background you need for poetry. Or for cavorting.

I'm no poet and I never was a cavorter. Obviously. I see now I may have let you down there.

I'll think further on it all, now I'm back safe. Finally saw a young fella purporting to be a doctor about five o'clock yesterday, told him I was taking myself off home for some peace and quiet. He looked terrified, clearly couldn't deal with me, he went and fetched a nurse at least twenty years older than he was.

Two against one—VOICES RAISED in objection—and they told me I was shouting!!! Leg condition needs to be stabilized, hospital best place, support yet to be arranged for return home etc etc.

In the end I had to mention most important point—ie getting back to you, dear. I said all support necessary was waiting at home, thank you very much, and further interference neither required nor welcome, please give your time and attention to those in greater need, I'm aware there's pressure on resources.

Predictably this threw them quicker than you could say Psychiatric Assessment, in fact it proved to be a proper old poke into a hornets' nest. People wandered through with clipboards and forms—not about me, it was all about a Care Program, social services, community nurses, meals on wheels, whole shooting match. And that was only the start, there was this or that or the next thing they couldn't do till tomorrow or day after or until so-and-so got back from vacation. I got so tired hearing them go on and on I fell asleep. I'm sure they slipped me something.

Fooled them, however! Was awake nearly all night as usual and up and dressed and ready to be off when staff were changing over this morning. There's even a taxi line outside, I didn't have to navigate the bus routes.

Couldn't escape the welcoming committee, though, Mrs. M and Co—taxi not home two minutes and there they were. They must've had the place staked out. But now I'm back I'll go on thinking about it all. The pictures, the words. Where your life gets put, if you're not very careful, by other people. What you're meant to do with all the things you remember. Should I be worrying that maybe I remember some things that aren't true, and forget others that are? Does it matter, if nobody would know but me? I only want you to know. I want to talk to you.

I'll have a sleep now and think about it all later, toward the time when the sun's setting. That's when I wake up and that's a good time for thinking. Thoughts pop up out of the dreams I have, though I don't remember the dreams.

I want to hear from you on these and other subjects, when I'm more myself.

When I'm less myself, is what I should be saying.

Affectionately

Arthur

Where's the harm in it? By staying here I can give him, in this discreet way, the help he needs. If I'm now Ruth, does it matter? He's happier, and he's clean and eating again. Considering what I've taken away from him, some small measure of well-being is little enough to be giving back. And since that's all I do give him, how could I take that away again?

I can't risk an appearance so I can't do much about all the visitors. I feel like writing to the damn nurses and the neighbor to say that while he may seem to them to be losing ground, actually he is being restored to life. But why would I owe them any explanation? And would they understand it? No; I would have to write it like a sick note composed to veil the whole truth. "Please make allowances for Arthur if he does not seem quite himself but he is more himself than ever and should be excused."

It can't be done. I would have to puzzle over it, pondering what it was they needed to know and how they needed it said, and concoct some version of his condition that would both satisfy and conceal. I would have to write with insincere respect for an established belief that I have long known to be false, which is that when people die, they depart; I would have to write it as someone other than Ruth, and that's impossible.

Dear Ruth

Your Della phoned. This story of yours, am only now appreciating the scale. Of your ambition, I mean. Della wonders if time is now right to ask if I would let them put some of it in their next "Work in Progress" collection, they do one every two years.

What do you think of that?

She also said you had just about finished it. Well I haven't come across anything beyond page 93 so where did she get that idea from? She said you were planning to read something from the second half to the writing group, they thought you might have had it ready for them that day. You know, the day it happened.

Also I keep finding poems. Folders and envelopes marked with year of composition. Wish you were a more meticulous filer. I claim, if I may, a little credit for meticulous filing, and like it or not you have to admit it would have done you good if a little of my example with check stubs, bank statements, and paperwork generally had rubbed off on you.

I'm no fan of Della's as you know, and common sense prevailed just in time, the phone was still in my hand. I was on the point of telling her about all the poetry I still haven't gone through, but I stopped myself just in time. Nearly said would she come round and be here with me when I read them, as if poems were a bit of a hazard, too risky to read on my own. Most of them I won't understand anyway. I banged down receiver just in time.

By the way I like the story. At least I understand it.

I suppose you would have told me about it once you'd got a bit further on.

Re: poems. I do like this one. When did you write it? What else did you think that day, what else did you say that day, and where has all that gone?

Green bird sits
Looking at me
From the green shelter
Of the lilac tree.
Doesn't it know
Doesn't it see
How much I wish
That I were he?

Shouldn't that be "was him" in the last line, strictly speaking? I can see it wouldn't rhyme then, but Della says rhyming's not necessary.

Couldn't fathom what bird you were describing, either. I finally tracked down the big bird book. When did you stick that and other works of ornithological reference in the attic, by the way, because I don't recall so much as a by-your-leave.

Now don't take this the wrong way. I'm just trying to help. Only I don't see what harm it could do to know what bird we're talking about. "Green" isn't much to go on. I'm skeptical, moreover, that you were sure it was a "he," but it would narrow it down a bit. Male and female plumage differ, as I know I have pointed out to you in the past.

Main possibilities are these (in order of likelihood acc. season, distribution of species, and population numbers, figs. as calculated by RSPB survey 1988):

Greenfinch
Willow warbler
Wood warbler
Goldcrest
Siskin

I grant you're the poetry buff but you'd concede I have the edge where ornithology's concerned.

Do you remember, many's the time at Overdale Lodge I was first to get the binoculars out? It became a bit of a joke! Mr. Mitchell and his binoculars!

I still maintain that as long as a teacher commands respect then he can take a little friendly standing joke against himself, in fact it shows he's human.

Education by stealth, we used to say, remember? Give the opportunities to all; and some will partake. Oh, we didn't expect to convert the kind of town kids we took to Overdale in the space of a week, but many's the hardened case was interested in learning how to use the binoculars. Many's the tough nut who was pleased to learn something about the lesser-known native species. Education by stealth.

At least in those days we managed to get them as far as Overdale. All that's gone and it makes my blood boil. Give the opportunity to all and some will partake, that was a good enough philosophy in our day and it still should be. Horses to water.

Overdale has been on my mind, since looking out photos etc etc from old times. I put one up, where Della's memorial left a hole in the wall.

Class 3C Aug 1973 it says on the back in your writing. Our fourth year, a year after we got married.

The kids in that picture are nearly fifty now. I wonder who that lanky fellow with all the dark hair and the sideburns was, he looks oddly familiar!? Clue—the one with the binoculars round his neck!!

You don't look any different.

I was looking for the lilac tree in the garden, thinking of your poem. It's over by the shed. It's the white kind, not the lilac lilac. No bird in it of any color in the middle of the night, but I looked at the blossom for a while. It's turned brown, as if it's been under a grill. I do notice some things.

Your touches around this place, I notice them, too. Thank you. You *don't know the difference you make. I never have been much good at telling you, have I? Maybe that's something that will change.*

With affection & gratitude

Arthur

I don't know what to do about his letters. He writes page after page every night now and leaves them around the place, sometimes whole sheets scrawled on both sides but most often scraps, disjointed bursts of words thrown down and torn off and shed everywhere like fallen leaves. On these clear warm nights I open windows and doors, and in the currents of air and the tread of our feet they drift and mass against baseboards and in the corners, so we walk the house as if following each other along a festooned path whitened by moonshine and rustling in a night breeze. I pick them up after him and stack them tidily so at least he'll know I've read them.

Things may settle after a while. I won't leave. I'll look after him as before, and I'll go on letting him know I'm here, by quiet observances and little signs: a footfall, a murmur, dishes done, floors swept, and windows opened to the moonlight. I hope it'll go on being enough. We've got it working nicely now.

Dear Ruth

*I think the time has come to acknowledge that we're on something of a different footing now, you and me. A different **plane** you would say, going for an airy word over a solid one, but footing will do for me, always preferred terra firma, and that being so, let's be clear about one thing. Which is—in one important way, of course, we're not on any footing at all.*

Because I know the reality of the situation, you only have to go back to my first letter to see that. I would hardly be talking about the flowers at the funeral if I didn't, would I? By the way, that woman who got me writing the letters in the first place, she's dropped off the radar, come to think of it. Thank God, one less. Can't remember her name, doesn't matter.

Also, I have been to the spot where it happened, some weeks ago now. Seen it with my own eyes. The Great Tony and Mrs. M took me, they doubted the wisdom etc, but I made them. And I made the police show me the photos of the bike. After, not before, I'm talking about. Plus I could hardly have gone through all the church and cemetery rigmarole and come out the other end not knowing the reality of the situation, could I? Strikingly obvious.

But you and I both know that doesn't alter the other and equally obviously striking fact. Doesn't mean what's happening isn't happening. You have come back.

Things are always happening, whether you know they are or not.

A thing can be true even if you don't understand it.

I must say, that's a very "you" remark! Doesn't sound like me at all. Occurs to me I've been making your kind of remark a lot lately, because you weren't here to say them anymore. Or so the Mrs. M's of this world would have us believe.

And that's the point isn't it, that is *the point. You see? I'm perfectly* au fait with the realities. But at the same time I'm quite au fait with the other reality, ie YOU ARE HERE.

You are here. Even if you aren't actually saying anything.

I KNOW YOU ARE HERE. I have not taken leave of my senses, despite what Mrs. M and The Great Tony and bloody nurses might say. I am sick and tired of their opinions and interference. Narrow minds.

You may have noticed I'm doing more to protect myself from that kind of thing. I have to. I can't have all and sundry turning up. Between them they're capable of pushing a fellow close to the edge. It wouldn't take much more than what I'm already putting up with to tip a sane person right over.

What they have all proved themselves consistently INCAPABLE of doing is grasping what's really important. THEY refuse to see certain things, NOT ME!!! Something IS happening in this house and whenever I mention it, they purse their lips and start up again about leg bandages and casseroles and fluid intake and letting visitors in. All diversionary tactics, of course.

I won't be put off.

Arthur

PS You could always leave me a few words, you know, just so I'll be CERTAIN. I'm leaving this letter out. You could add a word...that would shut up THEM and any other doubting Thomases, this world is full of them!

Dear Ruth

Well. It didn't seem so very much to ask. Still doesn't. Just a word, plus signature would have done. Nurse showed up yesterday, saw her coming up drive, was just in time to hide. But legs more troublesome so I reconsidered and let her in.

It was the English one so no escaping the interrogation. The Pole at least just gets on with legs.

Not feeling very chatty today?

Not feeling like getting dressed today?

I'm not too busy today, would you like a hand getting dressed? Can I help you find some clothes? What did you have for breakfast today? Shall I get you a cup of tea?

Next thing she does amounts to assault. She's sly about it of course, doesn't let it LOOK *like that.*

She's fiddling away at legs and she says, I just need to move your coat so I can get to the problem area here, oh look your papers they're about to fall out, can we put these somewhere or maybe you want to hold them—voice dripping saccharine of course—and she GRABS THE PAPERS STICKING OUT OF MY POCKET.

I'm not so frail on the pins I can't jump up, bandages or no bandages, and I told her where to get off. I told her these weren't JUST PAPERS *they were original writings,* PRIVATE LETTERS TO MY LATE WIFE *and her* ORIGINAL WRITINGS. *She missed the point but it was enough to see her off.*

Later on:

here's the POINT.

You're not my late wife, you're my wife. And very glad I am about that. Thank you dear, especially for the efforts you've been making since what happened to you in April.

I haven't thought to ask if you get impatient in the same way as before, or if all that kind of thing changes after a person isn't any longer—you know, any longer here in the usual way, present in their earthly body. It seems to me you're everywhere, and always busy—so the spirit doesn't seem to need to put their feet up for half an hour with the paper. You see I DO notice things!

With a grateful kiss

Arthur

After his return from the hospital I lost track, somewhat. It was as if I were waking from a dream of my life and realizing that the passing of the years had not been real. Time reeled me back and set me down at a stage that more properly belonged in childhood or adolescence, though I had not experienced then, nor at any period in my life since, what I was now feeling. I think it was adoration, simply.

My life now pivoted on a single fulcrum. Arthur's appearances and absences and habits were my entire study, all their tiny modifications and variants, the balances and counterbalances governing my every move. A sudden disappearance to the sitting room might mean he wanted me to change his sheets. A discarded sweater would prompt me to open windows. I scrutinized every act for clues that would enable me to preempt his desires, laying out the minutiae for interpretation: salt left on the side of his plate, three not two wet bath towels, a cup of tea left unfinished: what did these tell me? With diligent sycophancy I amassed scraps of data and archived them in my mind in lists of every aversion and predilection.

I began to concern myself again with his weight. Every night by candlelight I laid out his meal in the dining room and on my way back to the kitchen I would swing my hand gently across the wind chime in the hall to let him know it was time to eat. He didn't always come down very promptly, and he didn't have much of an appetite. Occasionally I had to sound the wind chime again, rather insistently, but I was determined he should not let his dinner go cold. He was a conservative and fussy eater, even a suspicious one. When he finished what I had given him I was grateful, as if a delicate creature had fed from my hand; if something remained untasted, my displeasure was intense. It called for patience. Gradually I learned his likes and dislikes. He left beets right in the middle of the plate along with some potato and a piece of ham that were stained bright pink with them. I concluded that his loathing of beets extended to anything that touched them.

I was both watchful and exhilarated, nervy and tearful, and also astonished to find that living in such a state of anxious devotion was quietly satisfying. But I did not want to be satisfied, I did not want to be rewarded. He could never forgive me for what I had done, of course, but the thought that he might allow me to comfort him reduced me to tears, and then I was ashamed at having been moved by the idea of my own gratification. I craved only his permission to enter the circle of his grief and the chance, thereby, to prove it not utterly unyielding, its widening rings not unstoppable.

During the day I stayed up in the attic, sleeping or drowsing, and often brooding about the nurses I could hear downstairs. They had taken to arriving in pairs so that, I had no doubt, one could attend to

Arthur while the other snooped around. I resented their unearned and undeserved power to administer to him. I imagined their irreverent hands on his skin and fumed at the squandering of such a privilege; they were ignorant of the value of what they were being allowed to touch.

If I had happened to sleep through until the evening, I could tell as soon as I woke that they had been in the house. From the top of the stairs, the eddying of Arthur's lately unheeded protests tautened the air; I would follow the wraith of his spent distress wafting from room to room. The wrong doors would be hanging ajar, chairs disarranged. I could also tell at once where in the house Arthur had chosen to lie to recover from their invasions. He didn't make any noise; I knew his whereabouts from waves of silent keening, as if from someone contemplating his wounds after the aggressor has moved casually on. This was when he would be at his quietest and most elusive. Not until I had got to work and begun to wash the memory of the intrusion out of the place would he be able to stir. Then I would hear him come back to life, creaking along the landing to the bathroom in his slippers, dropping papers, whistling birdcalls above the noise of running taps.

The nurses also kept leaving letters and forms and leaflets to do with evaluations and qualifying for things such as transport and home care. There was no end to it. On most of them they had already done the filling-in except on the line awaiting Arthur's signature, which they fenced at each side with bright red crosses. Arthur left these out for me, next to his letters, and after I'd read them I tore them up and threw them away, as he clearly intended I should.

Dear Ruth

Was caught going down for drink of juice around 4 pm. Mrs. M hovering at the front and she sees me through the door. She's got a saucepan in one hand, MAD look on face, frantic bitch. I'd ignore her as usual, only she starts calling out and banging till I fear for the glass, pays no attention when I shout at her to go away. So I open door to shout again and make sure she hears. Doesn't even look at me, barges past to the kitchen, she's says she's got something hot for me and she has to put it down before it burns her hands. Transparent ruse to get in and nosy around.

Anyway once there—oh, transformation, face lights up. Sniffs. Sticks bosoms out, actually wiggles them (sorry you have to hear this dear, but you ought to know the kind of woman she is). Then she says, Well, you ARE full of surprises! I'm impressed!

She says, Obviously you're getting somebody in! and then, smirky smirky—Naughty of you keeping it dark, I haven't seen anybody coming or going.

And does she have to remind me—finger wag wag—all I had to do was ask her for a hand, I needn't have gone to the length of paying someone. I don't answer, just look in her saucepan.

Brought you some soup, she says.

Some soup. Smells of sausages boiled in grass. I make no comment. Wait for her to leave, but no, hands go on hips and speech coming, I can tell. She just wants to help and Ruth wouldn't like to see me like this and no good just giving up and just makes you more miserable hiding yourself away etc.

Still, she says, looking round again, she won't scold anymore, as this is a VERY GOOD START.

I tell her yes, I have got somebody coming in. And I've told you that till I'm blue in the face, I add. And I've told the nurse, I've told all of them including the foreign one, what's her name, something like Clinger but it can't be that. I've been telling you all for weeks somebody's coming in and none of you listen to a word I say.

SHE'S *coming in.* RUTH'S *coming in.*

All I get is her Oh-we've-been-here-before face.

Now look, she says. Don't undo all this good work (waves hand around kitchen like she'd done it herself). Don't keep on with this silly talk. She moves in close and her voice goes quiet (I think it's because she thinks you might hear). Arthur, I'm speaking frankly now. You know this is silly, I know this is silly. But these people are trying to help you and they're getting the idea you're mentally ill. Arthur, you are your own worst enemy.

Ruth, if her and her ilk won't listen, why should I care? It's none of their business. So I tell her that, but does this have desired effect? Oh no, we're off again.

She wants to get off the silly *talk* and back to *sensible talk. If I won't tell her who I've got coming in, how much, may she ask, am I paying her, my mystery cleaner? She says, probably over the odds, because people have no qualms about asking what they think they'll get away with, it's criminal, there are people round here who get away with mur— oh, pardon me, she says. Oh, dear, poor Ruth . . . I didn't mean . . .*

Well? Didn't mean WHAT? *Get away with* MUR??? HAH!! *You tripped yourself up there, Mrs. M!*

She says, Well, clearly I've caught you at an inconvenient time. I'll call for the pan tomorrow.

I go to front door and open it.

I'll say good afternoon then, she says. Good afternoon!

And I'll say fuck off then, I say. Fuck off!

She pretends not to hear.

I know you *heard me, though. You were pretending it wasn't funny. You were trying not to laugh. You never liked the woman, did you?*

———

Still, you might have left a word. On the letter. I'm going to leave all the letters out so you can't miss them. Just add a little note, then we'll really show her.

Arthur

Later: That window cleaner turns up right outside kitchen window, radio on, blaring. That lump of rag he uses is filthy, how's that supposed to get anything clean? Looks like he's wiping the windows with a drowned squirrel.

He's very cheery. Thinks I've forgotten about last time. Shouts at me, am I keeping well? Say nothing, no point wasting words on the likes of him. I walk into conservatory so he gets full view, raincoat plus legs—I point down to my bandages. He says something, makes some gesture I don't get. So I open the door and tell him to fuck off, too. Leave him in no doubt.

PS Should have stayed in bed, going back there now.

PPS Leave me a sign.

―――――

THE COLD AND THE BEAUTY AND THE DARK
1956

Chapter 14: A Month in the Country

"Hurry up, Grace!" Evelyn cried, patting her hands over the surface of the eiderdown, trying to locate her other glove. She had just heard the honk of a car horn from the street outside. "Are you ready, love? It's here, the car's here!"

She found the glove and pulled it on. Her new summer gloves, bought for this special day, were made of some new stretchy fabric, non-wrinkle, fully washable, and, or at least as they had promised her in the shop, gleaming white. Today, Uncle Les was sending a car right to the door that would convey them to the convalescent home where, as he had written in his postcard, he was settling in fine after just a week and already feeling the benefit.

It was so long since Evelyn had been out anywhere that she was as excited as a young girl. When had she last gone for a spin through the countryside? It was years, and that was by bus. The thought of being taken in a private car was almost more excitement than she could bear. She was vague about where exactly Uncle Les's convalescent place was, but that didn't matter. In fact she liked the mystery. It was an extra thrill to feel that only the driver had to know the route. She could just sit back and be taken to her destination, like a duchess! It didn't do any harm to feel like a bit of a swell, once in a blue moon. It was only pretending, and life was ordinary enough the rest of the time for it not to turn her head.

Evelyn's good spirits survived, even when Grace refused to describe the car to her. Was it big and black and shiny, she asked, but Grace would say only that yes it was a car, yes it was big and black, just about all cars were, and as to shiny she hadn't noticed. Inside the car smelled leathery and expensive. When she leaned across and asked Grace in a whisper if the driver was in a uniform, Grace shooshed her impatiently.

They drove in silence. When the sounds of other traffic died away and she knew they were out of town, Evelyn wound down the window for some country air. But she enjoyed it for only a few minutes before Grace complained of the draft.

It was getting on for dinnertime when the car left the road and made its way slowly along gravel and finally came to a stop. The driver jumped out and crunched round to open the passenger door.

"Here you are, ladies, the Maud Braddock Memorial Home for Invalids," he said, handing Evelyn out so gallantly that she felt certain he *was* in uniform, complete with cap.

The air was certainly bracing, just what you would want at a place of convalescence, Evelyn said to herself, breathing it in. It was cool and mossy, and somehow watery, and there seemed to be a lot of it, more than you got in an ordinary lungful of town air. She could hear a fast-flowing stream not far away, and birds high in the sky. But Grace was tramping ahead over the gravel now, and Evelyn followed.

The place seemed half hospital, half hotel, hushed and smelling of floor polish rather than disinfectant. They were greeted in the hall and told that Mr. Hibbert was expecting them, and then they were led into a room so warm Evelyn felt she had stepped into a greenhouse. Indeed she almost had, as Uncle Les, who was waiting there, explained. They had entered a marvelous, newly built glass sun lounge, the last word in luxury, that stretched across one side of the front of the old Edwardian building, originally used as a hunting lodge.

He went on to tell them that the Maud Braddock Memorial Home for Wounded Servicemen had been set up here during the War. Now there was no further use for it in that capacity, and it was now catering to a different clientele altogether, convalescents and invalids who would pay for the best and insist on getting it.

"Like your sun lounge, for instance," Uncle Les said, waving his arm. "Deluxe. No expense spared."

A proper sun trap it was, apparently, where most of the patients lay on reclining chairs surrounded by potted palms for much of the day, basking in the warmth.

"Blowing a gale outside and you could be on the Riviera, lying here," Uncle Les said.

"Don't you want to get out, though, into the fresh air?" Evelyn asked. Uncle Les explained that half an hour out of doors twice a day, morning and afternoon, was as much as he was allowed. Well wrapped up in blankets, he was wheeled along by a nurse and encouraged to walk for five minutes at the beginning and the end of each session. Next week he was going to walk for ten minutes each time, and he was also planning to try the steam bath in the Home's brand-new hydro facilities.

Perhaps once they'd stayed for lunch (and the food was excellent, he assured them), and he'd had his afternoon nap, Grace would be so kind as to do the honors and push him along in his wicker chair for his afternoon constitutional? That's if, Uncle Les said rather tightly, she would deign to honor them with her presence? He'd only glimpsed her at the door, and then she'd disappeared. Where had she got to?

Uncle Les called a nurse and asked if Grace had been seen wandering about anywhere, and might she be informed that her uncle was ready to be her host at luncheon. Evelyn said nothing. She hoped Grace might just have taken herself off outside to explore and go for a walk, since the opportunity to enjoy country air was a rare one for Grace as much as for herself, but still she felt uneasy. Once the nurse had been dispatched to find Mr. Hibbert's mislaid visitor, Uncle Les began telling her, in a low whisper, about some of his fellow patients and Evelyn tried to concentrate, frowning.

Half an hour later, Grace still had not been found. The nurse reported back to them that she thought the lady must have gone for a longer walk, and she would ask the kitchen to keep aside something for her luncheon, which was now about to be served.

But when the meal, braised liver and onions with cabbage, with a glass of milk stout for Les, followed by ginger pudding, was over, there was still no sign of Grace. After coffee, Les was wheeled away for his hour's rest, and Evelyn was invited to sit in the sun lounge.

It was while she was there, feeling the sun on her face through the glass, that the commotion began. The same nurse who had looked for Grace came running in.

"Oh, excuse me, madam!" she began. She seemed not to know what to say next. "Oh, madam, your daughter, she is your daughter, isn't she? Oh, thank goodness you're here. Oh, what a shock! We need to contact her husband at once! Matron doesn't think it's going to be very long!"

Evelyn was mystified. "Why, whatever is the matter? Where is she? She's all right, isn't she? *What* isn't going to be very long?"

"Oh, madam! She's doing fine, it's all going to be fine, though Matron says it's early. The gardener found her in the little summerhouse, we got her indoors at once, of course, lucky there was a room vacant. And Matron's a qualified midwife, thank goodness! Though she's rusty, she says. Of course we've rung for the doctor. But we need to contact her husband to let him know!"

Evelyn sat silent for a moment. "I understand. I see. Yes. Yes, now I understand," she said quietly. "Let's not get hysterical." She paused, thinking. "Her husband can't possibly get here in time. He isn't available," she said firmly, "but we'll deal with that in due course. The main thing is that she's all right. I'm very sorry for this inconvenience, but yes, it *is* lucky she's here. Take me to her, please. It won't be long, you say?"

They walked swiftly into the hall and the nurse began to lead her upstairs. She was nervous and seemed unable to stop talking.

"It's the little room at the top. Quiet. You know, nice and private, right at the back. Well, Matron says that's better, in case there's to be any, you know, commotion. . . . Well, what with the other patients, I mean they're here to rest, aren't they, when all's said and done? There's a nice little fire lit and it's got a nice view of one side of the garden, and—"

Evelyn interrupted her. "Another thing. Please don't wake Mr. Hibbert. There's no need to disturb him. When he's had his rest, would you take him for his walk as usual? I don't want him upset. I'll give him the news later. Afterward."

A little over two hours later, Evelyn sat by Grace's bed holding the almost weightless bundle in her arms. The baby girl was tiny, but healthy. Although about four weeks too soon, it had been a quick and straightforward birth. Just as well, Matron had said tersely to Evelyn, since they weren't equipped for childbirth. And it was a great pity, in her opinion, that the father was working down south and would have to be informed by telegram once the mother had returned to Aldbury, where she had left his address. Then, with a click of her tongue and a murmur that seemed to indicate she was softening, and was perhaps rather proud of having delivered a baby safely, she had left the mother, new daughter, and grandmother alone.

Tears flooded down Evelyn's cheeks as she cradled the new arrival. It was no use, she was never going to know. Grace was too exhausted to be as hostile as usual, but she was refusing point-blank to name the baby's father.

"A baby out of the blue. A beautiful baby and no father to give her his name, it's a scandal," Evelyn said, feeling quite at the end of her tether. "Why didn't you tell me you were in trouble? Wait till your Uncle Les hears. Or does he know and he didn't tell me? Maybe everybody on the street knew you were expecting, everybody but me. Why did nobody say?"

"Nobody knew," Grace said sullenly. "I made sure of that. I didn't hardly show and I'm always behind the counter anyway. I thought I'd have it without folk knowing and get it adopted."

"Without folk knowing? How were you going to manage that?"

Grace sighed. "I don't rightly know," she said. "I was trying not to think about it. Anyway, folk'll have to know now, won't they? Because I'm keeping her. I'm not having her adopted. I'm keeping her and nobody's going to stop me."

There was a silence. "Aye, and I won't try and stop you, lass," Evelyn said gently. "It'll be hard going, mind. And I don't know what your Uncle Les is going to say. I'm warning you he won't like it. He's a respected businessman. He'll get it out of you, who the father is."

"Oh, never you worry. I can handle him," Grace said stoutly. "You leave him to me. *Nobody* is going to stop me keeping my baby."

Just then there was a soft little mewl and a tiny splutter from the baby. Evelyn wiped her eyes and smiled. "All right, then. We'll take one day at a time," she sighed, handing the baby over. "One day at a time."

Grace was right. She could and did handle Uncle Les. By the evening, after she had spoken to him alone, he was quite reconciled to the child's existence and, to Evelyn's further amazement, he accepted that Grace was never going to divulge the father's name. They discussed the matter in the sun lounge over tea while Grace and the baby were asleep upstairs. Matron had spoken to the owners of the Maud Braddock Home and had softened even further. Grace would stay on for another few days before going back to Aldbury, but for now, she needed rest. It was unheard of, a newborn baby at the Maud Braddock, but now that they were getting used to it the staff were enjoying the novelty and word had gone round among the patients, too. It seemed to be giving everyone a lift.

"But, Uncle Les, the fellow's got to face his responsibilities, whoever he is. He's fathered a child," Evelyn said. "Even if he won't marry her he has to take responsibility. It's only right he should provide."

But Uncle Les was very uncomfortable about pursuing the matter any further. "The child will be provided for, never you mind that. Grace is twenty-three, she's a grown woman and if she won't say, she won't say," he said with finality. "So we let it drop. You hear me? Bad for the child otherwise. You need to bring her up so it's natural to her she has her mother's name and no father. Bring her up believing he's dead. She won't know any better. Then she won't hanker after him."

"But—" Evelyn had opened her mouth to protest, thinking how she had never stopped missing the father she barely remembered, but Uncle Les silenced her.

"Nay, there's no more to be said. There's an end to it. It's not to be discussed again in my hearing, or in the child's. Have another scone, they're homemade."

Evelyn drank some of her tea thoughtfully. "It's not just the *father's* name," she said, trying to lighten her voice. "There's the name of the place an' all. Have we to put 'the Maud Braddock Memorial Home for Invalids' as place of birth on the little mite's birth certificate? That'll look peculiar. Whoever heard of a baby getting born in an invalids' home?"

Uncle Les gave a short laugh. "We won't need to. It's not been the Maud Braddock that long. Round here it's still known by the old name. We'll put that. The locals call it Overdale."

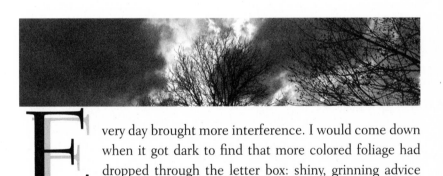

Every day brought more interference. I would come down when it got dark to find that more colored foliage had dropped through the letter box: shiny, grinning advice about hearing aids, time-share apartments, stair lifts, handy "systems" for "maximizing priceless storage space." The downstairs rooms became ragged and spoiled with torn envelopes, unfinished lists, unsigned forms. I would stumble across the paraphernalia of Arthur's leg treatments: towels, open tubes of ointment, bandages and socks left where he had pulled them off. The kitchen filled up with the neighbor's unrecognizable food in plastic containers, with notes attached: HEAT GENTLY, WILL SEPARATE IF BOILED. JUST POP UNDER GRILL TILL BROWNED. Some lumpy homemade biscuits turned up from somewhere along with a brochure about assisted living. Della left a potted plant and more poetry (just the slant of some people's handwriting can arouse fury). One night, stuck on the fridge door under magnets, I found a drawing in crayon of a lady with a halo and wings riding a bicycle, surrounded by clouds and flowers. Underneath was written *"from Amy and all the Watsons (at No. 48)."*

In dealing with these and other invasions I was holding back, I now see, not merely a tide of encroachment but also the notion that any such staying action could be only that, and would prove, in the end, unavailing. By definition, after all, the besieged have nothing more to play for than survival, and quite possibly the demands of that particular game, all the plucky, ingenious, and inconclusive stratagems to hold off ultimate depletion, are what distract us from its futility. So our way of living did not seem to me so frail that its final breach was inevitable, and I turned over in my mind, with no particular urgency, only the wisdom or practicality of this or that small refinement for its protection. I wrote a note discouraging circulars and callers and stuck it on the door. I left the neighbor's food out, untouched, on the front step. I did not consider that perhaps a play for time was all our arrangement was or ever could be; I failed to understand that no matter what I did, by little corrosive steps one person or another would be the first to bring it to an absolute end.

Ignoring every portent, I was attuned only to what seemed significant: the watchful and desirous duet between Arthur and me. After all, it was all we needed, and was surely its own fluent justification—though no justification was owed to anyone—for the simple necessity of two, the impossibility of more than two.

Dear Ruth

The baby, Ruth. The baby in the story. What happens to the baby girl?

It's nice having you around again. I wouldn't say I'm relaxed about it, it takes some getting used to. DOES NOT HELP, *does it, these fools popping up. I can understand why you make yourself scarce in daytime. Why* WE *do. I can't avoid them altogether because of legs. Keeping curtains closed sends out the general message though.*

Apart from only being around at night, you haven't come back in what one might call the standard ways, have you? You're not what anyone could call your average haunter. You're not scary or tragic, not even mildly SPOOKY, *to use a Della word.*

In fact, you don't seem all that deceased. You're pretty much as you were. Practical, comfortable, always got something to do. Not saying anything—that's the only big difference, apart from the fact that I can't see you, not in the old way.

Though on subject of seeing and not seeing, this story. I'm getting on well with it now. I keep thinking about that baby.

What I wonder is would you have shown it to me? I mean if circumstances were otherwise, in the ordinary way? Doesn't really matter because you have shown it to me, now. You directed me to it. And I know you're pleased that I'm reading it.

I like this new way. I like US *this way, suits us better than the old way.*

More soon. I even like writing to you, now. I like writing to you when I can hear you around the place and I know you're nearby, downstairs or in the next room or along the landing.

Arthur

I t came, inevitably. It came when we felt safest, on a calm, honey-warm early September night. The doorbell rang. As was our custom, Arthur was upstairs and I was in the kitchen, just starting to think about getting his dinner. Neither of us moved.

The bell rang again and went on ringing. Then came a series of bangs on the door and a man's voice. He sounded a bit drunk.

"Hey! Can you put a light on? Come on, Arthur, I need to talk!" He pressed on the bell again, and then we heard another voice.

"Tony, leave him alone, it doesn't matter! Tony, leave him alone!"

"I'm not leaving him alone, it's for his own good! He got a fucking invitation! Hey, Arthur!" The voice dropped to a placatory, treacherous singsong. "Come on, mate, barbie time! You gonna come and enjoy yourself or what?"

"Tony! Stop it, please—"

"Tell you what, Arthur, I got a drink right here for you. Get you in the mood, mate. Come on, s'only us and a few friendly faces, what's your problem?"

"Oh, Tony—have some consideration!"

"Wha's the matter? Look, Mum, does he or doesn't he need a firm hand? I'm only doing what you said!"

"I didn't say bully him! Leave him alone!"

The ringing and banging subsided and eventually stopped. Then the bell sounded again, tentatively, and above it came the woman's voice again.

"Arthur, it's me, Rosemary. Mrs. M! It's all right, Arthur, don't worry. He doesn't mean any harm. It's only Tony. Arthur? Arthur!"

He was still upstairs. The voice became wheedling. I began to tremble.

"Arthur, would you open the door a minute, dear? I'm so sorry, he didn't mean it. He wants to say sorry. Arthur, could you please come to the door?"

The man's voice added, "Yeah, sorry, mate, didn't mean no offense. OK?"

Arthur didn't stir.

"Arthur, it's Rosemary. I can't go till I know you're all right."

The man called, "OK, so how about you put a light on, Arthur? Show us you're okay, mate. OK?"

Only a few feet lay between us and the front door. Those people were just on the other side of it. If Arthur didn't go down to them they could burst through it and be upon us in seconds, yelling and cajoling, pulling him around. Suddenly I saw that all my efforts to protect us had been pointless. In the end, doors and locks and walls stand for nothing and against nothing. They are only the weakest of defenses against any purpose, including urgent and violent goodwill.

I stood with a tea towel in my hand, straining to hear above the shunk of the washing machine behind me and the hammering of my heart in my throat. Then I heard Arthur's tread at the top of the stairs. Without thinking about it, I knew the best way to protect him. I ran out to the conservatory and through the sliding door into the dining room. The door from there out to the hall was closed; I opened it a fraction and pressed close against the wall. Through the gap I could see the outline of Arthur's body, halted on the stairs. Shapes moved under the porch and shadows dappled the hall floor. The woman's voice came at us again.

"Arthur, I have your spare key here, dear. I'm coming in, all right? Just to see you're all right. It's just me and Tony. Tony's with me, we just want to see you're all right."

I heard Arthur whimper as the lock turned. Feet clumped across the threshold, lights flashed on. They were in the hall, just out of my sight line. Arthur had slumped down on the stairs.

"Arthur? Oh, Tony didn't mean any harm. Did you, Tony? He just wondered why you didn't answer our invitation."

I pushed the tea towel against my mouth to stop myself from screaming. Arthur pulled himself up and came unsteadily downstairs.

"Here you go, mate. Lager OK for you?" I heard the snap and hiss of a can. "Oops! There you go then. Get that down you. Do you good."

Arthur cleared his throat, giving up an attempt to protest. He had his back to me and I fancy I saw him retreat from them, inclining a little in my direction, to protect me, to explain to me perhaps that he was accepting the drink just to stall them there. He had to submit to their interest in him, not so far as to encourage them to think themselves welcome, but enough to get them to leave with both neighborly impulses, prurience and conscience, satisfied.

"Thing is," Tony said, "Mum's just trying to help. She's done this whole barbecue, see? And bugger me, there's all of us in the garden over there just trying to be friendly and you don't turn up. Not very polite, mate."

"Barbecue?" Arthur's voice sounded tight with confusion. "What do I want with a barbecue? I don't know anything about any bloody barbecue!"

"I did tell you, Arthur," the woman said. "We said it'd be good for you to see a few of the neighbors. You agreed. There were proper invitations, dear."

"I'm busy. Sometimes things slip my mind."

"But I wrote it all down. You said you'd come."

A few days ago there had been a handwritten card with a drawing of a smoking hamburger and a glass of wine on it. I'd torn it up.

"Mum's gone to a lot of trouble. It's a lot of work, a barbecue. Hey, mate, you OK?"

Arthur had started to sway on his feet, probably because he'd just tipped his head back to swig some of his drink. I saw him grope for the banister and the can fell from his hand. Tony marched forward and grabbed him and Mrs. M let out a wail. "The carpet!"

"Whoa, there! OK, mate, let's get you sat down," Tony said.

"Leave me alone!" Arthur said, recoiling. "Don't touch me! I just got light-headed for a second. Slight loss of balance. Comes and goes."

"Need a decent meal, I'd say. You *know* you're naughty." Mrs. M swung past Arthur toward the kitchen. "Where's there a bucket, dear—under the sink?" He stared after her, ignoring Tony's arm going round his shoulder. She called out over the sound of the taps, "Shouldn't stain if I get straight at it. I can pop over for my stain remover if you haven't any."

Of course we had stain remover. She returned, sank down on the carpet between Tony and Arthur, and began dabbing with a sponge.

"Went to your head, probably," Tony said with forced cheerfulness. "Sure you're OK?"

"Yes. Yes, thank you," Arthur said, stepping out of Mrs. M's path. "I'm all right now."

"She's got a point, though. You need a steak inside you," Tony said. "Red meat, nothing like it. Sets you up. I'm the same."

"He is," Mrs. M grunted from the carpet. "Always has been. I mean, don't ever give him chicken," she said, "because he won't thank you for it." She got to her feet. "As for fish, practically a dirty word. Well! That won't take long to dry. Fingers crossed. Sensible color for a hall. Is it 'Sahara'?"

I imagined Arthur staring at her and trying to puzzle out what on earth she was talking about. I realized I didn't really know what his eyes looked like. There was a silence. Then Tony said, "There's a few still over there, in the garden."

"Yes, you want to be getting back to your guests," Arthur said.

"Well..." Mrs. M sighed. "It doesn't seem right. Wouldn't you like someone to be with you?"

Tony took Arthur's elbow and gave it a shake. "Tell you what, Arthur, why not come on over now? Get another beer. There's plenty left. You could use a burger."

She joined in. "Go on. There's peach pavlova. Just for a while."

"I'm in my slippers."

"Don't matter just to cross the road. Tell you the truth, mate, I don't feel right leaving you," Tony said. "Neither does Mum."

"Thank you. Well, that is kind," Arthur said. I could tell from his voice he wanted to refuse, but then they might not leave; they were wrangling, disruptive, insistent people, ready to trample wherever they liked. "Very kind indeed. Thank you."

This pleased them. They led him away, one at each elbow, and he went quietly.

Dear Ruth

Where's the rest of it? The story. What happens to the baby? I want to know what happens to the baby.

I like it now, thinking about the early days.

I should have put a bit more effort into getting the point of the poetry and I'm sorry for that. This seems like a second chance.

I've been thinking. More comes back about Overdale the more I think. That first night. We lay there looking up at the stars, didn't we? It was so clear and so cold, and by then I had my arms tight around you trying to keep you warm.

I remember pointing out some of the constellations. You only knew the Plow. It was after I'd shown you how to spot the Great Bear and the Little Bear and was just moving on to Orion and Andromeda, and you suddenly told me to stop talking and close my eyes. Why, I said, I like looking at the stars, don't you?

Yes, you said, but you also liked closing your eyes and not seeing them but knowing they were still there. And when we were lying like that, eyes closed, you said, can't you just feel where we are? Can't you just feel the size of the mountain around you and the sky above and just feel the millions of millions of gallons of water flowing through the reservoir down below? Technically speaking Kinder Scout isn't a mountain and the water in a reservoir doesn't flow, it's stagnant, I said, and you punched me in the chest and told me to shut up. Playfully.

I want to live here, you said. I want to live on a hillside somewhere, surrounded by higher hills and mountains and with water at the bottom. I want to hear the wind on the mountaintops and the water lapping down below every minute of every day and all night long.

Of course I went along with all that. I said I'd like to live on a hillside, too, and just then I meant it. But I wasn't thinking only about living. I was so happy at that moment that the thought of death suddenly came to me. That's to say I allowed it to come, because I felt so free and strong that I didn't need to keep it away—I knew it could not pin me down and make me feel ordinary and discouraged, just then. I thought—I could die at this moment. If I died on this hillside right now, I'd die with my life well spent (though I was glad I didn't).

But if I had, I'd have died knowing all I needed to know—that I loved you completely, and that I was holding in my arms, wrapped up against the cold, all that was, or ever could be necessary to me now.

Arthur

I hadn't seen before that he can barely walk. In the house it doesn't show so much. I was watching from the bedroom window and I saw them come back across the road and up the drive, Arthur's feet edging along in little shuffles, his back bent. Tony, with professional tenderness for the slow and sick, was supporting him by the elbow, taking it slow and letting him rest every few steps. When they paused Arthur would look up and gaze ahead as if the house and I were miles distant and he would reach us only by the greatest exertion.

As they came through the door Tony snapped on the switches. In the burst of light Arthur vomited, suddenly and lavishly, on the floor. The sour, curdy stench rose instantly through the hall and up into the darkness of the stairs. I had come out to stand on the top step, and I craned forward just far enough to see him being steered, groaning and stumbling, toward the kitchen. I wanted to dash straight down but I didn't; I would be needed later, and only then would I be of real use.

Tony returned and cleaned up the mess, his scrubbing brisk and ill-tempered. When he went back into the kitchen I crept a little farther down the stairs, and listened. I could hear snatches of Tony's voice saying something to do with "doctor" and "urgent attention" and "tomorrow," but I couldn't make out Arthur's replies. Then Tony spoke sharply. Arthur, he said, wasn't being very cooperative.

"You're not doing yourself any favors, mate," he said. "Maybe it's time you accepted some help." He paused. "Look, I know what you're going through. Loss of spouse, it's bloody awful. I see it all the time. And it's worse for you. Everybody knows . . ."

Arthur began to shout. "You know nothing! You have no idea, you hear me? Nobody knows what this is like!".

"Hey, hey there! OK, OK—I'm sorry, I put that the wrong way. Look, steady on now," Tony said. "It's OK. It's understandable . . ."

Again Arthur interrupted. "Why don't any of you listen? I don't *care* if it's understandable! I'm going to kill the bastard! You hear? Some fucking bastard took her away and none of you do anything about *that,* do you? You're useless, the police are useless. You're all fucking *useless!*"

"Look, hold on a minute. I can see why you feel that way, honest I can. But the police are doing their best. They might still get him. We're all doing our best, mate."

"So bloody what? That bastard's going to get what's coming to him. I'm going to get him myself and strangle him with my own bare hands, it's the only way to get justice in this bloody country! Now leave me alone, will you? Fuck off and leave me alone!"

As the kitchen door opened I darted back upstairs into the darkness. Tony came out and paused in the hall, blowing out his cheeks.

He rubbed at the carpet with his foot, turned back for a moment as if he had one last thing to say, but thought better of it and left.

A few minutes later Arthur appeared. He raised his head in my direction but I don't know what he saw. He fumbled along the wall and switched out the lights in the hall. He seemed to have aged. I ventured down far enough to see his outline against the street lamps' aura from the door but I remained in the shadow of the turn of the stairs and did not move. Then, in the dark, he called for me in a breaking, plangent voice—*Ruth!*

That was all. We both listened to the sound of it dying on the air. He called again. I didn't go to him. He was sending out the name like a flare. He was experimenting, testing the house Ruth had arranged and kept for half her life to see if it would withstand the speaking of her name, if the sound of its one syllable wafting through the darkness to the edges of the walls and curving back would lapse and cease eventually, or would prove restless, an unruly echo roused easily from the corners. The quiescent, returning silence was like watching a white curtain fall back to stillness after the air has been disturbed.

He had called out for me at last.

Still I didn't go to him. I stayed in the dark of the stairwell, unable to move. Arthur swayed across the hall below me and disappeared into the kitchen. I guessed he had gone out to sit in the conservatory. I slumped down on the stairs, leaned my head against the wall, and waited.

After a while he returned, clutching the letter. He dropped it on the floor, looked up, called my name again, and shuffled away. The borrowed light in the hall was somehow absorbent; he seemed to be sinking and losing form in a way that might be irretrievable. I hurried down and read what he'd written in the glow from the street lamp.

Dear Ruth

I've called for you and you won't come, but I know you're still here. I know you're still here.

I have to talk to you. TALK.
PLEASE ANSWER.
It's all up. Done with.
Still you're not answering—you're here, aren't you?
We've got to do something.
Ruth, they'll be back in the morning.

The Tony fellow. I hadn't got my bandages on, that was the start of it. I was minding my own business, getting through a burnt sausage in a bun. Was perched on their swinging garden seat thing so ankles on display, and T leans forward, grabs my trouser bottom, pulls it back, and says AHA! *As if finding a leg inside a pair of trousers required some special brilliance.*

Thought so! Chronic ulceration!
Very officious.
There's your National Health Service for you!
You know the way people get offended when they find out something they think you should have told them? Especially when it's none of their business?
I tried to stand up for myself but it was no good.
Chronic ulceration! he says again, meaning "I'm the medical expert round here and don't you forget it." Here's a condition directly related to personal care and nutrition and what's the Primary Care Trust's answer to that!

He was the only one not embarrassed. Even Mrs. M (she of elephant hide) said, Now Tony, Arthur's here for a nice quiet time, you leave him alone.

Which didn't shut him up.

Bloody PCT hasn't bloody got one, that's my point! Look at the poor bugger!

Then even HE *knew he'd said enough. Mrs. M starts flapping around offering people more of everything. The women start making stupid remarks in big surprised voices, mainly about the food—you'd think Mrs. M invented potato salad. Tony leans in and says, Sorry about that, mate, but I'm not letting this go, we're gonna get you taken care of, right?*

Other people still milling around, laughing too much. I just ate my pudding and took no notice. You were the one for the small talk and the laughing. Mrs. M gave me a second helping of peach pavlova and when I'd finished everybody had gone. The Great Tony insisted on walking me back over.

You saw.

Ruth, where are you?

And then I was sick in the hall. Too much excitement, I suppose, not used to rich puddings. Tony cleaned up.

But I WOULD NOT LET HIM *help me upstairs and* I LEFT HIM IN NO DOUBT *that I could get into pajamas unaided—did not reveal that I have no need of pajamas as am generally up and about while others are snoring their heads off.*

But Tony says he'll be back over again first thing and he's going to phone the doctor and get something done. He says he'll be making a strong case for hospitalization because I'm deteriorating, and if the doctor doesn't visit and arrange it ASAP he'll call an ambulance personally. Or he'll get me into an ER himself even if it means picking me up bodily and shoving me in the back of his car.

We've got to do something. Nobody listens to me and they'll take me away again.

I can't leave you again. We've got to stay together.

You'd have liked that pavlova. Wish you were around more.

We have got to do something.

With love

A.

So I went to him at last.

He was rocking to and fro in an armchair. I kneeled down and pulled his hands away from his face, and closed his arms around me. He wept, and clasped my head against his neck. I could taste his tears and feel the loose, mulchy lips and his cheeks, so flimsy against the faintly rotten flaps of his mouth and the chipped bones of teeth. I embraced him as was my due and my right. I kissed his face and head, I pressed my mouth against the salty hide of his neck and chin, the skin flaking and wrinkling like cloth over gristly bones, over transparent veins and blood vessels like pulled threads. I

breathed him in as if I were swallowing all the minute ebbings of fluids, the smells of wax and little trapped signs of age and illness, the
thinning muscle that would one day slough and fail.

We said nothing. After a while his weeping subsided, and in one
movement I drew away, took his hand, and led him upstairs. In the
bedroom we arranged ourselves as if resuming a lifelong pattern after a
period of abstinence or absence. I took him to his side of the bed and
settled him on the pillows with a single kiss and a stroke of his hair. He
smoothed the sheet for me and turned and smiled as I got in. I
watched him fall asleep and then I lay awake thinking, trying to still my
breathing.

I let them form, the thoughts that are born of the middle hours of
the night, I let them grow firm and real in my mind and become the
plan for what I realized was now the only possible course of action
against our circumstances. Everything had been leading to this, though
nothing had prepared us for it, but no matter; it was as if we were making our way into an obscuring white mist that would disperse before us
and show the way ahead. I could see that our path had been there all
the time, merely hidden.

Before it was light I got up. First I climbed the ladder to the attic.
Apart from the nest of dusty curtains where I had been sleeping, there
was hardly a space not strewn with rubbish: papers, books, journals
baled and tied with hemp string, plastic binders of *Reader's Digest* and
National Geographic, but mainly notebooks and photographs and loose
typed sheets, covered with crossings-out and annotations. I was
pleased that Arthur, in all his rummaging and ransacking up here, had
not had the strength to dislodge the heavy things. There was furniture:
a kidney-shaped coffee table set upside down, its spindly gold legs
splayed like antennae, a chair half recaned, two dismantled beds
whose slats, poles, and headboards lay sloping in against the roof
beams. Everything was threaded together by wispy brown loops of cob-
webs. I also found, stashed behind a bundle of tied tent poles, more
than I had hoped for: a mattress with rusty-edged stains, and shaded
with what looked like charcoal or soot. I cleared the books and papers

off the floor with the edge of my foot and shoved them into heaps against the walls, then I hauled the mattress onto the floor. It fell with a *whump*, raising a cloud of its own sticky dust that smelled of dead grass and feathers and dried blood.

I went back to the spare room and collected bedding, which I pushed up the ladder ahead of me. I returned to the kitchen and made sandwiches and two flasks of tea. I found a jar for milk, and filled a large plastic jug with water. All these I carried up the ladder and set neatly next to the mattress. I got cups and plates and paper napkins, biscuits and fruit to go up, too. We could have nothing hot to eat, I had decided, in case the smell carried. I liked to give Arthur a hot meal every night, but he would miss it only this once. As soon as it was dark again we'd be on our way.

There was one other practical consideration that could not be ignored. I brought out the largest bucket from under the sink, emptied half a bottle of disinfectant into it, and added some water. I got the bucket up the ladder and set it in a corner behind as discreet a screen as I could devise from stacked boxes and an upended decorating table.

It was now after five o'clock and the sky was yellow. Birds were already screeching. The new day was burning the condensation off the skylight and soon would be reaching in and pasting the mattress with a rectangle of buttery sunshine. I pulled one of the old curtains from the pile of carpet scraps and burlap and underlays, and rigged it up against the glass, wedging it in tight. It was patterned in red and yellow and green; light shone through and cast glowing jewels across our bed. Suddenly I feared that Arthur might wake and find me gone, so I hurried back down.

He was asleep on his back. My entering the room roused him. At once his eyes were upon me, searching and finding, and they closed again.

Ruth? he said, though he seemed still asleep. Ruth, Ruth. I whispered to him that it was time to wake up. His eyes opened, and closed again. His mouth wriggled and settled into a thin pout.

Come on, I said. Wake up. It's time. I pushed the bedclothes back.

He turned over, gathering what was left of sleep tight into himself. I stroked his arm and gave his earlobe a little pinch.

Wake up, Arthur, I said. It's time.

I pulled his feet to the floor and drew him upright but he kept his eyes closed, and when I let go he sank back into the pillows. To the east on the other side of the house the sun was almost risen; through this eclipsed window the light had begun to gleam sullenly.

Arthur, wake up! Come on, it's time to go.

He didn't say anything or even open his eyes, but he allowed me to help him up again until he was sitting on the bed. I found his slippers and fitted them over his feet, as stiff and gray as dead flounders. There was a delta of purple veins reaching across both of his ankles. I pulled him up by the hands and he stood swaying and unquestioning as if he'd given up all resistance and all sensation in his desire to stay asleep. When I led him along the landing and indicated the attic ladder, he went on ahead of me without haste or curiosity. By the time I had drawn the ladder up after us and dropped the trapdoor in place he had crawled onto the mattress and was lying curled and still.

I expected Tony to be a man of eager habits and that we would not have long to wait. It was still early when I heard the doorbell. I waited for some other sound, fearing something rushing and cataclysmic, some rapacious incursion, but at first there was nothing, not even the key in the lock. Then came the sounds of Tony and his mother talking and moving, it seemed casually and at random, through the house: feet on the stairs, opening doors, calling from one room to another. By degrees, voices were raised and grew urgent.

Have you checked the bathroom? See if he's got stuck.

Wait. Look in there.

Arthur! Oh, God, where's he got to?

I'll try the garden.

Maybe he's had a fall.

Go and check the bedrooms again. Check the sides, in case he's fallen out.

The sounds receded for a while but I knew the two of them were still there. They would be thorough. Even after they had finished searching, they would not leave. They might check the hospitals to see if somehow Arthur had been transported away in the night. They would probably call the police. We had hours still to wait.

I did not dare move for fear of the floor creaking. I watched Arthur, praying he would go on sleeping, but he shifted and turned, groaned and woke up. For a wild second or two after his eyes focused, he didn't know where he was. I leaned across, smoothed the side of his face with my hand and quieted him with a finger to my lips. I pointed downward and pressed the finger to my lips again, and then placed it gently on his lips.

He nodded. Nosey parkers, he whispered.

They can't stay forever, I said. They'll go soon.

Then it'll be just us, he said, smiling.

I reached for his hand. It felt dry and loose as if his finger bones were afloat in a paper glove.

Around us the attic air grew gray and silky, and the sounds of voices and movement resumed in a dreamy way and swam like warm dust in the ether. Later, there were new voices and more footsteps, and the searching began again. All this was progressing at a time when we were used to sleeping and so we listened only half awake, half dreaming, to these warnings we didn't need, that below us, another day had got people in its crass and ruthless grip and was propelling them through the hours, using them up with things that didn't matter. We listened, and waited, and rested together untouchable, answerable only to each other.

A ll is quiet. Arthur is turned away from me, on his side. Now and again his hand flutters on his hip and a soft whistle or scraping noise emerges from his throat. I lie awake in the stained glow through the curtained glass and think of the shimmering sky and the surface of life beyond the strange warm altar of our mattress. Around me the air ripens with heat, and atoms of dust spin and glitter in it, and I sense a thousand secret quickenings in our attic universe of abandoned things and all their gummy folds and crannies and crumbling fibers, all the microscopic barbs of disintegrating matter on which the tiniest living things will catch and cling. Below me the house sighs with solitary, daylong weariness.

So we sleep, or wake and lie looking at the slopes of the roof, and turn to each other sometimes, and twice we stir ourselves as if by agreement and sit up and eat together, shyly at first and then with the silent, slight formality of people accustomed to sharing food but a little reticent and tongue-tied about the sharing of pleasure.

Arthur and Ruth conduct themselves over their meals with the same good manners that would attend all their mutual habits, with a decorum that, whether governed by constraint or by orchestration, is certainly consensual. She unpacks everything and arranges it on the mattress. He looks to her to preside. He waits while she chooses what he is to have and passes it to him. He starts to eat before she has arranged food for herself, this being a picnic after all, but he waits until she has finished before he judges it not inconvenient for her to provide him with what he wants next. He points to this and that—another sandwich, a tomato, a cracker with cheese—and eats them in that order. At the right moment he leans across and takes charge of the flask and cups. His fingers cannot grip properly. He brushes his hands across his chest several times and shakes them and blows on them to get rid of the pins and needles, and tries again to unscrew the top. He can't see to pour properly, either, and a considerable amount of tea falls on the mattress and wets his clothes, which he dabs with a napkin. I am watching anxiously but I don't interfere, any more than Ruth would step forward and relieve a tremulous priest of the Communion cup and bless the wine herself.

We sleep again, and later I wake to a darkness that presses on my eyes. Even though I think Arthur is still asleep I whisper to him to lie still until I come back. I clamber over the floor, lift the trapdoor, and send the ladder down on its squealing metal slope to the landing. I hear the thud as the feet hit the carpet but I can't see anything clearly. I wait for a moment before launching myself down, each tread heaving a creaky sigh. From the bedroom window I see that lights are on in most of the houses in the road. It's not nearly as late as it seemed to be in the attic. The sky is a milky violet and the trees along the avenue are restless in a breeze. A few doors down a woman comes out with a watering can for the hanging basket on her porch. A young man walks past under a lamppost, hands pushed hard into the pockets of his short jacket. Mrs. M has not drawn her curtains.

By now I can work well enough in the dark. I start to search out heavy warm things. Ruth of course keeps a methodical eye on the storage of clothing and when I reach deep into the shelves in the spare bedroom wardrobe I find paired thick socks, woolen sweaters put away for the summer, and winter blankets folded in plastic bags. I pack as if we were about to depart for another time and season which, in truth, we are; perhaps something different, something tenuous and icy and autumnal, has entered the wind tonight.

Arthur doesn't wait for me. I hear him lurching down the ladder and meet him on the landing. Down here, he looks worse. His hair is swirled and matted as if he's been half drowned. When I approach and press my lips to his cheek, he trembles, and his skin is sweaty and sharp with salt and a trace of vomit. His mouth harbors a sour, fly-blown smell and would be dark and sticky inside. One of his eyes wants to close. He wants to speak, I think, but he has trouble controlling his tongue and so lifts a hand into the air instead. He is listing a little to one side and stays on his feet as if standing up were a painfully achieved trick of balance.

But he nods at me and turns away to the spare room and soon I hear him paddling around among books and papers. He comes out with an untidy bundle and holds it out to me, mumbling. A string of saliva wets his bottom lip and descends in a slow cascade to his chest. He wipes at it with the papers in his hands and that's when I see that he's holding pages of maps, and when I take them from him I discover there's also a battered paper folder.

He manages to say, Just to be on the safe side.

The folder is labeled Group Leaders Information Pack: Overdale Outdoor Education Center. I open it and find a mass of photocopied drawings of birds waiting to be colored in, some homemade booklets, loose pages, and stapled sheets. Arthur starts sifting through it all. He lifts out a sheet headed *Directions to Overdale* and waves it at me. I close the folder and hand it back to him.

Arthur moves off down the stairs. He hasn't finished; I hear his feet sifting through the papers littering the hall and sitting room. When I've finished packing I follow, bumping the luggage down the stairs. There is a note for us in the kitchen. I find it on the floor; it must have been swept off the table in a draft from the door.

> ARTHER
> PHONE ME WHEN YOU GET THIS (07834 793922) OR BETTER COME AND KNOCK ON MY DOOR, I'LL BE IN.
> V worried to know you are alright. Couldn't find you and doctor wasn't notified so Tony called police. They sent someone but as no sign of forced entry they can't do anything. Told them you NEVER go out but they say adults entitled to leave own home without notice and to wait another 24 hours. Tried to make doctor talk to them re yr mobility, legs etc. but no go. Well later on nurse turned up for yr legs, she said not to worry as it's not Alzhimers, you're a bit confused but still independent, also they've been encouraging you to get out so you probably have.
> ARTHUR WE WANT TO KNOW YOU'RE ALRIGHT, IT WILL WASTE POLICE TIME IF YOU DON'T LET US KNOW, I'M SUPPOSED TO LET THEM KNOW IF YOUR STILL AWAY BY TOMORROW. WILL KEEP EYE OUT FOR YOU.
> HOPING YOUR ALRIGHT Rosemary (Mrs. M)

Arthur has nodded off, waiting for me in the conservatory. While I was packing he has been round the house collecting up more papers, and now he sits with them clutched against his chest; clearly he won't be parted from them. Even asleep he looks fierce, like a little boy ready to put up a fight if the adults try to say it isn't sensible to bring his stamp album to the seaside.

I've never touched the car keys but I know they're hanging on the line of hooks just inside the kitchen door. We leave by the conservatory and enter the garage from the back garden. There's an old-fashioned mechanical smell of oil and linseed and rags and grass. When I've loaded the trunk Arthur lets me help him into the passenger seat. There isn't enough room to open the door properly and several parts of his body encumber him. His left leg is uncooperative; once he is seated half in, sideways, he drags it after himself as if it were made of wood. The shin scrapes slow and hard against the door edge and his foot flaps about uselessly, but he doesn't flinch.

I'm trying to think methodically. The car hasn't been driven for months. What if it won't start? I climb in and turn the ignition, and it does. With the engine running, I get out again and open each of the garage doors as quietly as I can. But the bottom of the first one screeches in its worn semicircle in the tar of the drive, loud enough, possibly, for people to hear. Now there is no time to waste. I don't bother fiddling with the hooks and brackets in the ground that hold the doors open, so I shove them back as far as they'll go and throw myself back into the driver's seat. Before I can move forward they are already shuddering and swinging back on us but there's nothing I can do about that now. Our departure is announced by two loud *thwacks* as the garage doors glance off the sides of the car. All I can do is keep going. I drag the gear lever into second, then third, and we roar off the drive, straight toward the garbage can that's standing at the far end, slap bang in the middle under the trees. Those bastards. I forgot today was garbage day. It's too late to stop and move it, and it's also far too late to miss it. My hands turn numb and over it goes with a bang. The car veers into the wall with a horrible rasping noise but I grip the wheel and swing us past the splintered can and pell-mell into the avenue. My left-hand turn is more of a swerve and isn't tight enough, so we clip the side of a car parked invisibly on the far side of the road; the other thing I've forgotten is to put headlights on. I can't slow down to find where the switch is, so we have to lurch along for now, avoiding obstacles if possible. The trick is to keep going. Arthur tips back his head and lets out a whoop that scratches his throat and turns into a fit of coughing. He stamps his feet on the floor and turns to me with a mad spark in his eyes. Then he starts to clap one hand down against the other that lies dead in his lap.

Four hours later we drive into the canopied artificial daylight of a service station on the M6. As I fill up the tank I study the docile shuffling of people inside, queuing at the registers and swaying among the shelves and cabinets. I wonder that they seem unembarrassed to be so lumpy and dark and heavy in a place so garish and streamlined. They appear quite undisturbed by the lights, and I want to learn how they do it so that I will look, when the time comes for me to go in, not as though I belong there (because none of them manages that) but just enough like one of them to pass without notice.

But before I'm ready, Arthur is wheezing his way out of the car. He needs a bathroom, he says, and sets off across the forecourt in a bizarrely careful way as if he thinks he is elsewhere, perhaps walking sideways down a flight of stairs. He's lost one of his slippers. I retrieve it from the foot-well of the car and catch up with him at the entrance and we go in together. He halts, flinching, overawed by the piped music and excruciating light. He seems about to collapse under the glare. The toilets are at the back. Once I've got his slipper back on I steer him across the floor, concentrating on finding the shortest route between the stands of magazines and banks of candy and bins of DVDs and thermos flasks on special offer. Through the music and the plopping of the cash registers I sense people in mid-transaction going quiet and turning their eyes on us, but maybe I am only imagining it.

I push Arthur in the direction of his place and take myself to the ladies' room. There's a long mirror at the entrance that I can't avoid, and that's when I realize I probably wasn't imagining that people were staring. I haven't seen my own reflection in a while. I've changed. My face has puckered and turned a bready white, and my eyes are different, too, both faded and darkened. Rings have appeared around the irises, which are now a filmy watercolor blue. The pupils are sunk and tiny, like punctured holes. My mouth has the clamped, institutional look of someone whose incarceration, wherever it is, is chronic but no longer open to question, like a sanatorium patient or a life prisoner. Most dramatic though, is my hair. It's grown, of course, and looks like gray, drought-stricken grass, but I hadn't realized how flatly it sticks to my skull or how it sprouts up at the ends for being left unbrushed. The clothes could be better, too. They are plain enough and should not attract attention in themselves, but I am now aware my proportions have changed. The trousers flap at half-mast and the sweater seems empty in front and the sleeves hang over my hands to my fingertips. I see that I am wearing earrings, and the very idea of a surface such as mine being decorated in any way is preposterous. And being indoors so much has made me careless about footwear; the sandals don't fit and never would have fitted, and the brown socks practical enough for an evening in the house seem here both to demand and to defy explanation.

Arthur's getup, as I notice when I come out and find him leaning for support on the plastic dome of a pay phone bolted to the wall, is filthy. In this light I see that his purple sweatshirt with *Let's Cruise* emblazoned on the chest is crisscrossed with stains from our picnic in the attic, and his trousers are spotted with the dribbles and spills of innumerable little accidents of one kind or another.

His free hand is fumbling with his trouser front and he's oblivious to all else. I grab his other hand and pull him away, and he sets his eyes firmly on his feet and concentrates on getting them to move. We're conspicuously slow. The attention we're attracting is unmistakable now, and all I want is to get us through the door and back into darkness where the car is waiting. I'm trying unsuccessfully not to drag Arthur faster than he can go. We very nearly make it.

Hey!

I look up and see that the boy in the red T-shirt behind the register is talking to us. He has cinnamon skin and lustrous eyes. He can't mean any harm.

Yes, what? I say pleasantly.

'Scuse me a minute!

Now the whole queue is turning to look at us—why? We're not doing anything wrong, I know that, so the best thing we can do is ignore them. I grip Arthur's arm and tug at him so hard he nearly falls over, but I have to get us out of this place.

The boy glances over his shoulder and calls into a little office behind the counter. Another man in a red T-shirt appears and swiftly crosses the floor in front of us. When he's in position between us and the door, the boy speaks again. His eyes gleam like wet plums.

'Scuse me, madam, these premises are protected by surveillance cameras. I have to inform you that you and your car—

What? What's the matter?

He pats a few computer keys and his machine makes some pucking and scratching noises.

I have to inform you that you have been recorded on the company's
CCTV security equipment getting gas. Pump number 8, right? That's
twenty-six pounds eighty-seven, please. The company operates a strict
zero tolerance policy with regards to nonpayment. Cash or credit,
madam?

I simply forgot. It's an honest error made in a moment of absent-
mindedness, brought on, no doubt, by the strain of events. In my past
life, if such a thing was ever to happen, that's what I would have been
assumed to be: honest and absentminded. Now I look like a thief.
They think I'm a thief, and suddenly I feel like one, so how can I do
otherwise than act like one? I thrust the money over as if I were paying
a fine. I don't say anything; if I try to explain I just made a mistake I'll
sound like a liar, then they'll think I'm a liar as well as a thief. But saying nothing makes me seem stealthy and even more guilty; it's confusing me, being both exposed like this and wrongly accused, and my
confusion, too, looks like guilt. I try an apologetic smile but that must
look guilty, too, because the boy's glare shifts from me only long
enough to exchange a knowing look with his colleague. Arthur is shaking.

We make it out the door and back to the car. As we drive away it
strikes me I've made another mistake. We'll have to stop again. I should
have bought food there. If I had, I wouldn't have been able to forget
about paying for the gas. Now we've got next to nothing to eat and I
can't let Arthur starve. I am more unnerved than I can say; the thought
of braving such a place again fills me with absolute dread.

We drive for many hours. At around three o'clock in the morning we leave the motorway, and immediately the rushing in my brain eases. Arthur's head is lolling back, and as I turn up the exit ramp and steer around the roundabout, it tips and rolls and he wakes up. Just off the junction there's a long lay-by with a couple of parked lorries and at the very end a food van, lit and open. I pull over and stop. Arthur staggers out and pees against a tree while I buy four of everything: burgers, sausages, bacon rolls, kebabs, chips—enough to keep us going for a while, appetizing or not, stone cold or not.

For the rest of the journey we are traveling into the light. Arthur is cheerful now. He fishes out various maps and points all over them with a pen from the glove compartment, though he isn't saying much. Somehow he has three pairs of spectacles in his pockets and tries them all, finally using two pairs by wearing one and holding the other halfway between his eyes and the page on his lap.

Ruth, he says, making a face, the old B596 is no more. I'm rerouting us west of Bakewell, we can't be doing with all this bypass nonsense.

His words are muffled, as if he is chewing on a mouthful of wet paper, but I obey his directions and he settles back and says, Isn't this nice?

I agree it is. He beams and places a hand on my arm. Oh, isn't it nice? Going back?

It's lovely.

Going back together, he says with satisfaction, and we drive on until I have to start singing to keep myself awake. I wind the window down to let in some cold air. We're climbing higher; the rushing wind has lost the oily tang of the main roads and has the magical pricking sweetness of cut fields and a heavy, early autumn dew. Arthur laughs and joins in with "Green Grow the Rushes-o" and when we finish that he starts up at once with "Jerusalem," as if he knows a hundred songs and can pick one without thinking. The words come easily, and give him delight.

And did those feet in ancient time
Walk upon England's mountain green?
Remember, Ruth? *Jerusalem?*

Just in time, I do.

Fourteenth of June, 1972, I say, and he smiles at me and squeezes my hand on the steering wheel.

But still I can't stay awake, and although it's very nearly light and it can't be far now, I pull off the road into the opening of a rutted track. Across it just a few feet back from the road there's a barrier of barbed wire and baler twine, stretched between fence posts set in old concrete-filled paint cans. An electrified livestock fence is drawn across a couple of yards behind that. Beyond it, at the horizon, the sky is solidifying to a pale solid gold, like cooling beeswax. I tip the seat back and close my eyes. Arthur sighs and settles beside me and takes my hand. Except for the occasional soft buffeting of air as a vehicle roars past us, it is quiet and still.

The sun on my face wakes me up. There's a tight ache around my ribs. The day is already garish but when I get out of the car to stretch my body, I discover it's also windy and cold. By the side of the track, sparse and stemmy weeds dusky with exhaust fumes wave back and forth, and here and there in the ditch the meager yellow stars of a wild-flower dip among cigarette packets, bottles, and shreds of paper and buckled cans. Miles above us, a few birds fleck a giant, chaotic sky.

Arthur wakes in a bad mood. Of course, he says, peevish and flatulent, he will remember the turnoff out of Netherbarn Cross for Overdale, but we drive three miles too far before he admits in an injured voice that I have missed it. His stomach is upset; he wriggles and scratches and fidgets with the window. I turn the car around and we crawl back the way we came but still he can't find the turnoff because, he says, he can't be expected to recognize it approaching from the wrong direction. We persevere, but after more studying of the maps and the tattered hand-drawn directions from nearly forty years ago, twice he chooses the wrong track. One takes us into a farmyard; the other ends at a barred and padlocked brick building stuck with aerials and antennae, property of the electric company, sitting at the base of a pylon.

It's not as if you, Arthur says sniffily, as I reverse the car and we start to bump our way back to the road, were ever a natural at map-reading.

I'm too exasperated to reply so we drive on saying nothing for a while, back in the direction of Netherbarn Cross. We pass the same small garage we've seen half a dozen times; the situation is getting so desperate that I am steeling myself, if we have to drive past it again, to go in and ask for directions.

Still, he says, I suppose you'd better take a look.

I park at a disused turning that looks as if it might once have led to a hopeless golf course that never prospered. It's a derelict little place that we've passed and repassed in the last hour, but while I'm peering at the map Arthur is staring hard out the window.

Those trees are new, he says eventually.

It seems we're here. We've found it by accident. It's the trees that threw him, a line of conifers on each side behind low, curving brick walls that also, he says, never used to be here. The old Overdale track has been transformed into an entrance, and the entrance is now in disrepair; in front of each of the two trees nearest the road stands a pair of upright, rusting metal struts, buckled and stricken. One set is quite bare and from the other hang the stiff plywood shreds of a sign long ago ripped away.

And another thing, Arthur grumbles, waving a hand behind him: How could I be expected to find it when everything else is so different? The garage never used to be there, either. And they've widened the road and stuck those things in the middle.

There are barriers between the two traffic lanes and a long white-hatched space in the road where buses can wait before turning. His memory of the old hazardous junction is useless, and the old directions no longer make sense.

They've flattened out the bend, he says, aggrieved. No wonder I missed it. After all, you missed it, too, didn't you?

I start the car again and we set off up the track. The posts of the brick entrance have fallen away and lie crumbled and biscuity on the ground, and across the walls zigzag fissures in the mortar skew the brickwork. There are gaps in the rows of white copestones. Where the conifers end, the way reverts to a country track through fields. A tall green line of weeds grows down the center of it and swishes the underside of the car. Every few yards we drive over ruts that have been filled with stones or patches of tar, but not recently; thistles and dock sprout through puddles and cracks. I have to stop and get out to move a coil of wire and a sheet of corrugated iron out of the way, and about half a mile on we come across a burned-out, rusted car, tipped halfway into a field. The front wheels and hood are missing and its trunk gapes open. Nettles stretch up through the engine.

Gradually we leave the tussocky fields behind. The hills on either side of the way begin to climb toward the sky. As they rise into slanting mounds and suave, tilting cones they assume new distinction and character; they acquire the presence, even sentience, of sculpture or of people standing peripherally and very still, alone or in deliberate clusters. Light brims over the shoulders of the eclipsed hills to the east and pours itself over the opposite side in cold, showy pinks and yellows. The track rises ahead and then dips, and in the distance disappears round a curve into the dark swell of a valley. I glance at Arthur. His eyes are running with tears and his mouth opens and closes wetly.

Nearly there, I whisper, and he nods.

After another mile or so the wide pebbly stream that is now running alongside the track veers away extravagantly. We round the next curve and Arthur cries out. I stop the car on the edge of an apron of pitted tarmac tatty with weeds and the mangled remains of benches and litter bins. The building before us is a small redbrick mansion with a miscellany of dark elaborate turrets and impractical chimneys and gabled windows, set into the hillside in front of a sparse plantation of twiggy shrubs and trees. Even derelict and vandalized, it looks pompous.

The whole place is surrounded by high chain-link fencing, bearing warning signs about trespass and the hazardous state of "these premises." I leave Arthur weeping quietly in the car and walk the fence. I go as far as the ruin of a modern single-story extension, not visible from the car, that abuts on the far side of the lodge. Here is where two sections of fencing have been forced apart and where, against the walls of the extension, fires have been set. Smoke stains snake up the boards nailed over the front doors as far as the asphalt overhang of the flat roof. The blistered, prefabricated panels under one of the windows have sheered off and now curl outward. Like all the others, this window had been boarded up, but now it's a jagged dark rectangle. Traces of another fire on the ground underneath it reach as high as the sill. The window board itself, prized off and split and partly burnt, lies nearby in a bed of broken glass.

I'm stepping through the gap in the fence, twisting my way through a web of cut and buckled wire, when I hear excited screams from Arthur.

Ruth, Ruth! Quick! They're still here!

I run back round to the car, but it's empty. He shouts again. He's way over by the front porch of the lodge, waving at me. I follow his gestures and he guides me along the fence to where it curves up the other side and around to the back. It's adjoined clumsily to a wind-stricken tree whose trunk lists toward the ground, leaving an easy gap. Arthur beckons me through and I hurry down to him. The original pillared porch juts out squarely from the double front doors. There may have been benches set into the sides of the porch once, but they're long gone. Some of the colored diamond floor tiles are still in place under drifts of leaves and rubbish, and the walls are ornamented from top to bottom with panels of glazed brick set between carved pilasters and small empty niches. High on the walls a bas-relief frieze of acanthus and birds, bordered by a pair of deep ledges decorated like cake icing, runs along all three sides. Arthur is holding up a set of keys.

Knew they'd still be here! He's clanking them on their ring and he's gabbling and spitting with pride.

You remember? The secret spares! The porch ledge! Bill what's-his-name got them made in Matlock, remember? We'll soon be in business, he says, thumbing through the keys and selecting one far bigger than the others. Aha, here's the mortise. Proper locksmith's key, that. Feel the weight of it.

He hasn't noticed, or maybe he just doesn't see, that the front doors are now secured top, bottom, and middle by three hinged metal bands whose hasps are chained and padlocked.

Come on, I say. I think there's a way in round the back.

It's difficult, though. The broken window of the extension is impossibly high for Arthur and it takes time and a lot of strength for me to haul the vandalized benches and litter bins round to the break in the fence, get them through, and fix them under the sill so that he can climb up and step over.

We find ourselves in a bare classroom. It must always have been warped and thin and damp, but it now looks as if water has flooded through it. Mold stains streak the walls and the ceiling is buckled and slack. White deposits of mineral salts encrust the crumbling cladding material. The floor is gritty with it, and also with bird droppings and cigarette ends and burnt rubbish. There's a trapped, soaked stench of rain and ash and urine.

Through the door and across a corridor is another room, identical except that there's a heap of rags and bottles in one corner and it's darker because the window boards are still in place. The sun is bleeding through the gaps, casting wavering needles of light onto the far wall that's covered by a painted, chipped relief map studded with arrows and circles and crosses. Arthur gazes at it, enraptured. He wanders across with a hand outstretched and stabs at a point between some brown ridges and an irregular dark blue oval.

He strokes a fingertip across it and then touches his finger to his lips.

Here. Just here, he says, replacing the finger with tender and tremulous precision back on the exact spot on the map. Here, Ruth.

Then he moves into a shaft of light that illuminates his face abruptly and dazzles him so that he has to squeeze his eyes shut, and he loses his balance and begins to stagger. His eyes fly open in fright. I rush to take hold of him before he falls, and our bodies fold together. He shakes in my arms. I watch the light tremble on the floor and across the walls. Then I take his hand and lead him out and along to the end of the corridor where there's a solid old door connecting the extension to the main house. Arthur produces the keys again, and finally we find the one that fits. Beyond that is a kind of long scullery and another locked door, but it turns out we have the key to that, too.

He meanders through the house, raising dust. All the rooms are bare and dark and seem to me even more abjectly and irretrievably abandoned than the classrooms; their emptiness is sadder and deeper in a way I can't explain. But for Arthur it is pure reunion, unalloyed by melancholy. Behind every heavy, squealing door is something, or someone, he is delighted to see. In a room with a wide bay window he tries to draw my attention to the fireplace.

Remember! he says. Remember? We thought it so old-fashioned, that old marbled ebony, the maroon tiles! Worth a fortune today, old painted tiles like that.

He gazes at the wall admiringly as if the fireplace, rather than the raw gap where it used to be, were actually here. He takes me into the stripped-out kitchen that still holds a brackish vegetal smell, and from here into what he calls the eating and recreation quarters, now blank and damp. On the linoleum floor there are black streaks and dented circles where rubber-tipped chair and table legs were set down and scraped back in the clamor of innumerable institutional meals. Arthur stoops forward as if to catch again the trooping of children's feet from serving hatch to table, the crash of plates and dishes, the clang of dropped cutlery. A dartboard still hangs on the wall.

As we go on he grows spry, pointing out this feature and that: the deep cornicing and baseboards, and in the stairwell, where now hangs only a length of tied-off electrical cord, the original Edwardian brass electric candelabra with the little parchment shades. He leads me upstairs and first we inspect the teachers' accommodation on the floor between the girls' and boys' dormitories. He remembers the room I slept in but not the name of the red-haired phys. ed. teacher I had to share with. I don't, either.

Then we look over the top floor and the first floor, each one with five or six featureless rooms where, he reminds me, the kids bunked up in sixes and eights. He shows me their bathrooms with lines of collapsed shower stalls and basins clogged with dead insects. His fatigue has lifted; he walks the whole house, openmouthed. I follow, answering his excitement with a quieter pleasure.

I'm assessing each room, thinking about practicalities. Most are completely empty but here and there I note the hulks of furniture that must have been too heavy or too worthless to move. On one landing stands a gray metal cupboard without doors that still has pillows and some cardboard boxes of cleaning fluid and toilet paper in it. Nearby, three or four narrow bed frames with broken slats are upended against the wall.

It's broad daylight now. I drive the car round to the hole in the fence and we unload, Arthur fairly trotting up and down with the lighter things. I've settled on the darkest room to sleep in, a small one with a boarded window on the middle floor at the back that lies in the shadow of the hillside. It's probably going to get very cold; there's a little fireplace but I'm too tired to think now about whether or not the chimney might still work. I'm also too tired to drag in a bed frame. I fetch some of the pillows and put them on the floor and cover them with the thickest of our sweaters, and we arrange blankets over us. We lie close together.

Trees are being pushed to and fro outside, and light through the gaps in the window boards flows across the walls and ceiling in a shadow show of shifting irregular beads, the fuzzy little ghosts of moving leaves and branches. I watch, listening, and Arthur is watching, too; I glance at him and catch sight of his fixed open eyes glistening in the room's pale darkness. His mouth gapes and his breathing is rising and fading with the sweep of shadows reaching in, keeping time with the swoosh of the wind.

Yet something in all this swaying and ebbing of his breath, and of the trees and the wind, seems sly and mocking; something in or maybe beyond the room protests, wants this pattern of heartbeats and pulses disturbed, their rhythms arrested and rearranged. It is as if a tight, mewling voice is struggling through a tiny mouth and a knotted throat to say something unfinished and tremendous and full of sadness, perhaps anguished and violent. Arthur turns to me.

Ruth?

What is it? We should try to sleep.

There's something you have to tell me.

It's a statement, not a question, so I don't reply.

Now that we're here, there's something you should be telling me, isn't there? Something about what happened.

About what happened? Where, when? To the baby, you mean? The baby in the story?

He grunts. That, yes. But something else as well. What happened to you.

To me? Oh! Oh, what happened to me, that'd take too long to tell, now.

Don't say that. You have to tell me. What happened that day? You want to tell me.

Yes. Maybe. But I can't.

You can. You want to. You know what happened. You know who killed you.

Yes.

You have to tell me. Why won't you tell me? You're afraid of what I'll do.

No.

Then *why* won't you tell me?

I can't. Because knowing will be worse than not knowing.

Worse? That's nonsense! How could it be worse?

His voice rises and he thumps a fist on the blanket. Worse, who for? He should pay the price. He deserves to suffer!

Maybe they are suffering, I say dreamily. They are. Not in the way you do, but in their way. So much has happened. Go to sleep.

I turn over on my side and nestle down, but Arthur yanks me around furiously.

How can you be so calm about it! I want to know! I have a right to know! What about me?

He is leaning over me and his eyes are fierce. His mouth is clenched and lopsided, and his breath hisses from it and dots my face with spittle.

What about *me*?

Shhh . . . now, dear. It's all right. I'm here now. I'm here. Aren't I?

And we're back here. At Overdale, together. Everything's all right. You're tired. Lie down and try to rest.

I have to speak in this way for several minutes, and eventually he grunts and sighs and settles back.

I won't be able to sleep, he says, and starts to shiver and pick at the blankets with the fingers of one hand. Just as I think he's falling asleep he starts up and bursts into tears and rocks from side to side, wailing and coughing.

I can't sleep. I'm cold. I'll never sleep. Not till I know, not till you tell me. You've got to tell me.

I talk to him some more, and then tuck the blankets close around him and snuggle in to still his body and warm him. I run my hand over and over his forehead and shush him like a baby.

I'm cold. You've got to tell me, he says. Promise you'll tell me.

All right, I say. All right, I promise. I'll tell you, but not now. This isn't the time. Or the place.

Promise? When? When, Ruth?

Soon. I'll tell you very soon if you promise to rest now. Go to sleep.

After a while he stops shivering and sleeps. I am almost warm enough. Inside the room the darkness grows dreamy; from outside comes again the sleek rustle of the trees around the house and the rattle of the metal fence, and from time to time the wind carries the faint creaking calls of water birds flocking somewhere not very far away.

There's a grainy frost on the tarmac. Our footsteps grate as we walk across it in the dark toward the trickling and oozing of the stream. Behind us the lodge is a uniform black, before us the hills seem pulled upward by the moon. The moon pulls us along, too, casting our scissoring shadows ahead of us on the path and over the wet pebbles and shingle at the edge of the streambed, lighting the wavelets plashing over them with winking dots and ridges. A tree has fallen and blocks our way. I help Arthur clamber over it, then I return and break a length from a black, dead branch for him to use as a stick. We walk, and we walk. Some of the stones sit heavy and smooth and dun under their sheeting of water and some look bleached and jagged, like bits of tooth. We find lying half-submerged a white blade of animal bone, Arthur says most likely from a sheep. He cuts the air with it, sprinkling an arc of water drops into the moonlight. He has a notion to keep it but it turns ashy in his hands.

As we go higher the stream breaks into channels around bigger stones and small lodged boulders that split the runneling water into angled, restless swords of silver and dark and silver and dark. We rest often, in places as far out of the wind as we can find. Here and there the bank of the stream bellies out where the water turns in a slow spin and collects in deep level pools, and falls almost silent, and turns viscous and as impenetrable as mercury, so that when we pause we might hear only a ghostly plocking and gulping from under the surface. Though we stare down trying to see something move on the bottom, even just reeds in the current, the black membrane of water gives back nothing but shivering fragments of reflected sky.

We tire. As we go farther the stream breaks into smaller and smaller streamlets until it is a web of tangled strands across a field of stones and reeds stretching outward under the moon. We stop again and I pull Arthur's hands from his pockets and rub them between mine, and draw them inside my jacket to warm them. They are freezing, his face is freezing, his mouth is locked with cold, and his mind is quite elsewhere. When I speak to him about gloves and tell him I've got blankets in the rucksack, he gives me a kindly look, but he is puzzled, as if I am butting foolishly into another conversation and steering it in some new direction that he finds eccentric and tangential.

Though he is cold and weary, he is the leader. We move on when he is ready, we pause when he chooses. Sometimes he stops and raises his walking stick, listening for a faint sound he thought he heard to be repeated, some cry from a bird or an animal, and I have to wait until he decides it wasn't a living creature at all, just some indistinct whistle borne along on the sifting, chilly breath of the night itself.

We are deep in the hills now and although we are still able to make our way by its light, the moon has disappeared over a ridge. We are walking into a wretched wind and I start to feel afraid. I don't know where we are going, or maybe I don't want to know. I want to stop or turn back, but Arthur goes on doggedly, just ahead of me. Soon the path divides and he pauses, then points the way toward the lower fork that does not go to the top of the hill but cuts a gently downward slope around the curve of it, through a stand of scrubby trees. He tramps on and I follow close behind.

Within ten minutes we have rounded the side of the hill, and everything changes. We're in the shelter of the summit now. We have to call above the roar of the wind but we do not feel it so much; it sweeps over the top of the hill above us. The moon has reappeared and shines directly on the reservoir a long way below. Arthur plants himself on the ground to gaze and I realize we're not going any farther.

I unpack the rucksack and try to get him warm; I hunker down next to him and wrap a blanket around us. But he doesn't seem to feel the cold anymore. He's got his arms pressed tight into his sides and he is staring down onto the surface of the water, crimped and silvered by the wind and moon. He starts to point out the old landmarks.

There's the path through to Boar Clough, and if you go on over the top it levels out and another six miles takes you back to Hayfield. And this must be where the old sheep gate was, he suggests, gesturing vaguely down to a path far below us, and then he yawns and looks and considers again, shakes his head, and with a wide swing of his arm murmurs that it could have been anywhere. It doesn't matter. He turns to me and pats my face and smiles.

I reach into the rucksack for the pack of food and a picnic knife. We ought to be drinking something hot and sweet, like cocoa, but all we've got is fatty cold meat and onions in chewy bread, and some water. I cut off pieces small enough for him to manage and hand them over, and I eat the lumps that are left. When we've finished I say, I wish we had a tent, but Arthur gets to his feet and pulls out all the bedding, fixes the rucksack expertly as a windbreak at our heads, unrolls the blankets, and spreads one out on the ground.

Lie down, Ruth, get comfortable.

I do as I'm told. The ground is bumpy and damp but at least we are lying on a mattressy layer of heather. He arranges himself beside me and wraps us up.

We'll soon get warm, he says, and he takes me in his arms. He brings our last blanket over our heads like a giant hood, enclosing us in a stuffy sack that smells of the food we've been eating. It's also prickly, but once my eyes are closed I'm able to feel only his arms and his neck, and then his hand inside my jacket and on my waist, moving over my skin and pushing up my clothes until my breasts are bare under his fingers. He is so thin now, his mouth is loose and bristly, but he curls in and presses against me and kisses and nuzzles and rests his lips on my nipples, and I stroke his head. I feel his hand reach for mine and he draws it down inside his clothes. He has the beginning of an erection. With no urgency and with no words, we find our way through the layers of blankets and clothing to each other's bodies, and we make love. My body receives him, and that is enough.

Later when I whisper his name there is no reply, but then I feel his mouth forming words against my skin and his hand tightens in the dip of my waist. He is asking me something.

Ruth, what happened? Tell me what happened.

I don't know what to answer.

I say, Tell me something. Did you mean it? What you said you'd do to the person who did it, if you got your hands on them?

I said I'd kill him, he says. He sounds slightly embarrassed. I told everybody, I said I'd strangle him with my bare hands.

Surely that was just the heat of the moment, I say. You wouldn't do a thing like that. Not you, Arthur. You couldn't.

Arthur considers this. No, he says almost regretfully, you're wrong. I meant it. I could do it. I would. I'd have to.

No matter who it was? Even supposing it was somebody very young, only a kid? Or suppose it was a woman, or just somebody who'll never recover, somebody who'd do anything to put it right if they could?

I can hear fear enter my voice but Arthur doesn't seem to.

Put it right? What the hell does that mean?

I just mean . . . maybe it's someone who'll never, who won't be able to rest until—

He turns and presses himself down hard on my body, pinning me to the earth as if he's afraid I'll escape. His breath comes in hot, salty gusts.

I don't care! Put it *right*? So they feel better? Why *should* they be able to rest? Think what they did to you! They shouldn't even go on living, not after that!

All right—no, they shouldn't, I say. It's just I hate seeing you so upset. Please don't be upset. But I know, some things are too wicked to be forgiven.

He is silent. He releases me and eases himself back. Then he says, That's what I'm saying. And you do know. You put it in that story. Uncle Les, the bad fella. He was asking for it, a bad end.

It was only a story, I say. But I expect he got it.

Now Arthur is lying on his back. His eyes are closed and his face is rumpling with the effort of holding back tears.

And the child. Tell me what happens to the child. The baby girl in the story, Ruth. What happened to her?

I kiss his mouth softly and I say, Don't worry about it now. You'll find out tomorrow. As soon as it's light again. I'll tell you everything.

You promise, he murmurs.

Soon I hear his breathing slacken into an unsteady, rasping sleep. I lie in his arms, knowing that I will tell him everything. As soon as it's light. There will be no peace until I do. I feel, I think, a kind of welcome sadness at the idea that then at last his rage will rain down and spend itself on me, but I fear pain as much as anyone. I wish he were stronger or that he had a proper weapon. I hope oblivion will come quickly.

He wakes one more time and whispers, Ruth, I don't care what happens now. We're safe here, aren't we?

I don't know what to answer. Safe from what? In the morning I shall make sure the knife I brought is within his reach. I lie awake, afraid. For who knows what stalks us at a distance, circling in the dark? Who knows how inquisitive they will prove, how close they will come to see if we are lost children, if we are living or dead? What would they say to us? Suppose there are people still shambling along the path in the moonlight, and one strays from the others, and watches the distance grow between herself and her companions, and say that all in a rush she understands she will not see them again but no matter, for she has always known herself quite able to leave them? So she lingers at the gate and does not call out, nor even wave at their swaying backs, but turns her attention instead to the dark indecipherable shape on the hill. Suppose she has enacted this estrangement every night, in anticipation of us. Would we move to greet her? What would we tell her?

I don't know what to answer. But Ruth knows, somehow, and my grandmother knows, and all the others, the counted and the numberless, the remembered and the unremembered dead. They are around us now in their habitual, dreaming way, murmuring reassurances in the voices we know so well, and since we would not feel them if they touched us they stroke through the darkness with fond hands and stir the air into little vortices, sending flurries through the orderly night that shift the folds of our blankets by a fraction, or shake loose two or three leaves from the stunted trees on the ridge and cast them down the hillside into a wind that's no longer cold but soothes us in dull waves, and carries the scent of old vines and honey. By such tricks and currents they draw us on with kindliness, and though invisible they are not wholly unseen, they are not vanished.

I don't know what to answer. I lie awake shivering. I don't know how much strength there is in his hands. But I'll no more resist his vengeance, whatever form it takes, than I turned away when he reached for me and burrowed lovingly into my body.

Arthur's face was damp and yellow, I thought first of all with dew and the first light, but when I touched him his skin slid a little under my finger and it shone with a layer of some cool sweated oil, like putty. The wind had blown the blanket from the side of his head and a few leaves of hawthorn were fluttering against his hair. His mouth lay open toward me as if he had turned to speak. His eyes were half-shut and without meaning. The eyelids had become simply that, lids: a pair of formal, diminutive covers of skin interrupted in the act of blinking, but whether they had halted when his eyes were closing in sleep or opening under the glare of morning sky it was neither possible nor important to know. His arms were locked around me. I didn't move at once. I lay watching the little rags of birds in the sky over the reservoir, listening to their cries, and then listening to the silence beside me, wondering if it meant something more than not breathing, something more than absence, whether it could mean that a parting, perhaps this one, might be absolute.

I sat up and pulled myself clear of his arms but kept hold of his hand. How long could I stay; how could it ever be time for me to leave him? I pushed back his sleeve and watched the sparse hairs on his forearm rising and falling. His finger ends were turning blue and clawing at nothing. The lips of his moist monkey mouth were fluttering as if he had strange dead words to speak to the wind. Soon his face would sink in upon itself. All there was left to wait for now was the flecking and wrinkling of his skin, darkening into hide.

I closed his eyes. I rearranged his clothing and straightened his body. From the rucksack I drew out the pages of Ruth's unfinished story and placed them securely on his chest under his folded hands; I set his walking stick and maps close against his side. I kissed his lips and his forehead, and I settled myself close to him and placed a hand over his. I had promised to tell him everything and so I began to talk, and I did not stop until I had told him all I knew.

I began with what he also had known, that on that brittle spring day some force within her had marched Ruth right up to where the last moment of her life was waiting, a few minutes before noon on a country lane canopied by blossoming trees. There had been nothing she could do to prevent it, any more than I had been able to disarm whatever force in me had gone about its work that morning in delivering me to the time and place I would kill her.

The horror of what happened may mask, a little, its utter simplicity, or perhaps its very simplicity is part of the horror. Of course, if only we had known: if only I had been delayed by another minute, if only it had rained and Ruth had decided not to cycle. But all the *if onlys* in the world are grapeshot fired too late against the fact that on that day not one second's pause, not one extra breath nor the merest passing thought, had pushed themselves between our attention to some obscured notion of what life required of us from moment to moment, and the brutal second that death occurred. Ruth's life and the instant of my ending it were not separated by so much as a single additional beat of either of our two hearts.

Then I told Arthur it was not Ruth but I, the less beloved, who should have died. It would have mattered less. But although I was left still breathing, my life, too—that is to say any deserving I might have of my life—ended with the taking of hers. Her death brought to a close my daily enactment of a series of scenes, contained and infinitely repeatable, that for years I had been trying to string together into a semblance of a history that would bear the telling. My life's course had seemed always a delicate, waning story about which it was natural I should be sad and other people absentminded; in conversation my name was always the one they tended to forget. Now my story was finished. I had killed the person telling it.

Hereafter I would have no story, only a dishonored past. And what else could I do then, but begin to learn what it is to be dead before I actually was? I ended my own life in the taking of Ruth's, and in search of expiation I took her life again. What could I do but enter her story, and with the stealth and self-effacement of a ghost take it to its rightful ending here, with him, on a shining hillside she could not herself get back to?

Not that I quite understand endings, or beginnings. How a story begins is not why it begins, and how or why it ends is no more fathomable. Reasons buried in the accumulated past may be forever hidden from those whose reasons they are, or perhaps there are none, after all. Perhaps there are no reasons but only things that happen, attached to nothing, events that loom out of the dark and leave sometimes a series of blurry afterimages of what we thought vital at the time—what it will please us later to call our stories—imprinted on our blindness.

I paused, stroking Arthur's hand. The bitterness of his death was that it seemed a kind of absconding, a defection from one last neglected task. He would give me no shriving now; all the peace would be his.

The wind was sweeping shards of reflected sun across the reservoir like pieces of broken mirror, so sharp and blinding I could not see the water itself. And so it is that light passes back and forth over what I can't see as well as over this world of dark and changing surfaces, cloud shadows go on scudding across the wavering and inexact shapes of all the unended stories, casting angles and colors and all interpretations out of true. The sky will be always crowded and the earth forever alight with them, these unmediated details, the incongruent blunders as well as the mystic, the epic conjunctions, with the drifting and inconclusive atoms of the sparsest, no less than the mightiest, human events. I may lament all I like the lack of it, but there is no natural law in this world that can take such fragmentary and capricious refractions and make of them anything explicable and whole.

I swaddled his head with tender and particular care, wrapping a scarf round and round his face and eyes like a bandage. I covered him with the blankets and folded them in tight under his limbs.

That's how I left him, on the hillside with his face to the sky. I made my way back slowly along the path. On the curve of the hill I turned for one final look, and then I went on toward the rushing of the stream, shielding my eyes against the sunlight sparkling on the water.

All this happened some time ago.

I drove away from the lodge. The roads were deserted and the garage near the Overdale turning was closed. I left a letter there saying I thought he'd had a stroke. I said they'd find him out on the hill and I hadn't wanted to leave him but I'd wrapped him up safe against the wind and the birds. I didn't say that the last thing he gazed on was the dark water with the moon shining on it and the last touch he knew was the warm body of his Ruth.

I drove until the gas gauge was nearing empty, and abandoned the car at a railway station. I caught a train, where to isn't important. It was only a matter of hours before I understood that a person out of place is sentenced to be out of place everywhere, yet she has no choice but to keep going. And that is how it is.

Going from place to place at least punctuates a day with the dots and dashes of making a journey: the hurrying, the arriving, the synchronized languor of the intervals between connections. Waiting in cafés, I stack packets of sugar and trace patterns with a finger on the tabletop and look out the window; toward the close of afternoons I will find myself in another obscure provincial town, and thinking about nightfall, I'll start tapping on the doors of the kind of abject boarding-house that is never very far from the stations of such places. Sometimes I look for a trailer, off-season, or a room above a pub where I might stay for a week or so if I wash dishes. But sooner or later I'll begin again to study timetables, for precisely that purpose, to study time; and maybe also to assert, from my state of dispossession, a small degree of something akin to possession though it be of nothing more than the coming day, the passing of which I will determine and execute in measures of the routes between places I don't need to go.

Of course it's fruitless, the crossing and recrossing of these distances. How spacious the landscape between resting points, how unnaturally lengthy the days. And every twilight seen from the window of another temporary room confirms that the preceding hours have drawn me a little further from my mislaid life, for I never was going to find its vestiges here, nor there, nor anywhere visible.

When it's properly dark, I go out. I don't want to, quite, but it's become a habit after all this time not to resist how the night draws me to itself. And I am drawn sometimes miles away, to the edges of towns and the mistakenly built and put-aside streets of houses where people seldom flourish, where lives seem always precarious and marginal and lived against tides of more robust and purposeful forces.

There's a constant flow of vans and lorries to and from the garages and roadside mini-marts that thrum all night long on the borders of such places; the soft roar and sodium mist from bypasses and motorway interchanges muffle and cloud the darkness right over their roofs and pavements. There are a few people about on foot, some walking dogs but mostly they're foragers in the all-night shops, out for cigarettes or cans of drink or junk food, including, I've noticed, surprising quantities of ice cream for the small hours. Occasionally they're couples, more usually they're alone. But the lone ones aren't solitary in the entrenched way I am; something about them seems to say they've come lately from company of another or are hurrying back to it. I watch them cautiously. It's a matter of some pride to me that I do not look destitute, quite. But I think my loneliness can be breathed in, like an odor, and so that people won't pass by me close enough to detect it, I will cross the road or find a wall or doorway and wait. Then, without necessarily meaning to, I follow.

No, I don't really follow, not to begin with. I let my thoughts walk alongside them, that's all. I concern myself. I wonder if, say, the man striding by on legs that seem shortened from lack of use has cause to feel as pinched and aggrieved as he looks, and why he may be dismayed in his heart. I worry that the slow, sentimental-looking pregnant girl carrying bags of sweets has nobody to listen to her cravings and go to the shop for her, and hurry back to run her a bath and feed her licorice sticks or spearmint toffee, stroking her belly, as she lies in the deep warm water. I don't follow them; I just need to know they are safe, the lost ones, the wanderers. I like to see them enter rooms that will shut out the night that's lapping at the door. I'm anxious and hungry for their well-being, so I give in and let myself be pulled along behind them.

Not that I try to see into houses. I do not go searching for uncurtained rooms. But there are so many, and it is impossible not to look in through lit windows, for since I now truly know the dark, I want equal knowledge of its absence. I have to observe the places where darkness has been disallowed, where its opposite reigns apparent. Such brightness! I admit the brightness does enthrall me, though I gaze in dread because I can't separate it from what it illuminates: people in houses moored like toy lightships on the surface of the night, people tending

futile little eternal domestic fires the way I used to and the way Ruth
and Arthur did. I can hardly bear to see them so lit up, so impossibly
vulnerable yet oblivious, as if they thought their puny flares of artificial
daylight could prevail, as if any tiny guttering yellow flame could ever
withstand the encroaching black.

For hours at a time I watch them dappled by the light of television
screens, heavy and unmoving in their chairs. I watch them at tables
and mirrors, filling plates and eating with their hands, flipping through
papers, brushing their hair. They stand at sinks, lift telephones, open
and close cupboards. Children are put to bed and babies bundled on
shoulders are carried from room to room. I watch as they leave off talking and little by little grow dreamy and inattentive, and fond and slow.
How I envy them. Lights go out.

I want more. Now when a house goes dark I draw closer, right up
to the windows. I want to hear breathing. I like to picture people in
their beds and unaware that the day has run out on them, that sleep is
suspending every crisis, every flawed, unfinished striving, every word
said and not yet said in their particular small lives. I want to hear their
steady breathing because then I would know that until they wake their
stories are collapsed and upturned, dragged along in the depthless currents of dreams. I'd know that for a while at least their stories are as
lost to them as mine is to me.

So what harm would it do if at such a time, for such a short time, I
came closer still? I wouldn't invade anyone's dreams just by coming
within the walls. Nor would I try to steal anyone's story and take it for
my own, but may I not borrow it, during a few hours of darkness, in order to affect it for the better? I see enough in all these lit-up houses to
know I could do some good; there are always dozens of practical ways
of making a difference. I long to help, as I did before. And I wouldn't
take more than I give. I'd attach to another life to improve it, not to end
it or suck it dry. I'm not parasitic. It's symbiosis I seek, that poise and
purity and balance. I'm starving for it. I whimper at people's windows.

Yet I shy away. I haven't yet tried an unlocked door or unlatched a
low window and stepped in, though I think I'm bound to; it's only a

matter of time. I don't know what inhibits me, but I turn away long before it's light.

Tonight I wander back the way I came along the quiet roads but I'm not ready for sleep in the rented room that smells of bar dregs and disinfectant. I'll stay out even though there's a prickle of frost in the air and I should be in warmer clothes. Beyond the houses, the pavement widens and leads into a park with a few swings and a roundabout. I set the swings going as I stroll past and then walk on quickly so I won't hear their empty creaking. I slip through a line of trees on the edge of a recreation ground and strike out across playing fields. Ahead and around me in the dark I can make out the leaning white ribs of goalposts. When I've crossed to the far side I stop and stare back at the park and the houses under their yellowy bloom of cloud, looking for a sign that I ever set foot there. There is none, not so much as a dent in the grass. In front of me now is a fence and a scrub of bramble bushes and beyond that, over a metal gate, a stretch of plowed earth curving upward into faraway woods.

Once I'm through the woods I roam farther, across a patch of thin pasture and more fields. Then it gets steeper; paths end at stiles or slide over the horizon through gaps in hedges, land drops away behind scraggy stands of bushes and falls into hoof-rutted gulleys. The wind rises. Darkness lies trapped in the trees like black veils snagged on the branches, it ripples ahead of me and spreads over the swell of the hills. I follow it, climbing an old sheep path almost to the top of a hill high above the glow of the town, where moonlight strikes through the clouds and silvers the grass.

I shiver and settle myself down, hugging my knees. Suddenly I'm too weary to move any farther. My eyes close for a moment, though it's so cold I won't fall asleep. I wish I could. I need a place to lie, someplace to stay. Is it to be here, another hillside under the moon? I look back in the direction of the town.

Something feels near at hand. I force myself awake and try to make sense of the contours of the hill, but I'm drowsy and shapes loom and shift and nudge against me, benignly perhaps; the wind now has me wrapped in its cool rocking arms and I don't wish to be let go. I can't trust my eyes, but I strive to make out a gate half-open, half-closed, in the moonlight. I'm searching through the dark for signs of a throng of lost ones idling along the path, the wind ruffling dry leaves into a familiar tangle of hair, bearing the echoes of myriad remembered stories and the scents of old vines and honey. Will they wait for me?

Something is ending, or beginning. How long will they linger, my lost ones, my wanderers? They wonder, I think, why I stay away. Do they hear me when I murmur that I think it may be coming soon, the night when I venture close enough to see if the moving shadows on the hillside really are theirs, do they know how I yearn to catch a glimpse of patient, moon-white hands outstretched to take me with them? But again I make myself turn away and look down toward the town. Then it's as if I also see, motionless under the roofs of all the houses, the slumbering keepers of stories, the tender, infinite stories, so clamorous and so many and all of them unfinished, surrendered, waiting.

ABOUT THE AUTHOR

Morag Joss grew up on the west coast of Scotland. She began writing in 1996 when her first short story won an award in a national competition. She then wrote three Sara Selkirk novels, set in Bath, the first of which, *Funeral Music,* was nominated for a Dilys Award by the Independent Mystery Booksellers Association.

With her fourth novel, *Half Broken Things,* she won the 2003 Crime Writers Association Silver Dagger award. *Half Broken Things* has been adapted as a TV film and broadcast on UK national television, and *Puccini's Ghosts,* published in 2005, has been optioned for film. *The Night Following* is Morag Joss's sixth novel. She lives in Hampshire, England.